"A smart, witty, heartfelt, and riveting look at the infamous rivalry between Coco Chanel and Elsa Schiaparelli set against a gripping period in history. Mackin's powerful novel brings these characters to life and transports the reader, juxtaposing both the gaiety and tension of Paris on the brink of war. . . . The perfect read for both historical fiction lovers and fashion aficionados. Simply stunning."

—Chanel Cleeton, *New York Times* bestselling author
of *The Cuban Heiress*

"Sophisticated couture wars and looming world wars take center stage in Mackin's latest, with a plot that buzzes with love triangles and political intrigue. A gorgeous meditation on art, fashion, and heartbreak. Stunning."

—Fiona Davis, *New York Times* bestselling author
of *The Magnolia Palace*

"The contrast between the war over fashion and the war over the spread of fascism casts both in a new and unexpected light. . . . This is not only a vivid, compelling drama, it's historical fiction that will make you reassess what you think you know about fashion *and* World War II."

—Seattle Book Review

"A fascinating insight into a war of passion and ambition set amid the looming threat of the Nazi invasion of Paris. With elegant, vibrant writing, Mackin cleverly captures [this] infamous rivalry."

—Hazel Gaynor, *New York Times* bestselling author
of *The Last Lifeboat*

"Brings to center stage the fascinating life of Elsa Schiaparelli in a story that is as elegantly constructed as the clothes she designed. The combination of Schiap's fierce rivalry with Coco Chanel and the inevitable war makes for a palpable tension, and Jeanne Mackin ultimately delivers an ending that is beautiful, heartbreaking, and perfect in every way."

—Michelle Gable, *New York Times* bestselling author of *The Lipstick Bureau*

"A vibrant portrait of two designers cut from very different cloth, *The Last Collection* pits bold Coco Chanel and colorful Elsa Schiaparelli against each other in a fiery feud even as the ominous clouds of World War II darken the horizon. A captivating read!"

—Stephanie Marie Thornton, *USA Today* bestselling author of *Her Lost Words*

"*The Last Collection* is a skillful weave of compelling characters grappling for both fortune and affirmation, and is set against a vivid backdrop—first the glittering cosmos of Paris fashion, then the hardships of World War II, and then the remains of beauty after war. Beautiful prose and imagery enrich every page. Mackin is an insightful, engaging storyteller."

—Susan Meissner, author of *Only the Beautiful*

"Jeanne Mackin takes the reader on an enthralling journey, complete with such vivid descriptions of the clothing, you can practically see them on the page. Beautifully rendered and meticulously researched, *The Last Collection* is a must-read."

—Renée Rosen, *USA Today* bestselling author of *Fifth Avenue Glamour Girl*

"Chanel is all pearls and clean lines; Schiaparelli is bold color and invention. . . . By turns fascinating and tense, *The Last Collection* is a colorful and evocative novel about the price of loyalty."

—Heather Webb, *USA Today* bestselling author
of *Strangers in the Night*

"The famous fashion feud between iconic designers Coco Chanel and Elsa Schiaparelli is retold in splendid detail."

—*The Palm Beach Post*

"Iconic female feuds make for some juicy stories, and the high-stakes world of the fashion industry will lay the foundation for some seriously interesting conversation."

—Bustle

"Fans of Renée Rosen and Melanie Benjamin should enjoy this latest novel from Mackin. The designers' obsession with besting each other makes for fun, gossipy reading, while the tensions of prewar Paris and Lily's attempts to ease her grief through her art lend the narrative satisfying emotional depth."

—*Library Journal*

"A riveting story about two women and the time in which they lived."

—*St. Paul Pioneer Press*

"An exceedingly well-dressed historical catfight."

—Bookstr

"*The Last Collection* is more than a good story. It is a consideration of love, work, and art; war, freedom, and memory."

—BookTrib

"An in-depth tale of an enchanting, dangerous, and fascinating time period in Paris. Mackin's attention to detail and lyrical prose bring Chanel and Schiaparelli to life in a gorgeous and riveting manner."
                                                              —She Reads

TITLES BY JEANNE MACKIN

A LADY OF GOOD FAMILY

THE BEAUTIFUL AMERICAN

THE SWEET BY AND BY

DREAMS OF EMPIRE

THE QUEEN'S WAR

THE FRENCHWOMAN

THE LAST COLLECTION

PICASSO'S LOVERS

PICASSO'S
LOVERS

JEANNE MACKIN

BERKLEY

NEW YORK

BERKLEY
An imprint of Penguin Random House LLC
penguinrandomhouse.com

Library of Congress Cataloging-in-Publication Data

Names: Mackin, Jeanne, author.
Title: Picasso's lovers / Jeanne Mackin.
Description: First edition. | New York: Berkley, 2024.
Identifiers: LCCN 2023016620 (print) | LCCN 2023016621 (ebook) |
ISBN 9781101990568 (trade paperback) | ISBN 9781101990575 (ebook)
Subjects: LCSH: Picasso, Pablo, 1881–1973—Fiction. | Women—Fiction. |
Art—Fiction. | Women art historians—Fiction. |
LCGFT: Biographical fiction. | Novels.
Classification: LCC PS3563.A3169 P53 2024 (print) |
LCC PS3563.A3169 (ebook) | DDC 813/.54—dc23/eng/20230614
LC record available at https://lccn.loc.gov/2023016620
LC ebook record available at https://lccn.loc.gov/2023016621

First Edition: January 2024

Printed in the United States of America
1st Printing

Book design by George Towne
Interior art: Cubism abstract texture @ Maxim Ibragimov/Shutterstock

To Tim K

To find is the thing.

—PABLO PICASSO

PICASSO'S LOVERS

PART ONE

ONE
· · · · · · ·

Paris
1953

IRÈNE LAGUT

Pablo Picasso, my lover, the greatest artist who ever lived, almost didn't.

At birth, he was a blue-and-white wax statuette of a newborn who didn't move, didn't cry. "Stillborn," the nurse whispered. His mother was almost too exhausted from the birth to notice. But an uncle who had been pacing in the hall with Pablo's father had never seen a stillbirth before and was curious. He leaned over the infant, so close that the burning tip of his cigar touched the baby.

Pablo, white and blue, squirmed. He whimpered. His face turned angry red. He wailed lustily. The greatest artist who has ever lived—and that's not just my opinion, I assure you—decided to live. Fire brought him to life. Fire keeps him alive.

"Born of fire," I say.

"What was that?" Pablo, many years after that miracle birth, turns away from the washstand mirror and glares at me with those all-seeing black eyes. We had dined together at Café de Flore and spent the night at his studio in the Quai des

Grands Augustins. We had bedded down among the crates and canvases and statues, decades of his work crammed into the one space he had hoped would be safe from the Germans during the occupation. Mostly, it had been. In fact, they had come sometimes to buy from him, though their regime had declared him a decadent. He sold them a few paintings.

And he listened. Listened very carefully, in case he heard anything useful for the resistance. He made jokes to those German soldiers who marched down our avenues and sat in our cafés during the occupation, jokes in secret French slang, which the soldiers only pretended to understand. Those jokes insulted them, as Pablo intended.

People used to say of my lover that he lived only for art, that women and politics did not matter to him the way his art mattered. But people change. When Franco and Hitler destroyed that Spanish town, Guernica, Pablo changed. You cannot look at that painting, at the screaming mothers and murdered children and violence of it, and think, *This is a man who does not care about people and politics.*

And I have seen how his face changes when he speaks of Françoise, the woman who is leaving him.

"I think it will be a fine day," I said. "But come back to bed, Pablo. It is still early." I smoothed and patted the rumpled sheet that was still damp from our little bacchanal.

"The car will be here soon. If I'm not ready, Paulo will honk the horn and make a scene in the street. He's as mad as his mother."

"Has Olga really turned insane? I always thought she had that tendency. Though you are enough to madden any woman. Why don't you just divorce her?" I wonder what my life would have been had I married Pablo when we were young. *Not happy*, I think. No, I made the right choice. But still . . .

How good it is now to be away from maids and menus and all the domestic duties that eat away at a woman's life, that make it so difficult to work at her art. We aren't allowed closed doors, the way men are.

Pablo returns his gaze to his own image in the mirror and studies it, drawing the razor through the white foam on his cheek and making a curve, olive flesh showing through a white background. Another work of art.

"Hurry up and get dressed," he says. "Olga won't give me a divorce. You know that."

"So you have said for years. Perhaps it is very convenient, having a wife who lives separately and keeps you from marrying any other woman."

He throws a wet towel at me. "Get up. The car will be here soon."

"Listen to you, my love. A car. A chauffeur. I remember when you had holes in your boots, when you were my young love."

"That was long ago. And he's not a chauffeur, he's my son."

"Yes, much has changed." I roll over and light a cigarette, and the sheet falls away from my naked breasts.

I see where his eyes are, and they are not on my face, so I lift my shoulders and give my breasts a gentle push.

He grins. Gazes from Pablo are like brushstrokes. Some are long, lingering, full of texture and pigment. Some are short, shallow, even accidental. His gaze on me now falls somewhere between the two.

Once, his gaze would have found enough for an entire painting. He would have seen flesh, and the bone and muscle under the flesh, the question or certainty of the eyes. He would have seen past, present, and future and painted them in a way that made time irrelevant.

Yes, that was how he painted me. Everything and at once, all the angles and geometry of the body, and he made of me something eternal and always beautiful. That is what an artist can do for a woman. When most men looked at me, all I saw in their faces was desire, the urge to possess. When Pablo looked at me, his face filled with wonder waiting to be translated to lines and brushstrokes.

Spring, the second year of the Great War. I wasn't twenty yet, and had returned from cold, starving Moscow, where a loaf of bread cost as much as a silk dress. My protector, the Russian grand duke, had taken to sitting in his garden under the bare despairing trees and wringing his hands. He sensed his own ruination approaching. Most of the old aristocracy did. I did not care enough for him to face ruination with him. Back to Paris for me!

When Pablo first saw me, I was sitting on the rim of the Wallace Fountain in Place Émile, face turned up to the sun like a basking cat, enjoying the fine day and wondering what adventure I might find, and if my new love would be a man or a woman, and if they would have anything good to eat. It was early summer. I had stolen a bunch of cherries at Les Halles and a roll, but my stomach rattled.

I still had a fur cape I could sell, but I would need that for winter. I had a pearl necklace, but it looked so pretty on me that I could not part with it, not even for a good meal.

Pablo found me. I opened my eyes and there he was, this little handsome Spaniard with the black eyes, staring at me as if he had never seen a woman before.

I looked behind me to make sure there was nothing in the fountain capturing his attention like that, but no, he was looking at me. I sat up straighter and turned my face slightly to show off the better side.

Pablo and his friends had just finished lunch. I could smell the rosemary of a stew on their breaths. But while his friends were sloppy with cheap wine, Pablo was sober as a stone.

"Come with me," said this boy-man, extending his hand.

"I will not. Why should I?" I took a step backward, pretended I was not interested.

"Because I will paint you and make you live forever." He stepped closer and put his arm around my waist.

"Before or after bed?" I laughed, leaning away from him. I had no objection to bed, but I had just left a grand duke who gave me pearls before breakfast. Why take up with this fellow—an artist, judging by the paint under his nails—who probably hadn't a sou to his name?

I stepped out of his embrace and walked away. But we both knew something had begun.

Did he follow me or did I follow him? For a week, we bumped into each other almost daily—Paris is not so large that artists do not know where to find other artists, and I also had paint under my nails—and each time he said the same thing. "Come with me." And I said no.

Late one Saturday evening, I was returning to my room on Rue Lepic—I was singing in a café then, in exchange for free meals—when my handsome Spaniard crept up behind me and pushed me into a carriage. I was curious, not frightened. Where would he take me? What kind of lover would he be?

We went to an old villa outside of Paris. Missing doors, the smell of cat piss, ivy growing through broken windows into the faded, damp-stained rooms. When he opened the villa door for me to reveal those ruins, I laughed in his face. To go from a grand duke to a hovel! When he went out to find supper for us, I made my way back to Paris.

A week later, I still hadn't found any other adventure to my liking, and I kept thinking of his black eyes and the way he looked at me, the strength in his arms. I thought of sharing with him the bread and oranges he would put on the table, the slices of ham. I was more curious than ever to know what he would be like as a lover. So I found my way back to the villa, to Pablo. He was there waiting.

"I knew you would come back," he said. "I knew when I first saw you, this is a woman who wants to live forever."

He began a painting of me as soon as the oranges were finished, before we went to bed.

Thirty years ago.

"Would you like to paint me again?" I ask, getting out of bed and posing in a chair, one leg draped over the side, the other at an angle that the cubists used to adore.

He studies me. And then, "No, your face is too familiar. There is nothing new in it." But I can see his eyes moving, his right index finger drawing a small circle in the air. Some line in my posture has caught the artist's eye.

I laugh. "I will not let that hurt me, because that is what you intended to do. I will always be younger than you, Pablo. Remember that."

Some of last night's tenderness returns to him, and he smiles at me.

The razor still in his hand, he turns to stare back at the foam-covered face of the man in the mirror.

"At this moment of the morning, Françoise comes into the bathroom with my son, Claude. I make them laugh by dragging my finger through the shaving cream and making a sketch on my face. A clown with question marks over my eyes."

Pablo puts his razor down on the edge of the basin, and there is a suggestion of sadness in his proud face.

He does not spend a great deal of time in Paris, this older

Picasso. There is the house in the south, the sun, the woman, the children. He says the light is better there, but I think, too, the heat and sun feel good on his skin. We are both at an age of wanting comfort.

He tells me stories of the woman, Françoise, to make me jealous. Because he once asked me to marry him and I refused, his need for revenge is always there, in the background of whatever else we are feeling.

Françoise Gilot, dark-haired, black winged brows, long, strong limbs. His flower-woman. He has painted her, sketched her, sculpted her. Hundreds of times. Good paintings. I am jealous of the paintings.

Françoise, with whom he has lived for almost twenty years, who has given him two children, is threatening to leave him.

Poor little Marie-Thérèse, his lover before Françoise stepped in for the role. She was seventeen when Pablo first stopped to speak with her in front of the Galeries Lafayette. And she had never heard of him! He began painting her immediately, though, for decency's sake, did not bed her till she was eighteen. In his paintings of her, she is transformed into plates of fruit. The edible woman, the domestic woman.

Marie-Thérèse has been waiting for him to come back to her for years, and if she has heard the rumors, she must be ecstatic. Wrongfully so. He won't be returning to Marie-Thérèse or any of the others. When Pablo is done, he is done. Except for me. He comes back.

Still. Françoise leaving him? Impossible. Or is it? And who, I wonder, will be the next new woman, shiny and bright and devoted? Has he already chosen her?

Pablo, still standing before the mirror, finishes carving through the foam to reveal his face. An older face, but women still turn to look and whisper together as he passes.

Françoise is also an artist, and of all the portraits that have been made of him, hers is the best—even I admit that. She captured the look of his eyes: dark, large, questioning, assessing. Seeing and not seeing, because an artist only allows himself to see what will be useful for the art.

And only feel what is necessary for the art.

"Do you remember our villa?" I ask. "When you carried me off?" Of course he does. But I want a word of remembered love from him, a sentiment. After all these years, my pulse continues to race when I look at him. No other man has affected me like this, and I want his pulse to race, too. I want more than the artist's gaze: I want longing. But it is not there. Friendship, sometimes lust. That is all.

Suddenly restless, I leave the chair and, sheet draped around me, wander through the studio, the old wood floor creaking as I move. In one corner there is a row of canvases carefully placed back to front, front to back, in order of size. A thick layer of dust covers the top edges of the paintings, and as I look through them, motes climb up like swarms of tiny insects.

Some of them I recognize, cubist paintings mixed in with the semiclassical works. Early 1920s, I think, placing their chronology the way other woman remember the birthdays of nieces and nephews. All born about the time he did that painting of me, the one he called *The Lovers*.

"It's not you," he insisted, even as I was posing for it in his studio. "It's a woman I cared about. How could it be you?"

"Well, it's certainly not Olga or Dora or Marie-Thérèse or any of the other hundred or so. And that is my nose; those are my eyes," I told him. "You did care. Once."

"You've always been vain. Now be quiet and tilt your head. You've got the pose wrong."

"Yes, my master," I said, but in our lovemaking, I made him plead for mercy, not vice versa.

I want that painting as badly as I ever wanted a man. I want the *me* of that painting, the young, adored woman. And so I look for it in the studio, hoping, disturbing the dust on row after row of canvases

"Is it true you sold my painting to Sara Murphy's sister? That is what the dealer Kahnweiler told me."

"None of your business," he says, rinsing off his razor and packing it into his battered leather kit.

I am almost finished looking through the row of paintings when I find one that halts me. A girl sitting in a chair, looking to her right at something the viewer cannot see. The lines of her face are tender, delicate. Her folded hands rest in her lap, and there is a curve to her neck and throat that is almost heart-breaking in its perfection.

"Pablo, who is this?" I hold up the painting.

He is buttoning his shirt now. He stops, lowers his head like a bull.

"A girl I knew," he says, turning away.

"That much is obvious." And from the way he hid his face, his feelings for her, or at least the memory of those feelings, are also obvious.

"What happened to her? Who is she?"

Pablo pauses. Just for a second, but there is much happening in that second. It is the second that artists hate because the subject changes. It becomes an image of before and after, an image that cannot be painted. Well, not quite true. It is an image that Pablo could paint, but no one else, Pablo who can paint yesterday, today, and tomorrow in a single image.

"She disappeared. That is all I know." He finishes folding a shirt into the valise and slams it shut, pretending to be distracted by a piece of paper that has fallen to the floor, because he does not want me to see the emotion that crosses his face before he can erase it.

So. Another woman who left him. Pablo does not like to be left, and let's face it, he is more often the one doing the leaving. It is always so in these affairs. One loves more than the lover. Pablo's women usually loved him more than he loved them. Was it different for him with this girl?

He opens the window and peers out into the street below. Gray. But no rain. "I can't wait to get back to the sun," he says. "Why is Paris so gray?"

The city, since the war's end, remains a sad place, a place where everyone is still hungry and tired and trying too hard to unlearn the vocabulary of the past years, to forget the unforgettable images, the roundups and the starvation, the German soldiers marching down the avenues, the sandbags in front of the statues and monuments of Paris protecting them, the camps where so many of our men were deported to for forced labor, the camps where those hundreds of thousands died. We are trying to pretend that life has gone back to normal. It hasn't. It won't. War is one of those things that can't be undone, not even in Paris.

Now the streets and bars are filled with American boys and men who fought, survived, found their way to Paris, stayed. For the nightclubs and girls, the first taste of absinthe. The Left Bank, across from Shakespeare and Company, is lined with easels and amateur painters trying to capture the glint of leaden silver on the rippling Seine. Terrible work, most of it.

I go to the window and stand next to Pablo. I put my arm through his and rest my head against his shoulder.

Thirty years before, after the Great War, we leaned out a window in Paris and for the first time saw American GIs, mostly, still in uniform, full of hope while drowning in pain: physical, emotional—both from battlefield wounds. It was a different war. But somehow the people seemed the same.

Except for Sara, that rich girl from Long Island who came to Paris after the war, in 1922. There was a flood of Americans after the war, coming for the art, the food, the inexpensive apartments, the escape from that new-world Puritanism. A boy from Omaha explained it to me one night at Café de Flore, that sense of someone always looking over your shoulder, ready to judge. "In Paris," he said, "no one gives a damn. Do they?"

Sara said something similar when I met her. "I breathe easily here. My children laugh louder here," she said. "I love Paris. I love France. I think Gerald will paint here. He is an artist, you know."

"And what of you?" I asked her. "Are you an artist?"

She had laughed. "Me? No. I wish to be the one who makes art possible."

Sara, with her yellow hair and blue eyes, was more than pretty, as if she carried her own private sun and it radiated from her, drew people to her.

But not even well-bred, well-educated, and well-traveled married mother of three Sara could control the look in her eyes when she looked at Pablo. How had Gerald not seen it? Perhaps he had. And looked away.

Standing now with my head on Pablo's shoulder, I want to go back to that other painting of the girl, but my instinct warns me not to. He will be gone soon. Again. Let some memories sleep while I still have even a little of his attention.

The studio smells of turpentine and oil and smoke, a lovely

perfume. I hope this is what heaven will smell like. But because I am trying to forget the painting that made Pablo hide his face, it is all I can think about, and the memory floats up, unwanted.

Cap d'Antibes. The girl who never spoke, who kept her eyes on the ground. The girl who stayed in the shadows, the way people had learned to do during the war, who smiled only when Pablo smiled at her.

A honk from down in the street. Paulo is there waving up at us, laughing, ready to take his famous father back to the sun, to the sea, to Françoise, who may or may not be there waiting for him.

"When will I see you again?" I ask, keeping my voice light. He does not answer. No matter. I will go home to my husband and think of other things. And what will Pablo think of? Françoise, who is leaving him? The girl in the painting? There is a deep crease between his brows. If I painted him now, it would require a thick black line.

"What happened to her?" he wonders aloud.

"The girl in the painting? Do you care?"

"No," he says. "Just curious."

He is lying. Curiosity for a painter usually ends when the painting is finished. He still thinks of her and wonders. Pablo is self-absorbed and can be cruel. Nothing matters to him more than his art, his work. Yet he is not without feeling. I've seen the love and pleasure in his eyes as he watched his children playing, seen the pity sometimes when he speaks of Olga.

"Pablo," I ask him, "did you really sell my painting? *The Lovers*?"

"It was never yours," he says.

"I sat for it, as you recall. You promised it to me."

"Time for you to leave," he says. "Out, out," and waves his arms at me as if I were a flock of wayward geese.

"Without breakfast?"

"Without anything." He grabs me playfully by the hair, pulls my head back, and plants an exaggerated kiss over my protests.

"What will you do if Françoise leaves you?" I ask, leaning into the strength of his arm.

"What I always do. Find another woman. Put your hat on. Paulo will be here any moment, and I want to lock up the studio."

I reluctantly stand before the little cracked mirror next to the door and pull the brim of my hat a little lower over my right eye. I can tell he saw me searching again though the piles of canvases as he rummaged around the studio looking for something he needed to take back with him. A toy horse, crudely carved, puppy gnawed.

"What do you want that old thing for?" I laugh. "Do you now carry good luck charms?"

He growls something I can't understand, something in Spanish, and flings my gloves at me. "Go," he says. "I've had enough of you." Those, from Pablo, are love words. They are the same words I used when I refused to marry him, the words with which I dismissed him . . . and then called him back for more of what we had between the sheets. Husband, no. Lover, yes.

He means those words, I see. He really wants me to leave. He is standing by the door, holding it open.

Hat tilted rakishly over one eye, I clatter down the stairs, laughing and throwing Russian insults over my shoulder at him, curses still remembered from my time with the grand duke.

"Till next time, my love," I call, clattering down the stairs and into the street.

He's watching from the window. I can feel his eyes on my back, those huge black eyes that take in everything, including the way one of my shoes is pinching my toes and making me walk a little lopsided.

Will he now go back into the studio, those piles of canvases, and slide out what I had been looking for and couldn't find? *The Lovers.* My painting. A man and a woman, forever young and beautiful, forever in love. The young man looks at his beloved. She looks off to the side, modestly, submissively, as if she has not yet said yes. But a perceptive viewer sees it in her expression, the willingness, the desire.

The woman is me. Me, forever young and lovely and loved.

From the street behind me, an automobile horn blasts through the misty morning air. Three loud honks, and Paulo, his son, shouts up.

"Hey, Paulo!" I wave at him. He looks my way, gives a half-hearted wave, pretending he knows who I am.

"Come carry the cases," his father calls down to him.

When I first met Paulo, he was naked except for the sand covering most of him and carried a toy bucket and shovel. He was two, I think, and playing busily with Sara Murphy's children at the little beach in Antibes. La Garoupe, it's called. A postage stamp of a beach, though now it has been greatly enlarged to accommodate the tourists. Sara, the stylish avant-garde queen of the social scene had started a stampede south after that summer when she and her family went to Antibes.

Paulo's a grown man now, in his thirties, taller than his father, with brown rather than black hair. Good-looking in a predictable kind of way. He lacks Pablo's charisma. One can see it even from the way he walks, slightly leaning forward as if a strong wind pushes him back. Perhaps the wind pushing against him is his divorce from his wife, just completed I've heard. The Picasso men don't seem made for marriage, at least not loving ones or long ones. They seem unable to combine the two.

Paulo comes out of the building carrying two of his father's heavy valises, and he has the same worried expression on his face that he had thirty years ago when he was carrying that little toy bucket. He is one of those reminders of time past, the years that have flown by like migrating birds, except those birds don't return.

"Doves don't migrate," Pablo told me once when I made some misinformed comment about them. They stay all year. They are constant, like the north star.

The few times I've seen Pablo grow nostalgic, even a touch close to sentimental, is when he talks about doves, and by *doves*, he means the pigeons of his childhood, those cooing, prancing birds of the Spanish piazzas, where he and his father threw bread crumbs for them. He was a loved child, Pablo. He grew up in the sureness of that love, a child who was always picked up when he fell, rocked when he wept. Is that his strength?

My husband, the doctor, thinks that strength comes from good digestion. Pablo agrees, I think. He is careful with his diet, with his body. He intends to live a very long time. Pablo and his pigeons that do not migrate.

When the war ended and Pablo was asked to make a lithograph for the 1949 Peace Congress, he gave them *The Dove of Peace*. A white bird against a black background. Simple, naturalistic, memorable.

You see it everywhere now, even on Russian stamps.

But the print has its own secrets. Pablo drew not a dove but, yes, a pigeon, a pet bird that had been given to him by his friend Matisse. And the pigeon is an homage to his father, his first art teacher. José had taken him to the square in Málaga and taught him to draw doves when he was probably the same age as Paulo when he toted his little bucket.

The pigeon/dove is Pablo's symbol of peace, but also of himself.

There's confidence for you.

If I had married him, he would have destroyed me. That's what gods do, because we let them. No, better to be a good doctor's wife. Pablo will go back to his little villa in the south, and Françoise will or will not be there. For his sake, I hope she is. I will go back to my husband, who may not even have noticed I was away. He, too, knows what it means to love an artist. Art is all. Love is a pastime.

TWO
· · · · · · · ·

New York
September 1953

ALANA

I have a photo, faded and torn, of two women on a terrace. Their black jersey bathing costumes reach modestly down their thighs and up to their collarbones. Their hair is cut short in a flapper bob of the 1920s. The women gaze straight into the camera with a hint of defiance.

Beyond the terrace is a calm sea. Even in this black-and-white photo, the blueness of the water shimmers. Sailboats are caught forever on that sea, as are the women, ambered into eternal youth and beauty. Between the stone terrace and the sea are palm trees with fringed tops and grainy trunks.

If you look long enough at the photo, you can feel the Mediterranean sunshine.

On a table next to a moss-streaked pot of rosemary is a jumble of abandoned children's toys. A rubber ball, pick-up sticks, thin and dangerous as knitting needles. Toy animals, metallic and small. A cow, a sheep, a crude hand-carved horse, all lying on their sides as if exhausted from the hard play of children.

There is a secret folded into the shadows of the photo.

In the bottom right-hand corner, there is a third woman, blurred in motion rather than posing. The camera has caught her unaware. She wears a print dress, not a bathing costume; her hair is long and braided. The sun, directly behind her, backlighting her, makes her face impossible to see. The light halos the shape of her head so that she is everyone and no one.

Let's begin my story here. Beginnings are, after all, about discovery. About finding what has been lost.

My mother. A girl on a train going into France.

An everyday thing, the sooty smoke, rhythmic grinding of steel on steel from the wheels, murmur of conversation, shouts of bored children, rustle of newspapers.

This predictable commonality is the starting place of coincidence, which is another word for *miracle*.

She sits alone, separate from the other passengers, alone in the way that the dangerous and the unknown are, and so the others leave the seat next to her empty. The young wives with their babes on their laps sneak glances at her, noticing the wildness of her uncombed hair, her pale mouth and face.

She is running away from home to join her lover, Antonio. It is the first time she has been on a train alone without her mother or father or governess. Because Antonio did not meet her at the station, as he had promised.

Antonio has abandoned her and she cannot go home again. She has brought shame to them.

The train moves past trees, villages, dirt roads, a man beating his mule faster to market, children playing on the banks of a stream, wading into the cold frothing water. Coming to a railroad crossing, the train whistle screams a warning, then the train stops at the border. People stand, stretch.

A clatter of suitcases and trunks, shouting, the police coming through, checking papers, tickets. Her hands are trembling when she shows her papers, but they don't notice. The conductor blows his whistle; the train gives off great bursts of steam. They are in France. Out the window, the sea begins emerging through the greenery, the Mediterranean flashing its brilliant turquoise. Sailboats bob in the postcard-lovely harbors.

At the next stop, a woman wearing a straw hat shaped like a man's bowler and decorated with a silk rose that falls over her eye comes into the train car. She wears high heels and carries a rattan shopping basket. From this basket emerge tantalizingly familiar shapes and odors: bread, ham, oranges. A clank of bottles. The woman in flight looks up at her after ignoring everyone else for the past three and a half hours.

This is, after all, a beginning, and beginnings require change.

"May I?" the newcomer asks, looking at the empty sit next to her. Without waiting for an answer, she sits, puts her basket on the floor, crosses her legs, lights a cigarette. After a moment, she offers one to the girl, who accepts it. How can a foolish silk rose on a hat make such a difference in someone's life?

"Come far?" the new passenger asks.

"Not too far," the girl says. She turns back to the window and stares hard at whatever is passing by.

The other woman takes a newspaper from her basket and unfolds it, pretending not to notice that the girl opposite has turned pale. On the front page of the paper is a photograph of the Brown Shirts marching in Rome.

"He promises to drain the swamps, that man Mussolini,"

the woman says to herself as much as anyone else. She sighs and shakes her head. After that one comment, they ride in silence till the next station.

"My stop," the woman says, folding up the newspaper, rising. She hesitates, considering. "Look, I can see you are in trouble. Take this. It's the address where I'm staying. If you need a friend. The world needs kindness," she says quietly. She puts the card on the seat next to the red-eyed girl.

"Good luck." The woman rises, tucks her purse around her arms, and walks to the carriage door. She disappears into the steam of the resting train as the girl watches, fingering the card.

Beginnings, you see, are a flight to as well as a flight from.

At the last moment, just before the conductor shuts the door and waves the train on, the girl leaps from the train.

This is the story my mother, Marti, told me. How she ran away from home. But stories are inventions, especially stories that mothers tell daughters. My dark-haired mother who always pronounced her words so carefully, taming the rolled *r*'s of her foreign accent.

That is all I know of my mother's life before me. And it took all the curiosity and stubbornness of my childhood to excavate that much. There was a boyfriend before my father, a failed elopement. The stranger who did her a kindness. After me, there were to be no more risks, ever.

"Precious little pest," she would say, cradling me in her arms, even when I became a teenager and rolled my eyes at her. "I would die to keep you safe."

Many mothers may think that, feel that. But what mother says it aloud? Is there anything more frightening to say to a child?

Telling myself my mother's story used to calm me, make me feel like I was strongly moored to the facts of this world. This time, it didn't work. The steering wheel felt cold against my forehead. A smell of damp green lawns and fields rose up around me. It was an inky dark night, and I was alone in a car on the side of a road.

So I told myself the second story that is an anchor, one of my earliest memories. Warm sun, gritty sand, whispering ocean, and a pleasant, prickling scent I will later learn, during a cooking class, is thyme. I am so small my mother can lift me up under my arms and balance me on her knees. I am happy in the way that very small children can be when needs are simple and met. My mother's arms are around me, the air is warm like a bath, the sky is blue. The moment is rich and complete.

But now I was lost, in every way, and memories and stories weren't helping.

"Do something," I ordered myself, leaning over to look for a map in the glove compartment. It was early autumn, a time that always felt like endings, and so much was ending. My mother had died a few months ago, leaving me numbed to everything but grief.

Adding to that grief, I was having trouble paying the bills, and William, my fiancé, was becoming more insistent that we set the date. I was running out of reasons not to pick the day, buy the dress. But I couldn't imagine that till-death-do-us-part walk down the aisle without my mother there, giving me that special smile, mouthing the words "I love you."

My grief went beyond the personal. The Red Scare had taken over the country and the right wing was hunting for communists and communist sympathizers. The FBI was trailing after Albert Einstein because he had joined the American Crusade Against Lynching. Orson Welles, Charlie Chaplin and Martin Luther King Jr. had been blacklisted by the committee. That was how powerful McCarthy had become, how terrified of any hint of communism the country had become.

Senator McCarthy's House Un-American Activities Committee wouldn't care about a small fry like me. Yet I worried. I and some of my friends would be considered communist sympathizers because we demonstrated and marched for workers' rights. For desegregation. For world peace.

My old professor, Mr. Grippi, was about to lose his job at Columbia, thanks to the House Un-American Activities Committee. Professor Grippi was a world-renowned art historian, author of six books of art history, guest speaker at conferences in Oslo, Peking, and Milan. But he had added touches of socialist history to his art history classes, talked about the role of poverty and working-class struggles in the art of the Impressionists. But now his tenure was threatened, and several of his books had been banned and even burned because of their socialist view of progress.

And when he had picketed a restaurant on Fifth Avenue that refused to serve Blacks and Hispanics, I marched with him.

My mother had been alive then. She was both proud of and fearful for me. "If the police come to the demonstration, leave. Immediately," she said. "Promise? Stay safe?"

The police had come. And photographers. A marcher next to me was hit in the face, and I stayed long enough to wrap my scarf around his bleeding head before finding a side door into a department store and slipping through it. I was shaking so hard with fear and fury I could barely twist the door handle. When I ran past the perfume department, the salesgirl looked at me and nodded her head in the direction of the elevator. I spent the rest of the afternoon in the tearoom, trying to make my hands stop trembling. I had never before seen a man beaten by the police.

Sitting in the car, reliving that day, I realized I couldn't do anything about the House Un-American Activities Committee or my fiancé. But I could do something about my dwindling prospects of full-time work and my quickly dwindling bank account.

Get out the map. But maps only work when you already know where you are.

My plan had been gloriously simple: pack a bag, make sure the appliances were unplugged in my Pearl Street apartment, take my mother's Volkswagen up the parkway along the river to the exit recommended by Michelin. Drive to Sneden's Landing, that small and private town on the Palisades, and find Sara Murphy's house. Sara, who had been a friend of Picasso's.

I would knock on her door and ask for an interview. It would be after dinner, and if Sara was typical of her generation—the Lost Generation, Gertrude Stein had called them—then she would have had a few cocktails, some wine, maybe an after-dinner liqueur. She might be in a generous and talkative mood. If the interview lasted as long as I hoped, a couple of hours, I'd stay in some cozy country inn and then head back to Manhattan in the morning.

I'd return to New York with enough material to write my article, and that article would lead to more work. Even, I hoped, to a full-time staff position.

But after driving in circles past the same dark streets and byways for half an hour, I realized I was so lost I had given up and pulled over. Trucks roared by with a force that rocked my mother's little black car. Not hers any longer, mine now, but I kept finding reminders of her: pins under the seats, a lace

handkerchief in the glove compartment. Each new find a knife
thrust to the gut, I missed her so much.

Pablo Picasso had been my mother's favorite artist, her aes-
thetic touchstone. Reproductions of his paintings had lined the
walls of my childhood room. A hand holding a flower. Faces
with the eyes and noses misaligned. Circus figures. Guitars and
bullfights. Other children had Mother Goose or Mickey Mouse.
I had Picasso.

In our apartment, Picasso was an almost godlike figure, or
at least a giant figure, the greatest artist who ever lived, with
his various and prolific phases, his early cubism, the Blue Period, the Rose, the neoclassical—with its monumental figures,
the women with placid faces and eyes that never looked at the
artist when being painted, and so never at the viewer. Inexpensive reproductions covered the walls of our apartment.

"Too much history, too much past," my mother whispered
when we went to the Renaissance rooms at the Met. "Come,
let's go be in the twentieth century, where we belong," and she
would pull me by the hand, a small child who would have followed her mother anywhere. We'd go back into the street,
downtown to the Paul Rosenberg Gallery on East Fifty-Seventh
Street. My mother and I spent so much time there admiring the
Matisses and Braques, the Picassos, they knew us by name and
would bring my mother little cups of coffee as we sat and admired the paintings we could never have purchased.

My mother had led me to Picasso, and Picasso's art had led
me to David Reed.

Reed, editor of *Art Now*, had not wanted to give me an assignment. Some of the writers, all those bright young men fresh
out of Yale and Harvard and Cornell, let that slip during a

cocktail reception. "The board pretty much forced him," they let me know. "Say, were you homecoming queen? Did we meet at the spring festival bacchanal in sixty?" they asked. They never asked what my thesis had been, and sometimes their eyes never moved up beyond my chest.

I had been popular at that reception. But as soon as conversation turned to work, I was shunned. I was supposed to be home, minding the children, cooking dinner. Or at least staying in the typing pool, where I belonged. The war was over, and the men who were coming home were home, so women were very much less welcomed in the workforce than they had been during the war. Rosie the Riveter had been shunted into the PTA.

"Really?" I had complained when David Reed had first given me the Picasso assignment. "I know of at least three other writers who are working on articles about him at this moment."

"Then you'd better come up with something they can't." He shuffled some papers on his desk to indicate how busy he was.

"I think we should run an article about Irène Lagut instead."

"Who?" Reed asked, looking up and taking his pipe out of his mouth so that he could make an even more surprised expression.

"Lagut. Parisian. Showed with the surrealists. Great friends with Apollinaire and Picasso. Her work was very avant-garde, very influential. I saw some of her paintings last year at the National Gallery."

"Never heard of her. A woman. Too minor of an artist, I imagine. And I thought Picasso was the subject of your thesis." He struck a match to relight that smelly, irritating pipe.

"I have other interests now." The truth: thinking too much about Picasso made me feel that knife edge of grief for my mother.

And, of course, there was that other truth. Picasso was in France. I was in New York and broke.

"Not Lagut, Picasso. Take it or leave it," he said.

"Picasso, if it must be." I worried about not getting any assignment at all. "Expenses covered?" I asked. "Travel?"

Reed laughed unpleasantly. "For a freelancer? Of course not."

"Then how . . . ?" I didn't finish the question because I already knew the answer. He wanted me to fail. He didn't want a woman on the masthead of his magazine, his boy's club.

He smiled across his desk at me. Not a friendly smile. More of a cat-about-to-eat-the-canary smile.

That had been two weeks ago, and I had spent every moment since then researching, reading, trying to find a way into this impossible assignment. Every word I read, every note I took, brought back memories of my mother, the excruciating fact of her death.

I decided to focus my article on two of Picasso's paintings: *The Lovers*, painted in the South of France in the early twenties, and his masterpiece, *Guernica*, painted in the next decade. *The Lovers* was personal, poetic. *Guernica* was a horrific statement about war, painted in 1937 following the bombing of the little Basque village fifteen years after *The Lovers*. *Guernica* was a painting filled with violence, a testament to the planned, willful murder of civilians as an act of war during the Spanish Civil War, and a premonition of the larger war to come in Europe between England, France, and the United States and Germany, Italy, and Japan.

When the huge mural had first traveled to the United States in 1939, when I was fifteen, my mother had taken me up to the

Valentine Gallery on Fifty-Seventh Street to see it. The gallery had been packed, and we stood in a corner for hours, trying to see it up close. We had to wait almost till closing, and then we walked the length of it, all twenty feet, slowly, the way my mother walked the stations of the cross during Lent. She cried, as did many viewers. This had happened, was still happening, in Spain, where Franco's military was murdering people, where the war we hoped would not happen had already begun.

"Sara. Married to Gerald Murphy," I explained to my friend Helen over cocktails at our favorite bar on West Fourteenth Street. "Rich girl from Long Island. Presented at court in London, house on the shore, ponies, tennis. But also a free spirit, it seems, or became one. She was a friend of Picasso. As far as I can tell, Picasso painted her several times. His *Woman Seated in an Armchair* is a portrait of Sara. And her husband painted, too, when they lived in France. She had three children, but only one survived, the daughter. Her two boys died."

The bar was busy for a weeknight. Helen and I sat at the wooden bar, as close together as we could to avoid the elbows and spilled drinks of the other customers.

"Sad," Helen said, taking a cigarette from the pack in her purse. "How did you find out about her?"

"Papers in my mother's desk. There was a newspaper clipping, a story of Gerald and Sara selling their villa in Southern France, with a few sentences about the Murphys and their glamorous social life, their friendships with Cole Porter and Scott and Zelda Fitzgerald . . . and Pablo Picasso."

I'd also found unpaid bills, letters waiting to be answered, a note from the building super saying they'd be painting the hallway. I'd had another of those moments confronting the reality of her death and had wept for the rest of the evening. I had felt like a trespasser, going through her things until I had realized that now they were my things. My bills. My letters needing answers. My job to remind the super about the hall.

"Perhaps if I can track down the Murphys, they'll give me some new Picasso material for my article. Can we afford another round?"

"Why not? Who needs to eat tomorrow?" Helen waved her empty martini glass, and the bartender headed for our end of the bar.

"Gerald had a brief career, a minor splash really, in Paris in the twenties," I said, shouting a little over the barroom din. "No major work, but he knew everyone, as did his wife. And now they live in New Jersey."

We were two working girls, scrimping to buy stockings and lipsticks and waiting for our big breaks. We knew that we might be called girls and still be waiting for those breaks many years down the road, right up until we were called bitter old maids, because those breaks might never come. And at almost thirty years of age, we were close to that line already.

Helen toasted me with her martini. "I can't wait to see Reed's face when you hand him this."

"Me too. But first I have to convince the Murphys to speak with me."

And there was that other problem. My mother's ashes, in the urn in the bookcase, waiting to be dispersed. Except she had never told me where. Another of her many secrets. And William. Eager to wed, tired of waiting, of me dragging my feet.

"It will be good to get out of New York for a day or two," I said. "If anyone calls for me when I go to talk with Sara Murphy, Helen, just say you don't know where I am, okay?"

"Even William?"

"Even William."

"If your name is on one of McCarthy's lists, this would be a good time to get married, to change it," Helen said.

"Probably." We finished our martinis and put on our coats.

"He's a communist, you know. Has been for years," I said.

"Who?"

"Picasso."

D avid Reed, I thought, sitting now in my car on the dark side of Palisades Road, had set me up for a fall. He knew how impossible it would be to find fresh material about an artist as famous as Picasso, especially since I couldn't interview him in person. David Reed didn't want a woman's name spoiling his magazine. I spent a lovely five minutes daydreaming my revenge, my many articles, my Pulitzer, the board offering me the position of editorial director of the magazine. Firing Reed. *Take that, Mr. Reed.*

The traffic was thinning. It was almost eight, and I could hear night sounds weaving gently in and out of the stronger noises: an owl, and wind making a strange moan as it ran past the Palisades above the Hudson River. Twilight had turned the blazing autumn leaves to a rusty gray, but now black night was erasing all color.

It was too late to knock on Sara Murphy's door, even if I could find it. Just drive, I decided. Damned if I was going to sleep on the side of the road.

THREE

· · · · · · · · · ·

ALANA

Minutes later, I took a turn off the main road onto a smaller one and then an even smaller road. I passed a large Queen Anne house, yellow silhouetted against the lavender twilight. There was a sign in front of it. I did a quick U-turn and pulled into the graveled drive.

"Brennan's Inn" read the sign planted in the front garden. Steps led onto a wraparound porch. Lights poured from several windows, and somewhere a dog barked. I grabbed my overnight case and headed for the front door.

Inside, I was welcomed by a wood-paneled hall, Oriental carpets, walls full of bookshelves and art. The paintings were vintage Victoriana, lots of little girls with kittens and mothers bending tenderly over cribs. A few seascapes, though, were good imitation Turners.

The reception desk had been built in at the bottom of a beautiful mahogany staircase.

A family was checking in ahead of me, mother and father, two little girls, speaking Spanish quickly and quietly with each other. When one of the girls, a child of about six, whirled around and bumped into me, the mother was profusely apologetic. "No problem," I said in her language. "She's a lovely child. *Niña encantadora.*"

"How many nights?" the clerk asked when it was my turn. He wiped his hands on a dish towel tied around his waist and reached for the guest book. "Doesn't matter. Plenty of rooms. Sign here. Off-season." He pushed the register toward me. "Not that we have a season."

I was too tired to laugh at his weak joke. "How far am I from Sneden's?"

"Just down the road. Three miles." He handed me a key attached to a yellow plastic tag. "Number six. Upstairs, last door on the right . . ." He thumbed in the direction of the stairs. "Bar is that way, swimming pool, sauna, and massage room that way. Just kidding. We do actually have a bar, though, open to the public as well as guests. If you need more towels, there's a linen closet in the hall. Help yourself." He picked up the damp towel and headed in the direction of the bar. He was tall enough that he had to stoop through the doorway.

Through the taproom's open door, I saw the black-and-white television hung over the rows of dusty bottles. It was a news program. The sound was off, but I didn't need to hear the words. It was Senator McCarthy leaning into the microphone, scowling with frenzy and a cold hatred. McCarthy, who was looking for communists under every rock . . . and in many college clubs and groups.

Perhaps looking for me.

If David Reed found out, I'd never get another assignment. If he found out, he'd never run my article on Picasso, even if it did get written. Didn't matter what his beliefs were; association with me at any level would implicate him.

And I realized now that despite my original hesitance, I really wanted this assignment, wanted to think about Picasso, write about him. Picasso could help lead me back to my mother.

I went up the creaking stairs and unpacked my nightgown and put my notepad and pen on the bedside table. After a shower, I wrote Sara's name on the fogged bathroom mirror as a good luck charm. *Sara, speak to me*, I willed.

I wrote my own name next to Sara's: *Alana Olsen*. My father, who died when I was eight, had been a tall man of Norwegian ancestry, but I got my looks from my mother, who was small and dark-haired. I wrote *William Greene* next to my name, remembering how I used to enclose both names inside a heart and then wipe it away before William could see it so that he wouldn't accuse me of being too sentimental. This time, I wiped our names away without having enclosed them in that heart.

I willed myself to feel the love and the desire that a wife would feel, but instead, there was only that numbness that had grown worse since my mother's death.

"Make up your mind, Alana. You're not getting younger," he'd said at our last dinner date. "And I can't make partner till I'm married." His tone of voice made it clear that becoming partner was uppermost in his mind, not our romance, if romance it was. I tried to picture myself in a little day dress, apron tied on, greeting him at the door after a day at the office. Chicken in the oven, chocolate cake all frosted, cocktails ready to pour.

Tried and couldn't. I fell asleep in the huge old brass bed of the inn room trying to imagine William next to me, trying to imagine being his wife. I dreamed of my mother, of our last afternoon together. "You shouldn't be alone," she had said. "It is too hard alone." When I woke up in the early morning light, I was hugging myself so tightly my arms ached. The room was cold with autumn, and I dressed as quickly as possible, trying to forget the dream of loss.

It took me fifteen minutes of following faded carpets down different hallways to find the breakfast room. The inn was even larger than I had realized when I came across it in the dark last night. Large hallways turned into little ones; rooms emptied into rooms. Up a large staircase, down a smaller one. At one dead end, I found myself outside the house, on a small balcony. It was dizzying, but the view over the river was breathtaking. No wonder an entire school of art had dedicated itself to views along the Hudson.

"Found us, I see," said the man who had signed me in last night. He guided me to a table by a window overlooking a somewhat weedy garden. "The house is confusing as hell. Built in the time when big houses were like villages and all the servants knew the lanes and alleys." He had a towel wrapped around his waist and a pile of dirty plates balanced along his arm from his wrist to his elbow. "Eggs? Scrambled?"

"Sounds great. Coffee, please."

"I'm Jack Brennan. I'd shake hands, but they are full at the moment. Sorry I didn't introduce myself last night, but you looked pretty exhausted."

He smiled so that the freckles on his face spread wider, opening like a dim constellation in a pale sky.

"Hello, Jack Brennan," I said. "You work long hours. Both shifts?"

"Because I'm the owner. That's my good luck or curse, depending on how the plumbing is working on any given day. Inherited, along with the taxes and peeling wallpaper. Where you headed today?"

It was a friendly question but one with a hint of intimacy, as if we were old friends.

"Cheer Hall."

"To see the Murphys?" He looked at me more closely, a frown of curiosity and perhaps disapproval creasing between his brows.

"I will be staying another night, maybe two more," I said, I couldn't afford the trip to France I'd always wanted, but I could afford a few days of a working vacation on the Hudson.

"Great. Plenty of room," Jack said with enthusiasm. "Let me take these to the kitchen, and I'll bring out your breakfast."

"Thanks. And I need to make a phone call. Is there a pay phone?"

"No. Go ahead and use the phone on the reception desk. Not too long and not too distant, please."

A crash, a sound of breaking china, a muffled cry, came from a doorway at the end of the room.

Jack grimaced and headed to the kitchen disaster. When he hurried, there was a halt in his gait, a hitch and drag of the right foot.

He must have felt my eyes on him. He turned around again briefly. "South Pacific," he said. "Shrapnel."

After finishing the coffee and eggs, I went to the reception desk and used the house phone to make a quick call to Helen, who was temping as a copy editor at Manufacturers Hanover on Fifth Avenue.

"Right," she said when the operator connected me to her desk. "William has already called me twice. Where are you staying, and what's the phone number?"

I read her the number from the phone and then mumbled a question, turning my back to the noisy family that had lined up, ready to check out.

"What did you say? Speak up," Helen said. "And quick. I don't want to get fired for taking a personal call."

"I said, has anyone other than William asked for me?"

She knew immediately what I meant. "Nope. All clear."

"Great. Thanks. How's the job going?"

"Just fine, if you think correcting copy about the importance of savings accounts is fine. On the whole, I'd rather be writing about Jackson Pollock."

"Keep the faith," I said.

"You too. Good luck with Sara."

By ten, I was on the road and in good spirits, driving the country roads of pine stands, pastel-painted houses with front-yard oaks turning to gold and bronze, white stands of birch. It was so lovely I almost wished I had studied the classic landscape painters, not moderns like Picasso.

But now that I was only minutes away from Sara, from a conversation about Pablo Picasso with someone who had known him, I was feeling the first thrill of the treasure hunter who has found a Roman coin peeping up through the diggings. How well had she known Picasso?

For that matter, how well had Picasso known her? What kind of woman had Sara been? If this goes well, I thought, I might end up knowing more about Sara than my own mother. My secretive, beloved, infuriating mother.

I wondered if Sara had been friends with Irène Lagut as well. *Next time*, I told her in my thoughts, *Irène, you will be my next subject, once I have that job.* In a bookshop, I'd found a dusty catalog of her paintings from a 1923 Paris exhibit and had been struck by the colors, the shapes, her lovely images of women painted by another woman's eyes, not a man's. But, like Picasso, she was in France. How could I ever interview her?

Cheer Hall, when I found it, was a lovely old stone house, hugged by shrubs and towering trees and surrounded by ancient stone fences. Long porches lined the front of the house on both floors. A maid answered the doorbell, unsmiling and stiff in her white apron.

"Is Mrs. Murphy at home, please?"

"Maybe. Depends on who you are," the maid answered.

"Who's that, Martha?" a voice called from inside the house.

A woman, slender, dressed in tweed trousers and a black sweater, came and stood next to the maid. Sara. I recognized her from the few magazine photos I'd found. She was seventy years old that year, if the dates in the newspaper articles I'd found were accurate. Her curly blond hair was giving over to white. Round face, small, even features. She was still beautiful and looked younger than her age, but there was a sadness in her eyes. *Losing two children will do that*, I thought. When was the last time she had laughed?

"Good morning," I said a little too brightly, extending my hand. "I'm Miss Alana Olsen."

Sara Murphy shook my hand but didn't smile. "Do I know you?"

Her voice was vibrant and deep, like amber honey.

"Not yet. Are you Mrs. Murphy?" I smiled. "I'm very happy to meet you. I wondered if I could ask you and your husband for an interview. About your life on the Riviera. I understand you were friends with Pablo Picasso."

She stared at me with widened eyes, her hand going to her throat in that protective gesture we use when something unanticipated threatens us.

I hadn't called or written in advance. It's harder to say no to a person face-to-face than on the telephone or by mail.

Sara studied me for a long moment, her cool gray-blue eyes assessing me. From somewhere in the house, I could hear a radio playing a piece by Vivaldi. "I don't give interviews," she said firmly. She started to close the door.

"Please, wait a mo—" But the door was already shut.

I went back to my car and sat in it, thinking. A curtain opened at a side window overlooking the drive. Sara and I locked eyes for a moment. Though she had turned me away, her gaze wasn't hostile or rude. It felt like the look a friend gives just before she waves goodbye. It was the kind of gaze that required a smile, so I smiled at her.

I thought she was going to smile back, but just at that moment, her head turned away. The curtain flickered and she was gone.

FOUR

· · · · · · · · ·

SARA

I went to the window that overlooks the drive and peered at her from behind the curtain. Our eyes met. *She'll be back*, I thought. *She has a determined chin.*

After her car was out of sight, I regretted that I hadn't waved to her. Caution and cynicism still do not come easily to me, even after all these years.

And it was a surprise seeing her standing there, with that face so full of hope. She reminded me of so many things, the kinds of things that might be better forgotten, but your heart refuses to let them go.

She had looked like one of Pablo's paintings from the twenties, those lovely dark-haired women radiant and full of life. I was tempted to let her in, even though she had announced she was a journalist. I just wanted to look at her, to bask in that sense of a better future to come that radiated from her.

She reminded me of sand and sun. If only we had stayed there. The Côte d'Azur, La Garoupe, Villa America, our Riviera home. Blue sky, blue water, pale sand, and the bronzed children, the sticking sand turning their skin to velvet. And the lie that ended it all.

At first sight, I felt I knew her. But of course, that couldn't be. Could it? She was too young to have been there. But she looked so much like her.

Can the past be undone? No, of course not. But the more I thought about it, about her, it seemed an opportunity had presented itself to repair some of the past.

"Everything okay, darling?" Gerald shouted from his study, calling me back from the memory. "Did I hear the doorbell?" No, everything is not okay. That face full of hope has upset me, shook me the way a breeze makes leaves on a tree tremble.

Instead of shouting back, I walked down the hall and pushed his door open. The hinges squeaked a protest, but Gerald looked up from his cluttered desk and smiled. His sweet smile. His movie-star face, old now but still handsome, firm-jawed and noble-nose elegant.

"We had a visitor," I say.

"I thought I heard a car in the drive. And . . . ?"

"A journalist. She wants to talk about Picasso. I sent her away."

Gerald put down his pen and leaned back in his chair.

Beautiful Gerald, who had turned heads everywhere we went, male and female. Now slightly stooped, gray, with that sense of loss he carried that was more than the death of our sons. After Baoth had died, Gerald put down his paintbrushes and never picked one up again. He had reverted to that sense of incompleteness he had when we first met, that hollowness of the artist who does not make art, who has denied that creative part of himself.

Even Picasso had stopped making art for a while during the war. But with Picasso, making art was the same as breathing;

he could not survive without it and had quickly returned to it with even more driven intensity and determination.

I felt my own failure when I looked at Gerald. The failure of a wife who cannot heal the wounds of the man she loves more than her own life. *If only*, I thought again, *if only I could even get him to look at his old paintings, to see how good they had been.*

"She reminds me of someone. Maybe myself," I said.

"Maybe you should speak with her."

"We agreed. No telling tales, no gossip, no stories about Pablo and what he ate for breakfast, whether he swam well, how much he drank at dinner."

"Who he slept with," Gerald said. The tone of his voice was absolutely neutral. Innocence? Indifference? Sometimes they are the same thing.

Yes, we had agreed. We would talk about France as little as possible. We were modern people, and modern people live today, not yesterday. Not even when most of their lives are in that dark locked closet of the past.

"What's for dinner?" Gerald asked.

"I've asked the cook to make a bouillabaisse. We'll see how she does. And apricot tart."

He stood to hug me, my back to his chest, his chin resting on the top of my head. "Are you sorry we left France? The Midi?" he asked. It was years since we had lived in Antibes, but we had only sold our house there a few years ago. It had been hard, letting it go. So many memories, both good and bad. But lazy summers in the South of France had been replaced by years of travel and residences in Switzerland and Austria looking for cures, cures we did not find. And after we lost the boys, there was the war. Travel to France was impossible, and by the time the war was over, we had become New Yorkers again.

But some mornings, I still longed for the salt ocean air, for the smell of wild thyme, and for the turpentine fumes from Gerald's studio at the villa. For the time before the lie.

"We couldn't stay there, could we?" I said. "It was a time as well as a place, and it is gone. Remember the cook at Hotel du Cap?"

"I certainly do. She terrified me. Worse than any drill sergeant in the army. And that meek little daughter of hers."

"Anna. Except she wasn't the cook's daughter."

"Oh. Any mail today?"

Twenty years ago, he would have asked, "Then who was she?" He would have been curious. But that was before.

"You seem sad today." He turned me around and looked into my eyes.

"I distracted you, my darling. Back to work."

"He's about to change lovers again, you know," he said. "Françoise is leaving him." Gerald pulled a piece of paper out from the pile on his desk, Pablo's most recent letter. We had stayed in touch, all these years.

"So hard to believe," I said. "A woman actually leaving him. This is a first." I made my voice light, indifferent.

"The second. Don't forget Irène."

"Oh, yes, Lagut. The one who followed him down to Cap d'Antibes, just to irritate Olga."

"He loved having his women fighting over him. The scoundrel." There was true affection in Gerald's voice.

And thinking about Irène and Cap d'Antibes—that strange, wonderful, terrifying summer—made me think again of the woman I had just turned away.

There had been so much hope in her face, hope like a homecoming, like something familiar you hadn't even realized you missed. What was her name? Alana?

"Maybe you should speak with her," Gerald said again, just before I reached the door. "That journalist. See what she wants. Might be interesting for you."

"Perhaps. If she comes back. I may have discouraged her." *Please come back*, I thought. I wanted to see her face again, see the hope in her eyes. Hope is a rare thing, a wonderful thing.

"Has Honoria called?" Gerald sat down at his desk again and fussed with papers to hide his worry.

Our daughter, Honoria, had given birth to her second son in the summer, and his tininess, his newborn frailty, both delighted us and terrified us. Children are so vulnerable. When our sons had died, we thought we would never be able to carry more grief, and there it was, not grief but the fear of it. What if . . . ?

"I'll call her tonight," I said. "I'm sure all is well." But of course, I wasn't. We had learned and would live the rest of our days knowing that sometimes the worst does happen.

"Gerald, do you ever think of painting again?"

"Never."

When he had painted, that summer in Antibes, he had finished every work session by giving our boys piggyback rides to the beach. It had become part of his working process, and without that joyous ending of the day's labor, well, the day's labor of painting had become meaningless.

Death certainly cannot be undone. Grief cannot be put aside like an out-of-date dress. But if I could get Gerald interested in his art once again, perhaps there could be some healing.

And that woman, Alana . . .

"Gerald," I said, pausing in the doorway. "Do you believe in miracles?"

FIVE
·······

ALANA

When is a no not a no? She had shut the door on me. But then she had looked out the window, almost shyly. There had been curiosity in her glance. I could work with that. The table Sara had stood at when she looked out the window at me had had a bowl of fruit on it. Shiny red apples and green pears, all in a white glass bowl. Picasso had painted just such a composition in 1917, a year after his affair with the beautiful Irène Lagut, who was his student, according to the catalog of her work. I'd found another piece, an article on Apollinaire that said Irène had rejected Picasso's offer of marriage.

He had taken her to meet his family, and after, she had said, "No, I won't marry you after all." Picasso was not a man of small ego. That rejection must have gored him. And yet, when he painted her a few years later, he called the painting *The Lovers*.

If Sara wouldn't speak to me, perhaps Reed would accept an article on fruit still lives in early twentieth-century art?

No. He would laugh. And then show me the door.

Besides, I had roused Sara's curiosity, I thought. All was not yet lost.

On the way back to the inn, I stopped at a little store for cheese and a bunch of grapes. The cheese was unnaturally yellow and plastic-wrapped, but the grapes would do. It was my comfort meal, because it reminded me of an afternoon I'd spent with my mother years ago.

I'd been a child, very young, not even in school yet, and someone had died, someone I'd never known, but my mother had taken me with her on a plane, and after the plane, there had been a train ride through a countryside of forests and vineyards and pastures. There had been a smell that tickled my nose.

We stayed in a small hotel, and even though it was winter back home, here it was so warm we kept the windows open all night. I fell asleep to the sound of waves and woke up to the call of seagulls. Everywhere was the smell of flowers and bread.

Later that day, inside the dark, damp little church, I'd been afraid to see what was inside the open coffin. "A friend," my mother said. She was crying, and that frightened me more than the fact of death.

When I patted her hand and put my head in her lap, she said it wasn't just for her friend, those tears. Other people, too, so many had died in the war, but I was too little to know about them.

I was tired and fell asleep on the stone terrace on a pile of pillows. We were in a house, and people were talking quietly, the way they do when they don't want the children to hear, and when I woke up, we ate grapes and cheese.

Lunch is at one o'clock. Welsh rarebit, wedge salad, and choc-olate cake." Jack was behind the reception desk again when I returned from Cheer Hall.

"Okay."

"Your enthusiasm is not overwhelming" he said. "Not hungry?"

"Not really."

"That kind of day already?" He raised one eyebrow, tilted his head. "Kind of early to wave the white flag, isn't it?"

I retreated back to my room to plot and reconsider. Before I could think of a way to convince Sara to let me interview her, I fell asleep, soothed by the soft country air and murmurs coming from deep within the old inn. The extra sleep was welcome. I had been tossing and turning for weeks, thinking about William, about Senator McCarthy.

When I awoke, it was ten to one, and after running a comb through my hair and adding fresh lipstick, I went downstairs to the dining room.

"Hey," Jack said, coming over to my table with a basket of bread and butter. "No luck this morning at Cheer Hall? That what got you down?"

"Mrs. Murphy wouldn't talk to me."

"Talk? You're a journalist?" A deep crease of disapproval formed between his brows.

"Yes. Is that a problem?"

He paused, and I could see he was carefully considering his words. "We're all a little protective of the Murphys. People live in Sneden's Landing because they want privacy."

Jack sat at the table and stared accusingly at me. *What blue eyes he has*, I thought. The color of my mother's aquamarine ring and just as translucent.

"I'm not that kind of a journalist. I'm an art writer," I said, hearing the defensiveness in my voice.

He didn't look persuaded. "A career girl," he said, and I didn't care for the tone of his voice.

"The Murphys were friends with Pablo Picasso. I just want to ask them about him. Nothing invasive or too personal. And do you have something against working women?"

Jack folded his arms over his chest. A man at the next table was waving his hand in the air, trying to get Jack's attention, but he was ignoring him and still staring hard at me.

"You mean other than the fact that some of the GIs back from the war are still having trouble finding work? Still haven't found a way to support their families?" His eyes had narrowed.

"Look," I told him. "I need this interview to get a job. A good job from an editor who doesn't want to hire me because I'm a woman. I need to work for a living. No silver spoon in this mouth. I pay rent. My electricity doesn't come free."

"Not married," he said.

"Even if I were . . . I would want this. Haven't you ever wanted something that was more than putting a meal on the table?"

The hard line of his mouth softened a little. He nodded. I couldn't read what that nod meant. Without another word, he got up to take care of the next table.

He came back when I had finished lunch and was carrying a vase full of orange chrysanthemums and ferns.

"Flowers," I said, my voice flat with sarcasm. That comment about career girls had roused my defensiveness. "You shouldn't have." The flowers also reminded me that William hadn't brought me flowers in a year or two. "They just die," he said one afternoon when I stopped to admire some yellow roses at a corner kiosk. "Waste of money."

Impulsively, when Jack put the vase of orange mums on the table, I put one of my hands over his. He looked at me in surprise, his eyes meeting directly with mine, nothing in between us, creating such a strong feeling of intimacy that it shook me. I withdrew my hand. The moment passed.

"In a way, the flowers are for you," he said, taking two steps backward. "Take them to Mrs. Murphy. I know for a fact, since her gardener also works here twice a month, that she doesn't have chrysanthemums in this color."

"Thank you."

"You look like a woman who likes flowers. I'll have some put in your room."

"Thank you again." We were both working hard at not looking each other in the eyes. I liked his freckles, the pale blue of his eyes, his ginger-colored hair, the way he had to stoop at the doorways because of his height. It was a long time since I had been attracted to any man other than William.

I drove back to Cheer Hall later that afternoon, and when I knocked, Sara opened the door, not the maid.

"You're back," she said, and her voice was half friendly. "I thought you might be."

"For you." I held the flowers out to her.

"That Jack Brennan," she said. "You're staying at his inn, the postman tells me. I'm going to have a word with Jack. Well, since you're here. Come in. I can spare you a few minutes."

She took my coat and hung it on a hook near the hall mirror.

"Lovely scarf," she said when I handed her that as well. It was silk and floated between us for a moment, parachuting in a way that showed the brand name in the corner.

"A Marti design," Sara said approvingly.

"Yes. She was my mother."

"I hadn't known Marti was an actual person." She looked at the scarf again and then at me.

"Very actual," I said.

She laughed, a golden sound with bell-like vibrations to it. "We'll go to my sitting room. But we must be quiet. Gerald is still unpacking his books and rereads most of them before they get shelved."

There was a clatter from the back of the house, the sound of dishes and laughter. *The maid and cook*, I thought, *cleaning up from lunch or beginning dinner preparations*. My mother had entered such houses through the back door with the other servants before she'd worked her way into a job at Clara Designs in the scarf section.

Animal patterns had become her specialty, black spots over a tawny background, red and green feathers over a blue sky, designs that wore well with day costumes from Dior and Chanel. Grace Kelly wore them as headscarves; Elizabeth Taylor tied them around her throat. I was a teenager by then and had a hard time reconciling this woman who left the house every morning in a bespoke suit and high heels with the one who, in my earliest memories, had worn a maid's uniform.

"Anything can happen," she had said often. "Sometimes, even good things."

I paused in Sara Murphy's hallway. Now finally about to have a tête-à-tête with a friend of Pablo Picasso, I had lost some of my confidence. Every word would remind me of my mother, who had loved Picasso's work. We had quarreled before she died. My last words to her had been "Mind your own business" when she had asked me, again, why I hadn't set a date with William.

"You are my business," she had said.

Sara led me down the hall, past an elegant living room with stylish furniture and comfortable sofas, a study, a library room with crammed bookshelves, where I could see Gerald Murphy stooping over a pile of books, considering.

"Lovely house," I said, following a polite four steps behind.

"I like it so much better than New York." Sara smiled at me over her shoulder. "The quiet at night. Birds in the morning. You used past tense for your mother?"

"She died. This year."

"I'm sorry. Were you close?" Sara seemed genuinely saddened.

"Some of the time," I said.

"More of a daddy's girl, were you? Like my own daughter, Honoria?"

"My father died when I was eight." Car accident, my mother told me that night she came to my room weeping. Rainy night, bald tires because they couldn't afford new ones, oil on the road. She wet the top of my head with her tears. Later, after we stopped crying, she took out the family photo album, filled mostly with pictures of me, but on one page there was a photo of her standing next to my father, a tall man dressed in pleated trousers and a jacket. His arm was protectively around her shoulders. She leaned lightly into him, looking small and a little overwhelmed, but they both smiled into the camera. It was their wedding photo. After she died, I took out the photo and framed it, and put it on the bookshelf where I kept the urn with her ashes.

"Oh. I'm sorry." Sara turned at looked at me, hard, as if she were studying something. "That must have been difficult for your mother, becoming widowed so young. Come, let's talk."

She showed me into her sitting room at the top of the stairs, a small room with a sofa, two armchairs, a desk, and little else. It was cozy and comfortable, and when she sat on the sofa, she kicked off her shoes and tucked her legs under herself, as young girls do.

Sara had been extraordinarily beautiful in her youth, in the few photos I'd been able to find in newspaper and magazine archives. Young, burnt by the Mediterranean sun, smiling into a camera that might have been held by Picasso. Sara and Gerald, the golden couple of the Jazz Age.

"So, you want to talk about Pablo Picasso," she said. "What would you like to know? You may sit there." She gestured, palm up, fingers lightly curled except for the forefinger, at the chair opposite the sofa.

I sat, smoothing my skirt underneath me and positioning my yellow legal pad on my lap.

A maid peered into the doorway.

"Tea?" Sara asked. "Or something stronger?" The maid disappeared and returned just moments later with a silver tea service and bottle of Rémy Martin cognac.

A paperback lay open on Sara's desk.

"Have you read Agatha Christie?" she asked, noticing the way I was scanning the room. It spoke to a need for sanctuary, with its thick velvet curtains, the bookcase set up against an exterior-facing wall to help muffle sound. It was a good place for contemplation, for remembering, as well as reading. "*Murder on the Orient Express* is my favorite," Sara said. "The train. I've always loved trains."

"I do love Agatha Christie. But aside from the subway, I've never traveled by train."

"Never?" Sara raised an eyebrow. "Then you have something to look forward to."

She leaned forward and poured tea for us, and two small glasses of cognac.

"We took the Blue Train, in France," she said, "when we didn't drive ourselves. The one from Paris to the Côte d'Azur. Gerald sometimes dressed up as a train conductor to make the children laugh." There was a catch in her throat when she said *children.*

"I'm sorry about your sons." Her two lost boys, Baoth from meningitis and Patrick soon after from tuberculosis. Neither had lived into his teen years.

"Thank you. It was long ago when I lost them. But that kind of grief, you do not get over it. You live with it every day. It wakes up with you, sits down at table with you. But you're not here to talk about that." She sipped her tea and looked at me, her eyes soft with curiosity.

I took out my notebook and pen. "Did Picasso travel on the train with you? What year was that? When did you first meet?"

Sara leaned back into the sofa. "Paris, 1923. We were painting a stage backdrop for Diaghilev, one designed by Pablo. Gerald and I. Pablo was already very famous by then, and to have a famous artist congratulate you on your own work . . . Well, it meant a lot to Gerald. And to me. So I was already predisposed to like Pablo. You really want to hear about all this? Well. Since Jack sent you with flowers. He knows I love flowers."

Sara took a sip of her cognac and looked thoughtfully at where a sigh of an autumn breeze had billowed a curtain through the slightly open window. "You know, I haven't talked about Pablo to anyone other than Gerald in such a long time. Why are you interested?"

"Who isn't interested in Pablo Picasso? The most important artist of the century. And there is a personal connection. My mother loved his work. We had reproductions all over the apartment. Besides, I need work, and this is my best chance to get an actual job. I write about modern art. And if this doesn't work out, it's back to the typing pool. So, you see, this is very important to me."

Rule number two for a journalist: never appear desperate for a story. (Rule number one is never accept a no.) But something about Sara, her warmth and calmness, encouraged openness. I continued, hoping for the best, and told her about the magazine, about Reed.

"This is the assignment he gave me," I said. "To write something new about Picasso. Only he doesn't know I am interviewing you. My little secret."

She leaned a little closer to me.

"Let's see if we can find something in this jumble of my memories, then. I like to be a friend to other women. But some things will be under wraps, of course. My privacy."

"Of course," I agreed, already thinking about locked doors and the keys that open them.

"Since you brought me flowers, I will tell you of flowers," Sara said, "and Picasso and what might happen if there are no flowers."

She paused, tilting her head, letting a moment of silence flow between us. "When did she die, your mother?"

"Just a few months ago. I found you through her, a slip of paper she left in a book, about your friendship with Picasso."

"She had a paper about me?"

"It had been used as a page marker," I said. "Torn from a newspaper."

"I see." Her face lit up. "But now we will talk about Pablo Picasso."

SIX
......

SARA

I first saw a Picasso painting in a gallery window in Paris in 1923.

There it was, behind a grimy window, a simple vase of flowers glowing yellow and orange like a constellation of suns. All the grayness of the day transformed into something joyous. A moment of happiness that could not burst but would always be there. All you had to do was look.

The painting stunned you with its presence. You didn't look at it and say, "Ha! Here's something new." No. You saw it and thought, *This has always been here. It is as old as cave drawings.* But it was neither old nor new. It always was, always had been. A kind of manifestation of divinity, if you will. The eternal.

"It has changed my life," Gerald had told me the day before, when he asked me to walk by the gallery so I could see it, too. "If that is painting, that is what I want my painting to be." I hadn't seen him so moved since our children had been born.

I stood in the Paris rain, staring, the bread in my shopping basket getting soaking wet. It was a moment such as one I experienced years before, when I had seen Gerald, boyish and lanky in his swimming costume, walking down the East Hampton beach with his brother. Shy, beautiful, his lack of self-confidence showing in the way his head tilted down. I knew that I would marry him.

When I finally looked away from Picasso's painting in the gallery window, I headed home to our apartment on Quai des Grands Augustins. We had been there such a brief time that we still had mattresses on the floors for sofas, crates for tables, patches of paint samples on the walls. We had been traveling for two years since leaving New York. Connecticut. Boston. England. Versailles. And when we reached Paris, we had agreed. Yes. This is it. This is where our new life begins.

Within months, we had acquired a large circle of friends, many artists among them, but had not yet met Pablo Picasso. Paris delighted us, with its stately avenues, lively cafés and parks, the sense of bohemian fun that made our unfinished apartment seem pleasantly eccentric. But both Gerald and I had noticed that most of the young people in Paris were foreigners, Americans and Russians and Italians. So many Frenchmen had been killed in the Great War.

That day, passing the corner newspaper kiosk, I caught words of violence in Italy and Spain . . . demonstrations, students arrested, bystanders killed, Blackshirts marching in the streets. A new word, *fascism*. Spain had become a military dictatorship, and the generals, especially one named Franco, were clamping down on free speech, on anything that might limit their own power. The war to end all wars had ended just a few years ago, but violence was like the Hydra. Cut off one head and two others appear.

But then there is art, and art promises us a different world.

"Gerald," I called, opening the door to our little apartment. "I've seen Picasso's painting. And it is everything you said. And more."

Gerald took the shopping basket from me so I could embrace the children who ran to greet me, Honoria, six, with a headful of golden curls; Baoth, four; and Patrick, only three, who had a difficult time keeping up with his siblings.

"We will find a studio for you," I said. "And a teacher." I kissed the top of Patrick's head, breathing in the rich vanilla smell of his hair.

"I wonder . . ." Gerald arranged the apples in the fruit bowl.

"You can. You have a wonderful eye for color. Don't worry, darling. This is what you've been looking for."

The teacher we found was a Russian woman who barked orders at him but thought enough of Gerald's skill that several months later, he was invited to work, for no payment, for Serge Diaghilev, her Russian compatriot and the founder of the famous Ballet Russes. The Russian Revolution had made it impossible for Diaghilev to go back to Russia, so he, like so many artists, had made France his home. It was a great honor to be invited to work in his workshop.

Months later, after seeing the Picasso painting in the gallery window, Gerald and I were in Diaghilev's workshop crafting the set for a new ballet. I had been assigned the easy work, filling in backgrounds, cleaning brushes, running out for coffee. Gerald, though, on the recommendation of his teacher, was painting backdrops, doing actual artistic work, and I had never seen him happier, except on the days our children were born.

Picasso was in the studio, too, recognizable with his beret, his black eyes, that full sensual mouth. Though we hadn't met yet, friends had pointed him out to me in cafés or on the street. A woman stood next to him, a gorgeous creature with curling black hair and mischievous eyes. Picasso was doing his best to ignore her, but you could sense the current running between them.

"What kind of flower do you want?" I heard Pablo Picasso ask Diaghilev, pausing midbrushstroke. "A rose has too many petals, too much sophistication. It cannot shape-shift the way a daisy can. A child's daisy and the daisy of a woman about to commit adultery are two different flowers."

The woman next to him laughed. "Lagut," I heard one of the workmen mutter behind me. So that was the mistress Picasso had just before he met and wed Olga. The Revenge, some crueler tongues called Olga; the Mattress, because Lagut had rejected his offer of marriage and married someone else, a doctor, not an artist, and Pablo bounced into Olga's bed to ease his wounded pride.

Pablo refused to look at her. Instead, he looked over his shoulder at me. I had taken off my cardigan and draped it over a chair, and that movement had caught his attention.

I froze, meeting that gaze for the first time. He didn't smile, but warmth crept into his expression, and there was a question in his eyes, that old, old question that I had been ignoring from all other men since the day I fell in love with Gerald on that beach on Long Island.

"A flower that is about to become either a knife or a rose," Diaghilev answered, rushing away to shout orders at the carpenters. He had a streak of gray running through his black hair and a villain's mustache. His dancers and workers quaked before him. Not Picasso, though. He shouted something back in Spanish, his eyes still locked with mine.

When he looked away from me, I took a deep breath, as if I'd been running.

For Picasso, painting for Diaghilev was not so much an

honor as simply work. He was already well known in France, but painting for the great impresario ensured that even Parisians who weren't that interested in art would get to know Picasso through the stage settings of the ballet.

Gerald, standing next to me, paused from his painting and said reflectively, "A knife or a rose." I could see his mind working, trying to reconcile how the soft curves of a petal could shift to the sharp edge of a knife.

"A knife," said the dark-eyed woman. "Roses are a bore."

"Go away, Irène," Picasso said. She laughed and slunk away, her beaded silk dress making a chiming sound with every step.

"She's a devil of a woman," Picasso muttered, and I knew the comment was meant to be overheard. "Who are you?" he said to me.

I stepped forward and extended my hand. "Sara—Sara Murphy."

"An American," he said, and there was a teasing note in his voice. "I like Americans, though they are slow to buy my work. They will learn. You understand?"

He had been speaking in French, quickly, as fluent speakers do, but I had followed.

"I understand, and, yes, my countrymen will learn. This is my husband, Gerald."

Picasso turned to Gerald, and I watched them shake hands, saw my tall, fair husband lean slightly to Picasso, who was shorter. Two men who could not be more different from each other, yet each full of life, handsome.

"We will be friends," Picasso said to Gerald.

"Nothing would please me more," Gerald said, flattered.

"To work!" Diaghilev clapped his hands impatiently. The workshop buzzed with activity: ladders were moved, drop cloths rearranged, the smell of paint and turpentine filled the air, hammers and saws and shouting made any more conversation impossible.

Later that afternoon, Pablo came and stood behind me, where I was painting green grass on one of the backdrops. He watched, silent and unreadable. Then he took my hand in his, swirled my brush through a dab of black paint, and, with my hand still in his, drew one black stroke amid all that green. The field came alive. One stroke.

"Your grip is too tight. Like this," he said, firmly prying my fingers, one by one, from the paintbrush and repositioning them. After he had corrected my grip on the brush, his hand stayed on mine.

His touch was warm and dry and light. I should have pulled away. I did not. I stood still, waiting. For what? There was electricity in his touch, an invitation I hadn't responded to since falling in love with Gerald.

"Not a stab," Picasso said, leaning even closer. "A flowing. Think of the flowers moving in the breeze. Next time you are in a field, look. You may think you are seeing straight lines. Grass. Tree trunks. Stems. But no straight lines, if you look well enough."

Gerald looked over at us. He was painting clouds, and his face was spattered with a constellation of white spots.

Had he seen how long Pablo's hand rested on mine? There wasn't a jealous bone in Gerald's body. Sometimes to my dismay.

Picasso was forty years old that year and was the center of gravity of the Parisian art world. Gossip said he had a habit of walking up to pretty girls, complete strangers, and asking them to pose for him. By pose, he always meant naked. It was assumed that any woman who posed for him would also visit his bed. Pablo's wife, Olga, was not a happy woman.

Pablo didn't say a word to me before or after that single black brushstroke. But that night, I dreamed about a black line that formed into a rose and then a knife.

Gerald and I spent a week painting in the studio with Diaghilev and his stagehands. Picasso was often there and would wave hello to us and then return to his concentration, his work. There was no more conversation between Pablo and myself, but sometimes he and Gerald would sit together on the edge of a platform and talk quietly. That felt like a victory, seeing my husband deep in conversation with Pablo Picasso. I didn't mind that I had been excluded. I didn't.

When the ballet opened, it was a great success, praised in the newspapers the next day by the artists and intellectuals of Paris, and complained about by the bourgeoisie—always a good omen. The success of opening night was marred by a single incident, a disheveled thin man carrying a poster saying, "Food, not opera." He stood in front of the entrance of the theater, staring us down, until two gendarmes pulled him away.

"And you, you may host the party," Diaghilev shouted at us as a jubilant audience carried the maestro out into the street on opening night. He hadn't seen the protestor, nor the roughness with which the police had removed him.

Gerald and I already had a reputation for giving some of the best parties in bohemian Paris. Artists need release. They need food and conversation and cocktails. The war was over, but the memories of fear and hardship, the deaths of friends, lingered, and parties helped us feel that return to normalcy that fuels art. I was proud of my reputation, proud of how people enjoyed themselves, relaxed on the sofa-mattresses, chatted easily about everything from cassoulet recipes to the Greek philosophers, loved how they put their feet up on the crate-tables, left apple cores in the ashtrays. I had created a life so different from the stuffy, stilted days of my Long Island girlhood.

That Gerald and I had an income from my family and more money than most of our friends was a part of our social appeal. I knew that. And didn't mind. We had what others needed, and when we could, we shared and gave.

For Diaghilev's party, I decided that rather than rent one of the usual party venues, the Ritz ballroom or a park pavilion, I would put our party on water. We'd rent a barge on the Seine. It would be a party that no one would forget. I'd make sure of that.

The Sunday morning of our fete, the dawn over the Seine was azure shot through with gold. We left our flat early and rushed to the rented barge to begin the preparations. The empty Sunday streets of Paris reminded me, too late, of my mistake.

"There are no flowers for sale today," I told Gerald. "It's Sunday. No flowers at the market."

I sat on one of the folding chairs we had rented and put my head in my hands. One of the dozens of laundry boats that worked on the Seine passed us, and the barge rocked gently in its wake. "How can you have a party without flowers?" Inconceivable, a party without flowers. What would Diaghilev and his dancers, his musicians, the artists who had painted for him, think of a party that had no decorations?

Happiness is not in the large things of life but the small details, the untamable curl at the top of a baby's head, the breathing of your husband in the dark, the pristine whiteness of a fresh tablecloth. Flowers on the table.

Gerald was elated that morning. This was to be our grandest Parisian party, and the world was shiny and new as a Christmas toy.

"Why not buy birds and put cages on the tables?" Gerald suggested.

No. I couldn't stand the thought of anything in a cage.

"You'll think of something." Gerald put down the hammer he'd been using to tack up laurel wreaths on the barge walls and hugged me. Laurel, for victory.

It was already hot, and when the breeze came over the water, slightly refreshed, I could feel the two different temperatures warring on my face. In the distance, I could see the square towers of Notre-Dame. Overhead, wispy clouds floated off in the direction of Place de la Bastille, to the west.

Gerald was happy, so I was happy, even as I fretted over the flowers. And yet, there was always a shadow of something lurking in the corner, waiting to come between Gerald and me. Do all wives worry about that? As much as I loved Gerald, as well as I thought I knew him, there was a part of my husband that existed sometimes in an emotional place I could not reach.

A truck pulled up to where the barge was tied, and two men in striped jerseys and black caps began unloading the crates of champagne we had ordered. Gerald strolled over to them, pointed to where the crates needed to go, and joked with them about the heat.

Gerald shared that quality with Picasso, that center-of-gravity ability to attract and delight people . . . when he wanted.

The deliverymen didn't know what to make of movie-star-handsome Gerald. He was dressed in a torn jersey and rough wide-legged trousers, the kind the apache wore during their Saturday night bar brawls in the rough Marais district of Paris. He spoke French with a bad American accent, and his aloofness, when he was in one of his moods, was not bred in any sense of superiority but in his own sense of himself as someone separate, somehow different.

Picasso would be coming to the party that evening. I wanted to impress him. Some people's approval matters more than it should simply because their disapproval locks too many doors. I wanted all the doors of Paris opened for Gerald. His happiness was the basis for my own.

But how was I going to decorate the tables without flowers?

I wandered off alone to the Montparnasse bazaar to buy some new toys for the children, thinking that would help to clear my head and come up with an idea for the table decorations. I found a carved and painted cow for my daughter, Honoria, fire engines and trucks for the boys, Baoth and Patrick.

The toys I found in the market stalls were colorful—bright reds and blues and yellows, stripes and checks. They were cheap and some were badly made. The mismatched eyes on the dolls and the out-of-proportion angles on the trucks reminded me of the cubist paintings we saw in Kahnweiler's gallery on Rue Vignon.

On impulse, I bought armfuls of them. I returned to the barge followed by my loot and four wheelbarrow-pushing shopgirls, who joked behind my back about the crazy rich American.

The dining tables had been set up by then with all their plates and glasses and silverware. Gerald watched, amused, arms folded over his chest, as I arranged toys in the middle of each table, dolls and trucks and spinning tops all jumbled and sometimes upside down, as if they had been abandoned under a Christmas tree by weary children.

"Perfect," Gerald approved when I was finished. "Anyone can do flowers. This is original. Let the festivities begin."

"And never end. Never."

We stood, arms around each other, looking into a shared future with our children, our home, and wherever that home

was, there would be a studio for Gerald, for his days of painting, making his art. Days not spent at a desk staring down
profit and loss statements, negotiating prices of bales of leather
and gilt closures for the suitcases and purses made by the family business, Mark Cross Luxury Goods. Art mattered, and
home and our children and friendship. Not business, not a
desk. We would make our lives new.

That night, the barge on the Seine was full of our guests,
almost a hundred. The ballet corps, the orchestra, Cole Porter
and his wife, Linda. Diaghilev, still fuming, according to gossip, because his favorite lover and dancer, Nijinsky, had abandoned him and married a woman. Jean Cocteau, who boarded
at the last possible moment because he was afraid of being
seasick.

And Picasso and his wife, Olga.

I stood there on the barge greeting our guests. Olga, black-
haired and black-eyed, lithe in the way that only comes from
years of training at the barre, was splendid in rhinestone-
studded tulle. She was beautiful, dark, and Russian, like a Tol-
stoy character. Perhaps the gossip was true, that Diaghilev had
hired her not for her talent, which was modest, but for her
looks, which were fabulous and certain to lure wealthy male
patrons to the ballet performances.

Looking at her face, beautiful and hard as marble, the ten-
dons already straining on her neck as if preparing for old age,
I understood why the word *mad* was often used when speaking
of the Russian émigrés in France. The revolution, the civil break-
down, the nightmarish falls from aristocracy into poverty, the
midnight escapes—all of that would have been enough, of
course, to break anyone. But there was something else in Olga,
a sense that the slightest push would tip her into true insanity.

When Pablo came aboard the barge, he did not shake my

hand but instead gave me two quick kisses on my cheeks. Pablo was not a tall man. He and I were eye to eye. His eyes were dark and luminous, like a big cat's, and he had the muscular presence of a big cat as well, some creature silent and fatal, gliding through the green forest of other people's lives, pouncing when they least expected.

"I would not have chosen that color for you," he said, touching the silk sleeve of my yellow dress.

Deflated, I led them to the cocktail bar Gerald had set up on the upper deck and went back to greet the austere black-suited Stravinsky and his mistress, who was dressed in very little.

Night fell. A June evening full of laughter, the clink of glasses, and the rustle of women's evening clothes. The gentle rocking of the barge, rolled soft as a sleeper's breath, up and down. Music. The hum of happiness that falls over a successful party: a C-major drone occasionally interrupted with a B-flat flash of quarrel or high-C squeal when a drink is splashed onto someone or a hand strays too far. Languages: French and English, Russian, Italian. A cosmopolitan libretto.

"Happy, darling?" Gerald whispered to me, passing by with a tray of fizzing pink cocktails in his hands.

"Completely," I whispered back, meaning it.

At ten, we went belowdecks to dinner. Stravinsky had rearranged the place cards so that he was seated as far from Cole Porter as possible, and Linda, who still hoped Cole would become a classical musician, gave me an angry look, as if it were my fault. I shrugged. I adored Cole, but Linda could be a snob.

I was more interested in Pablo's reaction to my centerpieces, those jumbles and piles of toys.

"How strange," said Olga, and there was criticism rather than admiration in her voice.

But Pablo was delighted. He immediately began rearranging

the toys, looking as intense as he had in Diaghilev's studio. Moving from table to table, he created compositions and narratives for the toys. The middle of my table ended up with Honoria's little wooden cow climbing a fire engine ladder. In front of Gerald, a rubber horse straddled a wooden airplane as two marionettes looked on, their painted eyebrows raised in perpetual wonder.

The tables became works of art. People think of eccentricity and even insanity when they think of brilliant artists. Pablo had nothing to do with that, not with poor Van Gogh's true madness, that awful business of the ear, nor the syphilitic madness of Manet, nor the fake madness of Salvador Dalí, who fled Europe during the war and arrived in the United States wearing a loaf of bread on his head. Sufficient to say, some artists think a touch of madness makes them more interesting, or at least gives them more license. It certainly gives them more publicity. Pablo knew he didn't need license. All he needed was his art.

During dinner, I could sense Pablo's eyes turning toward me, newly assessing, considering. I pretended not to notice, pretended to be more interested in his arrangement of the toys than the artist, but we both knew this was a lie.

We drank so much champagne that night. Too much. I danced, I made sure no wallflowers were being ignored, I followed Gerald with my eyes when I wasn't actually standing at his side to make sure all was well. Poor little Cocteau wandered around with a lantern, moaning that the barge was sinking—it wasn't—and around four in the morning, someone took down the laurel wreath Gerald had hung from the ceiling. Stravinsky, that stern-faced bespectacled composer, jumped through it like a Russian circus clown, just to show that he could.

At five in the morning, when the sky turned pink behind the Eiffel Tower, Pablo came and stood next to me at the barge railing, where I was watching the sunrise and catching my breath. I don't know where Gerald was; the party had gotten close to mayhem, and all I could do was hope all would end well and safely. Maybe Gerald was with Cole, already plotting another party, another celebration.

People moved from party to party in those days, after the Great War, before the crash. It was a constant search for pleasure, for distraction. A running away from as well as a running to, and no one questioned too much what people were avoiding or looking for. Gertrude Stein called us lost. The Lost Generation. But we weren't. We were just eager.

"Well done," Pablo said, standing closely next to me at the barge railing. "The Parisians are green with jealousy."

He leaned on the railing, close enough that when the barge rocked beneath us, his jacket sleeve brushed my bare arm. It was getting chilly, in the way of very early mornings in June, so Pablo took his jacket off and draped it over my shoulders. We watched the first beams of dawn light up the sky with its palette of colors.

"The toys were your idea," he said, and the certainty of his voice annoyed me.

"Perhaps it was Gerald's idea."

"No. Yours. There is the beginning of the artist in your husband. You are not an artist, but a muse who brings ideas and inspiration. You will bring the apples that Gerald will paint. For some people, art is not what they make but what they live."

Pablo picked up my hand. He turned it upward and put a kiss in the middle of my palm. "Will you come to my studio?"

I was about to tell him that this muse was for Gerald alone, but Olga appeared just then, popped out of nowhere like a jack-in-the-box. Had she been watching us, listening?

She gave me an evil glance, retrieved his jacket from my shoulders, and folded it over her arm.

"We will go home now," she said, her voice menacing with that throaty Russian accent of hers.

Pablo made a growling sound from deep in his throat, but he let her lead him away.

I once had a tutor for geography, as I recall, who explained to me the three Chinese blessings. "And curses," she had said. "Often, a blessing and a curse are the same thing." May you live in interesting times. Well, the Great War had certainly been interesting. May you come to the attention of important people. Pablo? Easy for a woman, a happily married woman, to see how that could turn into a curse. And the final one: may you find what you are looking for.

I had found happiness with Gerald. And I was determined not to lose it.

People will be leaving Paris soon," I said to Gerald the next morning. "For the summer. We should, too."

Now that there would be no more days painting for Diaghilev, I wondered how we would fill our city days. A morning walk in the Jardin des Luxembourg, late lunch at Deux Magots, cocktails at La Closerie. We'd be like the expats I could set my clock by, predictable, automatic.

There was an undercurrent of despair in Paris that I had grown newly sensitive to. Perhaps it was terror left over from the war, or perhaps fear of another war to come. Cities concentrate our emotions, crowd them together like people on a full bus. It could feel hard to breathe sometimes.

And sometimes it was more than an undercurrent. Sometimes it felt like the despair would brim over into violence. The strikes, the demonstrations, marchers down the avenues of Paris protesting unemployment, low pay. Paris was still reeling from the war, but though treaties had been signed, it felt like peace was still a distant goal.

There had been riots and arrests in Spain and Italy, too, right- and left-wing workers and students throwing bottles and stones at each other.

"You watch," my neighbor Mr. Vedora said to me one morning. "It will get worse. Much worse. That madman in Italy, Mussolini. And in Spain, with the generals. Work and money. People need them, and the thieves in the big houses and government will not give. What did we fight for, eh? To make rich people even richer."

I wanted to be out of the city. I wanted paradise, the sense of angels floating overheard, the children playing in the waves, browned from sun and chubby from fresh fish just taken from the ocean and apricots plucked from the tree. I wanted to be elsewhere. Away from Pablo.

"Provence," I told Gerald. "The children look pale. You look pale, my darling." I took my husband's face between my hands and pulled it close to mine.

"Do debutantes go to Provence in the summer?" he teased, reminding me of the balls of my youth, my court presentation in London, the boring, senseless afternoons of calling cards and teas. He had saved me from that, just as I had saved him from his father's board meetings and profit statements, the drudgery of the business world.

"The Côte d'Azur." I was still holding his lovely face between my hands. "Antibes, or some other little fishing village. Just you and me and the children."

Gerald stood and looked out at the Seine. The red dawn reflected in the steel-gray water. It was going to be another rainy day in a long season of rainy days. Paris was already wide-awake, with a clutter of carts and carriages, the calls of vendors and blue-smocked laborers trudging off to work.

"It does sound good," he admitted. "Quiet. Sunshine. A painting studio and the whole ocean to ourselves. You and me and the children. And a few friends, occasionally."

"The Parisians will not come south for the summer," I reminded him. *And just as well*, I did not say. I wanted miles between myself and Pablo Picasso and those all-seeing black eyes of his. My happiness with Gerald, with the children, with being in France, away from our demanding, disapproving families in New York, had been a shield protecting me from the insecurities and melancholy of my girlhood. But when Pablo looked at me, I could feel the protective shield beginning to crack.

I did not want to change, to be forced into becoming a different kind of woman, the kind of woman who would love a man like Picasso. I liked who I had become with Gerald, his wife, the mother of his children. A sanctuary for them, a person who spreads warmth and calm and possibility. I did not think of myself as a woman who would betray a friend. Not then.

SEVEN
. . . .

SARA

The Hotel du Cap was the color of a faded pink rose, large and blowsy now that its customary English clientele had abandoned it for the season. Palms fringed the gardens, and giant aloes gave it an even more tropical air.

We convinced the hotel owner, Monsieur Antoine Sella, to stay open rather than shutter up for the summer. His eyebrows had risen so high they disappeared under the flat cap he wore. "In July and August? In the heat?" he protested.

"Yes," Gerald insisted. "Open. In the heat." A bank check for more than the rooms would cost even in high season quickly solved the issue.

"But the staff. Most have already returned to their homes for the summer," Monsieur protested. "Gone."

"A cook, a maid. That's all we'll need," I had reassured him. "We'll have our laundry done in the village, and the nanny will see to the children."

"Oh la." He had pressed his fists to his eyes as if he were going to weep with frustration. "Never can that work." But he folded and unfolded the check Gerald had given him. "Well," he finally agreed. "I will find someone. I cannot ask the cook to scrub floors and washbasins."

"I'll ask around," I promised, trying to mollify him. "We'll find someone."

At the hotel, Gerald and I soon created our own little world of sun and sand, afternoon siestas, quiet talks late at night on the porch, the scent of wild thyme and lavender filling the air. We held hands again, a habit we had stopped in Paris, where people walked too quickly and were always preoccupied.

In the mornings, porridge and then exercising on the beach, Gerald leading the children through a comical series of calisthenics as I watched from my beach chair, certain that there was no happier woman in the world than myself. In the afternoon, the nanny took the children for their naps and baths, Gerald would work on drawings for a new ballet set, and I would explore, taking buses and trains and sometimes hiking for miles to see the Grimaldi Castle, the gray tiny streets of Vence with their medieval flying buttresses and the Gothic church of Le Bar-sur-Loup, with its painted danse macabre.

The little beach near the hotel had been deeply buried in seaweed when we arrived. People in Antibes did not bathe in the ocean, so why clean it? But Gerald wanted a beach for us, so he began raking, cleaning the sand of weeds and litter, and we soon had a clean apron of soft sand for our sunbathing towels and the children's' games.

At night, after another day of sun and ocean, and the music of waves and laughter of my already nut-brown children, I lay next to Gerald and listened to his even breathing, the occasional mutter of one of the children caught in a dream, and a sensation would settle over me like a soft blanket, a contentment such as I had never known before. *Make this last* was my prayer.

Paris had been frantic and complicated. There had been so much partying, music, cocktails, loud quarrels ending in histrionic embraces, stumbling down the cobbled streets at dawn, making sure our guests turned in the right direction to get back to their own rooms.

Put the mail down and eat, Gerald," I said on our fourth evening at Cap d'Antibes. I unfolded his napkin and handed it to him. "We're starting with an omelet, and then there's a brandade of cod."

We were dining alone late in the evening at a little table set up for us on the terrace. The children were asleep upstairs. We held hands on the white tablecloth and listened to the murmur of distant surf and the night songs of the crickets, the gentle weep of palm fronds when a breeze caught them. There were occasional clatters and ill-tempered shouts from the kitchen. The cook who had been bribed back into service complained to us frequently about being called away from her sister's home and her *vacances*. I think she was secretly pleased. Her sister had seven children.

She stepped onto the terrace now, our Madame Lorraine, and glowered at our plates. She muttered something I couldn't understand, and her new assistant stepped out of the bulky shadow of the cook.

It was the girl I'd met a few days before on the train coming back from a shopping trip in Nice.

"I'm Anna," she said shyly. She looked different in her sprigged summer dress with the white apron tied over it. Her hair was braided and hung down her back almost to her waist. On the train, she had worn a good suit and worn her hair up. She looked much younger now, little more than a child.

"Anna," I said, "I do hope you'll be happy here." I gave the cook a look, indicating she was to be kind to this girl, but the cook ignored me. She was the law of the land in her kitchen, not me.

The cook muttered loudly in a dialect that I could never quite follow.

"She says you must eat it quickly, while it is hot," Anna said. "Otherwise, bad digestion." The cook nodded agreement so hard her chin tucked into her chest. Anna stepped closer to the table and with a deft twist of the wrist poured more Ventoux rosé into our glasses without spilling a drop. A practiced hand.

"Anything else?" she asked, stepping back into shadow. There was something furtive about her. All the pieces didn't fit right; she was like a cubist painting full of jagged edges.

"Your English is excellent," I said, and she heard the question in my voice. How had she come by such language skills?

She considered her answer too long. I knew whatever she said would be a lie. And so did she, so she said nothing.

But I had seen where her eyes had focused: on the strand of pearls I always wore, even at the beach.

I touched them instinctively. I'd be more careful about locking them in their case at night, the only time I didn't wear them.

She saw the gesture and flinched as if the imagined theft had already occurred, the accusation already made. From the shadows, her eyes, staring straight into mine, flared wide with the insult. I felt as if I should apologize. For what?

She made me even more uneasy. She was proud and sensitive, this girl, quick to take offense. *Trouble*, I thought, looking at her. *Here is trouble.*

That sense of trouble the girl gave me diminished over the days, though, as we learned the new routines, breakfast in the kitchen, the baskets she packed and handed to me for our long mornings on the beach. The children were not shy with her; they trusted her. So I began to trust her as well.

We had several weeks of slumbering bliss in Antibes, at the hotel and the beach. Time had stopped, and I wished we could go on forever exactly as we were. *May you find what you are looking for.* I'd never been happier, despite the occasional bouts of unease the new girl gave me.

I woke up one night from a restless dream of running, running from an unseen threat, and sat up in bed. I heard voices on the hotel terrace, the slamming of a car door. *Who could be arriving this late at night?* I wondered sleepily, but Gerald's arm reached out for me, and I curled back into his chest. I fell asleep again instantly.

The next morning when I went down to the beach, another family was there: a man, his back turned to me, unfolding a beach chair; his wife, overdressed in a linen suit; a small boy with gleaming black hair; a frazzled young woman who was obviously his nurse; an older woman dressed in the long dark dress of a widow.

Had Monsieur Sella found other paying customers? It was his hotel, after all. We hadn't asked him to close the place to anyone else. Still, I felt disappointed. Strangers would besiege our privacy. The children would have to be quiet in the dining room, not run in the halls. Gerald would have to remember to wear his bathrobe over his swimming costume when he came in from the beach.

"Mummy, who's that?" six-year-old Honoria complained, tugging at my hand. "They're on our beach."

"We don't own it, darling," I said, although I had come to feel as if we did. Baoth, four years old and carrying his toy pail and shovel, and three-year-old Patrick, carried by the nanny, pointed at a little boy who played at the shore's edge. But first

I saw the man sitting there. He wore a striped T-shirt, the kind sailors wear. Cigarette smoke drifted over his head. His back was to me, but I already knew who it was.

Pablo's little son, dressed in a striped swim costume and rubber beach shoes, ran back and forth from the shore edge to where his father sat.

Pablo must have felt the quick change in the atmosphere, just as I did, the disturbance of the air when someone else arrives. He turned and studied us for a long while before he waved. Black-haired, ramrod-postured Olga looked up from the blanket she had spread on the sand. She did not wave.

"Good morning!" I called, forcing a level of gaiety into my voice that I did not feel. "What a surprise!"

"Isn't it," said Olga crossly.

Pablo dropped the folded beach chair and walked up to me, very close, so close I could see specks of gold in his black eyes.

The sensation of a coat being dropped over my shoulders, the smell of pipe smoke and turpentine that was the smell of Pablo Picasso. Had he followed us down here? I vaguely remembered that he sometimes visited the Côte d'Azur with his family. But to show up on this particular beach?

"What a surprise!" I stupidly repeated.

"Is it?" he said, staring hard at me.

"I want to swim," Honoria said, pulling me away.

"Yes, darling. Of course." I smiled at Olga and spread my towel a good ten feet away from her blanket, as far as the little beach Gerald had created would allow.

"We are here for only a short time," Olga said, looking at no one in particular. "Days." She twisted the umbrella planted in the sand to keep the sun off her face.

"A few weeks," Pablo corrected. "With my mother, who has come from Spain." He waved at the older woman, all in black, seated in a beach chair on the other side of Olga. "She has not met my son before," Pablo said. "A vacation together for the two of them."

Olga rolled her eyes and spread cream on her bare shoulders.

Pablo helped me straighten the corners of my blanket, then returned to the newly claimed Picasso side of the little beach. We had established territories, like armies.

"Good morning, señora," I called to Pablo's mother.

She nodded and returned to the knitting she had brought with her.

"She doesn't speak English or French. Only Spanish," Pablo called back.

Honoria, cross at this turn of events, a new playmate for her brothers and none for her, gathered seashells and began making a line in the sand with them, a border between our two blankets.

I opened the book I'd brought with me and pretended to read, while Honoria, tired of border-making, splashed in and out of the waves. Baoth and Patrick were already crouching on the sand with Paulo, making a sand fortress with their pails.

Pablo and Olga talked in low angry murmurs like the buzzing of bees. I forced myself to look straight ahead at the waves, the fishing boats on the turquoise horizon. Presently, I reached that state where you are more asleep than awake, where the sounds of the children mixed with the surf as a musical score for a dream about flying. Flight.

Midmorning, Gerald came to join us, dressed in his swimming shorts and with a towel draped over his shoulders. He'd been working in the little shed he used as a painting studio, and there was a crease between his eyebrows as if the morning's work had not gone well. He paused when he saw the other blanket. The crease deepened, then disappeared as he recognized the husband and wife and child. He strode over quickly and happily to embrace Pablo and give him the two kisses on the cheek, Parisian-style.

They also patted each other on the back in a distracted manner, the way of men who are fond of each other but wary of showing too much emotion.

"Here for some beach studies?" Gerald asked. "To work?" During one of Gerald's visits to Pablo's studio during the gray Paris winter, he had seen some of the beach paintings from the year before, nude bathers with elongated legs and tiny heads so that they seemed to the viewer both near and far at the same time. Pablo had told him about a dream he'd had often as a child, of his arms and legs growing to monstrous sizes and then shrinking again, the people all around him suffering the same painful transformations.

"To work. Always. And to play a bit," Pablo said. That he did not look at me when he said that did not lessen its effect on me.

"Are you cold, darling? You've got gooseflesh," Gerald said, wrapping me in his towel.

Gerald and Pablo swam and, between bouts with the waves, helped the boys with their castle-building. I slumbered in my beach chair, the ocean singing me a soft lullaby.

"What are you laughing at, Sara?" Gerald asked, standing over me. The spray of salt from his hair had woken me. He cast a shadow of his face over mine, a planet creating our private solar eclipse.

"Lobsters," I said. "Only lobsters."

"Is that what supper will be? I'll be famished."

"You're always hungry." Thank god, he was always hungry. A good appetite meant good health, and I feared ill health in my family more than—I tried to think—more than hell itself, if such a place actually exists.

"And no, not lobster tonight. Grilled turbot with courgette flowers," I said, immediately worrying that perhaps Olga didn't like grilled turbot and would insist on something else. If they were staying at the hotel, they would be eating there as well, I assumed. I would have to confer on menus with her, and she would want rich food, Paris food, caviar and lamb and heavy sauces on the vegetables, not the light ocean-flavored Provençal cuisine.

Paradise had become very crowded. Yet I had felt a new layer of life fall over me when I saw Pablo running in and out of the waves, a silken layer that made me aware of the heat of the sun on my skin.

"Dow-dow!" Honoria called, using the children's nickname for their father. "I want to go to the movies today. Can we? Can we?"

There was one cinema in the sleepy little port of Antibes, and it opened only one day a week.

"There are no movies today, darling," I told her, sitting up. "Should we go shopping instead? We can buy new straw hats."

"I don't want a hat. I want a train," shouted Baoth, and the three boys began chanting, "Train, train, train!" Gerald laughed and swung Baoth around and around till they both fell onto the sand, tumbling together into the golden softness.

"You go," Gerald said to me, brushing a strand of seaweed off Baoth's browned chubby leg. "I'll stay here with the boys. And Pablo."

"Be sure they get their nap," I said.

Pablo turned and smiled at me over his shoulder. "Yes, I get tired, too," he said.

"I meant . . ." but I didn't finish the sentence. He was teasing me. When Honoria and I trudged up the sandy hill from the beach, I felt Pablo's eyes on my back but did not turn around.

Later that afternoon, we returned from the hat shop on the whitewashed, heat-shimmering Rue du Bateau. We'd had a small lunch in town, and Honoria was quiet with fatigue. We went into the hotel kitchen to find some *pain au chocolat* for her.

My daughter climbed happily onto a kitchen stool, dropped her new straw hat on the table, and ate the bread-and-chocolate roll the cook gave her, the little afternoon *goûter* that children enjoy in France.

"Smells wonderful," I said, lifting a lid from one of the pots. Madame Lorraine beamed. But her helper, the girl named Anna, looked up from the pile of potatoes she was peeling and scowled.

"There are other guests at the hotel. New guests," she said in her fluent but accented English. She did not sound happy about it. Her voice was deep and low, a cultured voice.

"We know them." I said. "We will dine together, probably, and that won't make much more work for you, I think."

"Eh!" the cook shouted at her. "Lazy! Peel more, talk less."

Gerald and the boys were still napping upstairs in our rooms, and the cook and Anna made it clear I was in the way. I sent Honoria upstairs to the nanny and went onto the hotel's terrace with its comfortable lounge chairs. The late afternoon shimmered with heat and the loud, creaking thrumming of cicadas.

There is a legend in Provence about the cicadas. The people of Provence were growing lazy in the afternoon heat and sleeping when they should have been tending the fields or making the evening soup. So the angels sent cicadas to sing so loudly they would wake everyone up, and the people would go about their work.

They had the opposite effect on me. I heard the singing cicadas over the sound of the waves and the seagulls, and I slept again, dreaming of protecting angels and a question I couldn't make out, something that added anger to the dream.

When I woke, the sun was setting, and a shadow had fallen over me. I looked up and saw the navy and white stripes of Pablo's jersey pullover. Behind him, the slender form of Olga shimmering with fury.

"Answer me!" Olga insisted, tugging at his arm for attention. "Is she here? That woman? Lagut?"

Pablo shook off her hand and leaned closer to me.

"Three more freckles," he said, ignoring Olga. "Good. Perfection is intolerable."

"Hello, Pablo," I said, sitting up. "Hello, Olga," I quickly added.

She was dressed to the nines in swathes of lace, her black hair pulled back so severely it had lifted her eyebrows. *More appropriate for a cocktail hour than a beach vacation*, I thought. Pablo's mother, Señora Ruiz, stood at Olga's side, a short, stout widow all in black, looking at everything and everyone as if they didn't measure up to her standards. She and Olga had that in common.

Olga, seeing the way Pablo was smiling at me, put her arm through his and clung so possessively that Pablo couldn't take a step unless she did as well. He seemed amused, and that, of course, made Olga that much fiercer.

We cling to things tighter when we fear we are losing them. My mother, who hadn't wished me to marry anyone, much less a merchant's son, albeit a very rich merchant's son, hadn't let me out of her sight during that last year of my girlhood, before my wedding.

"She wants to know if my mistress, Irène Lagut, is also

here," Pablo explained. He was laughing. Olga cringed but lifted her head higher, pulled him even closer.

So that affair wasn't completely over.

"I'm going up to dress for dinner," I said, wishing that they had stayed in Paris. How callous he could be, how indifferent to Olga's tattered pride. It would be a nightmare to love a man like that.

Upstairs, Gerald had already changed into evening clothes and was giving last-minute instructions to the nanny for the evening, picking out storybooks and games for the children from the large hamper we'd brought with us.

"Darling, you should have woken me up," I said, kissing him on his sunburnt cheek.

"You looked so peaceful. The children have had supper, and the cook is grumbling, always a good sign."

"Pablo and his family are dining here," I said, and he understood the trepidation he heard in my voice.

"They're staying here," he said. "Now, don't look like that. It's just for a couple of days." Gerald turned away from the departing nanny and peered into his shaving mirror, flicking away a bit of soap.

"Pablo says it will be for a few weeks."

"The hotel is large enough. We'll still have our privacy," Gerald said. "Don't you think? Besides, Pablo can be good company if we are willing to overlook Olga's tantrums. We can have long afternoons and evenings to talk about art together. I have so much to learn."

"But his mistress, too?" I protested.

Gerald laughed. "That scoundrel. So Irène Lagut is here as well."

"It's not amusing, Gerald. We came here for peace and quiet, to get away from that sort of drama."

"Everything will be fine," he insisted, giving me a quick hug. "His son and our children will be able to play together. They'll like that, won't they?"

"I suppose. I just hope . . ."

"What, darling?"

"That Olga won't be too difficult." That wasn't what I had been thinking, though. I hoped I would not be alone often with Pablo.

"She'll probably spend more time in Paris than here. Shopping, her lunches with the bankers' wives. All that. We'll make a party of it tonight."

I bathed and dressed in apricot silk, wrapping my pearls around my neck almost defiantly. Gerald and I went down to the terrace together, arm in arm, just as Anna was passing around a tray of cocktails. She gave me a quick glance, her eyes taking in my gown, the way I'd pulled my hair back and up, and there was approval in her look.

"Evening, Olga. Pablo. What a wonderful surprise. And you, kind and gracious lady." Gerald kissed Olga's hand as she expected and gave Pablo a pat on the shoulder. But for Señora Ruiz, he made a stately bow, sweeping an imaginary hat in front of her. She smiled, and for a moment, friendly warmth flashed on her weary face. Gerald had that effect on people.

When we went into the dining room, an hour and two sidecar cocktails later, the sun had disappeared completely, and Monsieur Sella had placed candles on the table. Pablo had talked most of that time, ignoring Olga and his mother. Most of his comments seemed to be directed at me—Was I a strong swimmer? Did I sail? Did the singing of the cicadas bother me? I couldn't blame Olga for the ice in her tone when she did get a word in.

Olga, needing a bit of the limelight, mentioned Diaghilev

frequently, in unfinished sentences interrupted by Pablo, who seemed disinclined to speak of the maestro. Pablo spoke of himself, mostly of the painting he was working on, something he called *The Lovers*, for which he was using Irène Lagut as the model. Olga stiffened and put down her fork.

"Lagut," Olga spat. "She is a nobody, a *potaskushka*."

Olga's tone of voice provided the only needed translation for the Russian word: *slut*.

Anna came out from the kitchen carrying a plate of olives and a pitcher of iced water.

"Who is she?" Olga asked suspiciously when Anna went back through the doorway.

"Anna. She works here. But I don't think she's ever worked in service before," I said. "Strange girl. She leaves books all around, and I've found her reading when she should be dusting."

Olga cleared her throat. "There will probably be a baby in a few months," she predicted. "And no husband." The thought had also occurred to me. It would explain her furtiveness, her habit of standing in the shadows.

Pablo's mother, not understanding a word, nodded in agreement and continued eating the grilled turbot that had followed the soup.

"It is too warm," Olga complained, fanning herself with her napkin. "Why we have come south in this season, I don't understand. Bad influences." She gave me a baleful glare. "And I don't care for this fish. I want roast lamb."

Anna had reappeared with fresh plates for the salad. She gave Olga an evil glance. "There is no lamb tonight," she said angrily. "Eat the fish."

There was a shocked silence. Olga blushed red with anger. After a moment, Gerald cleared his throat. Kitchen help shouldn't speak like that to guests.

Pablo laughed.

Olga threw her napkin onto the table and glared at Anna in outrage. Now Anna looked nervous. This would mean trouble for her.

"I'm sorry," she said meekly, but I could see the meekness was not sincere.

"Not your fault," Pablo said. "My wife can be difficult."

The moon was full and high and shimmering silver through the opened windows. The cicadas sang and moths flew around the candles on the table. Pablo looked at Anna, studying her. His eyes were already dilated from the night. They grew even larger.

Anna fled back to the kitchen, and a moment later, I followed her there, making an excuse that the saltcellar needed to be refilled.

Anna was wiping her eyes and turned her back to me when I entered.

"You shouldn't answer back to guests," I told her. "It could get you in trouble."

Anna didn't answer.

"Are you all right?" I asked her.

"Of course. Why wouldn't I be? And don't worry. I will remember my place from now on. And I won't steal your pearls."

"I didn't . . ." Didn't what? Think she would steal them? Anna was a stranger and certainly no cook's assistant. She might well be a thief, though I didn't really think so.

"Who is the Spaniard?" she asked. "The one with the horrible wife."

"Pablo. Pablo Picasso. And Olga isn't so awful . . ."

"The artist? Truly, that is Picasso?" Her nervousness disappeared in a flash, and she was all curiosity. "I would have thought him to be a taller man. Something to match the work. Pablo Picasso," she repeated quietly to herself. She was about to say something else but closed her mouth firmly, afraid to reveal any more.

"Bring out a fresh water carafe, please, Anna. And don't answer back to Olga. Stay out of her way."

For the rest of the meal, a long one with many courses punctuating Gerald's and Pablo's conversation, shoptalk about what the galleries were preparing for the autumn showing, which artists' prices were rising or falling, I sat mostly silent, listening and watching. Pablo's mother ate slowly, barely keeping pace with the courses, and never speaking, but as soon as she finished, she rose, smiled at her son, and left us for her bedroom.

We were alone then, Pablo, Olga, Gerald, me. Gerald's fair face, strong in the chin, animated, frequent smiles lighting his blue eyes; Pablo, darker, black-eyed, more reticent in his expressions except for those marvelous eyes that could not hide emotion . . . Such beautiful men.

More relaxed, I put my elbows on the table and leaned my chin into my hands, listening to Gerald and Pablo talk about the art dealer Paul Rosenberg's newest discoveries, the coming season for the Ballet Russes, and whether or not the Spanish composer, Falla, had finished his newest score, the rising costs of paints and canvas—all the Paris affairs we had come south to get away from.

There is, I tried to console myself, no such thing as true and complete escape. We bring our lives with us, and all the different parts of those lives. But at least here, we had sun and heat and waves.

An hour later, the table was cleared, and we took our coffee and cognac out to the terrace. The sky was sequined with stars, and it was good to sit and look at them, to smell the wild thyme, to let quiet conversation drift around like music.

I leaned back and closed my eyes, glad for the warmth of the Midi, the ocean sounds and smell of salt in the air. My children, brown from the sun, exhausted from fresh air and exercise, were sleeping safely upstairs. I was content.

The sounds of a woman's shrill "*Merde!*" followed by her laughter in the darkness made me sit up in surprise. We all turned to look.

A dark-haired woman dressed in a daring scarlet gown that dipped almost to her waist walked onto the terrace and held up her shoe. "I broke my heel," she said, shrugging, and I recognized her immediately from that day at Diaghilev's workshop when Pablo had refused to speak to her.

Olga moved forward to the edge of her chair, ready to jump up. *To run away?* I wondered. *Or attack?* Only Pablo spoke.

"Irène." When Pablo said her name, he expressed neither surprise nor pleasure, nor displeasure for that matter. Neutral. The voice of a man hiding his emotions.

"Am I too late for a little champagne?" she asked.

"Yes. Cognac will have to do," Pablo said. "Sara, Gerald, this is my model, Irène."

Irène Lagut—thin, fierce of expression, with bobbed curly black hair—was stunning. Not beautiful in the classical manner, but attractive in the way that some women are capable of when they live more fully than other women. More daring, more reckless, more passionate. It shows in the high coloring of the complexion, the fire in the eyes. Irène had the face she deserved, the wildness of a girl who left home at fifteen, who ran off to Moscow with a nobleman and, when she came back, caught the eye of Picasso and captured his affection. No easy feat with a man like Picasso. And then she had rejected him.

Pablo earned his reputation as a womanizer, a philanderer, an adulterer . . . but he himself had been wounded and abandoned several times. And men, I believe, do not recover as quickly or completely as women, who know they simply must get on with their lives.

So, his unwelcoming neutral voice. The ungentlemanly act of refusing to rise when Irène appeared. But I felt the new tension, a completely different tension from the one Olga had provided.

"Cognac will do," Irène said. "If there is enough of it. I left Paris so that we can finish the painting, Pablo. *The Lovers*."

No one thought to ask how she had found the hotel. She must have asked every person he knew in Paris to get that information.

Olga made a sound deep in her throat and lifted her chin. Her mouth was a thin angry line.

Irène ignored Olga and turned to me. "And you are Mrs. Murphy, I believe? I saw you at the workshop. Painting roses in a field. And you are Gerald? Since Pablo is ignoring his manners."

Gerald, who had risen to his feet, reached over and shook Irène's hand.

I murmured a good evening. "Yes, I saw you there." The night shimmered with new and uninvited energy.

Her pale skin and black curls glinted silver when they caught the moonlight. And I was jealous. It shocked me. I was so convinced my life was on a path of happiness and fulfillment that this new feeling made my hand tremble.

I felt like a tree suddenly caught by a strong burst of wind, so strong even the roots shook with it. *You do not want Pablo*, I told myself. I lied to myself.

Why did I ever suggest that silly game? I know I was restless and newly energized. Here we were, living in paradise and still so far from happiness. Olga, with her jealous nature, could never find the peace that happiness requires. Gerald, as close to happy as anyone I knew but somehow always holding back a little. Pablo, who had no more to do with happiness than does a bull ready to gore the matador.

And me. There was my mother's familiar disapproving voice in my head, belittling me—*not pretty enough, not sophisticated enough*—and there was Pablo, studying us like we were insects under a magnifying glass.

"Let's play a game," I suggested.

"Good idea," said Gerald automatically. "Lighten the atmosphere."

"What kind of game?" Irène asked suspiciously. She was sitting now on the railing precariously, something I wouldn't let my children do since there was a steep drop beneath it. Irène seemed to welcome the danger, the added tension she created.

"Truth or dare," I said. "We ask questions of each other, and we must answer truthfully or not at all. And if we refuse to answer, we must accept a challenge." This was a game I played often with my children, and the questions were playful things like "What color is the monster under the bed who isn't really there?" and "What food do you most dislike?" Why did I imagine grown-ups would have half as much imagination?

"I don't know . . ." Olga said. The evening had grown even warmer, and a hint of perspiration glowed on her smooth, wide forehead.

"Don't be a stick in the mud. It sounds like fun!" Irène cried. "I go first!"

"If you wish," I agreed. "What is the question, and who is it for? And remember, we must tell the truth or not answer at all, and accept a challenge."

Irène pursed her mouth and looked like a thoughtful child who has been asked to do a complicated sum in her head.

"Gerald," she said, pointing at him. "You."

"Me," he agreed, sitting up straighter and preparing for battle. "And the question?"

"Who is the prettiest girl here?"

Pablo laughed. "And do you have a golden apple to give the winner?" he asked. "There is danger ahead for you, my friend."

Olga at that moment looked devastatingly beautiful, despite the wary sadness on her face or maybe because of it. "The story of Paris," she said. "He must choose the most beautiful of three goddesses, Hera, Athena or Aphrodite, and give her the golden apple. The other two become jealous. It is how the Trojan War begins, yes?"

Gerald poured himself another cognac. "Yes, we have three beautiful women. But I know my choice." He raised his glass to me.

"Four," said Pablo. He pointed to the doorway.

Anna stepped back into the shadows. How long had she been standing there watching us?

EIGHT

· · · · · · · · ·

SARA

"Come. Join us," Pablo said.

Anna took a single step forward.

"The dark hair. The classical nose. Better than anything on a Roman coin. The eyes. Men go to war fighting over eyes like that." Pablo was leaning forward, smiling at her, studying her the way he had studied the piles of toys I had arranged for the barge party. But there was more in his face than artistic admiration. Desire.

Anna looked frightened, not so much by Pablo, I thought, but by the attention our entire table was suddenly giving her. She disappeared back into the shadows, and I heard her steps moving down the hall, toward the hotel kitchen.

"It's a stupid game," I said. "Let's have a walk through the gardens. We've been sitting too long." But no one rose. Pablo was still staring at the doorway where Anna had stood, watching.

"I'm going to bed," Olga said, the only one to rise. "I'll be speaking to Monsieur Sella about that maid. She does not know her place."

Pablo muttered something under his breath in Spanish.

"It's not easy," Gerald said to Pablo, when Olga was out of hearing range. "Being married to an artist. To a man who chooses art and fame, often at the expense of others."

"So, she wants to compete with me for attention, I suppose. Or tame me like a pet. Thank you, Dr. Freud." Pablo laughed.

In the bay, far below the hotel terrace, we could sense rather than see the white spume lashing the beach. I imagined the small crabs and fish being roiled by the surf, all that invisible life going on without us.

"So, we work on the painting, yes?" Irène asked. "That is why I am here, of course. As your model." She leaned forward and smiled at Pablo, a smile of sultry heat.

"Do you have a studio set up here?" Gerald asked. "You could use mine."

"Of course there is a studio," Pablo said. "I could not be here otherwise."

Gerald and I exchanged a quick glance, said our *à demain*s, and left the Mediterranean night, the stars, the cicadas, and the thyme-scented breezes to Irène and Pablo. I didn't turn around, but I could feel that his eyes were not on me as they had been when I left the beach.

Anna was waiting for me in the downstairs hall. She was wringing her hands. "I made a mistake," she said. "This is very bad. That woman will make trouble for me."

"I'll have a word with Monsieur Sella tomorrow," I promised. "Tell him that it wasn't your fault." Of course it was. The help does not speak back to the hotel guests. But both Anna and I knew she had no experience with this kind of work, and she had not known that she was to stay silent, always, unless asked a question.

There was a room behind the kitchen, a maid's room with a cot bed, flour-sack curtains, and a braided rug. I had peered in once and had seen how neatly Anna kept that little space. She had left an open book on the quilt-covered cot, Vasari's *Lives of the Most Eminent Painters, Sculptors and Architects*, a modern edition of the sixteenth-century book. Not typical reading for a kitchen assistant.

"Thank you," she promised. "That man. It is Pablo Picasso?" The awe in her voice would have flattered him.

"You know his work, Anna?"

"What student does not?"

Realizing she had just given information about herself, she frowned and turned to go back to the kitchen.

"Good night, Anna," I called to her.

"Come on," Gerald said. "I'm exhausted. Too much wine. A little too much drama." My arm around his waist, his arm around my shoulders, we climbed the stairs together.

I slept poorly. A car left the hotel—Irène's taxi, I suppose. Doors slammed; I heard Pablo creeping up the stairs to the room he shared with Olga. Angry words. Finally, I fell into a light, troubled sleep that ended too quickly at dawn, just hours after we had gone to bed.

By the time we rose the next morning, the nanny had already dressed and fed our children and taken them down to the beach. Gerald and I stumbled downstairs to the terrace. It was completely empty, no trace of the party the evening before. It felt like one of Gerald's Irish fairy tales, where a lost traveler happens upon the fairy folk and sings and dances the night away, but when he awakens, it's gone, all gone. The traveler is left bereft.

Why should I feel bereft? I sighed with aggravation at myself.

"Something wrong?" Gerald asked, leaning close to me.

"Nothing, darling. Just that I forgot my hat." The first lie. It was beginning, but I didn't understand my own feelings. How could I explain them to Gerald?

I went back upstairs for a straw sun hat while Gerald called into the kitchen for our *petit déjeuner complet*. In our room, I stared for a long time into the mirror, trying to see myself as Pablo would, trying to imagine him looking at me the way he had looked at Anna. I couldn't.

"I think Anna is gone," Gerald said when I returned to the patio. "Cook herself brought the coffee. She is in an even fouler mood than usual."

So, Olga was already up. And had complained.

When I went to find him, Monsieur Sella was sitting in his office, feet up on the desk, reading his morning newspaper. "No more coffee, thank you," he said from behind the paper, hearing my steps. I'd never been in his office before, not even when Gerald and I had asked him to stay open for the summer. He had come out to us on the terrace, bowing, smiling.

No such courtesy now. I stepped inside the doorway, noticing the piles of paper on his desk, the worn Persian rug, the smell of his pipe, and the dust balls in the corners. The office surprised me. He ran his little hotel with great efficiency, yet here was a sense of disarray. He was a man of contradictions, our Monsieur Sella.

"I'm not bringing your coffee, monsieur."

He jumped up in surprise. "Madame Murphy? Is there something . . . ? How can I be of assistance? A complaint?"

"Yes. Where is Anna?"

"Ah. You, too, wish to have a word about her. Madame Picasso has already done so. I have dismissed her. She is leaving immediately." He tugged at his ear in dismay.

"No. I do not wish a word, and I do not wish her to leave. May I sit down?" Anna was so young, so vulnerable I couldn't help but feel protective of her. She was a girl in trouble of some sort; she needed a friend. And that was how I saw myself, as a friend to people in need—artists, children, whomever. I did not create art, but I tried to create circumstances in which art may be created, in which people can live fully.

Monsieur Sella came from behind the desk and pulled the visitor's chair out for me.

"What happened last night," I began, choosing my words carefully because I did not know what Olga had said, how much detail she had given, "what happened was not Anna's fault."

Monsieur Sella sat back down, his chair creaking a bit under his girth, and sighed heavily.

"But certainly, when there is a problem between a kitchen assistant and a paying guest, it is always the assistant's fault," he said gently.

"Monsieur Sella, I assure you, Anna was within her rights to clarify what was on the menu and what was not."

His eyebrow shot up. "Is that all it was about? Yes, this is a different matter. Madame Picasso led me to believe . . ."

So Olga, too, had seen the way Pablo looked at Anna. Before Irène arrived. Seen it and decided to get rid of Anna for that as well.

"Only the menu," I clarified. "I wish her to stay. She is . . . she is under my protection."

"I see. Well. To please you, madame, then stay she will. She is still packing, I believe. Not that she has much to pack. These young women come from nowhere, leave, and go to nowhere.

Such a generation." He sighed again. "Just between us, I was very worried about finding a replacement for her. At this time of the year, everyone is either away visiting relatives in the mountains or already employed.

"But tell me, what do you think of this fellow?" He opened the newspaper to the page he had been reading. It was an article about one of Mussolini's rallies in Rome, the leader banging his fist on his podium, his followers standing grim-faced and wary behind him.

"They say he is doing good things in Rome. Draining the swamps to control malaria, putting people back to work, and ending the labor strikes," Sella said. "The last time I went to Paris to visit my cousin, you could barely walk in the streets, they were so crowded with strikers."

"Mussolini is also jailing students and imprisoning people who disagree with him. And that other one in Spain, Primo de Rivera, throwing crumbs to the workers as he jails students and laborers. They don't strike there. They are too afraid," I pointed out.

"Well, we could use a little order here."

"Not that kind, I think. I'll go tell Anna she is staying. Thank you, monsieur."

"Think nothing of it, madame. If it pleases you." I thought of the large bank check Gerald had given him. It had certainly made an impression.

Anna was still in her room off the kitchen when I knocked on the door. Her eyes were red, but her hair had been neatly brushed and pulled back into a low knot at the nape of her neck. Somehow, this hairstyle preferred by older women made her look even younger.

"It's all right," I said. "I spoke with Monsieur Sella, and you are staying. If you wish," I added.

She sat on the narrow cot that served as her bed and stared at the floor. When she looked up at me, her eyes were even redder, and she began to cry anew.

"I wish I could go home," she whispered.

I sat next to her and put my arm around her shoulders. I stole a glance at her belly. Flat. But still, she could be months along without showing.

"Why can't you go home?"

She pressed her lips together like a child holding back a secret. She shook her head and looked down at her hands folded in her lap.

When she looked up again, there was a warning in her eyes. "You are so lucky," she said. "Husband. Children. A good life. Maybe it is better not to take chances with it."

"What do you mean?"

"I mean Picasso."

Olga was already at the beach with Paulo when I arrived with the children later that morning. Pablo wasn't anywhere in sight. I was tempted to give Olga the cold shoulder for what she had done—tried to do—to Anna but decided détente would be the wiser course. It was a small beach, and if we were to share it, civility was required.

Instead, it was Olga who gave me the cold shoulder, ignoring my "Good morning" and turning her back to me. She twisted the umbrella around to shield herself from even a view of me.

Misery. Jealousy. She carries it around with her like a skin disease, I thought. Certainly, Pablo was difficult. He taunted her with his affairs, his wandering eyes whenever another woman entered a room. Yet my sympathy was more with Pablo, who was warm, not icy like Olga, and could be generous and encouraging, as he had been with Gerald. Still, I was thankful that my husband was faithful, that he never looked at other women in that way. Thankful that I and the children were all he needed.

Paulo, who had been playing with his bucket and toy shovel, gave a sudden wail of pain. Olga and I ran to him from our different sides of the beach and examined the swollen finger he held up to us. A crab scuttled away from the overturned sand bucket, and even though Olga gave him a candy to suck on, Paulo whimpered, tears flowing.

"I have some cream that may help," I said.

"Yes?" Olga said, raising one perfectly arched eyebrow.

I fetched the tube from the basket that held keys, books, apples, extra towels—anything needed for hours at the beach. After I messaged it into Paulo's tiny finger, he smiled at me and waved both arms in the air gleefully.

"Thank you," Olga said, and the ice was gone from her voice. She smiled, too. Impulsively, I gave her a quick hug, and she hugged me back.

"I saw it," Honoria whispered to me when she returned to our blanket. "It was only a little crab." Her shoulders were pink from the sun, her hair curling with ocean salt.

"But I'm sure it hurt, darling. Go play with your brothers and keep a lookout for crabs. Okay?" I straightened my beach towel and watched their play from under my sun hat.

When Pablo arrived later, Olga was asleep on her blanket. He smelled of turpentine. "You've been painting," I said, looking up at him from the magazine I'd been reading. "Did Irène model?"

He sat next to me on the blanket, and our shoulders rubbed together. I had to stop myself from leaning even closer. "Yes," he whispered, making our conversation secret, intimate. "Poor Olga. This will make her even more unhappy." He grinned.

"You could try a little harder with her, Pablo. Really, you could."

Pablo nodded. "Maybe. She thinks I should feel responsible for her unhappiness. I do not. I gave her all she wanted. Marriage. The child. Limoges plates so that she can impress her dinner guests." His eyes twinkled when he said that. It was common gossip that Olga was a social climber, that she liked her artist husband to wear tailored suits and pay for silk curtains in their Paris apartment in their very good neighborhood.

No more Bateau-Lavoir for Pablo, that crowded Montmartre artists' hovel where he had cooked over a single gas ring, slept on a mattress on the floor in a single room that was both home and studio, and washed at a fountain in the street. I think he missed it. I think it is easy to believe we are happy in poverty when in fact we are happy merely because we are young and our cares do not overwhelm us.

"Wives need more than fancy dishes," I said. "They need to feel loved." But Pablo had already opened his sketchbook and brought the pencil from his shirt pocket.

"Don't move," he said. "Don't look at me. Look at the ocean."

I heard the scratching of the pencil on the paper, felt his eyes examining the lines and angles of my face, my posture.

"You are the antidote to Irène," he said. "She is drama. You are calm. I will draw you often, I think."

But that first sketch was already finished, and he was distracted by the seagulls flying overhead, tracing their flight with his eyes and forefinger, no longer interested in me.

Poor Olga. To love such a man.

Gerald arrived soon after, followed by Anna carrying a basket.

"Picnic," she called out. "Peaches, bread, cheese. Lobster salad."

Olga, who had just awoken from her nap under the beach umbrella, turned and saw Pablo sitting next to me, and Anna, not dismissed as Olga had requested, unpacking the basket. Olga's face clouded over; she sank onto her elbows in defeat.

"I'm not hungry," she said.

"More for us," said Pablo.

Gerald and I exchanged glances over glasses of chilled white wine. I wished Olga and Pablo would go back to Paris and leave us in peace. And then I thought of the beach without him, that little burst of pleasure I felt every time I saw him, and it seemed the sun would not be quite as bright if he left.

Pablo watched as Anna bent and turned to spread out our lunch. He opened his sketch pad again. His eyes went from her to the pad, from the pad back to her, a flurry of movement, pencil moving quickly over the paper, and his face changed from that of an irksome, mischievous rascal to that of a child mesmerized in wonder.

Anna pretended to be unaware of him. She leaned close to me when she poured our wine and whispered, "Thank you for speaking to Monsieur Sella," but never looked Pablo's way. Never looked at the great artist, the famous artist, who was now studying, drawing her own image. But her face flushed.

There is a wonderful spiritual that Gerald and I sang together during those evenings in New York or Paris when our guests decided we should entertain each other, not just sit and drink to oblivion or quarrel over paint sellers and frame makers: "Come Down, Angels, and Trouble the Water."

I had brought my family to the Riviera for the beautiful calmness of the turquoise sea, for solitude. And here was troubled water. Because even as Pablo studied Anna, as Gerald dished out salad, as Olga turned her back to us, and as the children ran in and out of the waves, oblivious of the adult tension, I felt my desire for Pablo expanding like some exotic flower that has been given too much sun and water. It cannot last. But while it blooms . . . it cannot be denied. It cannot be unseen or unfelt.

And I was in that moment as jealous of Anna as Olga seemed to be of me.

I did not know before that morning that there could be electricity in the air without a storm to produce it. No, there was a storm. Pablo Picasso. Laughing at us, throwing balls for the children to catch. Posing, muscle-man style, as he felt our eyes on him.

And then returning to his work, his pencils and sketch pad. He could not look, could not see, without needing to translate what he saw to paper. And that summer, he saw women, playing children, beach scenes. Lovely things, but always that edge. In his paintings of that sun-seared season, the women are running. Are they running to someone or away?

I wonder.

NINE
· · · · · · · ·

ALANA

Sara, who had been sitting in her armchair, eyes closed, sat up suddenly, and her eyes fluttered open. She seemed surprised to see me, she'd been so lost in reminiscence. She brushed back a wave of fading blond hair and cleared her throat.

I had been there with her, it seemed. I had heard the cicadas singing, smelled the thyme and salt in the air, felt the warmth of a Provence night. I felt disoriented, suspended somewhere between 1923 and now.

"I can't believe I told you all that old gossip, rambling on," she said apologetically. "How bored you must have been."

I sat, breathless, so entranced that I had stopped taking notes.

"Please," I said. "Go on." She had spoken of a betrayal. Who had been betrayed?

"Have I made Olga seem like a witch? I didn't mean to. She was so beautiful. Elegant. I'm sure Pablo loved her very much. Oh, that's a lie, isn't it?"

But it hadn't been her reminiscences about Olga that had transfixed me. It was Pablo, on the beach, sketching Sara.

"Do you have any of the beach drawings he made that summer?" I asked, hope making me sit close to the edge of the chair. His paintings from that time were well known, but there was little information about the more informal sketches.

"Of me? No. Pablo kept them. I don't know what happened to the drawings of Anna."

That would have been too good to be true, I thought: unpublished, unseen sketches. That would have sold my article to Reed. Sara saw the disappointment on my face.

"I'll have a look through the trunks in the attic," she said. "We haven't unpacked everything yet from the sale of the house in Antibes. There might be something there that I've forgotten about."

"Thank you." I thought of something else Sara had said. "What did she mean?" I asked. "Anna. When she told you not to take chances."

"She saw the looks Pablo and I had exchanged. And Anna, though young, sometimes had an older woman's wisdom. Are you really getting anything from this, Alana? Are you understanding enough? I wonder. It was so long ago, so much has happened since then, but I can't help but think some of this is important for you. I know so."

Sara rose from her chair and went to her desk. She put her hand on the pull of a small drawer but then seemed to think better of whatever she had been planning to do, and the drawer stayed shut.

"It's great information," I reassured Sara, though in fact it wasn't enough.

"It surprises me that I enjoy talking about Pablo. We were close once. And he still sends letters occasionally, mostly to

Gerald. He admired Gerald's painting, you know. And he wasn't just saying that. Pablo is many things, but not a liar."

The afternoon had turned rainy, and the windows were beaded and streaked with water. A gentle tapping of rain on the roof filled the room with the peace of remembered childhood naps, wrapped in my mother's arms.

"You miss her," Sara said. "Your mother. Yes, the rain reminds me of childhood, too. What happened to her?"

"Cancer. She didn't tell me till it was almost over. We'd quarreled."

"Over the fiancé. Don't look surprised, Alana. There isn't much more for a daughter and mother to quarrel over, at least not until the children come, and then there's plenty to quarrel over. My mother was furious that I took my children to France. 'Barbaric,' she said. If she could have seen us, almost naked on the beach at dawn, throwing seaweed at each other and playing tag . . . well, it wouldn't have changed her mind."

Sara sighed. "She was more than a bit of a snob. Sometimes I wish she and Pablo could have met. I think the term is 'mutually assured self-destruction.'"

"They never met?"

"Good lord, no. She never visited us in France. She wasn't invited. Nor was Gerald's family. France was our refuge, our sanctuary. We were there because they were here. But let's talk about Pablo. I don't want to waste your time."

We sat and listened to the rain for a few minutes, locked into our own memories. There was a framed photo of her two boys, Baoth and Patrick, on a bookcase shelf, and Sara looked at it steadily, unblinking, but her unmasked expression revealed pain, sorrow, the grief that does not fade.

"So," Sara finally said. "Pablo. I was a little in love with him, you know. Most women were. He had such vitality, an

he did not lie about who he was. A womanizer. A man who would not be faithful. But also a genius. And sometimes, a little boy who played with toys."

"What kind of toys?"

"That night on the barge. The party, where I used toys as centerpieces. There was a little carved horse, a simple thing, carved years before by a father or older brother for a younger child. Picasso was entranced by it. It looked angry, he said, its mouth wide open in a scream, its head tossed back. He kept it, he confessed later. He carried it around with him. He had it there in his room at the hotel that summer. I saw it once when he asked me to go up to his room and fetch something."

"Why that toy? I wonder."

"Something about the lines. The rawness of the carving. The eyes were mismatched and one leg was longer than the other. It was a cubist toy, he joked."

Sara stopped pacing and returned to her chair. "I passed by Pablo's room one morning, and Anna was in there holding the toy horse, turning it over and over in her hand as if it reminded her of something. Maybe a childhood memory. She put it down when she saw me watching her. But I think that later Pablo gave her that toy, the one that I had bought in Paris. And I was jealous."

Jealous. A new possibility: much had already been written about Picasso's many lovers, but Sara Murphy had never been mentioned.

Sara shook her head, reading my thoughts it seemed. "I thought you were just interested in his art," she said. "I have been indiscreet."

"I'm interested in his art. And his muses."

A maid came in to clear away the tea tray. "Dinner will be

served soon," she said, giving me an unfriendly look. "Will there be a guest?"

I waited two heartbeats, hoping to be invited to stay.

"No guests," Sara said. "Tell Gerald I'll be down in a minute." To me, she said, "But you may come back tomorrow, if you wish."

"You don't mind? I mean, if this is bothering you . . ."

"I thought it would," she said. "That's why I was a little rude at first. You aren't the first person to come knocking on the door with questions. Gerald and I knew so many people who became quite, quite famous. And some who already were when we met them. It is difficult, being asked to witness other people's lives as if we are moons and they are planets. But you are a good listener."

There was particular warmth in her smile, the way she held my hand rather than coolly shake it farewell. As if I were an old friend. Yet we had met for the first time just the day before.

"You wanted to hear about Pablo's art that summer, and I've gone on and on . . . I've told you things I've never told anyone else, you know. My jealousy of that girl, Anna. My feelings about Pablo."

"I'm honored."

And I was. But she was right. I couldn't see how I could use any more than two or three sentences of the information she had given me. *Art Now* would dismiss most of what I had heard as tabloid fodder. They wanted to know about the art and might not see the connections between the women and the art. In a world where most of the art history books on the shelves have been written by men, it is taken for granted that there may not be much difference between women and still lives, those bowls of fruit and musical instruments.

She read my thoughts. "The art," Sara said, sitting up even straighter. "You want to hear more about the art. You probably know most of the work he produced during that phase. The neoclassical figures, rounded and full of volume, like Roman statues come to life and then retranslated to the page. But his figures were so much more than that. Statues don't move. His paintings and drawings . . . look at them sideways, and you could swear they are moving just as you look away from them."

I thought of his *Two Female Nudes*, a pastel drawing in reds and pale blues with the women, one seated and the other standing, leaning into each other. Sara was right: I'd experienced that myself, looked away from the painting and thought the standing nude had just whispered something to her seated friend.

And the lovely *Mother and Child*, the child sitting on his mother's lap, her mouth so close to the top of his head that you knew as soon as you looked away, she would put her lips there, kissing in the way all mothers kiss their children, inhaling the new-bread scent of her child's skin.

Pablo had created magic and mystery in those drawings and paintings.

"*The Lovers*," Sara said, "I think his finest neoclassical work. The girl's eyes are downcast. Her face is solemn. But she is about to smile. You can sense it. And her lover. He holds her so tenderly. But soon he will put both his arms around her and embrace her with passion. Or, perhaps, push away. That part is unknown. A kiss or a quarrel?"

Sara rose and stretched. "I'm tired. Let's continue tomorrow. I am so sorry about your mother," she added.

She stood aside to let me go through the doorway before she did and I smelled her perfume, a crisp green floral, almost girlish in its lightness.

I had been worried about reminding her of her loss—as if we

ever forget such things—and here she was, consoling me for mine.

The rain had stopped, but the autumn dusk filled the hallway with shadows.

"I hate this time of day," Sara said. "When the light dies and you have to learn all over again, every day, that the universe is not kind or malicious, it is merely indifferent."

Jack was behind the reception desk when I arrived, fiddling with a lamp that wasn't working.

"You have unplugged that, right?" I asked him.

He frowned and held up the cord, disconnected from the outlet. "Glad to see I inspire such confidence," he said. "How did it go with Sara this afternoon?"

"The flowers worked. Thanks." But he was distracted and fussing with the lamp.

"Something wrong?" I asked.

"Not if I can triple the room rates and stop paying the property taxes. Know anything about bank robbery?"

"Only that the robbers tend to get caught."

"Too bad. Chicken fricassee. For dinner. Lots of dark meat. Cheaper."

"Jack, can I buy you a drink after dinner tonight?" I said it impulsively, still mulling over Sara's story, what was said and what was not said, the intimacy and tenderness in her voice when she described what it was like, being seen, being drawn, by Picasso.

Jack's right eyebrow went into a full lift.

"Sure. Ten," he agreed. He twisted the lamp cord, running it through his hands like a fishing line, finding the frayed section where bare wires showed through.

"This will have to be rewired," he said, more to himself than to me. "Great. Another expense. I'd better check all the lamps in the hotel." He looked up at me as if just remembering I was still there. "Some of these lamps are so old they were converted from gas fixtures at the turn of the century. Only new thing in the place is my socks. And they aren't that new. By the way, there's live music tonight. Jazz. Local band, and pretty good, if I say so. I just hope they pass the hat instead of expecting cash from me." He stalked off to his office, closing the door behind him.

"Not a good week for him, I guess," said a woman's voice behind me. "I keep telling him he should let this place burn down and take the insurance."

She had shoulder-length black hair brushed away from her face in stylish waves and thickly lashed black eyes. She looked like Ava Gardner, and her suit was either Chanel or a really good knockoff. The overnight bag on the floor next to her was Vuitton.

"Janet," she said, extending her hand. "Janet Brennan. Jack's wife."

"Almost forgot to tell you, Alana," Jack called from the depths of his office. "Another message for you. There in the pigeonholes behind the desk."

I stepped behind the dark wood counter and pulled out the folded paper, very aware of Janet Brennan's eyes burning into my back, and of my own disappointment. A wife. A very beautiful wife. Ever since he had put that vase of flowers on the table for me, I had been, I realized now, looking forward to speaking more with him.

There had been a friendly warmth in Jack's voice when he called out to me about the message in the pigeonhole. Mrs. Jack Brennan had picked up on it.

"And you must be Alana," she said. Her smile revealed perfect straight white teeth and an ability to put a distinct chill in the air.

Jack heard her, that low mocking voice, and came out of the office. They didn't exactly run into each other's arms, I noticed.

"Hello, Janet," he said coldly. "You staying long?"

I pocketed the note, guessing it was from William, and left Jack and Janet staring daggers at each other. Upstairs, I took a long shower and then unpacked my Remington portable. I spent the next two hours tapping away, using my notes as an outline to fill out the afternoon's interview with Sara. When I reread it, I realized there just wasn't enough information about Picasso. How do you write about an artist you haven't interviewed?

I needed to go to France, to find Pablo Picasso, to ask him questions about that time.

Impossible. I could barely afford to put gas in my car. I budgeted to buy a pair of stockings.

When the day's interview with Sara was put down on paper, as word for word as I could get it, I reluctantly unfolded the paper and read the phone message from William.

Promotion coming in new year. Probably partnership. December good month for wedding. Come back so we can plan.

I sprawled on the bed, surrounded by papers and books, and put the towel over my face, the way children do when they are hiding. I tried to imagine a white dress, a walk down the aisle. My feet twitched of their own accord. Run, my brain told them. Like one of the women in the paintings Picasso made that summer.

That walk down the aisle. Who would give me away? No father and no mother. No brothers, uncles.

A sudden ridiculous thought, and I burst out laughing so hard the towel puffed up. David Reed? Now, there's a brilliant feminist move. Asking your boss to walk you down the aisle.

And after the wedding, supper on the table for William. Every night. How was your day, dear? A weight pressed on my chest just thinking about it. Why couldn't we stay as we were?

Dinnertime, I told myself, though I had lost my appetite. And then tomorrow back to Cheer Hall. *I am not wrapping this up so I can look through bridal magazines*. And then I remembered William smiling at me from under the bedsheets, the desire in his eyes that made my knees weak. A lifetime of that would not be so hard to take. He would take care of me.

My mother's voice had said that, inside my head.

Did I need to be taken care of? Probably. My mother had been right about that. Even if I did get the job on the magazine, I wouldn't be paid the same as the men. I'd be passed over for any raises, and there would be that monthly glance at my stomach, everyone wondering if I was pregnant yet, when I would be leaving the magazine to raise my family, and that would be the end of my career.

My mom had managed both work and motherhood. How? Perhaps because she'd been forced to after my father died. The unwritten rules were different for widows who had to earn their living.

I remembered some of my college professors who had so blatantly longed for the good old days, when education had been about men preparing for the world, not girls looking for husbands. Many of the professors had assumed that was why we were there: to find spouses. No other reason.

"Don't bother telling them about Rosie the Riveter," my

mother had advised one day when I came home from NYU
grumbling. "Men have short memories. Selective memories."
She had been sitting at the drawing table in the larger half of
the dining room she claimed as her studio. I had looked over
her shoulder at the new design, red and black geometrics with
yellow splashes.

"Calder," I guessed.

When she was preparing a new scarf pattern, she studied
individual artists, all their works. She let those works speak to
her, and she carried them forward into a new visual conversation, statements that women could wrap around their throats
and shoulders.

My mother had liked William. And so, in many ways, did I.
I wanted him. I didn't want him. And I wasn't getting any
younger.

William was a lawyer, the kind that big businesses take out
for three-cocktail lunches trying to recruit him. Currently, he
was working for the DA's office but had let it be known that he
was available for the private sector . . . if the price was right. So
far, he had been courted by a pharmaceutical company, a developer who was busily filling the outskirts of large cities with
row after row of the new ranch houses, and an international
bank. The developer had offered him a double deal: if William
would take over the legal section, they would also offer his
fiancée—that would be me—a secretarial job, if I insisted on
working.

"Just till the kids arrive," William had said. "Till then, it's
good money and steady work. You could afford to buy yourself
a decent wardrobe. What is that dress you're wearing?"

We'd been at supper at La Grenouille, the new French restaurant in Midtown that everyone was talking about, and William had already handed out six business cards. The restaurant

was, by my terms, outrageously expensive, but William thought of these evenings out as investments, a way to make even more contacts.

"It was my mother's. It's couture," I said. It had been worn during one of Givenchy's showings and had been slightly torn. They'd let my mother, who was allowed backstage because she was in the business, take it home.

"Maybe once it was couture," he said. "Now it's out of style. I don't think wearing your mother's clothes is particularly healthy, Alana. Reconsider, please."

"I don't want to work in the secretarial pool. I'm actually a lousy typist, William. I have a degree in art history, remember?"

"You never let me forget. And you wouldn't be in the pool. More on the order of executive secretary. Status. Just think about it. Promise? It would be helpful for me, for my work, if you were more visible, you know, friendly and chatty."

"What about my work?"

He hadn't bothered to answer. At that moment, a man approached our table. His pinstripe suit was expensive; his tie clip was gold and sapphires. The woman on his arm looked like a *Vogue* model with her dark hair teased up into one of the tallest beehives I'd ever seen and her eyes darkly outlined with liner that curled up at the corners of her eyes.

William stood and shook hands. He was trying to be cool, but I could see the eagerness in his face, so obvious it embarrassed me.

"Set a date," he'd ordered when he put me in a taxi that night.

"I will. Soon."

I was in love with him. I was. He was good-looking, generous, intelligent. And maybe he was right. Maybe I was wasting my time. Our time. His time. And time is precious.

"He's steady," my mother always said of him, as if that were the best thing a man could be. My father had been steady, too, before he died. But my mother and I, who wanted more than steady, had fought over William, and I wasn't with her when she died. I, her only child, her only blood relative, hadn't been with her.

I knew about the cancer. That day when I brought up the mail from the lobby box and she was in the shower. In the middle of the afternoon? She always had a bath in the evening. And there was the letter from a doctor's office, a doctor whose name I hadn't known. She'd admitted it reluctantly, toweling her hair dry in front of the little electric heater. "Inoperable," she added.

What she hadn't told me was how quickly the disease would spread. I had thought we had years. In our relationship with our mothers, a part of us is always a child. She has always been there. She will always be there. Death is not a possibility. So we'd wept that evening, over the letter, and then we resumed our routine, the good part, the tight hugs in the morning, sharing a piece of cake in the restaurant where the portions were always too large . . . and expensive.

The bad part. "You should marry William," she said again one evening after we'd finished washing up our supper dishes. "He is a good man. He will take care of you." Ever since the cancer diagnosis, she had become increasingly worried about what would happen to me after she was gone.

"Maybe I don't want to be taken care of," I said.

She almost growled at me. "The world can be a very hard place for a woman alone, a woman with no family. You think because you have been to bed with a few college boys—yes, I knew—you think you know the world, you know men. You know nothing. In this world, safety matters. Say yes to William."

"I don't want to talk about it," I said over my shoulder, checking the hall door to make sure it was locked, shuffling the magazines on the coffee table into a neater pile.

But she wouldn't let it go. We had the same argument over and over. And like a child, because she was pushing me in one direction, I went in the other.

"William called," she said one afternoon when I came home from work. I had a temporary job as a copy editor for a museum publisher and had spent the afternoon correcting captions for a Botticelli exhibit.

"I don't want to talk about it," I said.

"Poor Alana." She sighed, her anger swallowed by an emotion I didn't yet understand. Letting go. Of everything.

I took another freelance job when the museum one ended, this time for an art publisher in the Midwest, far from William, New York, and the apartment I shared with my mother, far enough away that I couldn't be expected home on the weekends. Time to think. And while I was thinking, there in that flat prairie city where the winter wind was like a cold slap from the beginning of time, she died . . . alone.

One of the last things she said to me was "Marry William."

Why was I thinking of all that? Because at dinner that evening in the dining room of Brennan's Inn there was a table occupied by a mother and daughter, two women of ages similar to mine and my mother's at the time of the quarrel. It was obvious they were both angry and not speaking to each other. A current of cold air seemed to circle their table.

I wanted to tell them about anger and loss and time you can never get back. But you can't say those things to strangers, and

even if you did, they wouldn't listen. The mother and daughter played with the food on their plates; they stared in faked interest at the ceiling, the curtains. Then checked their watches. Matching watches, as if that would bring them closer together. In my head, I talked to my mother and said, *I'm sorry*, over and over. And then I asked Jack, busily clearing tables, if I could again use the private phone in the office.

"Someday I'll have phones installed in the rooms," Jack apologized.

I finished my coffee and went to the little office behind the reception desk. His desk was carved mahogany, barely visible under piles of paperwork. Mid-nineteenth century. William preferred Bauhaus or Scandinavian contemporary.

He picked up on the fourth ring.

"Hey, William. It's me, Alana. I see you found me."

"It took some detective work." He did not sound happy. "I called Reed to find out where you were, and he didn't know, so yes, I called Helen. It was pretty embarrassing, having to ask a magazine editor where your fiancée is. Are you going to be back tomorrow? Or did you forget?"

I had forgotten. Tomorrow was Saturday. Dinner with the law office partners. Audition night, I called it. Audition, over and over again.

"I'm not finished here. I haven't even started," I said, wanting to kick myself for how weak, how defensive, my voice sounded. Like a child whining, "Please, can I stay up later?"

A long pause, anger crackling through the phone cord.

"Alana, this promotion means a lot to me. To us. More money. A lot more money. A bigger apartment, big enough so that we could start a family. That window gets a little smaller every year."

"I know," I said, anger now rising in my voice, matching his. He liked to remind me of my age, almost thirty. Well on my way to middle age and, soon, too old to have children. "But this article means a lot to me. To us."

"No," he said. "To you. Only to you."

"That's not fair."

"Think about it. Meanwhile, I'll make our excuses for tomorrow. Again."

"Can't you go without me?" I asked. "The dinner?"

"That's not how it works. Alana, listen. I love you. I want you to be my wife. To be the mother of my children. To be there for me when I need you. You have to decide what you want."

"I love you, too," I said. "I really do."

"Come home soon." His voice was softer, the anger gone. He hung up.

I decided to call Helen, too, check in with her. When she answered, I could tell by the slurring of her words that she was on her third martini.

"Shouldn't drink alone," I said.

"Who said I'm alone?"

"Oh. A date?"

"Not exactly. William dropped by. He left a few minutes ago."

"William came to your apartment?" He didn't like Helen. Or so I thought. "Did he just call me from there?"

"Yes. He's worried. I am, too, a bit. Two guys came to my office, very unpleasant fellows, asking if I knew you. Not police in suits, but definitely official. And they had a photograph. You in that march with Grippi in front of the restaurant. What's going on, Alana?"

I leaned against the wall, feeling the chill of its cold, damp tile seep through my blouse. When I was frightened, my mother

used to make me lie down, and she'd put a damp washcloth sprinkled with lavender on my forehead. I tried to imagine that scent of lavender.

"I don't know," I said.

"They asked if you knew a Professor Grippi. I told them you took his seminar on the French Impressionists and their influence on cubism. You and probably a thousand others."

I breathed into the phone as I slid down the wall into a protective crouch.

"Professor Grippi is a communist sympathizer. Maybe actually a communist," I said, and immediately wished I hadn't. The less Helen knew, the better.

There was a pause long enough that I thought we had been disconnected. Then, "Oh, Alana. What have you been up to?"

What have you *been up to, Helen? William was at your apartment?* What I said was a very watered-down version of that question. "You and William making friends? That's nice."

"Yeah. He's a nice guy. And no, there is nothing going on."

"Sorry. Of course not. It's just . . ." Just what?

"See you soon, Alana. Okay? Don't tell me any more. About Grippi and all that. I don't want to know." She hung up.

I found my way back down the long hallway to the taproom, keeping one hand trailing along the wall. If you're ever lost in a labyrinth, keep your right hand on the wall, never lose contact with it. That's how you find your way out, my mother had told me.

A December wedding?" Jack said. "Sounds nice."

The taproom smelled of spilled beer and stale cigarettes. A slow song was playing on the jukebox, and couples danced cheek to cheek in the small circle of bare wood floor that had been cleared of tables.

"Nothing definite. Nothing set in stone," I said.

Both Janet and Jack were sitting at the bar. *I'll have to buy her a drink, too*, I thought, *and she'll probably order champagne*. What a strange couple they were, Jack in his rolled-up shirtsleeves and worn corduroy work pants, that constant frown making his eyebrows almost meet over his freckled nose. And Janet, cover-girl beautiful and wearing an expensive tweed suit that would have been more at home in the Russian Tea Room than this country bar.

Janet had seen me before Jack did. She waved hello, then leaned over and gave Jack a kiss. *Point taken*, I told myself, forcing a smile on my face, forcing my feet to go in their direction. Jack's taken. Not that I was interested. I was engaged, after all. I wished I had thought to put on my engagement ring. William had given me a diamond so big I felt uncomfortable wearing it most places. But this evening, I would have loved to flash it in Janet's face.

"My husband tells me you're a writer," Janet said, lighting a cigarette.

The bartender, a young woman with hair even blonder than Jack's and the same long, aristocratic nose, made a face that Janet couldn't see, but Jack did, and the two of them laughed.

"Did I say something funny?" Janet, offended, blew cigarette smoke in the bartender's direction.

"Did the interview go well today?" Jack asked. He partially turned his back to Janet to face me.

"Sara is being wonderful. But I think I'll need more information than she can give me."

He drained his beer mug and set it down on the bar.

"Slow down, Jack," the bartender said when she refilled his mug.

I looked up at the small television bracketed into a corner of the bar. News. The sound was turned down so it wouldn't interfere with the music, but there was Senator McCarthy shouting into a microphone and a row of men sitting opposite him. Their faces weren't visible, but I was certain that was Professor Grippi there, in the middle of the row. Grippi, with his thin neck and his longish hair that he constantly brushed back with his hand. The man facing away from the camera brushed back his hair as if to confirm what I was thinking.

I froze in terror, not even breathing. My old professor had been called before the committee to answer questions. *Are you, have you ever been . . . ?* Would they ask him who had been with him in that picket line in front of the restaurant? Who had carried a poster reading, "End Segregation"?

"So, Alana. Tell me about yourself." Janet blew a second puff of smoke in my direction. The heavy gold charm bracelet on her wrist jangled when she picked up her martini glass. "How come you're working? Fiancé a little broke? Hard to start a family like that, and pretty soon, it might be too late, you know. Women over thirty . . ." Janet's voice was sweet as honey.

I looked away from the television into Janet's dark Ava Gardner eyes. Her mouth smiled. Those eyes did not.

"My fiancé is a lawyer," I said. "A successful lawyer." I wanted to look back at the television, to ask the bartender to turn up the volume, to hear what was being said. But it suddenly seemed very important to distance myself from it, to be just another hotel guest having a drink at the bar.

"Alana's a career girl," Jack said. He studied me for a moment. The teasing glint in his eyes was replaced by something that looked oddly like tenderness. "I'm glad today went well for you."

"I'm tired. Bedtime." Janet stood. "Coming up, Jack?"

"Not yet," he said. "I'll see you in the morning."

Janet slunk out, the eyes of most of the men in the bar following her.

TEN

·······

ALANA

Sorry about that," Jack said. "Janet can be direct, I'll say that for her. And this"—he nodded at the bartender—"is my sister, Tessie."

"Welcome to Brennan's Inn. Even if the manager is a jerk. Another glass of wine?"

"No, I'll have a sidecar, please," I said, wanting something stronger.

"Same," Jack said. "And put the drinks on the jerk's tab." When I protested, he shushed me by raising his hand, palm up.

"Your wife likes an early night," I said.

"She's only here to drop off some papers. Some tasks must be done in person."

"She likes to see him squirm," Tessie added, slinging the bar towel over her shoulder.

More customers came in, and Brennan's Inn Public Taproom became very busy. The band was setting up in a corner, and the occasional twang of banjo and high notes of a clarinet sang out over the murmurs and laughter of people enjoying the evening. The lights were low and intimate. The combination of Victorian wooden furnishings and candlelight with men in leather jackets and skinny ties and women in their full crinoline skirts was oddly charming, as if time itself had gotten confused.

"You run a good bar," I said to Jack, changing the topic.

"Thank you, ma'am." His eyes scanned the room, noting a group near the door that was a little too loud, a table where a teenage girl in bobby socks and a pink cardigan sipped a Coke. Her older friends gulped down beers.

"We'll have to keep an eye on her," he said to his sister. "Make sure those boys don't start giving her beer. In the morning, I'll call her father again."

"If it's a problem, why not ask her to leave?" I said.

"Because that fellow she's with, the big one in the leather jacket, would make a scene, maybe even bust up a few chairs," Jack said. "Better to just monitor the situation. The girl is Susan, well known hereabouts. Susan, fifteen going on forty."

His voice was protective.

"No kids yourself?" I asked.

"Nope. Mrs. Brennan isn't quite certain motherhood is for her. Might interfere with her social schedule. What about you? You and this William ready for a family?"

The band had finished setting up and sat at a large round table with a pitcher of beer before beginning their set. I looked at the television again. McCarthy was still there on the screen. I was tempted to ask Tessie to turn the sound up. What was he saying? What was Professor Grippi saying?

"Not certain I risked life and limb at Guadalcanal for the likes of him," Jack said, gesturing at the television. "He's even accusing army men of being communists."

I didn't say anything.

A few minutes later, when the band had finished their beers, they began their set with a slow song, one of the crooning Bing Crosby ballads that had helped keep spirits up during the war.

"Dance?" Jack asked, offering me his hand.

I saw Tessie look up, her eyes flickering with surprise, going from Jack to me and back again.

"Sure."

It was awkward at first. We both stood. Jack took a step toward me. I took a step toward him. There was a moment of hesitation till we agreed on ballroom style, my hand on his shoulder, his on my waist. After a couple of beats, we were moving together, right, left, swaying. He raised one arm and twirled me under it, then leaned me over his arm into a dip so deep my hair fell back.

You are here to work, I reminded myself. But I liked the feel of his arm supporting me, his chin close to my head when he swooped me back up. The awkwardness was completely gone, and we were close together, moving slowly, surely. A lovely sensation.

When the song ended, we stepped quickly apart.

"We'd better sit the next one out," I said. But neither of us moved apart, and we stayed like that, my hand on his shoulder, his hand on my waist, looking at each other.

William didn't like to dance. And he certainly wouldn't enjoy an evening in a taproom like this, loud and about to turn rowdy. But William carried certainty with him the way some men carry chocolate or flowers to their beloveds. Certainty and predictability last longer than flowers, offer more than chocolates. *Now you sound like your mother*, I told myself.

"There's a beer in front of Susan," Tessie said quietly so that only Jack and I heard.

Jack grimaced. He lowered his head in the direction of the

table where the too-young-girl sat. He looked like a bull about to charge.

He stalked over to the table, leaned down, and whispered a few words to the group in general. They laughed. When the boy in the black leather jacket tried to stand, Jack gently pushed him back into his chair and whispered something in his ear.

"Reminding him of the jail time for contributing to the delinquency of a minor," Tessie said. "Now he'll tell Susan that if she takes another sip, he's going to call her father. And it's over again. Same thing next week." She went to take orders from a couple at the end of the bar.

"Bedtime for me," I said. "Thanks for everything," when Jack came back to the bar.

"Yeah, me, too. Busy day tomorrow." He finished his drink in one long gulp. We walked away from each other, quick steps, no backward glances.

I had to pass Fifteen-Going-on-Forty's table when I left. One of the boys, the one with slicked hair curled over his forehead, had his arm around her shoulders and was sliding his beer toward her.

I'd known a few of that type, wrestled them off in dark movie theaters in high school and, later, avoided them at office parties or walks home from a kindly meant blind date arranged by friends.

I bumped the table when I walked by, and the beer ended up in his lap.

"Sorry," I said, smiling.

Tessie laughed from behind the bar.

I had a headache the next morning and was tired from a night of poor sleep. I'd been intrigued by the politics of handling Susan and her friends with neighborly discretion, and remem-

bering my own years of teenage rebellion, those late-night escapes to hear poetry readings at the White Horse Tavern or to
eavesdrop on the artists at the Cedar Tavern. Climbing out my
window and down the fire escape late at night and returning
early morning before my mother was out of bed. And sometimes I went to Café Society in Sheridan Square, where the city
communists liked to drink.

I thought I was so tricky, so clever. And all along, my mother
knew. She'd admitted it when I began college, and she'd decided
to have my room freshly painted to celebrate my scholarship
award. "Get rid of those scuff marks on the windowsill you
made climbing in and out," she'd said. When she saw my look
of shock: "I was young once, too, remember. I know about
sneaking out at night."

I woke up missing her, wanting to speak with her one more
time, to feel her hug me again, miserable with that need for her.
Gone, I told myself.

Breakfast that morning was served by Tessie, not Jack,
whom I had looked forward to seeing, to saying "Good morning" to. I wanted to thank him for his company last night. I ate
quickly and went back to my room. I worked at the little wob-
bly desk, jotting down impressions, notes about Sara and her
memories, Picasso's drawings and paintings of those years.

The twenties were one of Picasso's most fertile decades, not
that he had any fallow periods. But the work of those years
stretched from his early cubism to neoclassicism, from the
hard-edged and witty figures of the *commedia dell'arte* to the
softly sentimental mothers and children, and into the Dinard
Period, with the energetic dynamism that disassociates the
painted body from real-life figures.

And then, in 1928, he paints *On the Beach*. A work as close
to abstract as it can get, full of bright color and patterns.

Some art historians think this painting is a competitive response to his friend, his rival, Matisse. I wondered, looking through my notes, if he was thinking of the beach at Antibes, sitting with Sara on the sand, watching the children play, when he painted it. The energy. The joy. The heat.

But then, more than a decade later, he paints *Guernica*, the greatest political art of the century, from an artist who previously had not expressed his politics. *Guernica* with its cubist forms, the terrified and mourning women, dead children, destruction, all expressed in black and white, no color on a huge canvas. The ultimate anti-war statement painted after the Germans bombed a little Basque village at the request of Franco, who was willing to destroy his own country to secure his power. The bombing took place on a market day so that as many civilians as possible would be killed.

To go from the beach paintings and *The Lovers* to that. This was why my mother had loved his work. He encompassed entire worlds, could express anything with his pencils and brushes.

How much of an influence had Sara had on him? How much had that summer shaped future work to come? So far, I had many questions and a few pages of notes that felt as if they were circling rather than arriving at a truth. Sara was speaking freely but was also holding something back.

I went into the bathroom to put on some lipstick and brush my hair, preparing for the day. But while part of my mind was busy with Picasso, there was a dark corner of it filled with that image of Professor Grippi sitting in that chair, facing McCarthy.

My hands were shaking. Would he name names? Had he kept lists of the students who had joined him at those meetings at 35 East Twelfth Street, who had marched with him? All I could do was wait and see.

ara greeted me herself at the door that morning, rather than
sending the maid to show me in, and her smile was warm,
reaching all the way to her eyes.

"Got your notebook?" she asked, taking my coat, and then
looking more intently at me. "Those sidecars sneak up on you.
Especially if Tessie makes them."

"Lesson learned," I admitted.

She led me down the hallway, up the stairs, into her sitting
room.

"Tea is coming up," she said. "Did you notice the air today?
It has the last scent of summer in it. And that liquid smell that
sometimes comes off the river. It's not the ocean, not the Côte
d'Azur, but it has a similar quality sometimes. It reminds me of
the feeling of a wet bathing suit on a hot day. Did you swim,
Alana? As a child?"

The tea came in on a cart pushed by the maid.

"Darjeeling," Sara said. "I served this cold, to Pablo. He
only pretended to enjoy it, I think. Like a true European, he
couldn't understand the American fascination with iced drinks.
I remember his mother saying that chilled throats would make
the children ill. Even I understood that much Spanish."

That pause, whenever the children were mentioned, like
someone who has found herself at a cliff edge and pulled back
just before the fall. Thinking of those two sons, both lost.

When she looked at me again, the smile was a bit forced.
There was suffering in her eyes.

After those hours with her yesterday, I found myself drawn
to Sara, wanting to protect her. These memories caused her
pain. "No, we don't need to do this," I said. "If this is too

difficult to talk about, I'll find a different way to go about this article. Or maybe I'll just say no to the assignment."

"You mustn't do that. Stay," she said gently. "Sit down. We'll show that Reed. Is that his name? Women together, helping each other. There was little of that when I was in France. It was every woman for herself." She poured the tea and handed me a cup. "Besides, I'd like to talk about those years. I like speaking with you. It opens doors; some of them stay shut for a very long time, but some doors are lovely to look behind. And some stories need to be told."

She did something then that took my breath away. She took my face between her hands and studied it closely. My mother had done the exact same thing. It was a gesture of such tenderness that I felt tears starting to form in my eyes. Regret, loss. Shame.

"We quarreled, my mother and I. Just before she died," I said. "We didn't make it up."

"Then all the more reason for you to hear a story," she said. "A happy story. Happy at the edges, at least. You never know what you're going to find in the middle. Or at the end. Or who you will find."

"Picasso, I hope," I said. "Your influence on his work that summer."

"Don't overestimate me, please." She laughed. "Irène Lagut had much more influence over him. That magnificent painting, *The Lovers*, was for Irène. Pablo made that quite clear. I think that's what bothered Olga the most. Not the loss of their intimacy—I don't think she was a very sexual woman—but the loss of her husband's attention. She wanted him to paint only her. Perhaps when a man like Picasso paints you, that is as close as he gets to love."

We sat in the same chairs as the day before, Sara in a cushioned armchair, legs tucked up, me in a straighter but still comfortable chair, my notepad in my lap. Sun streamed in the window, a perfect autumn afternoon, the kind of day when my mother and I, in happier times, would walk down to the Battery and watch boats come and go.

"I saw a photograph of Irène Lagut in an old exhibition catalog when I was looking for information about Picasso, before I came here," I said. "The painting is not really a portrait of her, is it? Her hair was wilder, and from what her photo suggested, that meek downward glance doesn't really seem like her style."

Sara laughed. "You're right. *Meek* is not the right adjective for Irène. It is Irène as Pablo wished her to be. As he wished all women to be. Meek, loving, obedient. But now I hear Françoise Gilot is leaving him."

Gilot. The young painter who left her mother and father, her home, her art studies, to be Pablo's lover and eventually the mother of two of his children, Claude and Paloma. He'd been sixty-two when they met in 1943, during the war, and Françoise only twenty-two. They've been together ever since. Ten years.

"How do you know she is leaving?" I asked, intrigued.

"Pablo still writes to us once in a very great while. But mostly I hear news of him from other friends. Pauline and Ernest Hemingway, Dorothy Parker."

"Any chance I could see the letters?"

Sara paused and frowned. "I will have to think about that. They are personal, and I don't think Pablo would like them shown around. He can be a very private person, you know. But I admit I've taken a liking to you. I'll see if I can find one or two of interest. And now, Alana, you look as if it is Christmas morning. But we were talking about the painting he worked on that summer, *The Lovers*."

ELEVEN

. . . .

SARA

The days in Antibes passed quickly, a dance of emotion that carried through the hot days and the starlit nights. Olga's misery out of step with Pablo's free-spiritedness, his refusal to be tied down to anyone or anything but his work. Gerald, happy, working at his own paintings in his studio. Irène Lagut showing up at our lunches sometimes, always sitting or standing close to Pablo to annoy Olga.

I won't say Irène was malicious. But she was a troublemaker, one of those easily bored artists who, when they aren't painting or thinking about painting, enjoy manipulating others to see what happens. As if other people's lives can be composed and rearranged, like apples and pears on a table, completely indifferent to anything but their own curiosity and sense of play.

Like Pablo, Irène thought herself above any rules or norms that the rest of us felt obliged to follow. I sometimes envied Irène. I had never been that free. Not when I was a child playing in the toy-filled nursery of my parents' Cincinnati mansion, not when I was a young debutante constantly trying, and failing, to please my mother, not when I traveled in Germany and England and France.

Gerald brought me my first taste of freedom that day when I ran into my childhood friend walking on the beach in Southampton. I saw how good-looking he had become. And I saw how he looked back at me. He was walking with his back to the sun, so it radiated around him like a halo. This was a man my mother would never approve of. Not from the right set, would be her judgment. He had money, but not the right family. Irish. Catholic. Would not do.

But he was the one I chose, and loving him taught me to finally stand up to her. To say no to her when I wanted. To say yes to myself. Yes, I will meet Gerald and walk in the moonlight with him. Kiss him. Gerald asked me what I was reading, rather than told me what I should read. He sought my opinion on everything from Sunday menus to politics.

That was freedom. Loving Gerald became the only thing I wished to do, to make him happy and keep our children safe. Without them, freedom meant only emptiness. Loving a man like Picasso, though. That is the opposite of freedom. It would be more of an enthrallment rather than a choice. It would be all consuming.

I thought of Gerald holding me at night, and the children climbing into our bed at sunrise to get us up, the laughing and giggling, the warmth of their bodies, the scent at the base of their necks where they had been burnt by the sun.

And then . . . Pablo would brush by me or give me a look or a smile. He would pour a glass of wine for me at the table, leaning close enough that I could feel his breath on my neck.

"Sing that song, the one I like so much," he would say after dinner. "That spiritual. 'Come Down, Angels, and Trouble the Water.'"

Gerald and I would sing the old spiritual in perfect harmony, watching each other for the cues of how long to hold a note, when to take a breath. Never missing a note.

Sometimes I would see Anna standing in a doorway, watching, listening. Pablo sensed her, too, and their eyes would lock before she stepped backward into the darkness, out of sight.

Pablo and Olga and Paulo, along with the silent, sleepy mother, stayed at the hotel for several weeks before Olga decided she and Pablo should go elsewhere.

I went down for breakfast one morning, planning to take my bread and coffee out onto the terrace. Gerald was still sleeping, and the children were having their breakfast in the kitchen. I had woken from bad dreams, a restless night of mosquitoes and heat-damp sheets.

My children were just finishing breakfast, and when I kissed them, they tasted of oatmeal. They were arguing about what game they would play that morning. "Exercises first," I reminded them. Gerald spent a half hour with them in the morning on the sand, swinging their arms, touching toes. He taught them how to walk like Charlie Chaplin's Little Tramp, swinging an imaginary cane, how to leap like a tennis star swinging a high overhand at an invisible ball.

"Healthy minds, healthy bodies," he would call to them. "Jumping jacks!"

I poured myself a cup of coffee and headed to the terrace. Anna stopped me and suggested I use the little table in the side garden instead.

"She is out there. The Russian," she whispered. "In a foul temper."

Anna did not appear to be in a good mood herself. There was a crease between her eyebrows, and her mouth turned down at the corners. Cook was constantly yelling at the girl to work faster, to chop the parsley finer, mop the floor cleaner. I could tell from the way the cook was slamming pots that she and Anna had already had the first quarrel of the day.

"Then bring me some breakfast in the garden," I said.

"Do you like it here, working at the hotel?" I asked Anna when she brought me a tray of coffee and bread and jam. It was early, yet already very hot. The sun was a huge yellow balloon in the sky, and the herbs in the little garden gave off their scent of spicy thyme and sweet lavender.

Anna dropped the tray onto the table and gave me an incredulous look. She was often clumsy, and I would catch myself glancing surreptitiously at her belly. Still flat as a board.

"Like it? Here?" she said. "Always slicing carrots, picking up after others. You are the only person who is kind."

"Why did you leave your studies? Judging by the books you leave around and your interest in Pablo, I'd say you were studying art. No, don't go. I saw you reading Gerald's newspaper yesterday. The article about the demonstrations in Spain. Do you have friends there?"

"No," she said, but I felt it was a lie.

"You can tell me." She turned away and fled back to the kitchen.

I considered going after her. My children were often around her, and I had the right to know who she was. How had she ended up as kitchen assistant, this girl who in her free time read the classical authors, leaving Vasari and Ovid spread-eagled like downed butterflies on chairbacks and tables all over the hotel.

She was a refugee, I thought. *A runaway*. But from what? I thought of her accent and of those newspaper articles about Spain, the soldiers marching in the streets, breaking up demonstrations.

Perplexed by one woman, I decided to confront the other. Mystery does not appeal to me. Perhaps having children does that to you. The world needs clear answers, predictability. I finished my coffee and sought out Olga on the terrace. There was a half-emptied coffee cup in front of her, and she sat huddled in her chair, looking absolutely forlorn. When she heard my steps, she sat up quickly, reverting to that dancer's posture that sometimes looks haughty but is actually just the result of her early stage training.

"I do not like this place," she said. "Living in a hotel, always with other people. And the way he looks at you."

"Olga, my dear." I sat opposite her and put my hand over hers, touched by the misery in her voice. "Your husband is an artist. He looks at everything closely." Olga, with her dark, exotic looks and ballerina posture, was so beautiful. I felt my blond paleness, my softness, as a form of insufficiency.

"He doesn't paint me anymore," Olga said. "He does not look at me anymore. He draws you. And paints that woman, Lagut."

I wanted to comfort her, to say, "I'm sure your husband loves you very much." Instead, I pressed her hand and kept silent.

"We are leaving tomorrow," Olga said. "It is all arranged. And now I go to pack." She stood, pushing back her chair so that it scraped loudly against the flagstones. Momentarily, the startled birds stopped singing but then quickly resumed.

"We'll miss you," I said, thinking instead that I would miss Pablo, not bumping into him going up or down the stairs, not seeing him walking under the stars after our late dinners, that intimacy that comes with saying "Good morning" to someone over the coffee cups and "Good night" when two hands reach out to shut off the same hall light.

"Gerald will miss Pablo," I said.

"Well, we will not be far. Just in Juan-les-Pins. Close by." Olga took a final sip from her coffee cup. "Thank you. His women are often not kind to me."

"I am not his woman," I protested.

Olga smiled.

We spent the afternoon at the beach, as usual. Olga had finished her packing and spread her towel close to the waves. It was breezy, and little whitecaps danced to the shore, delighting the children. Gerald and Pablo spoke in quiet tones, seated in the sand in the middle, like an arbitration party between two enemy camps.

And there it was, the shadow over my contentedness. The gnaw of fear that I was not enough for Gerald, that when Pablo was gone, my husband would be unhappy. Gerald and I were two sides of the same coin. Sometimes I imagined that if I looked in the mirror, I might see him rather than myself. We were that inseparable. Yet sometimes it felt that no matter how close we stood next to other, even when we were in each other's arms, there was empty space between us.

I worried that if we were lost, if we wandered down a path to where it actually forked, we might never find each other again. And people did get lost. Anna was proof.

It was almost July, and even with the breeze, the heat was suffocating. I fell asleep on my towel and dreamt of my mother's chinchilla coat, the weight of it on my shoulders. And then my mother discovering me, snatching it off me, scolding me in her quiet, knife-sharp voice.

But it was Gerald's voice that called me back to awareness. "You've burnt your shoulders," he said. "You'll need some ointment on them." He kissed the top of my head and walked toward the children, calling them to get ready for their baths. Honoria, Baoth, and Patrick, their skin shimmering dark gold against the pale sand, protested, but Gerald herded them to the path leading to the hotel.

"Sara. You're as red as a lobster," Olga said that night at table, her first words to me since breakfast. She glowed in peach taffeta. Pablo, handsome in a white linen suit, looked every inch what he was: a man of great self-confidence and success, always wanting more of everything.

"Unwise to begin the evening with insults," Pablo said, and there was an edge to his voice that suggested a quarrel soon to follow.

"It was not meant as an insult," Olga protested. "Only that she should take care of her skin."

Pablo's eyes were on me, assessing, watching. He was in a bad mood. He'd had a letter that day from a friend in Paris about how badly some of his paintings had been treated during a spring art sale. The auctioneer had made jokes about the cubist paintings, and many of the artists had decided to abandon the dealer, Kahnweiler, and move to a different gallery.

"Will you move to Rosenberg as well?" Gerald asked, pouring wine for us.

"Not yet. The gallery owes me too much money, and if I leave, I will never get it." Pablo was staring at me so hard that I felt myself beginning to blush. "In front of a mirror," he said. "I should paint you sitting before a mirror."

He hadn't painted me yet, only sketched. He was asking if I would model for him.

Olga rose. "I am tired," she said. She smiled at me, but her eyes were dark with unhappiness and jealousy. Pablo sipped his water and smiled. From the doorway, I felt Anna's eyes watching, studying us.

"Are you coming, Pablo?" Olga asked.

"Later."

Olga nodded wearily.

"I'm tired, too," I said, leaving Pablo and Gerald to their discussion of art dealers and galleries, not answering Pablo's unspoken question of whether or not I would pose for him.

When Olga and Pablo moved out the next day, the tension in Monsieur Sella's hotel fell perceptibly. It was like the air clearing itself after a storm. It was pleasant and easy, the way I had imagined our summer in Antibes would be.

But there was little chance to actually miss Pablo. He spent hours every day at our beach when he wasn't working in his nearby studios. He sketched me over and over, and now when I felt him watching me, I remembered that unanswered question: Would I model for him in his studio?

It is useless to think of a story as something that happens by itself, in isolation. There are always other things going on in the background so that sometimes the background becomes a larger part of the story. Take a love story. We think it is the moonlight that matters, that first embrace.

In fact, it is that obscured face looking out at you from a darkened doorway, watching you, that might be the larger story.

It's like what Auden wrote in his poem, how that poor boy Icarus, the wax from his wings all melted, falls from the sky as people on the ground don't even notice him. The boy falls to his death. The plowman keeps plowing. The ship keeps sailing. The disaster, the death, are unremarked. What was that poem? "The Old Masters," I think. I read it once to Pablo, and he wouldn't let the tragedy of it sink in. He just said, "I wonder if Auden was thinking of Brueghel or Van Dyck."

I was in the sun, sleeping to the sound of the waves, delighting in my children, my marriage, the pleasure of waking up in the morning to yet another day of Eden. Sunshine, laughing children, my husband already plotting his work of the day, when he would go to the studio he had made in a shed at the hotel, and what he would paint.

But discontent grew in me like some spindly seed sprouting from the crevice of a rock, a sensation of wanting yet more that had begun that night on the barge when Pablo put his jacket over my shoulders.

One afternoon when Pablo and Olga had come to the beach together, the heat was like a blanket, sometimes comforting, sometimes suffocating, the sky white with the intensity of it. We were too heat-exhausted to even talk.

The sound of Pablo's pencils scratching over paper competed with the cicadas. I fell asleep on my blanket with a book spread over my face and woke to find Pablo's eyes on me, his pencil moving furiously over the page.

"Why do you wear your pearls to sunbathe in, and why do you wear them down your back, not over your chest?" he asked. It was an artist's question, lacking the intimacy of a friend or lover. He needed information for his drawing. That was all.

"I always wear them." I sat up and rubbed my eyes. "And I wear them backward to confuse the devil. He can't tell if I'm coming or going, and he can't catch me."

That was a joke, an old Irish story about why a man wore his cap backward, and it always made Gerald laugh.

Pablo did not laugh. He nodded and continued to draw.

"Let me see," Gerald said, rising up from the blanket and looking over Pablo's shoulder. The sun was a shimmering golden ball over his shoulder.

"It's you, Sara. Sleeping. Wonderful." The awe in Gerald's voice bothered me. It is one thing to be in thrall to a greater genius, but another when that genius is directed at one's own wife. For a moment, I wanted Gerald to be jealous.

"Let me see." I stood and brushed the sand from my legs and wrapped a towel around my hips before leaning over Pablo's other shoulder.

He had drawn me with a turban wrapped around my head and drapery falling over my legs and torso. It was a modest drawing, flattering and tender. A devil popped up in my thoughts. What would it feel like to pose naked for Pablo, as Irène had? But Irène, we all knew, was his lover—before and now again. It was there in the challenging sparkle of his eyes, the way he sometimes smelled of a perfume that Olga did not wear.

I forced myself to concentrate on the drawing and ignored that phantom feeling of a man's jacket smelling of tobacco falling over my shoulders.

Pablo's style was shifting that summer. He was always experimenting, always looking for different ways to reinvent what we see. That summer, his drawings were a reminder of classical sculpture, of those sturdy column forms that held up Greek temples and decorated ancient Roman baths. In his drawing, I had lost some of my softness, had veered toward the monumental, the classical rather than cubist.

"Let me see!" Olga said. She had come to the beach with Paulo that afternoon, probably to keep an eye on Pablo.

Olga looked over my shoulder.

"Such a thing will never sell. It is worthless," she said.

Pablo made a sound that resembled a laugh but was not a laugh. "Money. That is all art means to her."

Did Olga hear him? She paused midstep, the dark linen of her dress clinging to her long slender legs in statuesque folds.

"What are you saying about me?" she asked, her voice high and trembling.

Pablo ignored her and kept sketching. I lowered my head like a guilty child, though it had been his cutting comment, not mine, that had added ice to the balmy air. Olga stalked off, back to her own carefully demarcated place on the beach.

I was going to say something to Pablo, to remind him that Olga had known hardship, those nomad years after leaving Russia, that she deserved kindness. But I didn't.

"Don't speak," he said later when I woke from another nap. The sun was low. The beach was quiet. "Sit still. Like that, your head leaning on your shoulder."

Where was Gerald? And my children? Or do I only remember us being alone? Was my family nearby even as I sat in that bubble of solitude, shivering each time I heard Pablo's pencil tracing a line over his sketching paper, those quiet, caressing sounds?

There is nothing more sensual than being studied, having the lines of your body, the texture of your skin, translated into an object that is both you and not you. A work of art.

"I'm going back to the hotel," I told him, gathering up my towel and the unread book I had brought with me.

That evening, Pablo and Olga dined at the hotel at Gerald's insistence. Midway through the meal, Pablo spilled his wine, a full glass since he hadn't taken so much as a sip of the rosé that Gerald and I drank freely.

Pablo was abstemious, always sober long after his dinner companions had stumbled from pleasantly cheery to drunk. He ate well but little. And drank less. *Like a monk*, I sometimes thought. Saving himself for his inner life, his work.

But that evening he spilled his wine, staining the white tablecloth with a pink blot that looked like the continent of Africa. Pablo stood, watching it in delight.

Olga, dressed in creamy chiffon, rose with a little scream before the spilled wine could stain her dress.

Pablo glanced at his wife, a look of complete detachment, and returned his intense gaze to the spreading stain. From the doorway, I saw Anna standing in the shadows, her eyes on Pablo.

"Gerald, move those plates. I'm going to take the cloth in to soak," I said. Quickly, we rearranged the clutter on the table so that I could lift the cloth, first one side, then the other, and take it away.

In the pantry, I filled a large basin with soap and water and pushed the cloth down into it. I heard footsteps behind me and knew it was Pablo.

He took a step closer to me, and we stood like that, inches apart. His eyes, dilated from the darkness, roamed over my face, and I knew he was not seeing me, only angles and planes and shadows. He was the first to step back, to turn and leave the small room.

My hand rose up to touch his shoulder, to call him back.

It was automatic—no, it was animalistic, empty of thought and intention, one animal calling out to another. But he had moved beyond my reach. The relief I felt was so strong I was light-headed for a second. And then almost ill with disappointment.

Another floorboard creaked from the opposite side of the pantry. I didn't need to see her to know it was Anna. A second creak, a sound of rustling linen as she turned away, deeper into the darkness of the hotel hallway.

TWELVE
· · · · · · · · · · ·

SARA

Two days later, Gerald announced he was going to Venice.

"I may not tell Pablo till after I get back," he added. "Isn't that where he met Olga? Probably not his favorite city."

Gerald's work with Diaghilev in Paris had not gone unnoticed. Rolf de Maré, director of the Swedish Ballet, invited Gerald to create the scenes for his new ballet, an "American" dance based on jazz. Gerald, in turn, had convinced Rolf to commission his friend and fellow Yale classmate Cole Porter to write the music. Cole was in Venice with Linda, and the two men had agreed that Gerald would travel there for the collaboration.

"I want you to come with me," Gerald said. "I won't go without you."

I liked sweet, fun Cole almost as much as Gerald did, and Venice would be exciting. There was a nanny to take care of the children while we were away. Why not go? Except I didn't want to. I didn't want to leave the hotel, the beach, the beauty that surrounded me every minute of the day. The singing cicadas. My children. Pablo.

"Cole would love to see you," Gerald said.

I packed and wrote a note to Pablo, telling him that Gerald and I were leaving for a couple of weeks. It was a brief note, just a couple of sentences without sentiment. When I finished, I added a little drawing of a train and addressed the envelope to both Pablo and Olga. In case Olga should see it.

Downstairs, I gave the note to Anna and asked her to be sure it was delivered to Pablo's villa in Juan-les-Pins.

"If you wish," she said, but she avoided looking at me.

"And please call a taxi for us to take our bags to the station."

"How long will you be gone?"

"Anna, don't yell at the cook or talk back to Monsieur Sella. You'll be fine. And don't disappear in the afternoon."

That had happened several times already. The children would ask for a snack, or the cook would storm through the pantry shouting for Anna, or Monsieur Sella would have a question or a comment, and Anna would be nowhere to be found. I had assumed she wanted extra sleep and was napping in a quiet orchard or perhaps had found a friend in the village.

Once, Irène, her curling black hair standing around her head like a storm cloud, had charged onto the hotel terrace demanding to know where Pablo was. We had assumed he was in his studio, painting her, and told her so. Irène turned red with fury. "I haven't modeled for him in two days!" she said between clenched teeth.

"It is good you leave, I think," Anna said, putting my note to Picasso in her pocket.

Pablo didn't send a reply to my note. I hadn't really expected him to; I just wanted him to know why we wouldn't be at the beach for a while. That was all.

traded the brilliant turquoise of the Mediterranean for the muddy jade-green canals of Venice, the songs of the cicada for the shouts of the gondoliers, the scent of thyme and pine for the fetid fumes of Venice during the hot weather.

"Isn't it glorious?" Linda Porter yelled over the background noise and bustle, the shouting of gondoliers and haggling of merchants, the crying children and squabbling housemaids who were banging dusty rugs against windowsills.

Our gondolier guided the boat into the mooring of her "summer rental," and Gerald and I stared at it in amazement.

Linda had leased one of the grandest villas in Venice, a white marble palace called Ca'Rezzonico, on the Grand Canal.

"It was built in the eighteenth century," she boasted, standing up precariously in the gondola for a better view and holding on to her hat. She pointed at the many-columned facade of their summer home. I thought that it looked like an overdecorated wedding cake. I already missed our faded little Hotel du Cap.

"The plumbing proves it," Cole added, and he and Gerald laughed.

Linda gave him a scathing look. "It's historical," she said. She tapped a foot impatiently.

"But we're working on a modern ballet," Cole retorted. He looked dapper as always, in his white linen suit with a colorful scarf tied at his throat. "Could be a problem, you know. I'll be working on a theme of gospel songs, and here will come some moldy old ghost of a doge asking for his gout stool and demanding I compose on a harpsichord, not a baby grand."

Even the gondolier, with his limited English, laughed at that. We all laughed, except Linda.

"Darling, perhaps the ghostly doge will offer some help," Linda said. "And you should be composing classical music. A symphony. An opera. Something that will be remembered. Who will remember jazz? It's only good for the music halls."

"Today's jazz will be tomorrow's classical music," Cole said, blowing her a kiss. "They say Picasso's work is like visual jazz, and he is doing quite well with it, I hear. Financially." Linda looked at me and rolled her eyes with exaggerated impatience, but I knew she adored Cole despite his preference for jazz.

And Cole had known what he was getting as well. An American divorcée, a wealthy social climber. A beautiful woman who looked good on his arm, who gave him an aura of respectability.

There was love there. They just sometimes didn't get along all that well.

They reminded me of Olga and Pablo, who had also married for love but found growing incompatibility, that sense of one road forking into two separate ones.

Unlike and Gerald and me. We were so close, so in agreement, that some of our Parisian friends had called us "the Murphy," as if Gerald and I were one. We were.

Watching Gerald and Cole wrestle our suitcases out of the gondola, laughing when Cole pretended he was about to fall into the canal, I was glad I had come with Gerald. Happy to have left behind France and Pablo. Here, I wouldn't wake up with that memory of his eyes on me, that seductive, demanding gaze. There would be no distance between my husband and me.

"I love you," I mouthed to him as Cole loaded his arms with my hatbox and toiletry case.

Linda's idea of a summer vacation meant shopping every day: Canaletto prints from an antiquarian shop on the Rialto, custom-made travel cases from a leatherworker in San Marco, bespoke silk shirts for Cole from the Cannaregio. She navigated the narrow twisting streets with the unerring sense of a treasure hunter.

Mussolini's Blackshirts were everywhere in the streets, black crow omens of things to come. Mostly they were ignored. The business of Venice was pleasure, not politics, yet if you listened carefully, you could hear some shopkeepers and old men sunning on benches grumble about their arrogance, their strongarm tactics. No one complained too loudly, though. The most powerful men in Venice were Mussolini supporters. Mussolini and his rich businessmen were making Venice wealthy with their new grand hotels and monthly festivals.

La Serenissima, which had slipped into decay and poverty, was opulent again, glittering with newly applied gilt and scrubbed facades, thanks to the new leaders.

Those who spoke against Mussolini and against the rising movement of fascism found themselves on the wrong side of the city politics. Their trade floundered; their customers were often frightened away by gangs of pickpockets and muggers stationed by their customer entrances.

One day, shopping on the Rialto with Linda, we saw a man—a butcher, judging by his bloody leather apron—cornered by a group of Blackshirts, who were jeering at him, elbowing, and nudging him. The Blackshirts were young powerful-looking boys. Bullies. Five of them laughing at one old man.

Most people just keep walking by as if they didn't see. Linda and I stopped, and I took a step toward them, but a hand pulled me back.

"No," a voice said. "Leave it alone." It was the glove maker from whom, the day before, Linda had purchased a dozen white kid gloves.

"Will they hurt him?" I asked.

"Probably. And you, too, if you interfere." He pulled his cap lower to cover as much of his face as possible.

"But what did the poor man do?"

"Refused to hang a picture of Mussolini in his shop. Go home. There is nothing you can do here."

"Come on, Sara," Linda said, taking my arm. "He's right. Let's get out of here." Her hands trembled, and she had gone pale beneath the red spots of rouge on her cheeks.

We went back to the villa, climbed those expansive, expensive steps to safety, and shut the heavy door behind us. I spent the rest of the day filled with shame. I was an American, a woman of privilege. Perhaps I could have said something that would have stopped the beating that was about to happen. We had all smelled it in the air, the violence to come.

At cocktails that night, we dined at an outdoor restaurant where candles and lamps reflected prettily in the water of the Grand Canal. Gondoliers sang as they passed by. It was a chilling contrast with the afternoon events, a hint of the ugliness that often lay beneath the supposedly civilized surface. I'd felt that same surreptitious, even alternate, hidden world, sometimes in Paris. All those signs stating, "Reserved for Those Mutilated in the War," reminding us that the Great War was over, but no one could promise another one wouldn't follow.

Linda didn't mention what we had witnessed. I did, though I knew she wanted to keep the conversation safe and carefree, to talk about what the next opera season might be like at La

Scala. I told Gerald and Cole about the butcher and the Black-shirts, the glove maker who told us to go back to our hotel and not interfere.

"The glove maker was right," Cole said after a long while, interrupting.

"He was right. You might have been injured. I suppose this kind of thing happens after the chaos of war," Gerald said. "People want security, a return to some kind of normal. So they let strongmen spring up and take over. Italy and Germany are already feeling the convulsions with Mussolini and his imitator over in Germany, Hitler. Stalin. Spain will be next, I suppose. There are riots and troubles there as well."

Gerald put his hand over mine and squeezed gently. The old gesture, the comfort gesture: *I am with you. I understand.* For a moment, Venice had no longer stepped between us as Gerald's eyes met mine. As always, peace fell over me, and I felt a rush of animal comfort. But then Cole made a wisecrack, and Gerald laughed, and the moment ended.

I felt that, like Venice, I had two realities: one lovely and pleasant, the other secretive, buried, waiting to be discovered. In that first reality, Gerald and I stayed young and in love and happy—oh, so happy. But in that second reality, we were aging, we were changing. We were taking stock of who we might become, what changes might arrive. We were becoming different and separate, and I feared that more than anything.

Underneath the doubts, the fears, the love, was the memory of Pablo Picasso putting his jacket around my shoulders to keep me warm. The feel of his eyes on me at the beach, warmer than the sun.

Did Gerald notice how I sometimes fell silent and drifted away in my thoughts? I didn't think so. Yet Gerald sometimes seemed far away as well.

Each night, Linda entertained. Dinner parties for fifty and more, costume parties with hired chamber music quartets wandering from room to room. Grand style, to match the palatial Ca'Rezzonico.

"Tell us about Picasso," Linda would ask me in front of her dinner guests. "They know each other from Paris, and he has a villa close to where Gerald and Sara are staying in Antibes. What is he really like, Sara? Tell all."

"Go ahead, Sara. Tell us," Gerald would say, an edge in his voice that I didn't recognize. Had he noticed how close Pablo and I were growing? Noticed and not said anything?

I would repeat the same thing night after night. "Charming," I would say. "Temperamental as artists can be. Devoted to his son."

Linda would look at me, disappointed, and change the subject.

It was exhausting and tiresome. I missed the beach. My children. I wondered how Pablo and Olga were getting along and if Irène had gone back to Paris yet. I wondered if Anna was in trouble again at the hotel.

And I missed Gerald. I saw much less of him in Venice than I had in Antibes at the little hotel. He and Cole shut themselves up every day in the music room, which Linda had stuffed with carved mahogany furniture in addition to the two rented pianos. I did not begrudge them that locked door, that time given over to creativity, to work, but I was lonely.

I realized I had been brought along to keep Linda company, to entertain her as our husbands worked. I trailed after her through the sights of Venice, the art galleries, palaces, bridges. Spent hours with her in gondolas gliding from Piazza San Marco to Santa Lucia, where the water ended and the railway began. She had, of course, hired her own gondola and gondolier for the summer.

"Of course, it's not couture, like you find in Paris," Linda said apologetically, stopping in a workshop to buy a lace shawl so fine it could slip through a wedding band. "But the handiwork you can find here makes interesting gifts to send home to your friends." The shopkeeper who had been carefully wrapping the lace so it wouldn't snag on anything looked up in annoyance but said nothing.

"My feet are killing me," I complained to Gerald each evening when Linda finally retreated to her room for a nap before dressing for dinner. Gerald and I stole away to a little neighborhood bar for a cocktail, a quiet hour together. "And if I have to look at one more Renaissance oil painting, I may give up art for the rest of my life."

"Makes you appreciate Picasso and Braque and the other moderns even more," Gerald agreed. "Sorry, darling. I didn't know how hard this would be for you. I should have thought."

He sipped his cocktail and seemed preoccupied.

"I may not stay here," I said.

"Just two more weeks," Gerald whispered.

It sounded like an eternity.

Something was happening between Gerald and me. Our closeness, our knowing what the other was thinking, what the other wanted, wasn't as strong as it had been in Antibes or Paris or even Long Island. I knew he was preoccupied with the work, with working with Cole, but there was something else, as if the city itself were wedging itself between us.

Venice is one of the most beautiful cities on the face of the earth. But underneath the beauty, there was a hint of something dark and secret that summer, something pagan that emerged when people wear the masks of Harlequin, the seducer of young girls; Marinetta, full of rage and unfulfilled passion; Columbine, the adulteress trickster; and Pierrot, ever the simple-minded victim.

Costumes are a sign of our inner desires. Women want to be Cleopatra in her glory days. Men who think of themselves as lovers want to be Don Juan, and men who dream mostly of power appear as Cardinal Richelieu or Julius Caesar. Venice that summer was full of women begging to be seduced and men wanting more and more power. And their victims.

"How is the work going for you and Cole?" I asked, wondering if I could survive two more weeks of Linda and Venice.

"Well enough, I think. Cole has some great ideas for the music, but we aren't always in agreement on how the music will work with the sets."

"Is it making difficulties between you?" Cole was one of Gerald's oldest friends, a buddy going all the way back to their college days, when Gerald had convinced the farm boy from Indiana that his checkered suits, pink ties, and cheap wicker furniture would not be suitable for East Coast society. Gerald guided Cole through the intricacies of men's clubs and polite behavior, and they had been staunch and loyal friends ever since.

"Not as much trouble as Linda is making. She interrupts, she complains about the noise, she tells Cole he'll never make a name for himself, writing what she calls comedy revues."

The waiter hovered over the table, waiting for us to leave or order another cocktail. The shops were closing, and throngs of people wandered the narrow streets, studying window menus, looking for tables for dinner.

"Time to face the dragon," Gerald said. "Wonder how many dukes and duchesses Linda has invited tonight. Perhaps I shouldn't have asked you to come along. I know how bored you are. But I didn't want to leave you alone in Antibes."

Two days later, Linda gave her grandest ball of the season, an event she had been planning since her arrival in Venice.

The discomfort of Venice came to a boil. I wanted nothing more than to stay in my room reading a book or writing letters, but Linda insisted I join them in the Grand Ballroom, which had been decorated to look like a Versailles garden, with movable fountains and acres of potted roses and orchids lining the walls and interspersed among the tables.

Gerald groaned when he saw it. I clung to his arm and forced a smile, nodding at the few familiar faces I knew, murmuring "Pleased to meet you" whenever Linda introduced me to a duke or prince I had not yet met. The food was elaborate, the orchestra music dusty with old-fashioned waltzes. Some young people had crowded together in one corner and tried to Charleston to the music, but gave it up and drifted onto balconies and into stairwells to talk and flirt.

We were in costume, and the crowded ballroom was full of Pierrots and Columbines and the other villains and victims of the commedia dell'arte. Gerald, who enjoyed wearing costumes, had chosen to go as Il Dottore, the lecherous doctor with his huge black suit, white ruff, and bulbous-nose mask covering most of his face.

I had dressed in a white toga and laurel wreath to masquerade as Cornelia, the Roman woman famous for her virtue. It was a joke. I had heard gossip about myself in powder rooms that summer, how I refused to take a lover, how I loved only one man, my husband. How provincial I was.

Yet, in my white gown and rhinestone-sparkling wreath, I felt like a fraud. Just as I had smelled violence in the air when the Blackshirts had circled the butcher, I sensed a voluptuousness to come that did not involve Gerald. When I thought of the beach at Antibes or the hotel terrace, Pablo was always there. I could imagine his laughter at the inauthentic costumers, the affected poses.

There were several doctors there that evening, their black suits standing out against the vivid reds and yellows and purples of the other costumers. But Gerald was taller than the others, and even though the mask hid most of his face, it didn't cover his clean, strong jaw. I would recognize him anywhere, even in costume.

It was a long evening, and I felt tired almost as soon as it began. It wasn't the good and expected tired you feel after a long walk or too many sets of tennis; it was the fatigue of boredom and tension. The dancing, the drinking, the practical jokes, the inane conversation—it was all too familiar, almost rehearsed. A bad play that could not be improved but would only get worse.

Around two in the morning, I decided I was going to my bed, no matter how much Linda complained about my early departure. I looked for Gerald and couldn't find him. Not in the ballroom where the dancing was increasingly frantic, not in the supper room where the long tables of food had been ransacked, or the cardroom where fortunes were being lost, or the gardens.

Finally, after what felt like hours of searching, I saw him down at the gondola landing with Cole, smoking a cigarette in the dark, the glowing end of it tracing a flight in the darkness. He had thrown his doctor's cape over one shoulder so that he looked like a bird with a broken wing. Water lapped at the mossy stone steps, and there was a smell of dead fish and seaweed. There was a third man there, shorter than both Cole and Gerald. He wore the gondolier's striped shirt and flat-brimmed hat, and he had his arm around Gerald's waist and was leaning into him. Tenderly. His head against Gerald's chest, where I rested mine.

I stepped back into the shadows before they could see me. I watched for a few moments and then left without saying anything. The Venetian evening was warm, but I felt cold, numb.

So, that's it, I told myself over and over. The shadow I had always known was there. Why Gerald was so uncomfortable around our homosexual friend, Jean Cocteau; why he never stared at pretty girls the way other men did. How long? And what did this mean for me. For us. I was running then, back to the lights of the party, the crowd. Better to hide in a crowd behind a mask than in solitude.

It means heartbreak, a voice in my head said. *Did you think you would never experience it?*

Gerald didn't come to our bed until dawn.

"You saw, didn't you?" he asked quietly.

"Yes."

Neither of us said anything for several heartbeats, but when Gerald slipped into bed, he took me in his arms, turning my face onto his shoulder. The old embrace.

"I love you," he said. "I love our children. I promised to always keep you safe. To love only you. I will keep those promises."

I wanted to put my arms around him. My first impulse had been to console him. But the darkness that Venice had promised was there between us, and now it had entered me. The radiance of what I had felt for my husband had been changed to something less shining. I turned my back to him.

THIRTEEN

. . . .

SARA

A s soon as Pablo saw me, he guessed what had happened. No words were necessary. Gerald's struggle with his sexuality was fierce enough that it could not stay hidden from those who cared for him, those who were willing to see and accept, and Pablo clearly always had. I had suspected. I just hadn't admitted, not until Venice, when I had seen.

Pablo was at the beach, sitting on a towel, sketching his son, Paulo. He said hello without even needing to look up to know it was me standing between him and the sun, casting a shadow over him.

Seagulls cried overhead in a sky that was white with heat.

"You came back without Gerald," he said when I sat next to him. "Angels troubled the water?"

"More like figures from the commedia dell'arte than angels." I trailed my fingers through the sand, tracing spirals and zags. "All those damn Harlequins and Columbines. And gondoliers."

He didn't laugh, nor had I intended him to. Instead, he leaned over and drew a line through my spirals in the sand, then wiped it away. "Sometimes we reveal more of ourselves when we are in costume. We are freer."

"As long as you're here, go and sit on that rock," he said. Look over your shoulder. Not at me. If you look at me, I won't be able to draw you. It is inevitable now."

"What is?"

He laughed.

I sat on the rock, twisting slightly away from him in the three-quarter profile he preferred. He was wearing his Stetson hat—a habit of his, even at the beach—and tilted it to keep out the sun's glare. I couldn't see his eyes as he worked, but I could feel them on me. I burned with more than the heat of the sun. I desired this man, and having to confront Gerald's secret forced me to confront my own. It wasn't revenge. Really, it wasn't. Pablo was right. It was inevitable.

We became lovers that night, Pablo sharing dinner with me after the children were in bed. I didn't ask where Olga was. He didn't ask about Gerald. We shared coffee and cognac on the terrace under the stars until the time came, and he rose and went indoors. I followed.

As Pablo ran his hands over my shoulder and throat, feeling for the bones beneath the way a sculptor handles clay, then pulling my slip down to my waist to bare my chest, I could hear Anna downstairs fussing with things in the kitchen. She had watched us closely at dinner, Pablo and me. Her face was blank; she said nothing. But she had watched, sensed the new heat and tension in the room. She brought bottles of mineral water even when we hadn't asked for them; she leaned in the doorway, arms folded across her chest. Her disapproval was palpable. I didn't care.

Morning sun. Damp sheets. In the morning, I put my hand on Pablo's chest and felt it rise and fall with his breath.

"What are we?" I whispered into his ear.

"Lovers," he whispered back.

When I went down to breakfast alone after Pablo had left, Anna wouldn't look me in the eyes. We became formal with each other, cold. I didn't care. I had given myself to Pablo, given myself over to being his lover, his mistress, and my body was on fire with it. I didn't think about Gerald. When the children were with their nurse, I didn't think about them, either. I thought about Pablo's hands on me, his breath on my neck, the shuddering and sighing of our lovemaking.

Pablo, in the two weeks that we had together, painted me over and over. He mixed sand in with the paint so that the paintings weren't just images but physical reminders of our time together. Pablo and Sara on the beach.

When I posed nude for the first time, in his studio, it was like learning the pleasures of the body all over again. His eyes going up and down my figure, the brush matching his eye movements as he worked. Sometimes he scowled when he wasn't satisfied with an angle or curve. Sometimes he smiled and would not say why. "I'll show you later," he promised.

The painting he had been working on that summer, *The Lovers*, was on an easel in a corner, still unfinished, though sometimes I could tell the cloth covering it was hanging differently. He was working on it secretly. Irène had gone back to Paris by then, and Olga had resigned herself to being the wronged wife, a role she filled all too easily. She knew better than to come to the studio when we were there, and she would no longer even say "Good day" to me. I was content for her to keep her distance.

He could be so cruel, Pablo. He had a camera that summer, carried it almost everywhere with him, and one day he brought Olga to the hotel for lunch to taunt me, I suspect, but I knew his feelings for her were nothing to match our own fire. Pablo insisted that Olga and I pose for a picture on the terrace of the hotel.

Anna was still clearing away the lunch dishes, and Pablo clicked the shutter just as she was rushing past him. He did it on purpose, I think. Olga and I standing there with frozen smiles, Anna a blur, almost a ghost, captured by surprise.

She was furious and tried to snatch the camera away from him.

"What are you afraid of, Anna?" Pablo taunted her. "Is there a husband you have run away from? A convent that you had been forced into?"

"Stop it, Pablo," I said. "Leave the girl alone." Anna had turned white as a sheet. I realized that whatever she had fled had been real, and it had been dangerous.

"Don't worry," I told her. "You are safe here." She fled back into the kitchen, leaving the dirty dishes behind on the table.

My world reduced to a place of animal pleasure. The hot foreheads of my children after a little too much sun, the heat of Pablo's legs resting between my thighs at night, the salted slipperiness of oysters at dinner, and the sweet coolness of a ripe peach. My body became a vessel, an urn filled with pleasure and need that tasted of pears and sandalwood.

Even when we weren't making love, we were, Pablo and I. He called it our "mystic marriage," a union unblessed by man or church or society, a union of two animals obeying primal urges, thoughtless and cruel and as necessary as food.

When I thought of Gerald, there was neither hurt nor anger

in me, but only a great emptiness that was now filled by Pablo. We had no past, no future, only moments, one at a time, and that, with the salt water and the sun and the scent of thyme, was enough.

After that first night, we did not make love at the hotel because of the children, the possibility of their discovering us. Yet everyone at the hotel seemed to know. The cook frowned when she saw me; Monsieur Sella raised his eyebrows and was a degree less courteous, since I had changed my status to adulteress, a situation any hotelier is familiar with, but one that is not formally approved. And Anna. Her eyes burned into me. Only when confronted with Anna and that questioning, worried gaze did I pause and wonder what I was doing, what I was playing at.

But when Pablo brushed my hair or ran his fingertips down my spine to make me shiver, I stopped wondering and merely enjoyed. There was no past, no future. Just the moment to be lived.

It was two days before Gerald was returning to Antibes, to me and the children. He had telegraphed to say that he and Cole had made enough progress on the jazz ballet that they could put the final touches on it without each other's over-the-shoulder prompting or criticizing. He added a "Linda sends love" to the end of the brief message, and I knew that Gerald believed he was coming back to what had been between us, the love and certainty.

Linda most certainly did not send love. Gerald was making a joke, sending a private message of unity.

I folded the telegraph and put it in my sweater pocket. Two days. I should have been thinking, considering, planning. But two days was a long time, forever, and the moment would take care of itself.

The sun wasn't fully up yet, and the air had a freshness to it, a hint of summer's end. The unfinished coffee in my cup cooled quickly. Soon, the children would be up and eating their oatmeal before dressing in their bathing costumes to go to the beach. They were brown as walnuts, plump with good food and fresh air, and just looking at them made the world new and shiny. They were the constants, outside of the complicated, messy world the adults around them created.

Pablo would be at the beach for an hour of swimming before going back to his studio. And after lunch, I would join him there.

There should have been a sense of worry, of problems to come, but I had none. Gerald, my husband, was coming back to me. Pablo expected me at his studio and I would go to him. Two different men, two different worlds. I wondered how the choice would be manifested, what the cues would be.

"Anna, Mr. Murphy will be back tomorrow," I said when she came to clear the breakfast table. "Please make sure his mail is on the table for him and his laundry is clean and folded."

She nodded and looked preoccupied. Her long black braid had come loose, and strands of hair floated around her pale face.

"Are you well?" I asked.

"Of course." Her manner was stiff. She had no more smiles for me, no warmth.

Olga had decided, weeks before, that Anna was a runaway, a girl in trouble, and that was why she was alone, estranged from her family. There had been an affair. It was true that Anna had gained weight. Her face was rounder, her figure fuller. When she walked away, there was a new sway to her walk, a confidence. Perhaps she had simply found a boyfriend in the village, a fisherman's son who wouldn't mind if she came to him already in the family way.

"Anna, we are friends, aren't we?" I asked as she swept crumbs from the table.

She looked up, pale, and nodded but still did not smile.

The studio door was ajar when I arrived hours later at the studio after a swim with the children. There were noises from inside, not the sound of scraping, washing, muttering, the sounds a painter makes when working. These were sighs, murmurs, quiet laughter. The music of intimacy between a man and a woman.

Perhaps, I thought, *Irène is back from Paris*. Jealousy fluttered in my chest. *So soon*, I thought. I knew he would not be faithful, but so soon?

I paused in the doorway, wanting to run away but needing to move forward. Never had I believed he would be only mine, stay mine. Yet fact is quite different from expectation. So soon.

One step. The floor creaked. Silence, no more sighs and laughter, only the heartless thrumming of the cicadas in the afternoon heat. Two steps, three, four, and I could see fully into the studio, could see the glinting brass daybed with its rumpled white sheet and dented pillows where heads had lain. Two people sitting up now, looking at me. Pablo, naked and startled, looking like a satyr from one of his own paintings, with his mouth bruised and wet from sex. Was that how he had looked after enjoying me, victorious and exhausted and already needing to move on to whatever the next thing would be, the next woman?

Next to him was Anna. Clutching the sheet to her chest, her hair fallen over one side of her face so that only one eye looked back at me. I could not read the look she gave me.

The shock of it pushed me backward, as if I had been struck.

We did not speak. The situation did not require words. It was all perfectly clear. I ran out of the room, stricken. They did not call me back, did not follow after me, did not offer explanations or apologies or protests. I don't think I had ever felt more alone.

W hat's wrong, Mama?" Six-year-old Honoria came and stood by my chair at dinner that evening.

"Why do you think something is wrong, sweetheart?"

"You haven't eaten your artichoke, and it's your favorite." Honoria pulled off one of the leaves and dipped it in the mayonnaise sauce, as if to demonstrate how to eat an artichoke, as if I had forgotten.

"Mama's not hungry."

"Mama's sad." Honoria climbed into my lap, and we sat like that, me stroking her bright golden hair, Honoria cushioning her head onto my chest.

"Daddy will be home soon," she said. "Then we'll be happy again, won't we?"

Her words brought me back to myself. When you have children, you can no longer live for yourself. You belong to them.

"Have you been unhappy, darling?"

"Nooo . . ." She drew out the word. "But I have a dream sometimes that you are flying away, that you are a red balloon, and I can't catch hold of the string."

"That's a silly dream," I said, laughing into the sweet, salty fragrance of her hair.

"Is it?" She looked at me with such solemnity that guilt rose in me like that red balloon, floating up and up.

After the children were in bed, I sat alone on the terrace trying to make peace with the dark, with the night, with solitude. Pablo would not send a message for me to come to him, not if he hadn't already. For him, nothing had changed. He had his art, his women. His freedom. For him, all was as it should be.

And me? I felt hollowed out from loss and betrayal.

"Do you want a lantern? It is very dark." Anna's voice was soft, full of concern. She was standing just behind my chair. I hadn't heard her footsteps.

"No," I said. "It would just draw moths."

Anna sat in the chair next to me, uninvited.

"With such a man, love is not the point," she said quietly. "I was honored that such a great artist chose me, that he wanted to paint me and make love to me. He spoke Spanish with me. Like a friend would."

"How long?" I asked. Perhaps it was the other way around; perhaps I had stolen her lover, not vice versa.

"Weeks. I was just about to tell him that we couldn't meet anymore when you came back from Venice and went to the studio with him. I thought, 'If she sees me with him, she will see him as he is.' Yes, I knew you would go to the studio. But, Sara, that man is not for you. No, not for me, either. He is only for himself. And you have so much to lose. He will not love you, just use you. And what of your children? What are you willing to throw away for this man who will not love you?"

She had leaned closer and took my hands in hers. She had called me Sara, not Mrs. Murphy. My jealousy turned to anger and spite. *Too many betrayals*, I thought. Gerald. And now

Pablo and Anna. I withdrew my hands from hers and made my voice as icy as my heart felt at that moment.

"Who are you to speak to me like this? You shouldn't sit down with a customer unless you are asked, Anna. Stand up." *Friends no longer*, my conscience whispered back to me.

She heard the roused anger in my voice and obeyed. She gave me a long, searching look. Then she made a mock curtsy, lifted her chin, and left.

I couldn't sleep that night. Fatigue only deepened my anger. The chirping night insects, the birds at dawn, even the pink and orange sunrise deepened my anger, my sense of having been made a fool. When I saw Monsieur Sella going into his office the next morning, I didn't hesitate. I wanted my revenge. A betrayal for a betrayal.

"There is a problem with Anna," I told him, carefully closing the door behind me.

He looked up from his ledger, interested. "Something about her," he said. "I never trusted her. A girl like that."

"She has been sleeping with one of your customers, Monsieur Sella."

"That is strictly forbidden," he said, his eyebrows shooting up into his hairline.

But as soon as I said the words, I wanted to take them back. I knew what the words would mean. I shrank inside myself, ashamed.

"Thank you, Madame Murphy. I will take care of this." Monsieur Sella slammed shut the ledger and rang the bell that connected his office to the kitchen. I stumbled out of his office and went to get the children ready for their morning swim.

Anna was not there at lunchtime. Pablo was, though, storming into the dining room, anger flowing off him like heat from a radiator. He grabbed me by the elbow and marched me out of the room onto the terrace.

"What have you done?" I'd never seen him this angry. His eyes were like black fire.

"I don't know what you mean."

He drew back, and now his eyes were black ice. "I didn't know you could lie," he said, and I hated the disappointment in his voice. "Anna came to me this morning to say goodbye. Do you know what she said? 'Be kind to Sara.'"

"Sit," he said in the same tone of voice I'd used last night to order Anna to stand. "Sit, and I will tell you what you do not know, what she told me, so you will understand what you have done. She was an art student from a very good family. She joined a student group, a union. She had a special friend, Antonio. They protested and marched against Primo de Rivera. You have heard of him? He will create a dictatorship in Spain if he is not stopped, he and his generals. She marched in a demonstration with her student friends, and the police came. Some were arrested. She was beaten but escaped. That was why she left Spain. That is why she has nowhere to go."

His eyes were on one of the palm trees in the hotel garden. He wouldn't look at me.

"I . . . I didn't know." The enormity of what I'd done made it hard for me to breathe. "Oh god. We must find her," I said.

I borrowed Monsieur Sella's car . . . for an exorbitant fee, but time was crucial. That sense of having stepped out of time that I'd experienced with Pablo was over. Time, time. How far could she have gotten? And what would I do when we found her?

The question was irrelevant. Pablo and I drove all the dusty little roads leading in and out of Antibes; we searched the beach and the town cafés, the train station. But we didn't find her, and we never saw her again.

I was crying when Pablo left me to go back to his villa. "It is a bad thing you have done," he said.

That night was long and silent. When had the cicadas stopped singing? I sat at my bedroom window, not even attempting to sleep, feeling loss and as empty as a room with no furniture, no purpose, except to keep out whatever might try to get in. I would never outlive my guilt, never have a chance to make up for the harm I had done to Anna.

M ama! Mama!" Honoria called from my bedroom doorway the next morning. "Come see!"

The children's nanny stood behind Honoria looking tidy in her black-and-white dress and very apologetic.

"I told her to let you sleep," she said.

"It doesn't matter. Come here, my darling, and tell me what it is I have to come see."

Honoria ran to the bed and hugged me, and I straightened the pink bow in her hair.

"Come on, Mama," she said, pulling me by the hand.

She led me into the little side room where we sat on rainy days and played games. It was filled with roses. Vases and vases of them, red and yellow and white and pink, thickening the air with their too-heavy scent.

Pablo was seated on a chair smoking his pipe and sketching one of the vases of roses. He looked up at me and went back to his sketching without saying a word.

At first I thought Pablo had brought flowers and then remembered he didn't like roses. He preferred daisies that could cut like knives. And he had no reason to bring me flowers, not anymore.

Gerald, looking tired and disheveled, stood behind the

chair where Pablo sat. "I bought every rose on the Riviera," he said.

Part of me wanted to fly to my husband. Part of me wanted to walk away and never see either man again. My hesitancy did not seem to surprise Gerald. The world was not the same as it had been just two weeks before. We were not the same.

"I took the night train, decided to leave a day ahead of time. To surprise you," he said. "Perhaps it was a bad idea."

"No. No, it was a lovely idea." I went to him then, and we hugged. He rocked me slightly and kissed the top of my head.

"It's good to be home," Gerald whispered. "You are my home. Where are Patrick and Baoth?"

"Probably in the kitchen having breakfast."

"Let's rush them. I want to go to the beach. Good to see you, old man," Gerald said to Pablo, not questioning why Pablo was in the hotel rather than his villa. "Will we see you later?"

"I'm painting in the studio today," Pablo said.

"Well, if you feel like it, join us at the beach," I said. "But I don't want to interrupt your work."

Pablo nodded. He understood. What had been between us was over.

"I have a note for you," he said. "It was left at my villa last night." He handed me a piece of folded paper. I opened it. Anna's handwriting. I recognized it from the marginal notes she had made in some of the books she had been reading and left open on chairs and tables.

I will go to a friend and stay with her, in Guernica.
Do not come for me. Do not contact me.

I refolded the paper and gave it back to him. There was a sense of conspiracy between us, of secrets larger than infidelity.

Anna had returned to Spain. Perhaps it was for the best. But I felt my guilt, my betrayal of her; the danger I might have put her in would never leave me.

Pablo left. Gerald hugged me again and whispered, "I'm sorry. I'm so sorry."

"I know. I am, too." Gerald didn't ask why.

"I love you," my husband said. "You and the children are my world. Now put on your swimming costume, and let's take the children to the beach."

Barefoot and wrapping my house robe more closely around me, I followed Gerald and Honoria down the narrow stone hall to the hotel's kitchen.

Baoth and Patrick were at the long plank table, Patrick in his high chair and Baoth next to him in a regular chair so that only his shoulders and head were visible above the table. There was raspberry jam smeared all over Patrick's mouth and cheeks. Baoth had a thick milk mustache. My darlings.

Summer ended quickly after that. The days grew shorter, the evenings cooler. What had, weeks before, seemed quiet and peaceful now felt restless, as if we were waiting for a train that was late to arrive. Gerald and I talked late into the night about the year to come and what we would do with it. Return to Versailles, for one, back to Paris for the autumn and winter. Back to our friends, the parties, the long hours of studio work. We felt a new eagerness for all that we had—in the spring—been eager to leave behind.

We did not talk of Venice or those two weeks we were parted. If Gerald noticed any of the glances Pablo gave me when we met for supper or at the beach, he did not comment on them. We pretended everything was well between us, and soon everything was. We resumed our old lives, as if the things that had happened had been some masquerade, a party game gone wrong.

But of course it wasn't just a game. Harm had been done. I thought often of Anna. There were nights when I lay awake thinking of her, worrying about her, and my guilt was like a sour taste you can't get rid of.

FOURTEEN

. . . .

ALANA

And that," Sara said, "was how the summer ended. My beautiful, peaceful summer." Her eyes were enormous in her pale face. "Me, an adulteress, Gerald more confused than ever, Picasso furious with all women, it seemed, and Anna gone. Never to be seen again. Anna, whom I betrayed."

I shifted in my chair, easing the numbness from my right leg, which had fallen asleep. I hadn't moved, not even breathed deeply, for an hour and longer as I'd listened to Sara's story. From downstairs, I could hear the sounds of banging and laughing in the kitchen. It would be dinnertime soon.

"I'm tired," Sara said. "You know, I've never told this story before, not all of it. Not even to Gerald. Such a sad story. But come back tomorrow. I've more to tell you."

The room, with that firmly closed door for privacy, had grown cold. Sara shivered and put on a cardigan. "Tomorrow, Alana. We will finish the story. But now I must see to dinner."

———

At the inn, Jack wasn't at the reception desk, so I assumed he would be in the dining room. He wasn't. My disappointment was unexpected and sharp. Even after such a brief time, I had started to look forward to seeing him, the way he looked up from the ledger to say hello, his deprecating comments about the hotel, the way his smile turned up more at one corner of his mouth than the other.

Upstairs, I showered and sat at the old nicked oak desk, going over my notes, organizing them, putting question marks where I would have to do more research to round out what Sara had told me. And then coming to the page about Anna, her affair with Pablo, Sara's jealousy and betrayal. No, I couldn't use this for the article. So why had Sara told me all of this? It was confessional, when I had come to her for information.

I missed my mother, who would have sat with me at our kitchen table, who would have listened without interrupting, who would have forced me to come to some conclusion, right or wrong. But who might also have said, "The past is the past. Now matters, tomorrow matters."

And then she would have asked me if I was seeing William that night.

William. Sweet William, I used to call him, until our conversations became about his work, his promotion, setting the date. Until he began all the not-so-gentle hints about my giving up my career and becoming the homemaker I was meant to be, according to him.

There are so many forms of violence against women. Picasso, the serial seducer, represented one form. He could so easily make women want him, love him. And he did, without ever giving back as much as he was given, except perhaps in the case of Françoise Gilot—who was leaving him, who had decided that what Pablo had to give wasn't enough.

But there is another form of violence. William's. That insistence that I was here to smooth his path, to be his helpmate, that my own dreams and ambitions needed to be secondary to his. That I was secondary. *This*, I thought, *is the same thing Pablo did to his women*. He turned them into art; William wanted to turn me into staff.

When I had finished organizing my notes, I went down to the dining room. It was almost ten, and I was the last one there, seating myself at a table with a fresh white cloth and not-yet-lit candle, surrounded by tables with crumbs and stains littering the tablecloths, coffee spoons and cups with red lipstick marks still waiting to be cleared away. I could hear laughter in the kitchen, gentler murmurs of conversation from the hallway, where people climbed the stairs to the bedrooms.

"Not much left," Jack said, coming across the room. He leaned close to me so he could move the salt and pepper shakers closer to my place setting. "We usually don't serve this late and the cook has already left."

I put down the menu that had been propped against the water glass. There had been roast chicken and Salisbury steak, but I was hungry enough to settle for peanut butter and jelly if I had to.

"Sorry I'm so late," I apologized. "A sandwich, maybe? And a glass of wine?"

Jack looked tired. His reddish-blond hair stood up where he had run his hands through it, and there were shadows under his eyes. *A fourteen-hour workday can do that*, I thought, remembering the long hours my mother used to work in her design studio uptown, how she would come home to our apartment, throw her hat and coat on a chair, and close her eyes for a five-minute rest before dinner. I learned to cook when I was young, not even a teenager, so that she could have a longer predinner rest.

"I can do better than a sandwich," Jack offered. "And I'm glad you showed up at all. I was a little worried about you. How about an omelet and salad? And if you don't mind, I'll join you. I haven't eaten yet."

"Deal," I said, wondering why I was so pleased that he had worried, that he was joining me for dinner.

Because he's very attractive, I told myself. Because I like his smile, and the way he looks at me, meeting my eyes and holding them for long, steadying moments. Was this how Pablo seduced his women? With those dark all-seeing eyes? Jack's were pale blue but just as all-seeing, I thought.

A few minutes later, Jack returned with the promised food and a bottle of wine.

"You're a good cook," I said, taking a forkful of the omelet.

"Better with a pan and spatula than with hammer and pliers," he admitted. "I was a cook in the army."

"Tough days, right?"

"Very tough. If I get to know you better, I'll tell you some of the stories. They aren't easy hearing. For now, I'll just say I was very glad when the war ended and I left Saipan."

He put his fork down, as if memory had just robbed him of appetite. He started to light a cigarette, but I reached across our plates and took it from him.

"You should eat," I said.

"Right. Okay. But pour me another glass of wine and tell me what it's like to be a journalist. Tell me about this Reed guy."

I told him, making the stories as funny as possible to lighten his mood, letting Reed's pipe become a gag, Helen's penchant for too many cocktails a comic scene akin to something from

Gentlemen Prefer Blondes, a movie I'd seen in August with William. Being able to make Jack laugh reminded me of how I felt when I came home from school and showed my mother a medal I'd won or my A in geometry. A true achievement.

We talked much too long into the night, talked as the hotel grew quiet around us and the remains of our dinner grew cold on the plates and the wine bottle was emptied. Talked until our voices grew whispery with fatigue until Jack stood, stretched, and said, "Workday tomorrow. For both of us."

We parted at the bottom of the stairs, leaning toward each other and then pulling quickly away, that incomplete gesture leaving a question between us.

FIFTEEN

....

Alana

When the summer was over, we went back north and took rooms at the Hotel des Reservoirs in Versailles," Sara said the next day. "Close enough to get in and see our friends and the galleries every day if we wished, but far enough away that I could still hear birds singing in the morning. I love birdsong, don't you? We picked up the same routine from the year before: painting, cocktails, visits to the zoo at the Jardin des Plantes with the children. Sometimes we ran into Pablo and Olga; a few times we had dinner with them, usually at a loud bistro. I think Pablo purposely chose places that would irritate Olga. She preferred white tablecloths and violins to plaid cloths and accordionists."

Sara poured the tea for us. "Are you all right, Alana? You look tired."

"It was a long night," I admitted. "I didn't get much sleep." I hadn't. I had tossed and turned, thinking of William, of Jack, of my article, of the future. Of my mother.

Sara sighed. "You must take care of yourself. We are almost done here, but I need you to pay attention."

"I am. I'm listening to every word, believe me." I showed her my notebook, the dense writing on the pages.

"Good. That winter, Pablo worked day and night. Shadows under his eyes. Like yours. But, oh, what he was painting. All the colors of the south. The sun and sand, ochers and burnt reds. Compositions of guitars, dishes of fruit. As if he had taken our summer and distilled it into essences which he could then put on canvas. All of that summer and what had taken place.

"I have not told that part of the story, what happened after Venice, to anyone," she said again, emphasizing that this story was for me alone. I didn't yet understand why. "And it is not important for your article. You will not use it."

I hesitated, but Sara was right. Her personal story wasn't necessary for my article. In fact, I was wondering why she had given such personal information. "Agreed," I said.

She rose and went to the window, a gray pane filled with the sadness of a rainy autumn afternoon. "He and Olga finally separated later that winter. You can see what it did to their son, Paulo, in the portraits he made of him that year. The child is never smiling. In one of the paintings, he is holding a toy horse and looks as if he is about to throw it. Pablo also did several portraits of Olga that year, looking beautiful and very, very alone. Downcast. No portraits of Anna survive, or none that I know of."

"What about Irène Lagut and the painting *The Lovers*? Did Pablo finish that painting of her?"

"Later, yes. He showed it at the Rosenberg gallery, and it was a great success. Pablo had also been working on a large painting of me that summer, and I learned later that he had painted over it, painted me out of it, and left only a flute player. I think he meant it as a punishment for what I had done to Anna."

"What happened to her wasn't all your fault. One moment of anger . . ." I zipped my purse open and folded my hat into it.

"I murdered her."

The shock of that statement made me sit down again. What could she mean by it? And then it hit me like a gust of wind strong enough to blow a person over.

"You mean Anna was still in Guernica when the Germans bombed it?"

"I thought so, yes."

I could think of nothing to say. Living with that. All those years.

"Your coming here brought back all the memories," Sara said. "You know, when my sons died, I thought it was part of my punishment for what I had done. But sometimes we are forgiven; sometimes there are second chances. Gerald and I had our second chance.

"When the pain lifted, I realized I loved Gerald more than ever. Loved his incompleteness, the occasional dark moods, the source of which I now guessed. That is what Anna gave me. I would thank her if she were here. Pablo would have destroyed me, I think.

"And family is so important. The only important thing, really. When that summer ended, so did the last of my innocence. That was one of the last summers I could wake up in the morning not worried about my children. Their health. Even before Patrick's tuberculosis, I had these presentiments of disaster. Both of my beautiful little boys, dead. Thank God for Honoria.

And there was another second chance. We have two grandsons now. Honoria's children."

When you don't know what to say, sometimes it is best to say nothing. So I stood next to Sara at the window and put my hand over hers for comfort, just as she had—the day before—touched my hand when I spoke of my mother's death.

The air in the room felt dense and heavy with a sense of endings. "In two days, we are going to visit Honoria," Sara said when the moment passed. "She sometimes sat on Pablo's lap at the beach. He made faces at her to make her laugh." Sara arranged the folds of the curtains and let her hands drop to her side. She was smiling again.

"Gerald is quite mystical about it," she said. "Two for two. Two sons taken from us, two grandsons given to us. So now I think we are almost finished. So much talk of what had been. Too much past. I want the now."

"That is what my mother used to say," I said. "When I began my studies in art history, I wanted to focus on medieval manuscript painters. But she said no, I must value my own time, my place. The only early art she truly admired was Giotto's *Flight into Egypt*. She said it was a magical painting, that people could be fleeing such a terrible calamity yet be so calm, so certain of a safe outcome."

Sara looked at me intently. "Was your mother happy, Alana? What was her life like?"

"Hard. My father died when I was eight. He was much older than she was. And there was no other family, so she was alone with me to raise. During the war, she had to stop her design work because all the textiles were used for the war effort. She worked in a factory. Long hours, little money."

We could hear noises coming from downstairs, a loud

clanging as a pot was dropped, a door opening and closing, murmuring in the kitchen.

"There's a new girl helping the cook," Sara said. "Oh, how history repeats."

It was getting cold in the room without sun shining in the windows.

"The letters from Pablo?" I reminded her.

"None of them talk about that summer, and they are brief, just the keeping-in-touch kind of thing friends send. Little about his art, nothing that would be helpful to you."

Apparently, she was not willing to let me read them after all.

"I do have the two drawings I promised you, though, if you wish to see them." There was a hint of teasing in her voice. Of course I wanted to see them.

Sara went to the desk and opened a small portfolio that had been placed in the middle of the desktop, waiting for us. She untied the two strings and opened it.

"Come," she said. "Look over my shoulder. These are portraits of me done by Pablo that summer. These are just studies for the finished works, but even so, you can see so much of him in the work. The differences in his moods, in his demands for the individual images."

I stood at her side and looked down at the two pieces of paper, the two different images of Sara. One was of her face only, Sara looking straight ahead at the viewer, pensive, unsmiling. It was realistic and representational, part of his neoclassical work with no tricks of cubism to distort the perfection of her face, the huge eyes, the small mouth, her curling hair parted in the middle and pulled back to show the delicate cheekbones.

The second image was a seated figure of Sara, slightly turned to the side so that she was almost in profile, and again there was that sense of tranquility. Other works of that summer had been full of movement, women running on the piece, children playing. His pictures of Sara were about stillness, completion.

Perhaps he had loved her, not just wanted her, and that love was shown as a sense of homecoming and restfulness in her presence.

"This one," Sara said, holding up the seated figure. "I saw it when he finished the painting, and it was glorious. This was before our affair. He painted me all in deep red to contrast with the lightness of my hair, and my face is lit up like a Vermeer portrait. How I wished he would give it to me, to keep. He didn't. He kept all the portraits of that summer, except for these two studies."

Sara placed the portraits back in the portfolio and gently closed it again.

"If my article is used, may we reproduce those?" I asked her.

"Yes. Maybe that will help me make amends for what I did to Anna. If I can do something for you."

"Thank you." But why would helping me make amends for what happened to Anna?

"Also, have you seen this?" She pulled a scrap of paper from her sweater pocket. "Pablo's portrait of Stalin. *Les Lettres Françaises* asked him to draw a tribute to Stalin when he died in March. They put it on the front page, and Pablo has been in trouble with the French communists ever since. They say this is disrespectful, that it doesn't meet the ideals of socialist realism."

Sara handed me the clipped page of newsprint. Picasso's portrait of Stalin had a strangely youthful, almost feminine appearance despite the exaggeratedly thick mustache.

"Picasso had been a communist for decades. It was a choice

between right or left, nothing in between. And he chose the
workers' side, though Stalin proved even good intentions can
become evil. This picture is a criticism as well as a portrait.
Pablo demasculinized the man. Showed a softness that Stalin
denied in life, as do all tyrants. You may keep that."

Sara put her teacup on the tray the maid had brought hours
before. She carefully folded her napkin and put it next to the
cup. Finished, she looked at me, frowning, seeming to answer
for herself some question she wasn't posing to me. She opened
a top drawer of her desk and took out another small piece of
paper. "Come," she said, extending her hand to me. I stood
close to her, looking over her shoulder.

It was a yellowed brittle photo of two women standing on a
terrace, toys on a table on front of them, strong sunshine making halos of their hair. Their black jersey bathing costumes
reached modestly down their thighs and up to their collarbones. The women gazed straight into the camera with a hint
of defiance.

One of them was Sara. I easily recognized her, with that
golden, curly hair, the open, friendly smile. The second
woman—ramrod straight, her face a lovely cold mask—must
certainly have been Olga.

Beyond the terrace was a calm sea. Even in this black-and-
white photo, the blueness of the water shimmered. Sailboats
sailed forever on that sea in this photo, and the women had
been ambered into eternal youth and beauty. Between the stone
terrace and the sea were palm trees with fringed tops and grainy
trunks.

There was a third figure caught as a blur in the bottom
right-hand corner.

"That is Anna," Sara said.

"The kitchen helper? Picasso's lover?" I looked at the face of the girl, turned sideways to the camera so that her thick black braid had fallen over her shoulder.

"Doesn't she look at all familiar, Alana?"

"No. Why should she?"

Sara took a deep breath and put a hand on my shoulder. "I think Anna was your mother," she said.

"No." I shook my head. "Remember? My mother's name was Marti."

"Martina," Sara corrected. "Anna Martina was her name. She never told me her last name."

I was tempted to laugh, to accuse Sara of teasing me, of making a mean joke. But she turned me around to face the wall, where there was a small mirror over the bookcase.

"Look," she said. "How black your hair is. And the cheekbones. The jawline. The eyebrows, straight with no arch. But mostly, when you smile, which isn't often enough, I see Anna's smile. She, like you, did not smile much, but when she did, it was memorable. I can understand why Pablo found her attractive, irresistible, why Olga disliked her. And she was Spanish. Like your mother. You are like Anna, ten years older than when I knew her."

"This is not possible," I said.

"Think, Alana. How did you first learn about me?"

"A clipping I found in one of my mother's books."

"Could be a coincidence. But maybe she left it there for you?"

Sara put the photo on top of the bookcase just in front of me. Faceup, those three figures looking out at the photo taker, who might have been Picasso. I was aware, again, of how little my mother had told me about her life before me.

"Impossible," I said again. But was it?

"And do you see what this means? My Anna lived. She was not in Guernica. I was given another second chance." Sara hugged me. "She lived, Alana, daughter of Anna."

I had to accept it then, or at least pretend to, for Sara's sake. It still seemed unlikely, but I was tracing a possible trail left by my mother, her love of Picasso's work, her delight when I studied Picasso and wrote about him for my thesis, and then the newspaper clipping leading me to Sara. She could have been telling me after her death what she had not told me when she was alive. This could have answered some questions. But it posed others. Why hadn't she told me?

"Keep it if you wish," Sara said. "It should be yours." Instead of handing the photograph to me, she put it on the desk. She reached up and closed the curtains, shutting out the dusky early evening, and the lamp on the side table cast her faint shadow over the rug.

She had offered me a choice. Leave the photo behind. Pretend she never told me this. Just a coincidence. Or pick it up and take the photo with me. Take this history with me.

Anna. Marti. All those secrets, the history never told. The loving protective mother who said to avoid the past, to think of now, the future. She was very young when I was born, that I already knew, but there had been a life before me that I could never even have guessed at.

The noises from the kitchen below were growing louder. There was a sense of impatience in the air, of waiting. I picked up the photo and put it into my sweater pocket.

Sara nodded and walked me to the door, to the stairwell. I went down the now-familiar carpeted steps in a daze, and at the front door, she hugged me again and, for a moment, held my face between her hands.

"I am glad we met, Anna's daughter," she said. "I am glad

there was something from all that history that ended well, that my Anna lived on. Come back sometime. We'll talk more about Anna."

That is how my time with Sara ended. I went looking for Picasso and found my mother's story.

When I pulled out of the driveway of Sara's house, I saw her face looking out at me from behind the sheer curtain as she had the first day. Curiosity had been replaced by something more peaceful in her expression. Her friend Anna had survived.

R ough day?"
    Jack was at the reception desk again when I returned to the inn. There was more noise than usual, laughter coming from the dining room, loud conversation.

"You could say that," I said. Ever since I had recognized my mother in the photograph, nothing else had seemed real or familiar. I looked at Jack, wondering.

"More guests here tonight, several carloads in fact, so if you want dinner, you should be seated now, before we're completely overwhelmed. Your usual table?"

"I'm not hungry. Just my key, please."

Jack studied me for a moment. "You need a drink."

I looked at his sand-colored hair, the freckles, the persistent crease between his eyebrows. I didn't answer. Need is something a person familiar with reality feels, a person, say, who knows who her mother was, who doesn't find out at the age of twenty-nine that the woman who was her mother was a stranger, that her secrets were so much greater than the few facts she gave her daughter.

I had a feeling of sleepwalking through someone else's history, not my own.

"I'll have a sandwich sent up," Jack said gently. "Then meet me later in the bar. We'll talk." He smiled, and that warm electric current passed between us.

"I'm leaving tomorrow morning," I told him later, when we were seated at a booth in the darkest corner of the bar. I'd showered, tried to nap, gone over my notes, but the only thought that stayed with me was this: *Anna Martina. Anna. Marti.*

Jack's choice of a private booth was considerate. He had sensed that whatever our conversation was about to be would involve my tears, and he wanted to allow me privacy.

"Sorry to hear that," he said, and it seemed sincere. The bar was busy. The newly arrived guests had moved from dining room to bar. It seemed to be a family reunion, a large one, with grandparents and grandchildren playing pick-up sticks or card games at the tables while the parents, sisters, brothers, cousins, aunts, and uncles visit back and forth, sharing photos and stories.

All the family life I never had. When my mother died, there were moments when I felt like I was the last one of my species, completely alone. Not even William could dispel that feeling. Perhaps that's why I wouldn't set a date with him. Not even love can always make you feel less alone than you are.

"I've finished the interviews with Sara. No reason to stay," I said.

"Too bad," Jack said. "I will miss you." He said this in a low voice, almost a whisper.

We sat in tense, expectant silence, eavesdropping on the various conversations going on around us for distraction. His hand was on the table, long fingers like a pianist's but covered with ink stains from bookkeeping and a scrape on the side from some handyman mishap.

I wanted to reach over and take his hand, to feel contact with another person, something that would dispel this feeling of disconnection that had begun with my mother's death and had not stopped now that I knew more about her.

"Do you want to talk about it?" he asked when the wine carafe he had brought to our table was half empty. The wine was a Chianti, a good one that tasted of tart cherries, though William wouldn't have appreciated it. He didn't drink Italian wine, only French. I wondered if Anna, my mother, had liked Chianti. What wines did they drink in Spain?

And where to begin, to tell some of this to Jack?

"Turns out, Sara knew my mother. Before she was my mother. Or at least, she thinks she did."

I took out the photo of the three figures on the terrace and gave it to him so I could cradle my wineglass in both hands. They were shaking.

Jack looked. That permanent crease between his brows grew even deeper. He didn't hesitate. "The blurry woman in the foreground," he said, "looks like you."

"So it seems."

"Where are they?"

"France. Antibes. A hotel. She never mentioned living in France to me."

Jack considered before asking, "Does this somehow change things for you?"

"It does. And it doesn't. This woman"—I pointed at the photo—"has a history I know nothing about, knew nothing about, till Sara told me."

"Most families have secrets," Jack said.

Somehow this was beyond secret. This was hiding, deception about who she was and, therefore, who I was.

There had been so much she did not want me to know. Yet

she had left that clipping, knowing I would eventually find it. She had led me to Sara, who had revealed Anna Martina, the Spanish girl hiding behind the Americanized Marti. My mother had known that you may hide from the past, but it is still there, the monster under the bed or the welcomed unwrapped present, depending on what that past was. That still had to be discovered.

There was still incompletion, something unsaid that I couldn't put my finger on. That was what was upsetting me, an unfinished thought that I couldn't put into words, like the feeling when you have completed a jigsaw puzzle but one piece is still missing.

"Look." Jack put his arm around my shoulder. I wasn't crying, but I was close to it, not from distress but from the magnitude of what had happened earlier that day. "Look, your mother kept back some things. Maybe that's why, when we fall for people, we want openness. No secrets. To make up for those silences of childhood, for all that we never knew."

"And were there silences in your childhood?"

Jack tapped the table and shook his head before answering. "There is a room at the back of the inn that is never used," he said, "because my father kept it aside for his girlfriend. Top floor, private. He always told us it was too cold, too drafty, for customers. But when we opened it up after his funeral, it was the best room at the inn—private entrance, cozy, good view, wonderful oak furniture. And we found things, a woman's things. I don't know if my mother knew or not."

"I'm sorry."

"So am I. I grew up believing they had a happy marriage, a fulfilling one. That's why, when I found out my wife was having an affair, I told her we were done."

"Will you divorce?"

"Probably. We can't undo what has been done. And I don't know if I can live with it, the way it is now."

That, then, was the source of the hardness, the brittle humor, that he used to keep people at a distance. But we had danced, close, leaned into each other.

"Sara said we—I guess she meant our generation—made too much of those things."

"That may be true for Sara. Not for me."

It was eleven o'clock, and the late-night news came on the television. The bar guests had been playing the jukebox, the same songs over and over, Teresa Brewer and Marty Robbins, so the sound of the television was turned low.

But there he was. Senator McCarthy, glaring into the camera, his mouth twisted with threats. I thought of Picasso's portrait of Stalin, his affiliation with the communist party.

Jack drained his wineglass and made a kind of growl in the back of his throat. "I'm going to get rid of that damn thing," he said. "Come on." He took my hand and put his own dime into the jukebox.

We danced again to a slow ballad, and he pressed me close against him. I felt safe. The wine had lightened my mood, and I was able to push the secrets back into the box, to keep them for later, when my head was clear. The confusion of the day drifted away, leaving behind an ocean of possibility. I floated on the waves, light and indifferent to everything but the smell of Jack's bay rum aftershave. I wanted him. The revealed secrets of the day had made me a different woman, one who wanted a different man.

When the song ended, I took his hand. I led him through the bar, up the stairs, to my room. This was the only connection I wanted, needed, at that moment. No words. Secrets and truths were reduced to flesh on flesh, need meeting need, sigh answering sigh. Nothing in my life had ever felt that right.

"Alana," he whispered, running his hands over me. "Alana, as soon as I saw you . . ."

I silenced him with kisses and trembled with pleasure in his arms.

I woke up at three in the morning, Jack sleeping heavily at my side, his face flushed and one arm still thrown over me as if he would not let go. It felt natural, comfortable, like that. When I sat up, he muttered something and turned onto his other side.

I hoped his dream was a good one, because mine had not been. I had dreamed of a man leaning over me, making the sweet and silly sounds that fathers make to their infant daughters, the "There, now, it doesn't hurt that much, does it?" reassurance when I skinned my knee, the protective hugs during thunderstorms. Dreamed of those moments of childhood that perfect our connection with a parent. I had loved my father, been devastated when he died, taking too much of my childhood with him.

But in my dream, the man didn't have a face. I didn't know him, didn't recognize him.

This was the connection that hadn't been made, that Sara had left unspoken. It had come to me in a brief moment between sleep and wakefulness. My mother had had an affair with Pablo Picasso. According to Sara, that had been in July and August of 1923.

I was born in April of 1924.

I must have said something out loud, made some gasp of shock. Jack woke up and took me in his arms again. "Alana, what's wrong?"

"My father."

"What about him?"

"It might have been Pablo Picasso."

"The artist? The one you are writing about? That Pablo Picasso?"

"Yes."

We stared at each other, speechless.

Perhaps this was the reason for my mother's many secrets. She hadn't wanted to tell me about Picasso. Hadn't wanted to tell me that my father was not Harry Olsen but the most famous artist of the twentieth century.

PART TWO

SIXTEEN

· · · · · · · · · · · ·

Paris 1953

IRÈNE

All his talk about sun and warmth, the gentle southern light that makes anything ugly less ugly, anything beautiful even more beautiful, has made me restless. I watched Pablo drive away with that son of his, and for a moment, I wanted to shout, "Wait! Wait for me! Let me come with you! Bring me to the beauty!" I almost ran down the street after him, that rainy Parisian street, with its cobblestones running in a long line beside the Seine, everything in shades of gray or brown or dulled pewter, making color a mere memory.

But I didn't run after him. Irène Lagut does not beg. Irène Lagut remembers when the young not-yet-famous Pablo Picasso begged her to stay. Instead, I waved his car around the corner, walked to the baker's shop, and bought a baguette to have with my soup, which I would be eating in solitude.

At home, I paused in front of the hallway mirror and hat-stand, trying see myself the way Pablo had seen me. My reflection did not smile back.

I've reached that time of life when my child no longer needs me. She has her own life, her own cares, a life with more in common with my husband than me: hospitals. Patients. Laboratories. My daughter chose the life of a healer and does not think perhaps that art also heals. And, increasingly, my husband no longer desires me. He is tender. He is kind. He is busy. I am like the furniture or perhaps the madwoman locked in her attic painting, painting. Our apartment, which used to feel too small, feels too large.

What makes a woman beautiful? Is it youth? Is it a gentle asymmetry of the face, a certain tilt of the head? I ask this later, standing in front of my easel, trying to capture the way early morning light sends a flash of silver over a woman's cheekbone, trying to think about something other than Pablo and the light in the south, where blue sky meets even bluer water.

Thirty years ago, I followed Pablo to the south, where he had followed Sara Murphy, where we had acted out the Grand Guignol of love, of desire. It is a comedy, the Grand Guignol, full of fools and cruel tricks. And now, I want to follow him there again. But I think I will not.

Outside the window, autumn has turned the trees into scarecrow bristles against the gloomy sky. There is a constant threat of rain, of thunder. People rush down windy avenues, their faces buried in their coat collars like turtles as I hold my dripping paintbrush.

This woman I am painting has cheekbones that are soft rather than sharp, curved, made to exactly fit the palm of a loving hand. I saw Gerald Murphy do that with his wife, Sara, that summer when I followed Pablo to Antibes, to force him to finish my portrait, the one he calls *The Lovers*. Gerald, Sara, Pablo, Olga . . . they were sitting on the hotel terrace under the stars when I arrived uninvited. Sara was gracious; Olga was furious.

You can tell much about a woman by the shape of her cheekbones. Soft, gentle Sara, with her face as round as a child's. Sharp, dangerous Olga, with cheekbones that could slice bread. There was nothing Olga could do, though, about my uninvited arrival that summer. It was a hotel. Much as she wanted, Olga couldn't order me to leave.

"A cocktail," Gerald Murphy said to me, an order, not a question. "Take this chair. Pleased to meet you, Miss Lagut. Or should I call you Madame Cadenat? Do you use your husband's name?"

"Lagut," I said.

"The juice of a few flowers," Gerald Murphy said, pouring something violet-colored into a cocktail glass and handing it to me. "That's what Sara calls my cocktails." Gerald was impossibly handsome. He could have been a movie star with that blond hair, the tan, the fluid, athletic movements.

"It does taste like a garden," I agreed, wishing he had poured me a whiskey instead.

That was when he reached over and cupped Sara's pretty face in his hand. They gave each other the kind of look that excludes everyone else, a look of such intense love and intimacy it was almost painful to see.

I looked at Pablo to see his reaction. Because as soon as I saw pretty Sara Murphy, so in love with her own husband, I knew Pablo meant to have her. Pablo watched Sara and Gerald and grimaced. Desire. Jealousy. Possession. Admiration. It had been there in the atelier a few months before, when we were painting the backdrop for the ballet, an arrow of lust pointed at Sara. Now his desire for her was so large it sucked the air out of the night. Olga was gasping with fury at what she knew was inevitable.

And Sara. Was she as oblivious to it all as she seemed? I wonder. Can anyone be that innocent?

That night, someone watched us from the doorway. The hotel maid, her eyes huge, her black braid, thick as a wrist, hanging over her shoulder. Pablo sensed her presence. He looked away from Sara to the maid. Their eyes locked. And then she backed into the hotel doorway and disappeared.

I remember it like yesterday, because the silver sheen I am trying to paint onto the cheekbones of this woman on this canvas was the sheen of light I saw on the hotel maid's face just before she disappeared. She had a face that lingers in the memory, that *jeune fille*. The scar over her eye, still red and raw, made her face more interesting, not less.

It's freezing in the studio. I'm done for the day. This painting will not work, my thoughts keep wandering, and, more than anything, I want to be in the warm south.

My portrait, *The Lovers*, was not in the Quai des Augustins studio. Maybe Pablo has taken it with him to Antibes. Maybe I should make a little trip. I still have friends in Antibes. I can go catch up on the gossip. Torture Pablo a bit, show up unannounced as I did that night thirty years ago, though these days, it is more difficult to take him by surprise. He hides from the public he once courted. Fame does that.

Fame. Swallow the bitterness that fame comes so much more easily to men than women. How long since I have shown my work, since a gallery called and said, "We have put you on the calendar for the fall season. Do you have enough new work for a one-person show?" Too long since any dealer has said that to me.

I could pack away my paints and brushes. I could admit defeat. All artists feel it, that moment when perhaps it isn't worth the struggle. But there is the matter of a silver sheen on a woman's face, a problem to be solved, a moment of eternity to catch out of this landfall of moments sliding by, rushing into oblivion, into mortality. Try adding more titanium white to the palette. There. My silver sheen. I was trying too hard for transparency. Sometimes the best way to achieve transparency is by allowing opaqueness. Not all must be revealed.

But to chase Pablo one more time to the south? A waste of time, I think. I refused to marry him because I knew he could never give me what I most wanted: himself. Pablo Picasso belongs to his art, not his women. Aside from the lust, that wound healed long ago. Yet I am curious to know what is going on down there with Pablo and Françoise and Olga. The Grand Guignol. I will call my friend and get the news.

SEVENTEEN

· · · · · · · · · · · · · · ·

ALANA

J ack was at the reception desk when I checked out of the inn
the next morning. He looked tired. Neither of us had slept
much after I told him the story of Sara, Pablo, and Anna.

He smiled a quick, secret smile as I handed him my room
key. I wanted to lean forward and kiss him, but people were
coming and going, other guests looking for the breakfast room,
a cleaning lady lugging the heavy vacuum. Jack became the
innkeeper once again, accepting my key and check with professional courtesy, but a telltale blush lit up his face. That made
me want to kiss him even more. It's rare for men to blush. Jack
was rare. When he took my key, that electricity was there between us, even stronger.

"Visit us again," he said. A little pause. "I mean it, Alana.
When you're ready. I'd like you to. Very much. You . . . you
mean something to me."

I remembered the feel of his skin on my mine, the smoky
scent of his hair, the way he winced when his injured leg twisted
under him. I wanted to press his head to my chest again, keep

my arms tight around him, and it wasn't just passion. It was also possession. *I want this man to be mine*, I thought. *I want to be his*. It wasn't a decision to be made. It was a fact and I could not hide from it.

I'd felt so complete when he had his arms around me. I felt safe and accepted in a way I did not with William. Jack, I thought, was a man I could quarrel with, disagree with, but know that when the words ended and the differences of opinion had been aired, we would still be able to find each other, touch and accept. I could tell Jack about the marches and demonstrations I had participated in, and though he might not approve, he wouldn't sneer or judge. Not like William. But there were things to be done before I could think about accepting Jack's refuge, before I could accept exile into his life and away from mine. Before you could leave a life, you had to know what that life was. Who your parents were.

And William. What was I to do with William, whom I loved, whom I did not love?

When I returned to the Pearl Street apartment in the late afternoon, I fought down the persistent urge to call out "I'm home" to my mother. Instead, I unpacked in the lonely quiet of the place and then sat on the safe with a glass of wine. The urn with my mother's ashes glinted in the bookcase. "I met Sara," I said to it. "She told me the strangest story. I think you know it." Silence.

I finished my wine as the twilight deepened, turning the corners of the room into secret shadows. And then I turned on all the lights and systematically searched through every book, every cluttered drawer, to see if my mother had left other things behind, scraps of paper or photos that would prove once and for all Sara's story. I rummaged through shoeboxes at the back of the closet, the single photo album we had, the kitchen junk drawer. I gave up at midnight. I had found nothing.

Part of me was still arguing against what Sara had told me. She could be wrong. This could all be coincidence. How to prove such a thing, your own mother's unknown past, her life before you?

But first there was the draft of the article for *Art Now* to finish. David Reed to be faced. And William. I wasn't certain what that night with Jack had meant, except for one thing: I was not ready to be William's wife and perhaps never would be. That had been Anna Martina's dream, not mine. Marti, the mother who wished above all else for her daughter to be kept safe.

I wrote a note to Sara, thanking her for her time, the generosity of her reminiscences about that summer and Pablo Picasso. Professional courtesy required it, so I pushed aside the puzzled anger I felt over the betrayal she had confessed. I did not mention Anna Martina because that wound was too raw. No child, no matter how close to pushing middle age that child is, wants to learn that her mother had kept so very much from her or that her mother had been betrayed by a woman who had been her only friend in a dangerous time.

Instead of saying anything about my mother, I sent her three Marti scarves, carefully selected from the box of models and samples my mother kept in the apartment. Something to remember her by, though she had never forgotten.

For two days, I worked feverishly on the article, from seven in the morning to ten in the evening, dredging through my notes for more and more information, making late afternoon forays to libraries and museums to look at Picasso's work. Pablo. Refusing to think about the ending of Sara's story, the photograph.

My father? I didn't think about that. It was stored away in that locked chest to be opened later. In the late evening when I had finished the day's quota of work, I returned to my search of the apartment, opening and shaking every book on the shelves, looking through the pockets of her coats and sweaters, all the clothing I still hadn't packed up for the Salvation Army, the zippered compartments of her handbags.

But my mother hadn't left anything else behind, no more scraps of papers, no photographs or journals that had answers to questions that had never been asked. Children take so much for granted. Mommy is Mommy, a woman others called Marti or Mrs. Olsen. And that man we call Daddy is Daddy, the man who dangled a stuffed bear over my crib, who had a gray mustache over his mouth, who wore a scratchy coat that smelled acrid, a smell I couldn't identify until years later when I went into a café that was thick with pipe smoke.

There was a locked underwater sea chest of questions to be asked later, after the work was done. After a meeting with William.

I was working on a paragraph about Picasso's relationship with the Rosenberg galley when the phone rang. No one had called since I had returned from Sneden's Landing, and I had called no one. I knew before I picked up the phone who it would be.

"So, you're home," William said.

I was sitting at the little table by the window where my mother had sat in the evenings with her sketchbook, working. The phone line had to be snaked across the room to reach this table, but I wanted to sit in my mother's chair, anchored in a world that had grown strange, unknown.

"How long have you been back?" William asked, sounding both hurt and angry. No preliminaries. No "I missed you" or "How are you?" or "How was the trip?" Right to the heart of the matter. That was William.

"A couple of days," I said.

"And you couldn't be bothered to call?"

"I was working. And I had some things to think about."

A long pause. "I hope this means you've decided to set the date."

"Let's meet for dinner," I said. "Tomorrow? Agostino's?" I thought it better to have the conversation in a public space.

"I'm free tomorrow," he agreed. "But let's go to Pierre's. The wine list is better. Seven?"

I was early the next evening, and he was a few minutes late. I watched him come through the velvet-curtained entry, hand his coat and hat to the hatcheck girl, straighten his tie.

Those Cary Grant looks of his, the short, dark hair, the wide shoulders and lopsided smile, made me almost regret what I knew had to be done. William was the kind of man who makes partner by the time he is thirty. Next month was his thirtieth birthday. And I was about to ruin this for him.

I wanted to rise up from the chair where I had been waiting for him and run. Not to him, away from him. I didn't. I was not my mother. I was not in danger as she had been when she ran. I was just unwilling.

"You're early," he said, pleased. "That little vacation out of town must have helped."

It wasn't a vacation, it was a working trip, and I was tired of arguing this point with him, but I couldn't stop myself. I asked, "Helped what?"

"Don't start, Alana. You know what I mean."

I did know: *Get this irritating ambition out of your system.*

Understand a woman's role. Help me, my career; stop thinking so much about yourself all the time.

The waiter brought the menus—but it was William who would decide what our dinner would be—and the wine list. This, too, was part of the pattern that we had created, that we had allowed. The waiter made recommendations, and William agreed to the cream of asparagus soup, the veal chops, the pear financier cake for dessert, the bottle of pinot gris from Alsace.

To start, he ordered a Manhattan for himself, a sloe gin fizz for me. A very ladylike drink. I would have preferred a sidecar, one of the cocktails I had shared with Sara, but stayed silent.

"I think we should honeymoon in Miami," he said, clicking his cocktail glass against mine. "Or would you prefer somewhere else? Maybe Canada, Toronto. Good restaurants there. Or, if we get married in December, a Christmas wedding . . ."

December was barely two months away.

"If we get married in December, we can go skiing in Colorado," he finished.

"How about France?" I asked, already knowing his answer.

The restaurant had filled up, and we were surrounded by the murmurs of conversation, the sound of forks gently tapping against bone china, the ring of crystal wineglasses. I thought of the raucous sounds of the bar at Brennan's Inn, the loud laughter, the smell of beer and buttered popcorn. Jack. I missed Jack in a way I hadn't missed William.

William gave me the look. Gentle, patient, understanding. He reached to put his hand over mine, but I pulled my hand away.

"Alana, they still have food shortages from the war over there in Europe. It's a mess. And such a long way to go. I would have to be away from the office for weeks."

The asparagus soup arrived, mossy green in a delicate white

bowl edged with gold. I took a few sips, then put my spoon down and waited for William to finish his.

"Excellent," he said. "Not hungry?"

"I had a big lunch," I lied.

"Why a big lunch if you knew we were meeting for dinner? Really, Alana. Are we going to quarrel again tonight? I thought you had things all sorted out. Isn't that what your little trip was about?" He put down his spoon as well, and the Cary Grant charm was gone. His face was flushed and angry. This was the face he had never showed Marti, my mother.

"I don't want to quarrel," I said. "I just . . ."

"What? I missed you, you know. And you missed a wonderful evening at the Bishops'. Sylvia asked about you, a good sign. I think she'll be the perfect friend for you, someone to lunch with and go shopping with. She might even help you with a new wardrobe." His voice trailed off. He didn't want to quarrel any more than I did, but as soon as he hugged me an hour earlier, I saw the way his eyes took in what I had chosen to wear that night, a loose sheath rather than a tight-waisted dress, strapped shoes instead of simple, elegant pumps.

"I don't need a new wardrobe," I said.

"You will," he warned. "Alana, I love you. You look beautiful in anything. But I wish . . ."

He didn't finish the sentence, concentrating on his soup, careful not to drip any, not to slurp. Elegant. William was nothing if not elegant. When the soup was finished, with just enough left in the bowl to satisfy Emily Post, who had warned against scraping the dish clean, he continued his train of thought.

"John bought a billiard table for the recreation room and built in a bar. Sylvia pretended to complain about boys being boys, but I could tell she was pleased. Billiards. Perfect for relaxing, for talking casually about some of the things going on with the *Art Now* account."

"The what?" My voice was too loud. Several people turned to look at us, and William cleared his throat.

The waiter, who had just appeared with our plates of veal, took a startled step backward. I smiled apologetically at him, and he set the plates before us.

"A new client," William said. "The magazine. They are looking to acquire a literary journal, something that hasn't shown a profit in years, and asked for legal representation. It's a small account, of course, but a new foray for us into publishing. Could take us somewhere bigger if this goes well. Didn't I mention it before?"

The smell of the meat was making me nauseous. The mashed potatoes had been piped into precious swirls on the plate next to the meat and gravy. I was grateful for the potatoes. I could hide the pink undercooked veal beneath them.

He was going to be legal representative for *Art Now*. The news felt like a pill that had been swallowed but got wedged in the esophagus, burning and choking.

"William, that's the magazine I'm working with."

"Is it?" William cut into the veal. "Done just right, don't you think?"

When I first met William, he was finishing law school, and I was finishing my dissertation on Picasso. Neither of us had money, so we spent our evenings walking and talking, holding hands, dreaming about the future, the cases he would represent, the books I would write. We talked for hours and hours.

One night there was a blizzard, and we went out for our usual walk anyway, playing in the car-emptied streets like children, throwing snowballs at each other, making snow angels on Broadway in front of the Equitable Skyscraper, where streetlights still flashed red and green for the traffic that wasn't there. He caught snowflakes on his tongue and tried to kiss me before they could melt.

"I think the veal is underdone. Do you remember the night we made snow angels during the blizzard?" I asked him, pushing food around my plate.

"I remember you wore a red ski hat with matching mittens. And when the snow fell on your hair, I thought there couldn't be a prettier girl in the world."

"We have changed," I said.

"Of course, we have. Did you think we wouldn't?"

"William, you can't represent *Art Now*."

"Why, may I ask?" The beginning of a quarrel, a true one, that edge in his voice.

"Because it is the magazine that will, I hope, hire me full-time as a writer. I've been telling you about it for weeks. Haven't you listened to anything I said?"

The room grew dimmer. Nine o'clock. I didn't have to check my watch to tell the time. The restaurant always lowered the already dim lights at nine, believing probably that it was the time when diners might be more interested in romance and flirtation than their meals.

William went on cutting into the meat, lifting the fork to his mouth, chewing.

"Well," he said, after consideration, "of course I listened. I just forgot the name of the magazine. But you're right. That would look like a conflict of interest. You'll have to leave the magazine. Go to some other publication."

"I can't. There is no other magazine like this."

"What about *National Geographic*? They just published an article on, what was it, the Sistine Chapel?"

"I write about modern art, not the Renaissance."

"Alana, I need this account. I can't turn it down."

Stand up, I told myself. *Stand up now and leave.* But I didn't. I thought of the student catching snowflakes on his tongue, and I owed something to that boy, if not the man he had become. He had waited years for me, a fact he frequently pointed out. He had held me, comforted me, on the day of my mother's funeral, had stood up and said wonderful things about her as part of the eulogy. *He will keep you safe*, my mother had told me.

But was safety enough? Perhaps for my mother, who had feared going to jail, who had a child to raise. But for me?

Sometimes, absolute truth is the only solution. Sometimes you have to jump and hope there is something softer than rock at the bottom of that cliff.

"William, when I was in New Jersey, I slept with another man."

He froze in his chair, his eyes burning into mine with disbelief.

The waiter—oh, that poor waiter, how I was beginning to pity him—had just arrived to clear the plates and pour more water into our glasses. Had he heard? Did waiter training include this kind of problem, a woman declaring infidelity, her fiancé looking as though he were about to smash everything off the table and onto the floor?

"Are you ready for your dessert, or should I hold it for a while?" he asked quietly, keeping his eyes on the tray he balanced on his forearm.

William didn't bother to answer him, and the waiter, with a great show of composure, backed away.

I was the destroyer that night, not William. He forced his hands to be still, to stay carefully on the table, one hand close to his wineglass, the other clutching his napkin. I took it all in:

his familiar, handsome face, the face I'd seen change from boy to man; his expensive suit; his long, elegant hands.

My engagement ring with its large diamond caught the candlelight. William watched as I twisted it off and placed it on the tablecloth in front of him.

For one wild second, I was glad. I was free and weightless, and the future was full of endless possibility, no maps needed.

But I was wrong. The mapped future, the future William saw for us, for me, was still there.

"Think about it," William said, pushing the ring back toward me. He took out his wallet, threw some bills on the table, and rose. "See yourself home," he said, and started to walk away. But he turned around. He came back and bent over to give me a kiss on the cheek, and not just for show because other diners were watching us again. There was tenderness still there under the outrage.

"I'll call you. I can't talk about this now. Give me a few days to think. Finish your article. Then we'll sort this out. We belong together, Alana."

That was the man that Marti had wanted me to marry. That was the boy who caught snowflakes, who loved a girl in a red ski hat.

I walked home rather than take a taxi, enjoying the blare of traffic on Fifth Avenue, the lights and bustle. It had been so quiet at Brennan's Inn. But I had enjoyed that, too.

I walked, thinking I knew more about Picasso, whom I had never met, than my own mother, who had kept so many secrets. Who were her parents? Why had she kept a clipping about Sara Murphy and Pablo, but not her own birth certificate or wedding certificate? She had obliterated her past.

No. Not completely. There was a wedding photo. She and

the man I knew as my father. Marti in her full-skirted dress and flat heels standing in front of a church, looking small and a little overwhelmed but happy with the man at her side. I had looked at the photo a hundred times, wondering where that church was and, yesterday, looking at it freshly, wondering if I could detect a hint of pregnancy under that voluminous dress. Finally understanding why she was wearing flat shoes and not heels. Balance might have been a problem already for her, her center of gravity shifted by carrying a child. Me.

One photo. Now two. A wedding photo and an earlier photo of a girl, a blur on a terrace in Antibes. A frightened girl. A girl who had been beaten by the police, who could not go home because they might be looking for her.

I tried to imagine what it would be like to carry William's child. Children. He wanted several. So did I, and he was right, I couldn't wait much longer. After thirty is dangerous, my own doctor had warned me.

She couldn't have been ready. Not at that age, in those circumstances. I had always loved my mother even when we quarreled, but now there was a new feeling layered on that childish adoration of the girl who had so admired the mother: sympathy. Tenderness. I wanted to put my arms around that girl, protect her, help her, tell her it would be all right.

As I walked home through the autumn night, the blinking lights of Fifth Avenue felt like intruders into my thoughts. Just a few months before, I had walked down this avenue, stopped in front of this store window, with her. She had been walking slowly, stopping frequently to catch her breath. The department store window we stopped at had a display of spring fashions, tennis skirts, and short-sleeved dresses with full skirts. And Marti scarves.

"Mine," she had said smiling. "Not bad, are they, Alana?"

I missed her, wished we could still talk late into the night as we had sometimes done, discussing Sartre and modernism and all the other topics she had read up on, insisted I read about. *Now is all that counts*, she told me endless times.

But she was wrong. Then, and what happened then, matters, too. We had so much more to discuss. When I crossed Fulton Street, a different thought wandered through my mind, distracting me from my grief for my mother and the problem of William.

Sara couldn't be right. Or could she? Picasso, my mother's lover. Had he thought about her at all during those decades after her disappearance, decades when Sara thought she had been living and then died in Guernica? Is that what Picasso believed?

And the problem of my birthdate. Impossible. She'd had a boyfriend in Spain, Sara had said—Antonio. If she'd already been pregnant when she married, Antonio could have been the man who got her pregnant. I started counting again on my fingers but stopped. The math didn't work. Like William, I couldn't think about it now.

On Monday, I received a response from Sara, thanking me for the scarves. *I enjoyed talking with you*, she wrote. Just that. And below those words, an address in Vallauris, France. Pablo Picasso's address. She hadn't offered it before. Had the scarves changed her mind? I held the letter in my hand, wondering what she meant by sending it. But I knew it could only mean one thing. She thought I should go to France. She had sent me a challenge. And a gift.

How? was the question. I was broke and, more than that, not

quite certain I wanted to meet Pablo Picasso face-to-face, not now, not yet. Meeting the artist would have been one thing . . . but this other Picasso? The one who had been my mother's lover? Who might be . . . I stripped my bed and stuffed the dirty laundry into a canvas bag and took it to the Laundromat on the corner to spend the evening listening to the chug of the machines and thumb through old *Time* magazines.

William didn't call. He left me alone, and I was grateful, even though his silence was a sign that he was waiting for me to apologize. The days were easy for me since they were about work, only work. But the evenings were full of questions and confusion, and more than once, I found myself thinking about Jack Brennan, not William.

Jack and I had danced well together. Had made love in a way that made me tremble when I thought of him. But we were both on a train heading into a completely unknown future. William, on the other hand, knew every station, every stop.

I worked feverishly to finish a draft of the piece on Picasso. The Picasso I was writing about now was the Picasso I had begun with. This new Picasso was a man who had played a role, a large role, in my mother's life. Who perhaps had played an even larger role in mine, though I had never met him. His work had to be reconsidered, seen from different angles and possibilities, because I had new connections with it.

I tacked a reproduction of *The Lovers* on the wall and stared at it for hours, looking for new messages in the woman's downcast face, in the gentle way her lover reaches toward her. None of what Sara had said about my mother and her pregnancy could go into the article. But I could not leave my emotions completely out of it, so I ended up writing about Picasso with both tenderness and anger. And with those mixed emotions, I finished the article.

On a sunny afternoon, when the chestnut tree in front of my apartment had dropped its last leaf and left the sky open and bright, I hand-delivered it to David Reed's office.

The receptionist took it. She was an older woman, severe in a gray suit and bun twisted tight at the back of her neck. One day she'd shared some confidences with me, how she had wanted to be in publishing and took the secretarial job as a way in . . . and had stayed a secretary for the past twenty years. I think she meant it as a warning to me, but after that one single conversation, she had kept our interactions brief and formal.

"Mr. Reed is with someone," she said that afternoon. "I'll be sure he gets this."

She gave me a strange look, and as I walked to the bank of elevators, I saw her pick up her telephone and press a button. Word spreads fast at the water cooler, even in big companies. Had she already heard that my fiancé was to be the legal representative for *Art Now*? Was she already, as others would eventually, inevitably do, wondering if I had pulled strings to get work?

William was right. We could not both be associated with the magazine. Either William would have to turn down the work . . . or I would have to. All I had hoped for, worked toward. The other solution was obvious. End my engagement to William.

It didn't occur to me that her strange look might be a portent of a different type of problem. In the days I had spent with Sara and then back in New York working on the article, I had been living in my head, in the South of France, in those years following World War I, in sunshine and hope and stories of art and passion. I hadn't given McCarthy much thought, because he didn't belong to that time. I had, in fact, almost forgotten about him.

David Reed called the next day, early in the morning.

"We need to talk," he said. "Meet me at the Cole Bar at the St. Regis. Four o'clock." Click.

The tone of his voice brought me back to the here and now. Something was very wrong.

EIGHTEEN

· · · · · · · · · · · · · ·

ALANA

The radio was playing Eddie Fisher love ballads. I kept it turned on almost all day, waiting to see if there was more news from the House Un-American Activities Committee, if more names were mentioned. That day, there had been none. People were wearying of the witch hunt, I hoped. But my instinct was saying otherwise.

My best suit was a Dior look-alike with an A-line gray skirt and a jacket with padded shoulders. I put up my hair so that it wouldn't fall into my eyes. The effect was eerily similar to the look of Mr. Reed's defeated receptionist. My reflection frowned back at me from the mirror. I added a Marti scarf in a cream-and-blue print, tying it in a floppy bow at my neck. Better.

For added bravado, I took my mother's car, which had been sitting in the garage since my return from Sneden's and Sara. I drove myself uptown rather than take the subway, hoping to find a parking spot once at the hotel. If not, I would pretend I was a guest and let one of the hotel staff park it for me.

An autumn drizzle turned the roads and pavements shiny as

new coins. The air was fresh and cold, true New York autumn weather, harbinger of months of gray and snow and slush to come. Another winter to get through, my first Christmas without my mother.

I arrived at the St. Regis ten minutes early, when the King Cole Bar was still almost empty. Come five o'clock, when the offices closed down, the bar would be filled for cocktail hour. David Reed had chosen this earlier time for our meeting so that we wouldn't have to shout at each other. I wondered, though, why he hadn't asked me to meet him in his office, whether that was a good or bad sign.

There was a table for two in a dark corner off to the side of the bar, where King Cole wouldn't be smirking down at me from the mural. I chose that one and waited, feeling nervous and hopeful at the same time. The bartender gave me uneasy glances. The bar had only recently begun admitting women. It had been men only since its opening fifty years before, and women on their own were still not fully welcome, even if allowed.

Reed arrived exactly at four. Three other tables had filled by then, and it took a minute before his eyes adjusted to the dimness of the bar, before he saw me sitting in the corner, waiting. He had a folder tucked under his arm.

As soon as he sat down, he opened the folder and put my article on the table between us. He took out his pipe, filled it, lit it. Without a word. A cocktail waitress came and took our order for Bloody Marys.

"The silence is ominous," I said as he sat there puffing on his pipe and avoiding looking at me.

"The piece is incomplete without some direct quotes from Picasso. You need to speak with the artist," he said.

"How? Picasso doesn't come to the United States, and I can't get to France."

For a moment, Reed almost looked sympathetic.

"What you have so far is good," he admitted. "But you need to round it out, to at least have him confirm some of your suppositions about who he was painting in 1923, who his models were. Sara Murphy. Irène Lagut. You even suggest a hotel maid."

That maid was my mother, I didn't tell him. *And, oh, by the way, Picasso might be my father.*

"How?" I said again. "I have no travel budget and, even if I did, no assurance that Picasso would speak with me. But you know that."

Our drinks came. The silence between us deepened, more ominous than ever. Doors were closing in my life—my engagement to William, this magazine assignment—and that feeling of being lost fell over me again as it had that evening weeks before, when I had taken so many wrong turns on my way to Sneden's, to Sara.

"I know that," Reed agreed. "But the article feels incomplete. I won't accept it yet."

Reed relit his pipe, and his expensive silver Dunhill flared in the dimness like a torch. He opened the folder. "Let's go over it together." One of those closed doors opened again, a crack, enough to let in some hope. He moved closer to me, and we went over it together page by page.

He had made copious notes in the margins, and as he explained his questions and corrections, I found myself agreeing with him more than I disagreed. This was the first full-length article I had written for him, the first time he had personally edited my work rather than hand it over to someone lower on the ladder. And he was good. I saw the possibilities he was suggesting for the piece, saw the weaknesses as he saw them. Saw that if I worked in most of his points, the article would be stronger and richer.

And he was right. I needed to speak with Picasso. I had his address, thanks to Sara. But how to get there? How to convince him to see me? I shivered, thinking that I might be asking my own father to meet with me.

When we had finished going over the piece, Reed returned the marked pages to the folder, handed it to me, and moved back to his original position at the table opposite me.

"Something else has come up. Some men came to the office last week asking about you," he said. He looked worried.

"Not William, I hope. I'm sorry he called the office. I've asked him not to." I sat up straighter. Apologies call for a sense of dignity, or they merely look like weakness. "Won't happen again," I said.

"You mean that lawyer guy? He's your fiancé, right? We'll talk about that, too. But no, these men weren't friends. They had badges. FBI. Asked if you were the Alana Olsen who had been a student of Professor Samuel Grippi."

Does the heart really stop beating in those moments, or does it just seem so? I took a deep breath, forced myself to keep breathing, because I felt light-headed with fear.

"I told them I had no idea," Reed said. "Told them we'd only met once and I knew nothing about you, except that you were a fine writer from what I've seen so far and that you might be writing a piece for *Art Now*, that it still had to be decided."

His praise helped a bit, and I thought perhaps he had added that "fine writer" to give me courage. He seemed to be warming up to me a little, and I hoped it was because he had seen potential in my article.

"Look," he said, finally giving up on his pipe and knocking its embers into the ashtray. "I don't know what you got up to as a student. I don't want to know. But if you're in trouble with them, that puts the magazine in trouble as well. I can't hire a communist."

He spoke very quietly, almost in a whisper, because the bar was filling and he didn't want to be overheard.

"I'm not a communist. I was friends with some, and some of my professors were. But I . . ." How could I put it? I had stayed on the sidelines for the most part, not taking part in May Day celebrations or helping to distribute literature. Both my mother and William had insisted on that. "I picketed a segregated restaurant," I said. "I marched. That's all. I don't support Stalin or property redistribution or the rest of the Russian movement. Just equal rights for all Americans."

"I'll take your word on it. But if you don't want to be questioned and brought before the committee, I think you should take a convenient vacation out of town for a few weeks."

"I don't suppose you'd give me an advance," I said. Reed laughed but not loudly, not cruelly.

"Nice try. But no. Till this sorts out, till the article is finished and accepted, we don't have a formal relationship. And don't tell me where you are going. I don't want to have to lie for you in case they return to the office and ask more questions. But I hear Cannes is nice. Isn't that close to where Picasso is?"

Reed signaled to the waitress, who brought our check. He paid for my drink as well as his and rose to leave, gathering up his hat and umbrella. "Give me ten minutes before you leave so that it doesn't look as if we are together."

The look on my face made him smile. "That was a joke," he said.

So, David Reed had a sense of humor. Noted, though not appreciated under the circumstances.

Even though it was a joke, I waited ten minutes anyway, going over our conversation, jotting notes to myself about the article, clinging to that, to work, my raft in stormy seas, not thinking about men with badges. I realized Reed hadn't finished our conversation. We hadn't talked about William and his business relationship with *Art Now*, and what that might mean for me. It didn't really matter anymore, though. I already knew, perhaps had always known, I couldn't marry him. That had been my mother's ambition, not mine. And while there was much of my mother in me, there was much that was not her.

That evening, I sat in my apartment, my mother's apartment, in the dark, huddled under a blanket in the corner of the worn sofa, thinking. Worrying. I'd watched some of those committee hearings on television, had seen how people, professors, screenwriters, teachers, had been bullied and tricked into looking guilty even if they weren't. How people close to them had been made to look guilty just through association. It wasn't just my career at risk but perhaps my friends' as well: Helen's. William's. The last thing he needed was to be assumed guilty of communist sympathies simply because of his relationship to me, because I had been Professor Grippi's student and had marched against segregation and racism.

I huddled deeper into the sofa. My mother had been so proud of that sofa, with its stylish black-and-white print, the sleek modern lines. It was the first thing she had been able to purchase new, not used, and in the easier postwar years, before her illness and care emptied our savings accounts, she had added other furniture to go with it: a coffee table in light-colored wood with a shelf for magazines, a floor lamp with a bendable gooseneck, a rug in shades of gray and cream. All in the modern style, to match her passion for the moment, for ignoring the past.

She had drawn a line between then and now, between danger and safety. Anna Martina had run away and never looked back.

Or perhaps she had. If Sara had got the story correct, had Marti spent long hours thinking back to an earlier lover? I had thought Picasso had been her favorite because of his art. Perhaps there had been other reasons. Perhaps when she realized she was dying, she reconsidered this complete cutoff from the past. Had she left that clipping, that bread crumb, for me to find?

More information, David Reed had said. A convenient vacation. There was one solution for both problems: I would become "unavailable." They wouldn't be able to question me because they wouldn't be able to find me. *Unavailable* was the word I'd heard people use about themselves, about others, if they feared being asked questions they would rather not answer about their political activities, about picketing restaurants or going to meetings. They would disappear for a while.

I would go to France. I would find Picasso and speak with him. Didn't matter how impossible that sounded. It must be done. Perhaps I could also track down Irène Lagut and speak with her, begin another article for *Art Now* about the overlooked women artists of the 1920s. Somehow I would talk David Reed into publishing it, despite his initial lack of interest. It must be done.

But how? My bank account was almost empty, and I owned nothing of value. No, that wasn't true. My mother had left me her car. I could sell my mother's Volkswagen, and that would probably give me just enough money to get there and back.

I had never considered selling it before because it had been hers, had been one of the few things she had left me, other than the apartment furnishings and her box of scarves. When I sat in the car, I could imagine her next to me. Sometimes I thought I could still smell her perfume. And she had loved that car because, she said, it meant she would never have to take the train again. Words with new meaning.

The neon sign from the drugstore across the street flashed a wedge of light across the table where my notepad was. Using just that sliver of light, I began a list of what I needed. I already had my passport. I'd need to pack a few changes of clothes. Was it warmer in France than New York? Ask Helen to stop by the apartment once in a while to pile the mail on the table. Sell the car. The superintendent of the building had once asked if it was for sale. First thing in the morning, I would ask him if he still wanted it.

Such a short list of to-dos. How easy to uproot a life, to leave it behind. How extraordinarily painful to leave all that was familiar. How exhilarating.

I would have to send William a letter. I owed him at least that much. And Jack. Just thinking of Jack made me light-headed. One night with Jack had changed everything. And yet I hadn't called him since I left the inn. I had been busy with the article, with deciding about William. And there was some fear there, as well, that his feelings weren't as strong as mine.

Were he and Janet going to divorce? Even if they did, it would be a while before he would want to begin a new relationship. But we already had one. That much couldn't be denied. Whether or not there was a future for us was the question. A very large question, because I also remembered the disdain with which he had said *working girl* when we first talked.

I found the card with the inn's number on it at the bottom of my purse. This had to be done before I left. I couldn't leave, not knowing.

Jack picked up on the third ring.

"Brennan's Inn," his voice said over the line. A voice already sweetly familiar.

"It's me. Alana."

A pause. "Alana. After you left, I realized I didn't have your phone number. I've been waiting for you to call."

"Were you?" Joy flooded through me. "I've been a little preoccupied. Sorry."

"I know. Work and all that." No disdain in his voice this time. Sympathy. Regret.

"And the fiancé," he added.

"Jack, I'm not engaged anymore."

"Aren't you? Good. I mean, sorry. I mean, I hope it's not because of me."

"Largely because of you." I pictured him at the reception desk, leaning on it, his hair catching the lamplight, his shirt open at the collar, and his tie hanging loose at the end of a long workday.

"Good," he said. "I like the sound of that. I miss you, Alana."

"Jack, I'm going away for a while. I'm not sure how long."

"Then I'll have to wait. And I will. But I expect to be the first person you call when you get back. We have unfinished business, Alana. A lot of it. Maybe a lifetime's worth."

When I hung up, there was one thing about which I was certain. How I felt about Jack. I was in love in a way I hadn't been with William.

Think about that later, I ordered myself. *Now pack, get the apartment in order, and go beg Helen to let you stay with her a few days till you can leave New York.* If there were going to be any knocks on my door by men with badges, I wouldn't be sitting here waiting for them. My gaze went to the bookshelf opposite me, to the top shelf where the urn with my mother's ashes rested.

She had insisted on cremation, complaining that fancy caskets were a waste of money. That is what happens when you are a young widow raising a child in Manhattan. You worry about the cost of hamburger, next year's rent increase, the price of your own funeral.

I did not know where she was born or if she still had family somewhere. But I knew where she had spent three important months of her life, and I would take some of the ashes there.

Three months. With Sara and Gerald. With Picasso. What if that math was correct, and Marti had already been pregnant when she married the man who leaned over my crib when I was a baby, the one whose name I carried. What if . . .

We think we know the past because it is over. But we never really do. It will always have its secrets, just like my mother. And I was about to leave behind all that I knew and go into the unknown. I was going to get even more lost, to swim into an ocean of unknowns and hope the horizon might be revealed.

The unknown. I scratched a name at the end of my to-do list.

Françoise Gilot was leaving Picasso. His lover of the past decade, the mother of two of his children, was walking out on him, according to Sara. His mood, even if I found him, was likely to be less than gracious. I might not even get in the door. I must try. Think of what was over there in the Midi, the rooms of art, some of it still unexhibited, and the very presence of the man, the world's greatest artist.

My father, perhaps.

The packing and list making were done, I had loaded my purse with my passport and pen case and an extra notebook, and I was just about to change into my pajamas when a knock sounded at the door. An angry, impatient knock. On the other side of the door, framed like a cameo in the door's security peephole, stood two men with hard expressions on their faces.

McCarthy's men.

Even though they couldn't see me, I cringed away from the door. They knocked again, and that knock heralded the end of my ambition. A staff position with the magazine. Not possible.

And Jack. How could I see him again, allow myself to love him, if I would be doing him harm? Because I would be. His inn would be put under surveillance. He might be questioned. It didn't matter that he was a war vet. McCarthy didn't care about such details.

Get out of here, I ordered myself. *Now.*

Tiptoeing through the tiny living room, I picked up the small suitcase I'd packed. A board creaked. I froze midstep. The knocking grew more insistent. Through the kitchen, to the fire escape, clambering down to the alley.

I slept at Helen's apartment that night, and when I dreamed, I dreamed in Spanish. I spoke the infrequently murmured phrases of my childhood, when my mother would forget and say *por favor* to a store clerk instead of *please* or *lo siento* when she pulled my hair when combing it. A world of words had been stored in my memory, words she hadn't wanted me to use because they, too, were part of the past. But they were there, waiting.

A week later, I was in France taking the train down south from Paris. I had landed the day before, bedraggled from the Pan Am flight that had left me on a French tarmac tired and uncertain, my dress crumpled, my hair flying like storm clouds around my face, after that long night over the Atlantic.

People bustled all around, mostly French, but also American servicemen still in uniform, businessmen, a few wives traveling with those men, and their very young children, all in the same age group, it seemed, born in those years just after the war when getting back to normal meant home, marriage, family. Sara's generation had been the lost one, but there was a new generation crowding round my knees at the luggage retrieval station and in the restrooms.

Painfully aware of how little money I was traveling with and with no sense of how long I intended to stay in France, I decided to be as miserly as possible. No taxi for me. Balancing my suitcase and French phrase book in my hands, tottering on heels I realized were too high for traveling, I resolved to stick to the Parisian subways and trains.

Under the airport terminal, I found the metro stop that would take me into Paris, to Les Halles, where I would have to change trains and get on a different line going to the Gare de Lyon. I elbowed my way through the crowd and found a seat.

The people traveling by metro seemed a world removed from the wealthier airport groups heading for the taxi stands. They were a little more threadbare and exhausted looking. The bus fumes, the noises, the blue fog of cigarette smoke, the crowding, didn't affect them; they barely looked up when they heard an American asking an older woman in badly accented French if this was the correct train for the Gare de Lyon. I was as invisible and anonymous as I was in the New York subway, and this reassured me.

Blend in, my mother had frequently told me. *Don't call attention to yourself.*

I could have flown from Paris to Nice rather than take an all-night train, but with my budget, that was out of the question. Besides, Anna Martina would not have flown. There had been no flights when she fled, and I was making this journey for her as well as myself. Just being in France was already making me feel closer to my mother. The jar of her ashes in my suitcase never left my thoughts.

The Gare de Lyon, when I arrived hours later, was cavernous and beautiful with its huge arching glass vault and its restaurant with the gilded frescoed ceiling. It served meals that any five-star restaurant in New York would have been proud of, even if the shortages had kept the menu brief. I allowed myself a bowl of onion soup for lunch, a cup of strong coffee, and then browsed the magazine stands on the platform until the evening train departure. I bought a postcard of Notre-Dame and a stamp, and mailed it to Sara with no message on the back but *Thank you for the address*. She would know that I meant Pablo's location.

She wanted forgiveness from the daughter of the woman she had betrayed, and that would have to come in time. But what I felt now was my mother's hurt and fear after that betrayal. First, that must be put to rest.

Then I sent a second postcard to Jack. This was even harder to write. One night. That was what we'd had. And it had changed the trajectory of my life. *Miss you*, I wrote. Would he know how much those words actually meant?

Paris waited for me outside the station, but I was too tired and too focused on the purpose of this trip to be distracted by sightseeing. *Later*, I promised myself. *After I have spoken with Pablo Picasso.*

If I get to speak with him, if he opens that door. If he does, what will he see? A stranger, or Anna's daughter? Will he remember?

NINETEEN

· · · · · · · · · · · · · ·

Alana

The air changes when you reach the Midi, the South of France. It becomes soft and fragrant. South of Lyon in the early morning, I woke up to the smell of flowers and herbs. Warmth. Even in late October, the sun was so bright that shadows stood out like well-drawn silhouettes against the rumpled cushions, and magazines littered the floor of the train.

I had spent the night sitting up in the second-class compartment of the Blue Train. Not for me, those gilded cars and five-course dinners served in first class. My neck was stiff, my hands numb from poor sleep. Other passengers began to stir, stretching and yawning, unpacking hampers with thermoses of coffee, waxed paper packets of sandwiches. Children whimpered; little dogs jabbed the air with sharp yips.

I had never before woken up to the sound of fussy, demanding children, and the noise startled me. It was not unpleasant, any more than the sound of a baby bird calling for its mother is.

Once, when I was a child, a pigeon nested on my windowsill in a secret corner behind a pot of geraniums. When the nest was finished, I could watch her sitting on the two perfect eggs and then feeding the squeakers after they hatched. I couldn't open my window for that entire month, but waking up to the sound of tiny pigeons calling for breakfast enchanted me.

My mother watched with me and always hugged me closer as we sat on the bed together. "She will do anything to keep them safe," she said. "She is a good mother."

Good mother, good mother, the train wheels clicked over the rails.

Soon the air changed again to something more acrid, more urban, and the train passed through the rough-and-tumble port of Marseilles, a city of sailors and merchants and all the things that went with them, the taller buildings, grimy warehouses, laborers in leather aprons, streetwalkers in the train station.

The train made several stops before continuing on to Antibes, and Vallauris would be a short bus trip after that. Picasso lived in Antibes, but his studio was in Vallauris, and I thought I might try him at work rather than at home. There would be many people coming and going, I supposed. I might blend in for a while, get my bearings before I approached Picasso.

We followed the coastline, and I could see boats on the azure Mediterranean on one side, pines, olive groves, and fields of lavender planted in neat rows on the other as we passed by. My mother, who had come from Spain, would have looked out a similar train window and seen the same olive groves and fields of flowers, boats floating on the impossibly blue waters.

This had been Vichy France during the war, unoccupied by the Germans but ruled by Marshal Philippe Pétain, a collaborator who followed the Nazi plan to turn all of France into an anti-Semitic, conservative, traditionalist country. *Pétain and Senator McCarthy would have had much to talk about*, I thought. *Much in common*. Pétain had been tried for treason after the war and sentenced to death, but De Gaulle commuted the sentence to life imprisonment. The old general had died, insane and feeble, just two years before in a prison citadel on a small island in the Atlantic.

My mother had read the death announcement in the *New York Times* and left the paper folded open to that page for me to read as well. "This kind of man," she had said, "men who want everyone to look alike, think alike—they killed the avant-garde in France. Except for Picasso. No one can destroy Picasso."

In Sara's story, my mother is speaking from experience, not opinion. During my years of graduate school, researching Picasso, studying his works, my mother never mentioned she had known him. She spoke kindly of him yet never acknowledged a relationship with him. He had been part of the past she had walked away from.

In the late afternoon, I arrived in Antibes. the ancient town first built by the Greeks, my little guidebook announced, a town of fig trees and artichoke beds, cobbled hilly streets. After the Greeks had come the Romans and then medieval architects who left behind Romanesque towers and castles. Later, Napoleon had walked its narrow streets. His nobly born mother, impoverished by the revolution, had washed Napoleon's linens in a stream here.

Across the bay was Nice. The two cities faced each other like welcoming old friends or warring enemies, depending on the politics of the times. The bay is called the Bay of Angels because it is shaped like wings. Angels' wings. What was that song Sara had mentioned? "Come Down, Angels, and Trouble the Water."

The woman at the information desk in the Gare de Lyon had warned me that finding accommodation in Vallauris would be difficult. "It's just a village," she had said. "Full of potters and workmen and their families. Most of them work now for Picasso in the ceramic studio. No," she said, "you had better stay in Antibes."

"With the other Americans," I heard her mutter as I walked away.

She had been right about that. Antibes, now that the war was over, was full of Americans come to enjoy the sun, the beaches, the restaurants, to follow in the footsteps of the Greeks, the Romans, Napoleon.

Sara probably knew from her correspondence with Pablo and other friends in France how her sleepy fishing village of the 1920s had been changed into a bustling resort town of the 1950s. The little secret place where she had been happy with her husband and their children was gone now, and with it, one more tie to her dead boys was severed. I felt that as keenly as Sara must have. My hours with her had given me a stronger sense of the past than my mother had given, and with that sense came a quicksilver grief for what had been lost. *That sadness*, I thought, *was what my mother had tried to protect me from when she insisted I always face forward to the future.*

The tiny beach that Gerald had created by raking away sand was greatly expanded, I suppose, and full of strangers' towels, little bottles of suntan lotion, copies of *Look* magazine carried over in luggage. The private little shore filled with seagull cries and the laughter of three small children—four if I include Paulo, Picasso's son—would be filled with the shouts of strangers.

I decided to find a little hotel or guesthouse as far from the expensive beachfront hotels as I could get. The price would be better, and I wouldn't be inundated by all those American voices with accents even worse than mine, asking their way to the Bastion Saint-André on the ocean ramparts, the gardens of the Villa Thuret, and the lighthouse that is in the center of the little peninsula that is Antibes.

I found Madame Rosa's guesthouse in the late morning after an hour of poking around corners, taking wrong turns down narrow streets, lugging my suitcase. It had been recommended by a man in a magazine kiosk outside the train station when I asked about inexpensive guesthouses. Madame's house, tucked away in a palm-tree-studded garden at the top of a gentle hill, was small and apricot-colored. Her pet parrot sat on a perch by the front door and welcomed me with a loudly squawked "*Vos chaussures! Vos chaussures!*" an instruction to remove my shoes. I was grateful. My toes were covered with blisters.

I stood in the doorway waiting, and Madame Rosa came hurrying down the hall, her bright red hair flying behind her like a banner. She was of a certain age, as the French kindly say of older women, and her hands, when she reached over to take my suitcase, were mottled and gnarled, yet she lifted the suitcase with ease.

"Ignore him, that rude bird," she said. I barely followed her heavily accented French, and when she saw my confusion she switched to English. "The bird, he is left here by my Japanese friend," she said. "He come often, but not now, not since the war. So I get bird."

"And parrots live a very long time, I understand."

She laughed. "He will live past me," she agreed. "Maybe you take him with you."

There were four guest rooms, and I took the last one available, an attic that once had probably been servants' quarters. But the room was clean, the bed was soft, the linens smelled of lavender, and the sun streamed in a window framed with faded blue toile curtains. The sun was so warm when it touched me

that it felt like a blouse just come off the ironing board, and I
had a flash of memory, my mother ironing my school uniform
in the early morning, quizzing me on the rivers of the world as
she worked.

"I'll take it," I told Madame Rosa.

"Good," she said. "With board? My cook makes the best
cassoulet in Antibes. For how long?"

"A week?" I guessed. "Maybe longer."

"You stay longer," Madame predicted. "I can tell by the
look in your eyes. Are you making your holidays?"

"Yes," I said, too tired to go into the truth of why I was
there.

Helen and I had decided on a simple plan: if two weeks went
by and there were no more appearances of strange men asking
for me, it would be safe to come back home. She couldn't know
if they went to my apartment or not, but she could keep track
of Reed's office. He had agreed to tell Helen if he had more
visits. I hoped that by the time I returned, the professor's appearances before the committee would have come to an end
and they would have moved on to other prey or, better, realized
that they were doing more harm to democracy than good.

There was always the chance that they had been looking for
me to testify against Grippi, not to defend myself. But if he had
named me and other students, then the follow-up would be
swift . . . or not at all.

None of this was to be discussed casually, certainly not with
Madame Rosa, who reminded me of the women who sat on my
apartment stoop in the hot weather gossiping. Also not ready
to be discussed casually with anyone were the matters of my
plans to meet with Picasso or my plans for my mother's ashes.
There was no way I could set a timeline for the resolution of
either of those things. I was in unknown territory, physically

and emotionally. Perhaps I was learning why people keep secrets: say some things out loud and it might close the door to other solutions and possibilities. And other things are kept secret because they are dangerous.

Madame Rosa's comfortable guest room reminded me of Brennan's Inn. It smelled the same, of lavender sachet pods from the hall linen closet and stale smoke and the dust of many years, accumulated where dusters and vacuums couldn't reach. Madame Rosa brought me a pile of fresh towels and a bottle of water for the night table. When she closed the door behind her, I fell onto the bed exhausted. My dreamless sleep lasted for hours. When I woke, the room was dark, and a crescent moon hung in the square of sky framed by the window.

There was a gentle buzz of conversation coming from downstairs in the guesthouse and from the street outside the window. The low vibrations of crickets played their gentle percussion for the evening. The air was warm and soft, and even this far from the shore, it had a tang of salt. *I'm in France*, I thought. *I'm in the town where my mother had been. How strange. How wonderful.* I had always planned to come to France, but money had been a problem, William didn't want me to travel without him, and he had no interest in visiting France. I had been broke and busy with work and William. But now I was here.

And then I caught a scent on the evening breeze, sweet and tangy, and memories flooded back, that old and shapeless memory of being on my mother's knee, the same scent tickling my nose.

She had brought me here as a child, as an infant. I was sure of it.

The realization made me sit back on the bed in shock. Why had we come here? And why had she never mentioned it afterward, made it part of the secrets we had lived with. I felt like someone who is asked to explore an unknown room while blindfolded. I could only move forward hoping for eventual clarity, for the truth of my mother's life.

My stomach rumbled. I had slept through lunch and dinner, and I was hungry. The toilet and washroom were down the hall, and because I was occupying the only guest room on the floor, I had them to myself, so I took a long shower of mostly cold water. I dressed in a fresh shirt and skirt and, with wet hair bundled on top of my head, went downstairs.

"Ah, our American is awake." Madame was on her front terrace, smoking, her cigarette making orange designs in the darkness. "Did you have a good sleep, yes?"

"Very good." Now that I was more alert than when we first met, I noticed that she was even older than I had first assumed, in her seventies if not more. Her hair was dyed an impossible Titian red, and she wore bright scarlet lipstick painted in a bow shape that ignored most of her natural lip line. Her eyebrows were plucked and arched. She looked like a woman who had found her style many years before, in the flapper era, and stuck with it. It was not an unpleasant appearance. In fact, it had a nostalgic charm to it that put me at ease.

"Hungry?" she asked. "Dinner ended hours ago, but I put some aside for you in the warming oven. Stay. I'll bring out a plate for you and some wine."

We sat on the terrace together in the warm evening air, and I ate fried codfish with olives and green beans with garlic as Madame, with little urging from me, told me the story of how she had come to the Midi from Paris and why she stayed. There had been a lover—so many of her stories began with lovers—and she followed him to the Antibes, where he tried to find work as a chef. But he burnt the roasts and curdled the custards. Once here, she realized she loved the Midi more than the man, so when he returned to Paris, she stayed on.

"That was in 1922, and I am still here," she said, lighting another cigarette. "It was very hard at first. There was so little here. Just a small town, everybody knows everybody. There were a few small hotels with short seasons, fishing boats, mad Russian émigrés trying to work at any job they could find. Me too. Maid, cook, governess. I did it all. Badly, I'm afraid."

When she laughed, she choked a little on the cigarette smoke, and I worried that it would be overfamiliar of me to slap her back, so I waited for the coughing spell to end.

"There were other men, of course," she said, winking. "I married, and that is how I came to own my little hotel. It was his mother's house, and when she died, we opened guest rooms. We were one of the first guesthouses in Antibes. Other than us, there were only the bigger hotels, a handful, closer to the ocean. We were friends with Monsieur Sella. He had a hotel, pink like a rose, just a short walk to La Garoupe, the beach. Sometimes he sent people to us, people who could not afford his hotel. So we do okay. And then my husband died."

La Garoupe. Sara's beach. And Sella's hotel was where she had stayed. My mother and Picasso, too.

"You knew Monsieur Sella?"

"Yes, of course. Everyone here knew him."

"Did you know an American woman, Sara Murphy? She was here in twenty-three. With her husband and children."

"Murphy? No, I don't remember."

"There was a maid at the hotel then . . ."

Madame Rosa interrupted. "There were many maids at the hotel. Mostly they didn't stay." She grew silent and finished her cigarette. "Sad thing, to be alone at this age. This is why I talk so much. Are you married?" she asked when that cigarette, too, had been crushed under her shoe.

I didn't answer, disappointed that Madame Rosa didn't remember Sara or my mother. To be so close and still so far.

"No? Perhaps . . ." She didn't finish the sentence.

"I was supposed to be married. At Christmas."

"I don't often talk to strangers like this," she said instead. "But I like your face. Brides don't usually frown like that when they talk about their wedding."

"I think you are right." I had finished my dinner by then and pushed the plate away. The night was dark in a way it never was in New York except during the war, when we had closed our curtains and the streetlamps were not turned on in case of German planes. This darkness had a very different quality from that wartime darkness: it was velvety and comforting, not menacing. I leaned back in the creaking wicker chair and breathed deeply.

"Be careful," Madame Rosa said. "You might end up like me, staying. My friend Irène, the painter, always says she will stay—she likes it here very much—but then, after a few days, she goes back to Paris, to her husband, and to painting."

Irène is not an uncommon name in France. But I had nothing to lose, so I sat up straighter and leaned closer to Madame so that I could speak softly. There were noises now from inside her little hotel, people talking, laughing, in a room close to the terrace.

"Not Irène Lagut, by any chance?"

"You know of her? Yes, her."

The shock of this good fortune made me wish I hadn't eaten quite so heartily. I felt a little queasy.

"That was her name before she married," Madame said. "For many, many years now, she's Madame Cadenat. Her husband is a doctor. She married him in twenty-three, just after Pierre and I opened our guesthouse. She stayed here soon after her honeymoon for a rest."

Sara had mentioned that Irène had married after refusing Pablo Picasso's proposal. That must have left a scar. Had Sara sensed that perhaps some of Picasso's sexual restlessness that summer had been because of the rejection, that betrayal of Irène refusing him but marrying another? Antibes, in that moment, became the center of my world. Most of what I wanted was here or had led me here. Pablo Picasso. Irène Lagut, whom I had wanted to write about, but David Reed had insisted I write about Picasso. And here was at least part of my mother's secret past mixed in with Sara Murphy's.

Madame Rosa pursed her heavily lipsticked mouth and blew out, puffing her cheeks. "That woman. Rest is the last thing she wants. Energy, energy! Never have I met a woman with more energy."

Irène had come to the Midi that summer. She had taunted Olga, whom Picasso had married after Irène had rejected him, and Picasso had painted a portrait of her that summer in the studio.

A flush of hope washed over me, soft as the evening air. If Picasso wouldn't speak with me, perhaps Irène would. I could interview her, write about her, and somehow convince David Reed that it was time for *Art Now* to feature an article about Irène Lagut, the overlooked French artist who had known Picasso, who had been part of that wild and furious post–World War I avant-garde, experimenting with art and life, making images that shocked with their boldness, their untamed colors and freedom.

"Does Irène Lagut still visit?" I asked.

"Not as much. Her husband is a very important man, a

surgeon, a member of the Legion of Honor for his work. She has a daughter, also a doctor. There is much for her to do in Paris. But sometimes, yes, she comes to Antibes and visits with me, her old friend. I am good at keeping secrets." Madame winked.

"I would like to write about Irène Lagut. About her art," I said. "But my editor wants a piece on Picasso."

She threw up her arms in delight. "When you leave, you must go to Paris. You must meet. I will arrange this for you."

Something small stirred in the shrubbery near the inn. There was a hopeful *meow*, and Madame Rosa took from her pocket a piece of fish she had saved from dinner. An orange cat with ragged ears emerged and took the fish from her hand. She waited for it to finish the scrap. When he sat and watched her, hoping for more, she patted his head. He purred loudly.

"This is Tomas," she said with affection. "A great hunter. No mice in my kitchen."

From the doorway, the parrot squawked in alarm.

"Hush," Madame shouted back. "I'll *vos chaussures* you!"

"What about Pablo Picasso?" I asked, feeling as hopeful as the cat waiting for a second helping of cod. "Do you know him, by any chance?"

"Ah, the great man. Very great, though when I first saw him, he was not so great. We have met, yes. In the old days, when Antibes was still a *petit village*. He would come into town and eat in the café sometimes. With his friends. Some Americans who came here in the summer before all the others started coming here. It was so very quiet in the summer, you understand, before then. When first I came here. In the nights, all you could hear were the cicadas singing."

Madame Rosa lit another cigarette and gazed off into the distance.

As far away from the beach as we were, we could hear the low hum of music and laughter that came from the hotel terraces, even in the off-season. "Sometimes," she sighed, "I miss the quiet. Why do you want to know about Picasso? Isn't it enough to see his paintings?"

"I think he was a friend of my mother's." How strange that still sounded to my ears. I had barely said aloud to anyone, even myself, that he might be my father. "They met here in Antibes. That would have been in 1923." I didn't say that I would be writing about him. People can grow very quiet when they learn you are a journalist, that you are taking notes.

"And she did not tell you all she could about him? Why is that?" Madame lit another cigarette.

"She kept secrets."

"Ah. That is a hard thing about secrets, that you don't know people have them till you begin to discover them, and suddenly you must question so much. What is the truth if so much has been hidden? So you make a pilgrimage to find out what your mother did not say. *Bien*. This is what I know about Picasso. Very good-looking man. He had what they call in your Hollywood sex appeal, yes? Women could not resist him. Those eyes, so dark. He was quieter than most men in the cafés. He did not drink heavily. He stayed alert. He watched. He listened. Sometimes he would take out a pencil and make a sketch on the paper tablecloths." Madame Rosa made a drawing motion with her hand, tilted her head back, and looked at the drawing she was seeing in her memory.

"He drew me one evening," she said. "Very pretty. But Pierre, he was jealous and tore it up. Aieee. We could have sold it, had some good money for it. Already Pablo was so well known that the innkeepers would save those sketches. They were worth money, but Picasso, he drew because he must. And he liked to look at the girls. In that, he was like the other men, but you could not tell which girl would take his interest. Always he looked, I think, for the interesting nose or mouth, not just the prettiness. Me, for instance, when my friend Jean-Marc first-time introduced me to him, Picasso looked at my birthmark."

She pointed to a brown spot over her right eyebrow about the size of the nail on my little finger.

"It is shaped like Spain," he told me. "Very nice. I used to wear my hair in a fringe, to hide it. But after that, I let all the hair grow, I show my forehead. I have a mark shaped like Spain, and Pablo Picasso admired it."

"And?" I prompted.

"You wonder what else happened between me and the irresistible man." She laughed. "Nothing. I was busy, I was in love; he was busy, he was in love. We meet, we say hello, and that was all."

"Who was he in love with?"

"Not his poor wife, we all saw that. At least no more. I heard he was even bored on his honeymoon. And still in love a little with Irène, though he was very, very angry with her. Bitter. But not so bitter he would throw her out of his bed. No, he did not allow himself to suffer. There were women. He was very busy that summer."

Madame laughed, and Tomas the cat, seeing that his meal would not include seconds, stalked back into the shrubs.

"Do you ever see Picasso now? In town?"

"Now? No. He has grown older. We all do. But he has become so rich, so successful, he begins to avoid people. And his woman, Gilot, has just left him, so he is not in the best mood. He is tired of all the people who come here looking for him. The people from the papers. People with their cameras. Now he wants his privacy. He stays in his villa, in his workshop. Away from us and the tourists."

I was glad I hadn't mentioned I was a journalist.

But Sara's news about Pablo was out of date. Françoise wasn't thinking of leaving him. She already had. My heart sank. I had come all this way to speak with a man who was angry and bitter and avoiding people. Who already disliked journalists. A man. Maybe my father.

"Now," Madame said. "You sleep some more. Get rid of those dark patches under your eyes. Are you ill?"

I spent the next day orienting myself: walking, eating salty, thick-crusted *pissaladière* from corner kiosks, thinking, planning. Antibes, despite its many tourists, charmed me with its cobbles, its old walls and Romanesque church. But it was the ocean, always the ocean, that drew my attention. I walked streets that led to it, sat on benches that faced it.

How does water get that blue, the sails of boats that white?

It was warm enough in October that people were still swimming and sunbathing, and I wondered how much time Picasso spent watching sunbathers, those girls in their new stylish bikinis. The seawall was dotted with men of all ages gazing with hungry eyes. Desire and sexuality added tang to the ocean air, making me remember that night with Jack. There were moments when I felt weak from desire for him, but that was quickly followed by shock that William had never had that effect on me.

He will keep you safe, my mother had said of William. She never asked me how I felt about him. Had my mother loved the man she called husband? Marti, Anna Martina, had insisted that safety and security were the most important things in life. She had never mentioned love. She kept secrets.

She had left France and Antibes already carrying a child inside her, another secret. Sara had suspected that she was a girl "in trouble" when they first met on the train, but if the puzzle she put together is correct, Anna became pregnant after fleeing to France, not before.

Later that afternoon, I sent a telegram to Helen, letting her know where I was and the name of the guesthouse where I was staying so that we could stay in touch. New York seemed very far away. A world away, and I was in France doing something my mother had always warned against: looking backward.

But also forward, I argued back with her in my thoughts. The future could grow out of one interview with Pablo Picasso, who did not want to speak with journalists. *He will speak to me*, I decided. *I'll find a way*. And that made me think of Jack, who had given me flowers to bring to Sara, and the flowers had opened the memories for her, made her willing to speak with me.

I sent a telegram to William, too. I hadn't seen him since that evening at the restaurant, when he wouldn't take back the engagement ring, wouldn't let me end the engagement. "In France for a while," I wrote. "Talk when back." I chewed the end of the pencil and considered. "Not wearing the ring," I added.

When I returned to Madame Rosa's little guesthouse hours later, tired from walking and sunburnt because I had not worn a hat, there was a message already tacked to my door. William had gone to the trouble and expense of making a transatlantic phone call.

That gesture moved me more than anything else William had done, more than the bouquets of roses on my birthday, the expensive dinners out, the large diamond of my engagement ring. He wanted to know if I was safe. He wanted me to know he missed me.

Our quarrel, my infidelity, had been pushed aside, and he was my William again, forgiving and generous. I felt gratitude. And knew that wasn't enough.

I had dinner at the guesthouse, both to please Madame Rosa, who was eager for me to experience her table and the skills of her cook, and to see what the other guests were like. I needed some distraction, because tomorrow was going to be a very important day. Tomorrow, I would try to meet Pablo Picasso. The great artist. My mother's lover, perhaps.

That evening, the table in Madame's dining room was full. There were two English ladies in their sixties who had come to see the Romanesque church and the old Greek walls of the town, a couple from Paris whose doctor had recommended the ocean air for the husband's health, and a salesman from Philadelphia who was in Antibes to convince the grand hotels they absolutely needed to buy his American-made porcelain dinnerware.

When I entered the little dining room, they looked up at me and murmured faint greetings before returning to the conversation they'd already started. Marie, Madame's maid, ladled soup into my bowl and put a roll on my bread plate.

"But, monsieur, we make very fine plates here in France," the Parisian woman said, raising her thin, arched eyebrows. "Why would we want yours?"

The salesman grinned. "Ours are affordable," he said. "And they don't break as easily. Hotels don't need heirloom quality," he told the table in general, "they need a good bottom line."

As soon as money was mentioned, the English ladies decided the conversation needed to be steered to loftier topics.

"I hear that artist Picasso lives nearby," said the one who wore her hair in a bun. Her companion had styled her hair into a cloud of gray curls.

"All that strange modern stuff," said her companion, sipping delicately from her soup spoon. "Never understood it. Give me a Renoir or Monet any day. Look at those, and you know what you're looking at."

Madame Rosa, sitting at the head of the table, winked at me over her wineglass. She had dressed for dinner in a straight sheath whose beaded fringe sounded like gentle rain on a roof when she moved. Between courses, she twisted cigarettes into an elegant ivory holder and blew smoke rings into the air.

The man from Paris turned red. "But," he protested, "we must live in the time we are given, not someone else's time," he said, visibly moved. "Why look at art that was made for people who lived so many years ago?"

It had been my mother's argument, and I liked him instantly.

"But isn't that the whole point of museums?" said the English woman who had started this conversation. "To see history, to experience what others saw and felt and experienced?"

"Museums. Warehouses," said the Parisian woman, patting her already smoothly brushed-back hair into even sterner lines. "Fine and good for what they are. But we must pay attention to our living artists, not just the dead ones."

"Picasso," said the salesman, obviously irritated that the talk had excluded further promotion of his tableware. "The guy who puts noses on foreheads."

Madame Rosa laughed. "Yes, that one," she agreed. She was a good hostess. She would not correct a guest. But when the apple tart with cream was brought out, she gave him the smallest portion. I wondered if Jack, at his inn, ever resorted to that kind of revenge for irritating guests. One piece of bacon at breakfast instead of two.

"What is funny, mademoiselle?" asked the Parisian woman, because I had laughed out loud at Madame Rosa's vengeful portions. "You are from New York? Do you know the Rosenberg gallery?"

"I have spent quite a bit of time in the gallery," I said. "My mother and I often went there."

"Such a crime, the war and the Germans made Monsieur Rosenberg move to New York," the Parisian woman said. "So many crimes. So, you know Picasso's work? What is your impression?"

"I know his work well. He's a genius." Such a simple statement hiding so much. That I was there to force a meeting with him. That he had been my mother's lover. That he might be my father. *Not really dinner conversation*, I thought.

"Bad reputation," said the plate salesman. "Hard on the womenfolk."

"As are many artists. And bankers, for that matter. Or plumbers," said the Parisian man, and his wife lowered her eyes to her plate of apple tart.

"Picasso's paintings can be very challenging because he was fearless," I told the salesman. "But he could also be very gentle and even traditional. You should look at his very early work. *First Communion*, for instance, painted when he was still in Barcelona. It would please even you."

"As an American," the Parisian husband asked, "what do you make of this McCarthy type? He who hunts down all communists and their friends? A strange country, yours, maybe not so free as some like to say."

"Here, we openly discuss such things," his wife agreed. "Here, it is not dangerous to speak of politics."

"Some might disagree with that statement," said one of the English ladies. She said no more but had a distant look in her eyes, and I wondered what she was thinking of. Whom she was remembering.

"Picasso is openly communist. Has been since the war, when one had to choose between being fascist or communist," Madame Rosa added.

"I agree it is better to be open, that people should be free to speak their minds. And live their ideals," I said. I did not add that it seemed I was one of those people that McCarthy's men wanted to question.

TWENTY

·············

ALANA

In the early morning, bathed in a strong yellow light already warm with the promise of noontime heat, I stared hard in the mirror at the stranger that was myself. She stared back, looking both skeptical and amused. But her hands were shaking so much she could barely button her blouse.

"*Valor,*" I heard my mother whisper. Courage. That had been her answer to difficulties.

Imagine, I ordered myself, *how Pablo Picasso may feel about this situation. You cannot walk up to him and say, "Hi. I'm your daughter, I think. Your American daughter. Remember that hotel maid?"* He would assume I wanted something. Perhaps money. But it was truth I wanted, my mother's secrets opened to daylight.

The stranger in the mirror had a warning in her eyes, the same look my mother gave me when she thought I was taking too great a risk, walking alone late at night or refusing a job with secure income so I could continue freelancing as an art writer. *You are not here to confront a man who might or might not be your father*, the woman in the mirror warned. *You are here to interview the most famous artist of the twentieth century because you need this interview to write that article, to get that position at the magazine.*

But part of me wanted to say that one word to him: *father*. It's primal, I suppose. Children need to know these things. But I was not a child. I'd be thirty soon. I had lived all my life thinking of, knowing, Pablo Picasso as a great artist, the subject of much of my studies in art. Nothing more than that.

Right, I said back to the mirror image, who was no longer a stranger but my mother looking back at me. I hadn't realized how much I looked like her. *I'm here to interview an artist so famous he now shuns the press and journalists and most strangers in general, it seems. And I've come just when he's been wounded and rejected by his woman, Françoise Gilot.* Could I have picked a worse time? But then, I didn't exactly pick this time. I left New York because I needed to, and quickly. *But, Françoise, couldn't you have stayed with him just one more month?* What a difference it could have made to me, to have Picasso in a happier frame of mind.

Birds sang outside the window. I smelled coffee and bread fresh from the bakery. Madame Rosa's voice filtered up from downstairs, a high-pitched staccato. She was agitated, as she usually seemed to be when she discussed food. "The fish we had for lunch yesterday was not fresh enough," she complained. I had enough college French to understand that much. After even just two days in her guesthouse, I knew she would be waving her arms for emphasis; her Cupid's-bow mouth would be pursed.

The cook muttered something I couldn't hear. A door slammed. The day was beginning at Madame Rosa's. My day was beginning as well. I would walk to the bus stop and take the local to

Vallauris, to the ceramics studio that Picasso had established there, where he produced pitchers and plates and statues with noses on their foreheads, as the salesman had said.

Highly inaccurate, of course. I had seen photos of the ceramics, and they were largely representational, with recognizable people and animals as subjects. They were joyous and primitive images, sometimes using as few as seven brushstrokes to render the subject. They had the energy and joie de vivre of young things. Moreover, they could be produced in quantity, and Picasso had made it clear throughout his career that he did not value poverty.

"The hair," Madame Rosa said, looking up when I entered the dining room. She had been folding napkins but came over to me and retied the scarf I had put around my neck. "The hair is not right," she said. "Perhaps more like this." She pushed my hair behind my ears and twisted it into a single very unfashionable braid that reached to the back of my neck.

"There. Now you could be a pretty woman from anywhere, anytime." She stepped back to assess her work. "Better to show your face. And don't forget to take your lunch at my brother-in-law's café. In the market across from the Church of Saint Anne. It is easy to find. He will give you a good price and a good meal."

"Café of the Dancing Goat," I repeated from the information she had given me last night, after dinner. I had told her I planned to visit the ceramics factory, and she had nodded vigorously with approval, then given me a long list of instructions. Where I was to eat. What I was to eat and when. What to say to the bus driver, who might not leave me at the right stop.

"And don't talk to strangers on the street," she had concluded, making me feel as if I were a child again, still under my mother's care.

The bus from Antibes to Vallauris took almost half an hour to travel the five-mile distance. We stopped at every corner, it seemed, for people to get on or off. At every curve in the road, which were many, the bus slowed to a crawl. The scenery was beautiful, unlike anything I had ever seen before: little hills dotted with the top-heavy umbrella pines of the Midi, fields of cultivated lavender, sheared now of their fragrant summer flowers, and long, straight blue-gray rows in the reddish-brown earth. Diminishing ocean vistas would appear and disappear again, inviting and taunting, as the bus moved us farther inland to the hillside *balcones* of Provence.

I thought perhaps tomorrow I would walk instead of taking transport, the better to enjoy the landscape. I would not be able to stay in France long and had no idea when I might be able to return. And that word, *tomorrow*, reassured me. It promised that the interview would continue not just over hours but over days.

The little town of Vallauris, surrounded by vineyards and groves of olive trees, had the distinctive Provençal fragrance of heat and herbs and flowers. After the bus deposited me in the town square, I turned a full circle to take it in, the narrow main street lined with cafés and a few shops, with cobblers and dry goods stores, a vegetable and fruit stand, the ancient stone church at the head of the street presiding over the town like a matriarch.

On my left in the square was a statue of a man carrying a sheep. It is not uncommon to have art in public places, especially town squares, but this piece was unique and unexpected. This strange statue had begun as a series of drawings by Picasso during the occupation of Paris, then had been cast in plaster. After the war, when metals were again available for peacetime use, the statue had been cast in bronze and donated to Vallauris. The man carrying the sheep is naked, emaciated, but larger than life. The lamb he carries looks terrified, with its elongated neck and protruding eyes.

It is not an easy statue to look at. In it, I could see Picasso's reactions to the war: the fear, danger, and death. The lamb looks like a sacrifice about to be made, not the rescued animal of the New Testament, safe in the shepherd's arms.

It was impossible not to be moved by it, not to imagine what the war must have been like for these townspeople who had survived it. My war had been so much easier than theirs; for a few years, I'd done without new clothes and favorite foods, had walked through the blacked-out nights of the city when we listened for the German planes that never arrived. Vallauris had been part of free France, unoccupied France, but they had suffered hunger and cold and fear. The townspeople walked past the statue now, busy with their everyday chores, but there it was in the middle of the town, in the middle of their lives. The reminder, if reminder were needed, of all the war had done.

I had meant to go straight to the pottery studio where Picasso was working. Instead, I decided to acquaint myself with the town first, to walk its narrow cobbled streets, visit the old church, take a meal at the Café of the Dancing Goat. Think about what would come next. How to approach the great man. Here, in France, so close to him physically, I felt the enormity of what lay ahead. And I felt very small.

I drank a coffee at an outdoor café, where golden-tinted red leaves from a chestnut tree scuttled down the street like hurrying mice. What would Marti—Anna Martina—make of this? I wondered. Her daughter, here in France, in the Midi, retracing at least some of her footsteps and preparing to meet the man who had, for a brief time at least, been her lover. Preparing, perhaps, to meet her father.

My courage failed me. When the afternoon bus came and I boarded it once again, I had visited all the public buildings of the town, had an excellent lunch of a spicy chicken stew with lentils, even lit a candle in the church, though I was not religious. I had done everything there was to do in Vallauris except visit the Madoura pottery studio and find Pablo Picasso.

Tomorrow," said Madame Rosa when we were again sitting outside after dinner, she smoking and me feeling ashamed, suffering the sting of failure. Madame knew I was upset because I had not been able to eat much of the splendid dinner at her table and had not joined in the conversation.

Outside in the soft Provençal night, after she had given ragged-eared Tomas his portion of roast pork and scolded the bossy parrot, I told her of my day, how I had avoided the very pottery I had come to visit, the artist I most wanted to speak with.

How, after hours of hesitation, I had returned to Antibes. Was it just jet lag? Fatigue? I felt a new sympathy for my mother, who had wanted above all else to stay safe, to stay in the present. Yet my mother, Anna Martina, Marti, had left a telltale scrap of paper for me to find. Had sent me here to France, to her past, to what had been left behind.

"It is different for men and women, courage," Madame Rosa said. "Yes? Men must be able to fight, to defend. Women must be able to allow them. That was what the war was like, seeing our men of the town go off, for the women to stand straight and not weep, though we knew some would not return. My nephew and me were very close; he did not come back."

She exhaled a large plume of smoke and was silent for a long while, remembering.

I had waited, too, during the war. William was never sent overseas but had become a radio instructor stationed in Alabama. Many of my college friends and colleagues from my early working years had not been safe or fortunate. One boy I had dated briefly died on the beach in Okinawa. Another friend went down with his plane over Midway. Susan, who had planned to earn a PhD in Italian Renaissance fresco paintings, had joined the Red Cross and died at Anzio, in Italy. I thought of Jack at the inn, the leg injury that created the strange gait he had. Would he tell me about it someday, the details of that day, that attack?

"I see strength in you," Madame said, grinding the stub of her cigarette into the grass. The cat took this as a hint that his meal had ended, and he slunk away, tail high, a gray shadow moving into a deeper shadow. "Today I think the stars weren't right. You will go again, try again."

But I woke up the next morning to the golden sound of church bells. Sunday. The pottery and most of the town would be closed. No point in going there. My relief belied what Madame Rosa had promised. My courage was still slumbering. I spent Sunday walking along the ocean promenade, sitting in cafés, jotting thoughts in my notebook, enjoying the smells and sights and textures of Antibes.

Monsieur Sella's pink hotel was there, somewhere close to the beach. I was avoiding it, saving it for some later moment, the right moment. I would know when.

But even as I enjoyed my hours of tourism, spending money only on stops for coffee at sidewalk cafés when I was tired, I wondered what was happening in New York and at Brennan's Inn. I worried that Jack was being careless about rewiring lamps or, worse, falling back in love with his wife. *Wait for me*, I said to him. *I'm coming back soon.*

On Monday, I returned to Vallauris, walking the five miles of dusty road in a pair of canvas espadrilles purchased in Antibes. The shoes were cheaper than the bus back and forth, and the rope soles made the walking easy. The slower pace, the quiet of my own steps instead of the noise of the crowded bus, became almost trancelike. *There is nothing to lose, and much to gain*, I thought. *I can do this.*

When I arrived at the town square in midmorning, it was busy with rushing people in clay-covered aprons, artists and artisans with hands chalky with white slips and clay glazes. The pottery stores in the square were open and doing good business, selling the plates and kitchen vessels the town had been famous for since Roman times, when Vallauris pots and plates had been found in kitchens in all the towns of the Mediterranean.

The Midi pottery had gone out of fashion after easier, long-lasting metal pots and flasks became available at the beginning of the twentieth century. But later, the abandoned factories had begun to reopen during the German occupation because of the shortage of metals. Now the old pottery workshops had been rediscovered and put to use by a new generation of potters and artists who, following Picasso's lead, came to Vallauris from all over France.

Much of the work shown in the stores was a testament to bad taste, produced too quickly and with too little artistry, thanks to new electric kilns and the use of cheap white clay brought in to replace the local red clay that had been used for centuries. Shop displays were filled with souvenirs, clumsy little things that shouted, "I have been to France!" There were many things that were mere imitation Picassos. The worst were the little figures of women that, one shop owner told me, were meant to be portraits of Françoise Gilot, Picasso's woman. Gilot, who had just left Picasso, so that he was becoming reclusive in his bitterness. I put the clumsy, imitative figurine back on the shelf and moved on to the next pottery store.

In the shop closest to the town church, opposite the statue of the man carrying the sheep, was a window displaying Picasso's works: an amphora painted with a goat, plates decorated with a rim of centaurs, another one with sea urchins and eels, a large platter painted with olive branches. A small statuette of a woman that reminded me of an ancient Chinese figurine.

The designs were modern and almost prehistoric at the same time. Picasso had obliterated time; he had made work that stood outside of it. I went in the shop and asked about them but of course could not afford them. And I wouldn't have risked simply putting one of those precious pieces in my luggage and taking it back to New York.

"He requires they be used," the woman in the shop told me. "Not just looked at. They are for the table, not the wall." The doorbell clanged and another customer came in, so she left me standing there admiring them. My mother would have loved these pieces, would have wanted to translate the olive branches into a textile pattern for one of her scarves.

After lunch at the Café of the Dancing Goat, I decided I would go to Picasso's studio. *Just go there*, I told myself, *and see what happens*. Picasso worked there every day, the shop woman had told me. The workers made the plates and urns, and then Picasso would reshape them, paint them, turn simple terra-cotta dishes into art.

I followed her directions and walked up a stony hill away from the town to a low, large-windowed industrial building on

Rue de Fournas. It had once been a perfume factory, but Picasso had converted it into a studio. This was a more isolated part of the town, with fewer passersby and no tourists. I felt and was conspicuous standing there, studying the building as if I needed to count the bricks in the walls.

It was quiet. I could hear the cicadas, those noisy insects that Sara said came to rouse people from midday slumber. When I knocked at the heavy wooden door, the cicadas grew silent for a second, as if I had interrupted their conversation. No one came to the door, even after I knocked two more times.

Across the street from the studio was another old industrial building, a former pottery studio that had been converted into a chair factory, it seemed, with examples of strange things made from iron and rope set outside, I suppose, to attract customers. The chairs looked more like sculptures than chairs and very uncomfortable. A young woman came out of the building to water a pot of geraniums, and when she saw me sitting on a stone by the street, she asked if I was lost, if I needed a glass of water.

I accepted the offer. We sat together, balanced on two of the impractical chairs, and I told her that I had come to speak with Picasso. She didn't ask why, only made that puffing sound and shrug of the shoulders that could indicate any of a hundred different emotions.

"You don't look like a delivery boy," she said. "Or a buyer. But it is not my business, right? He is not so easy, these days. He is angry. More water? You are welcome to sit here and wait, if you wish."

So, there I sat, precariously balanced on steel and rope, and waited. The sun blazed overhead. The cicadas sang, keeping me alert. After an hour or so, a woman came out of Picasso's stu-

dio. It was not Gilot. As crude as the portrait figurines of her
in the town shops had been, they had indicated a round face,
brown hair, eyebrows like circumflexes. This woman had black
hair and a squarish face with prominent cheekbones.

The woman leaned against the studio wall and stared up at
the cloudless sky, not noticing me at first. She stretched and
yawned as if she had been working very hard and for a very
long time in the master's studio. As she probably had been.

When she saw me watching her, she stiffened and dropped
her arms to her side. Her gaze was hostile. She muttered something in French.

I stood and took a step closer. "I would like to meet with
Monsieur Picasso," I said.

Her gaze grew even more hostile. "Not possible," she said.
"Go away." She turned so hard her skirt flared out and then she
went back into the studio, closing the door behind her.

The young woman from the chair factory, who had been
watching us from her chair, shrugged. "Not today, it seems,"
she said.

The woman is Jacqueline Rogue," Madame Rosa said after I
had returned to Antibes, covered in dust and defeat. "I have
heard of her. She is a tough one, that woman, and she will be
Françoise Gilot's replacement. Probably already is. What he
sees in her . . . Well, she is beautiful, of course. And they say
she is complete in her devotion to the master. How you say?
Hand and foot. She waits on him. And possessive. Like a ter-
rier. He has decided to be a recluse, and this Jacqueline keeps
out the world so that he may work."

"Is she the reason why Françoise Gilot left?" We were in

Madame's kitchen shelling peas together, the last of the mottled pods from the garden behind the house, where she also kept a rabbit hutch and chicken coop.

"Perhaps." Madame tossed a pea into her mouth. "There were many women. Françoise would have known this, tolerated it as long as she could. But after a time, it gets to be too much. Françoise Gilot is an artist, too, you know, but living with a man like Picasso, there is no time for your own life, only his. This I learned from my Pierre, the chef."

She used her lacquered red fingernail to slit open the last pod and then lit a cigarette. She had tied a towel over her frizzed red hair, but little wisps of it crept out, falling in her eyes. From the front hall we could hear the parrot talking quietly to himself and squawking occasionally for emphasis.

"Someday, maybe I cook that bird," she said, but I had caught her kissing him on the beak when she thought no one was watching. "This article you write about him. Why?" The question was blunt and direct.

"Because he is well known, and people are interested in him."

"Irène maybe I could arrange. But Picasso I cannot arrange." She took a deep, satisfied draw of her cigarette, and ash fell into her chipped white bowl of peas. "No harm," she said, puffing at the ash to blow it away.

The next morning, I repeated my walk into Vallauris, had my coffee at the little café, and by midmorning was seated again outside Picasso's studio on Rue de Fournas. I'd brought a book to read, a thermos of cold lemonade from Madame's kitchen, a notebook, a pen.

I knocked at the door, knowing it would not be answered, so I sat down again on the strange chair I'd sat in the day before and waited.

Time passed. The sun rose higher in the sky, giving off that strange palpable warmth that was like a garment. I sketched the yellowing clumps of grass, the rocks and grainy soil, the distant gray-green umbrella pines, learning those things better by studying and trying to duplicate their lines, their textures. I had watched my mother do this, take out her sketchbook while sitting on a bus or in the park, shopping—anywhere, really—when a line or color caught her eye.

At noon, when the church bells rang, I had filled many pages of the sketchbook, and my stomach began to rattle. No one had come or gone from the studio; I had seen no faces peering out at me from a window. I considered going back down the hill for lunch. *Stay*, something ordered me. I rubbed my aching back and longed to lie down in the low shrubs and wild herbs, to be engulfed by their soft fragrance. Madame Rosa had warned me, though. There could be scorpions, little brown ones that weren't very dangerous, but a sting would hurt nonetheless.

A few minutes after one o'clock, just as I was about to give up and go for lunch, a girl trudged up the street, leaning against the weight of the hamper she carried. I recognized her from one of the cafés where I had taken coffee. She set the hamper on the step in front of the studio door and knocked. Picasso had had his midday meal delivered.

Jacqueline opened the door and looked warily around me before picking up the hamper. She was wearing a tight white blouse and a full skirt that swayed when she moved. Her lips were painted bright red. She looked like a woman who intended to hold a man's gaze. Picasso's gaze. She saw me sitting there again, and her face turned hard with annoyance

"Go away," she said.

I heard a male voice from inside the studio, asking in French what was wrong, what was happening, ordering her back inside.

Jacqueline said something over her shoulder and glared at me again. "He will not see you," she insisted. "Go away."

More orders from inside: a man's voice, irritated, impatient. Footsteps.

Picasso came to the door. He was older, shorter than I had anticipated, but easily recognizable in his black beret. It must not have been warm enough for him inside his studio, away from the Provençal sun, and he was dressed in heavy trousers, a checked shirt, and a vest. There was a scarf tied tightly around his neck. Deep lines like parentheses framed his face from his nose to his chin, and where the beret didn't cover his head, short bristles of gray showed. But age sat well on him. His movements were quick and precise, like a matador's, who must know in every instant where danger might come from.

There was a paintbrush in his hand, and it dripped onto the floor, a round drop of green like a piece of leaf or a petal that would never grow brown and shriveled. It was a bold green that my mother had favored in her designs.

He hadn't seen me yet. Picasso said something to Jacqueline in French, something angry and impatient. She whispered and gestured with her hands toward me. He followed her gaze, looked where she was looking. Both of them now standing in the doorway, heads turned in my direction.

On impulse, I called out to him, using one of my mother's phrases. "*Necesitamos hablar.*" We need to talk.

His expression changed from annoyance to something different when he saw me, when he heard me. Disbelief? Pleasure? I couldn't tell.

"Anna?" he said.

He stepped out of the shaded doorway into the bright sun. He dropped the paintbrush, and when Jacqueline bent to pick it up, he waved her way, back into the studio, and shut the door behind her.

"Anna?" he repeated, and there was both surprise and pleasure in his voice.

So, he remembered. I took a few steps toward him slowly, as if he were something wild I didn't want to frighten, or perhaps did not want to be frightened by.

"I'm not Anna. I'm her daughter," I said, stumbling through my high school French. Madame Rosa had reminded me that Picasso did not speak English. "Anna. Antibes. The summer of 1923."

"Impossible," he said, but there was now more pleasure in his voice than surprise. He studied me, his eyes moving from feature to feature, from my eyes, my neck, the braid in which Madame Rosa had bound my hair. "*Oui*, I see. There is a difference. Not much." We both had moved closer and were now face-to-face. He reached out as if he would touch my face, then thought better of it.

"I thought she had died," he said. "Guernica."

"She may have gone there when she left Antibes," I said. "But she did not stay. She was gone before the bombing."

"All this time I thought she was dead." Anger now in his voice. A deep crease between his steel-gray eyebrows. "Why did she let me believe she was dead?"

"I don't know."

"Did she ever speak of me?

"Only as an artist. Not as a friend. She never told me that you and she . . . that you had known each other."

We stood in the bright sun studying each other. This man in front of me, with his lined weathered face, his paint-covered hands, his fierce black eyes, had been my mother's lover for a short time. The time before me, the time of the secrets.

What was he seeing? A woman with a black braid and eyes as dark as his own. A woman who reminded him of another woman he had once known. A woman about to break open some of those locked cabinets of the past, to invade his privacy.

And perhaps to give him some answers to his own questions, he realized.

"Come," he said. "Share my lunch. I have questions."

"So do I."

TWENTY-ONE
. . . .

ALANA

Jacqueline muttered a protest, and there were fast angry words between them, but Picasso won the battle. "Leave us," he told her. "Come back later. I will need you again in the studio." Like he was dismissing a servant or a temple acolyte.

She glared at me, and I knew I had made an enemy. She nodded meekly at him, picked up her sweater and purse, and stormed out, her blue skirt whirlwinding around her knees. Once Picasso and I were alone in the studio, I told him what I thought he needed to know at that moment, the apparent official purpose for my visit. The other matter would wait till the ground felt steadier beneath my feet. Anna's daughter had learned some caution.

"I am a journalist." I held up my notepad for him to see.

A look of distaste, of wariness, crossed his face.

"Even so," he said after a long moment of consideration. "Journalists, too, must eat." He made a sweeping arm movement as if he were waving a cape, and when I walked past him to the

table where the hamper sat, I felt his eyes on my back, studying me.

Giving me frequent sideways glances, he opened the hamper
and spread the lunch over the worktable: a bottle of water, a
smaller bottle of white wine, a flatbread dotted with olives and
rosemary and spatters of green olive oil, a bowl of tomato
salad, a plate of cold meat. He spread it evenly between two
plates, giving me Jacqueline's share, but poured the wine only
into my glass, not his.

Picasso had wonderful hands, not large but in proportion to
his height, strong and flexible, with rounded nails and pronounced white crescents at the top of each nail. He handled
things—the plates, the serving spoon and fork—with quick
sureness, the movements of a man who does not drop things or
make clumsy gestures.

I watched him, barely breathing, afraid to break this spell,
the sense of closeness already building between us. I had been
afraid that he wouldn't even remember Anna or accept that I
was her daughter. He would turn me away, and that would be
the end of the story. And here I was, sharing his lunch.

"Anna had an American daughter? You are Anna's daughter?" he asked, putting a plate in front of me. His phrases
slipped between French and Spanish, sensing which I would be
more liable to grasp. "You speak some Spanish?"

"Very little. My mother spoke only English at home, except
for a few phrases."

I am Anna's daughter, I thought. *Am I yours?* Would that
possibility occur to him?

"Tell me, Anna's daughter," he said.

"Tell you what?"

"Everything. She left at night. I went to the hotel one morning, and they said she was gone. No note. No explanation, except that she would go a friend's house, back to Spain. Why?"

He put a wineglass in my hand, and more of the cool reserve I had expected of myself melted. But for all I knew, he had seduced and abandoned my mother. *Do not trust this man; be careful what you tell him*, I thought. This man who might be my father.

"My mother did not tell me much of what happened that summer," I said. She had told me nothing, in fact. "All I know was told to me by Sara Murphy. Sara met with me, spoke with me."

"So, Anna never mentioned me?" His eyes flared with disappointment. Is there anything worse for a lover's pride than to think he has been forgotten?

Picasso cut a slice of cheese but put it on my plate, not his. "From sheep's milk. Very good," he said. "If you can't tell me why she left, tell me what happened after she left. What became of her? She disappeared before I could finish the painting of her."

There was a painting of her? Of course. Sara had found them together in the studio. From what I had learned of Picasso, the studio always served two purposes, not just one: Seduction. Art. Hand in hand for Picasso.

"When she left Antibes," I said, "and after leaving Guernica, she ended up in New York City. She married an American, Harry Olsen."

The man I had always thought of as my father, who was my father in the ways that most matter, who had dangled toys over my crib, taken me ice-skating, helped me build school projects and memorize the multiplication tables.

And this was part of the mystery. How and where had they

met? My mother never told me. "He took me dancing," she said once. But where? When? Children are the center of their own universe, and, like most children, I hadn't questioned the obvious, that my mother and father loved me. They'd had lives before me, lives I knew almost nothing about. There was a place called Wisconsin, where he'd grown up, but we never went there. No grandparents. "Heaven," he told me. No aunts or uncles or cousins. A world unto ourselves, Harry and Marti and Alana.

"I don't know where they met, my mother and father. She never said. She didn't like to talk about the past. He died when I was eight. She didn't remarry."

Harry Olsen had adored her, that much I knew. There had been flowers on her birthday, my father putting his finger to his lips and whispering to me, "Let's be quiet and let your mother sleep in," on Sunday mornings.

I lifted a piece of tomato to my mouth and let its sweet acidity distract me for a moment from the pain of this conversation and the joy of it as well.

"So, your home is New York." Picasso, too, lifted a forkful of salad to his mouth. "I have never gone there, not even during the war, when Paris was occupied, when many artists went there to be safe. I did not go even for the big showings of my work. I think that man, Hoover, and his FBI would make my visit difficult, no? They would not like my politics. Nor does the generalissimo. I will not go back to Spain as long as Franco is still there. I think they keep a file on me, like on my friend Charlie Chaplin."

"They keep many files," I agreed. Perhaps even I have one, I did not admit.

"What happened to her then?" Picasso asked. "Anna, in New York, with her American husband."

She had me, I didn't say. That was obvious. He didn't know my age yet. He couldn't be doing the math yet.

I took off the scarf I had tied around my throat and handed it to him. It was a Marti scarf, a green-and-yellow print of leaves.

"She became a designer," I said. "This is one of hers."

He fingered it, studied it. "A little clumsy, maybe," he decided. "She made too much effort to make the design appear naïf. And too busy. But the colors are good, the leaves are good."

"She became quite well known for her designs," I said, stung by the criticism. "People collect these, like art."

My eyes had grown accustomed to the dimmer interior, where the filtered sun came in pronounced yellow streaks through dusty windows. I could take in the details of the studio, the canvases leaning against the walls, pedestals of clay sculptures, a long wooden table filled with pieces from the Madoura pottery, waiting for the maestro to finish them with his shaping of the still-plastic clay, and to paint the surfaces with rims of goats, centaurs, olive branches, women's stylized masklike faces.

Pinch yourself, I thought. *You are in Picasso's studio*. Marti, who had pulled me by the hand through the New York museums and galleries of Picasso's work, had finally led me here. No, Anna Martina had led me here. How would I ever make the two women one?

"Was Anna happy? Before she became a widow?" he asked. He was studying my face again, his index finger tracing a design in the bread crumbs on the table. "Did she try to be happy? Did things go well for her? I was angry, you know. She left without a word. We were . . . friends."

Friends. He had hesitated before using that word. Had carefully considered.

You were more than that, I thought. But I'd wait till later for that conversation. I wasn't ready.

"Some things went well. Some did not. When my father died, that was hard for her, raising a child on her own."

"Yes. I knew she was alone, no family. Or maybe she had family and couldn't go to them. I don't remember." He poured more water into his glass and drank thirstily. "Family can be good, but they can also confuse a woman. Françoise's family . . ." He stopped in midsentence. "They encouraged her to leave me. Her friends encouraged her to leave."

"Tell me what you know about Anna's family," I said. I didn't want to hear about Françoise Gilot; I wanted to hear about my mother. "Tell me all she told you."

He pointed to my notebook, lying next to my plate. "I thought you were here to talk about my art." There was a hint of annoyance in his voice now.

"Yes," I said. "But also to speak of my mother. She spoke of you; she said you were the greatest artist of the century."

"She did?"

The annoyance and wariness left his eyes. Satisfaction lit them up now, pride.

"What do you know of Anna?" I asked again. "You remember more than you are telling me, I think."

Picasso took a long sip of water and pushed away his half-eaten meal. "She was very young when we met in Antibes. A student. She had been granted a scholarship to the school of fine arts in Barcelona, La Lonja. I, too, once studied there before I saw that I already knew more than my teachers. She knew my work long before we met, had studied my cubist paintings and the Harlequin and circus paintings. But when I let her paint a little in my studio in Antibes, the work was too immature. She had found little in herself yet. Or maybe she was too afraid; she was locking things inside herself."

That sounded more like my mother, all those locked doors full of secrets.

There was a commotion outside, and Picasso went to the door, frowning at the disruption. Rapid-fire French I couldn't understand, another man, his voice thick with apology, a cart being wheeled in with plates and urns ready for the master's finishing touch.

"I need Jacqueline here, she is to inventory this," Picasso complained, gesturing his impatience.

Françoise Gilot, who had only been gone a few weeks, had already been replaced. Picasso seemed to use up and then discard women the way other men replace automobiles, always on the lookout for the newest model. I felt an overwhelming tenderness for my mother, realizing this. Whatever had been between them, I hoped she had not loved him enough to be wounded by him. I hoped she had been the heartless one, that eighteen-year-old, so vulnerable and alone.

Picasso signaled to the man to place the plates on an almost empty table, and he held one up for me to see. "A blank," he said. "A nothing. But when I have finished, it will be everything. It will have found itself."

"True, maestro," said the man who began unloading his cart.

"Why did Anna leave her studies?" I asked, determined not to be distracted. I had meant to stay cool, to be the journalist, not the daughter, but the need for answers became like a hunger. "Was it for an elopement? Why was she afraid?"

Picasso said a few more things in his rapid-fire French to the deliveryman, who hurriedly arranged the plates and urns on the table and then backed out of the studio, out the door. Only when we were alone again did Picasso speak. "The boy in Spain, you mean. I don't remember his name. No, she didn't leave because of him. Other reasons. There are still things Spanish families do not discuss. Political things. She had gotten in trouble."

He was referring to Francisco Franco, the general who, with his Nationalists, had overthrown the republic in Spain and established a dictatorship. Whenever his name appeared in the papers or on the news, my mother had winced in distaste and something else I saw now had been fear, even though she was very far away from Spain. Franco's politics reached far, and there were many in the United States who supported his dictatorship since it punished and imprisoned communists. McCarthy was a supporter of Franco, I'd heard.

"But my mother left Spain before Franco came to power."

Picasso stared at a slant of light coming in through one of the windows, and I could sense his eagerness to be back at work. "There were troubles already before Franco," he said, getting up from his chair. "Primo de Rivera, the Spaniard who wished to become like Mussolini, in Italy, was already there. The students marched against him because they knew when he came to full power, he would destroy the constitution. He would put the country under martial law. They were right, the students."

"So Anna marched with the students."

"She had a cut over her right eyebrow when I met her. Deep. It had bled a lot, she said. She had been hit by a police baton."

I knew that scar, had traced it with childish fingertips as she made up story after story about how she had acquired it and then told me, at the end of each story, that the past did not matter, only the future did.

"So, after the police beat her and her friends and that boy, she knew she must leave Spain. She could not go back to her university room or her family. Some of her friends had been arrested and taken away, and she was afraid they would come for her, too."

Picasso broke off a piece of bread and put it in his mouth. "Yes," he said. "You look very much like her. What she would look like, when she was older."

Ask me my age, I thought. *Ask*. But he didn't.

"Probably her family disowned her because of the dishonor of a daughter running away. In those days, daughters of good families did not even go shopping without having a maid or brother escort them. It had taken her a year, she told me, to get her father to allow her to study art at university instead of with a tutor at home. She had gone on a hunger strike, like prisoners sometimes do, and so he finally gave in, her father."

"She studied, joined a student movement, and then had to leave Barcelona. She worked at a hotel in France that summer. In Antibes. Monsieur Sella's hotel. Where you met her," I said. "Sara Murphy told me about that summer."

"What else did Sara Murphy tell you?" The wariness returned to his voice, and he studied me even more intently, trying to see what I knew, what I did not know.

"She told me much. She was generous with her time."

He laughed, a kind of admission of defeat. "Sara is, let me see how to say, not a gossip, I think."

"But she was in a talkative mood."

A deep frown line appeared between his brows. "Then you already know all you need to know. More. We both do."

Not quite.

"I know why my mother left Antibes," I said. "Sara told me that, too."

He pushed away his plate and took another swallow of water. "Why, then?"

"Sara saw her in the studio. With you. And she was angry and jealous. So she told Monsieur Sella, and Anna was fired."

"So, it was about me." Was that satisfaction in his voice? The ego of the lover who must always be the cause, the center, the focus?

"I think it was more about Sara and my mother. The betrayal," I said.

He considered that for a moment.

"You are here to talk about art," he said. "Let us begin." And like that, Anna was no longer our topic. She had been dismissed in the same manner in which Jacqueline had been dismissed half an hour before. I had learned some, but not enough. Too much was still in shadow, leaning in a doorway, watching.

TWENTY-TWO

. . . .

ALANA

I opened my notebook. "We'll begin. You were born in Mála-ga, Spain, in 1881. What month?" I knew this already, but it was an opening question, a lead into the interview.

"October. And my first word was *pencil*. I was stillborn, did you know that? No crying, no movement, until my uncle touched me with his cigar and made me cry. My grandfather, too, born that way. It is something that runs in the family." Picasso put the cork back in the water bottle and arranged it in the lunch hamper, clearing the worktable.

I hadn't heard this before about Picasso. This was something new, something that would make Reed sit up and take notice, the artist famed for the action and movement of his work had himself been born unmoving. "Is that true?" I asked.

He glared at me. "Everything I say and do is true. Especially my paintings."

I waited a second and said, "I was born in New York. In 1924. April."

"And what was your first word?" The numbers hadn't reg-
istered with him. But I had planted that seed.

"*Mama.* That was my first word. Tell me about your
childhood."

We talked for an hour, Picasso telling me about the early
drawing lessons his father had given him, the pigeons in the
square that he had thrown crumbs to, his early years of going
back and forth between Spain and Paris before he had established himself, the ice in his washbasin in his studio in the
Bateau-Lavoir in Montmartre, his friends Apollinaire, Gris,
Leo Stein, who introduced him to his sister, Gertrude. He
talked about painting *Les Demoiselles d'Avignon*, the cubist
painting that began what is known as modern art and his own
reaction to it, that strange starting point of the avant-garde. It's
a composition of five nude women in various poses, all flat
planes and dangerous sharp angles. Their faces are like masks,
unreadable. It is one of the earliest, perhaps the first, works of
art inspired by African traditional art. And because African art
became admirable, people also began reconsidering the people
who made the original art, the ancient peoples who were, in
America, being refused service at lunch counters and being sent
to the back of the bus. The people Professor Grippi had marched
for. Picasso, with his art, had helped start a civil rights movement decades before.

"It was an exorcism, for me, that painting," Picasso said. "A
way of getting rid of the past and its rules, its academic requirements. Matisse was angered by it, a good sign, don't you think?
He thought I was making fun of the modern movement. Ha."

Picasso used his hand to make an expressive, dismissive
gesture.

Like many people confronting age, his memories had wandered back to his earliest years, the time when everything was

possible, not the later years when all the paths have been charted. But I wanted to hear about one year in particular.

"Tell me about the summer in Antibes," I asked. "I would like to concentrate on that time for my article. It has not been as frequently written about, I think."

"I have passed many summers in Antibes, in the Midi. And now winters, too. I do not like Paris in winter. The light is better here."

"Nineteen twenty-three. You drew and painted many beach landscapes, women and children, the neoclassical, and you worked, I think, on a painting you call *The Lovers*."

"After the war. The Great War, they call it. Cubism died because it looked too German; it reminded people, not that they forgot, but we did not want to look at or paint the anger. So, yes. Neoclassicism, though the title is inaccurate. Titles are like boxes, meant to be broken open."

He had left the worktable and had gone to stand in the beam of light that had captured his attention, and was trailing his hand through the dust motes, leaving a design in them. I watched, my notebook butterflied open on my lap. Suddenly, he came over, took me by the hand, and pulled me out of the chair.

"Look," he said, pulling me to a different worktable, one covered with objects. "That is what you need to do. Look. You talk too much, ask me to talk too much. This. What do you think?"

He picked up a vessel that had been painted with a woman's face, her eyes huge and black, her eyelashes like rays emanating from a child's drawing of the sun.

My French wasn't up to this task, trying to find the adjectives that would describe the power of the object he held. I struggled and found only school words.

"Power," I said. "Ancient. Modern. Both. One woman. All women."

"Yes," he said, nodding, satisfied. "And this?"

He walked me through the studio, picking up object after object, asking me what I saw, to simply respond, not to think. Sometimes there was a gentleness in his voice, sometimes impatience with my slowness.

"Art is not for the brain," he said. "It is for the senses, for the dreams. You will sleep well tonight, I think. And these"—his arm swept through the air—"these are so that everybody may have something to fill their dreams, to remind them of forgotten things. To find what has been lost. Not just rich people."

It was a disingenuous statement, because Picasso's pottery would become sought after by wealthy collectors as soon as it was offered for sale, and he knew it. But I understood what he meant. It was not art they could put on their walls; it would have to be used. I thought of the vessel he had shown me earlier, the woman's face, the primitive mask of it, and tried to imagine it sitting on a table laden with precious eighteenth-century Sèvres china and crystal goblets. It wouldn't work. Whoever tried to own and use that vessel would have to rethink so many other choices. The pottery, like most of Picasso's work, was also subversive.

There was something else in the studio, though, that caught my eye. A little hand-carved horse missing an ear and the end of the tail after years of children's hard play with it. It was the toy horse I'd seen in the photograph that Sara had given me. He'd kept it all these years.

"And this?" I picked it up.

"A toy, something Sara found for a table decoration when

there were no flowers." He paused. "Your mother, Anna, liked that toy. Take it. I meant to give it to her but did not have the chance. Take it. Something for your children."

"I don't have children."

"You should."

I let that go and put the horse in my purse. "Thank you."

After two hours of showing me the work, the plates and platters, urns and vessels, painted with Roman and prehistoric motifs, with olive branches and fish and mythological figures, Picasso's voice started to soften, to tire. He was, I reminded myself, seventy-two years old. And he himself was losing interest in this interview. There were several long silences. He began to clean a brush, to look for the drying rag, to act as if I weren't there because he no longer wished me there.

There was a tilt to his head, a suggestion of solitude and of living inside his own thoughts that looked strangely familiar to me. I heard William in my own thoughts, saying, *Alana, where did you just go? Are you ignoring me?* It was the same tilt my head automatically fell into when I was distracted. When we both had our hands on the table, I had mentally compared them, the length of our fingers, the width of the palms, both our hands made for strength, not delicacy.

"May I come back tomorrow?" I asked him. "With my camera for some studio photos?"

"Yes, yes," he said impatiently. He was at one of the worktables. He picked up a blank, a serving platter, and traced a pattern on its rim with his finger, considering, his attention completely focused on the object, not the woman standing next to him. The interview was over.

Over, and I hadn't touched upon the part that mattered the most: his relationship with my mother.

"I'm sorry," he said, when I opened the door and stepped into the bright sun. "Sorry that Sara and your mother quarreled." Nothing about his part in that quarrel.

*T*omorrow, I told myself during the walk back to Madame Rosa's. *Tomorrow I will tell him that Anna was pregnant when she left Antibes. That he might be my father.*

It was late afternoon, and the afternoon Midi heat felt like a blanket. The path I took through the low hills was dusty, and my throat was scratchy from it. I was tired, physically and emotionally. But jubilant. I had had my first interview with Picasso. It hadn't gone completely as I had hoped, but he had spoken freely and at length; tomorrow we would talk about his neoclassical work and that summer in Antibes. And the women of that summer. And that my mother was, I believed, pregnant when she left Antibes.

Tomorrow, I would interview the other Picasso, my mother's lover. How would he react? He remembered her and still felt some pain because she had left him without a word.

Why had she? *That*, I thought, *was the question I could never answer.* Perhaps being yet one more of his many mistresses did not appeal to her. Perhaps she had known their affair was too tenuous, that he would not welcome her and her child into the more private and protected corners of his life. Perhaps, because she could not return to Barcelona and her family, and because her first love, Antonio, was in prison, she decided to put even more distance between herself and the danger in Spain, to go all the way to New York, as some did in those early years of fascism.

There, in the bright Provençal sun, I tried one more time to probe all the secrets of Anna Martina, Marti, and came up empty-handed. That empty-handedness, the not knowing, was part of my grief at losing her. To mourn and to eventually move away from that mourning, you must know who you mourn. My mother was still two separate people. I needed the whole. The exhilaration of my meeting and interview with Picasso disappeared in a fresh wave of grief. I sat on a rock and wept for my mother—the one I had known and the one I had not.

The fit of weeping made me feel a little better, a little stronger. Tomorrow. I would let him know the part of her story he did not yet know. Me, her daughter. His.

But the next day, when I went to the studio full of hope and determination, it was closed and locked. I stared at the heavy iron bolt with the lock hanging from it first in disbelief and then with dawning awareness.

Jacqueline. She did not want me there, did not want me talking to her Picasso, distracting him with memories of other times, times before her. She was plainly in love with him, and her love was possessive as well as passionate.

I knocked and kicked at that door. I rattled the lock and threw pebbles against the windows. Nothing. When I had to accept that no one was inside, I tried to pretend that locked door was accidental. He had forgotten. Perhaps, I hoped, he was simply arriving later. So I waited. For two hours, I waited, and each minute of that long time was an eternity. *You must be here*, I told him. *You must come. I still have things to tell you.*

After several hours, the young woman who had the chair workshop across the street came out and gave me a glass of water as she had the day before. There was pity in her eyes.

"I have not seen him today. If he were coming, he would have been here by now," she said. "Come back tomorrow, I think."

I finished the glass of water and handed it back to her,

wanting to wait even longer but knowing she was right. He wasn't coming.

"Jacqueline is very jealous," the woman said. "Perhaps you are too pretty. Now that Françoise is gone, Jacqueline means to have him for herself, I think."

I stood and walked back to the town center slowly, hoping against hope that I would meet him coming up the path. I didn't.

Back in the town square, the girl who had delivered our hamper lunch of the day before was sitting at one of the outdoor tables of the café, having a coffee and cigarette. It was late afternoon, the quiet time between lunch and dinner, when the black iron café chairs are full of old men nodding over newspapers and glasses of *pastis*. She looked up with only mild interest when I said "Good day" to her.

"Monsieur Picasso," she said, when I asked if she had delivered a meal to him that morning. "No. His woman sent a note saying he would not be there, not to bring his lunch. They have gone to Nîmes for the *corridas*. The bullfight. The last one of the season."

He had not mentioned going to a bullfight yesterday when we spoke for more than two hours. This was a last-minute decision. Who had made it? Jacqueline had studied me closely in a way that announced her immediately as foe, not friend. Maybe she had seen more in my face than he had, some resemblance that set off all her alarms, the shape of my eyes, so like his, my nose, smaller and similar. And now Picasso and Jacqueline were gone.

"Are you all right, mademoiselle?" the girl asked. "Can I bring you something? Are you hungry? No? As you please." She returned to her coffee and lit another cigarette.

"It did not go well," Madame Rosa said, greeting me at the

door of the guesthouse. Her parrot squawked and ruffled his feathers, hopping from foot to foot on his perch. "I see it in your face. Courage. There is tomorrow."

"Yes," I agreed. "Tomorrow."

I returned to Vallauris the next day and the next. But Picasso did not return from Nîmes, or wherever he had gone.

"Maybe they have gone up to Paris for some business," the girl in the café said. "Or Arles, or to see that other old painter, Matisse. They visit him often. Another coffee, mademoiselle?"

A cold wind was sweeping through the town square, the infamous mistral of Southern France that sweeps down from the Rhône Valley. The weather had changed. The sun was brighter than ever, the sky bluer, because the mistral blew away all clouds and mist, Madame Rosa had told me the evening before. By that time, our after-dinner hour of her smoking her cigarette, me rambling about New York, my mother, had become an established ritual. I told her everything . . . except that my mother had had an affair with Pablo Picasso and that I thought Pablo Picasso was my father.

I was starting to understand, I thought, why my mother had been so secretive. She had wanted to protect me from the pain of that closed door, the rejection.

Madame Rosa, in turn, taught me about the important things of life in the Midi: of what foods to eat and when and which wines were best. She told me about the thirty-two winds of Provence, the Rousseau, Levant, Auro-Bruno . . . but most importantly, there was the mistral, the wind that blows away everything that is not properly attached or weighed down. When it is strong, it will blow the tail off a donkey, Madame Rosa told me. Patio furniture, laundry on the line, roof tiles.

Gone. And when it is very strong, it will give you headaches and insomnia, and if doesn't stop in time, it will drive you mad.

I could imagine my mother, Anna, in her bed in the hotel the night before she fled, the night Monsieur Sella said her service was no longer needed. She would have known it was Sara who had betrayed her. Would have known that protective friendship had turned to animosity just as a summer breeze turns to the maddening mistral.

Sitting at the café in Vallauris the third and last time I went there hoping that Picasso had returned, I asked for my usual coffee, thinking the caffeine would ease my headache. But when it came, it tasted off, and I couldn't drink it.

"It is good, like always," the café girl insisted, offended. The wind lifted up and carried away a newspaper that one of the patrons had left behind.

"Oh, là," she muttered, chasing after one of the café's white napkins. It scuttled down the street ahead of her as if an invisible hand pulled it.

I pushed the coffee cup away with one hand and held on to my scarf with the other as the wind kept trying to blow the fabric into my eyes and mouth. As if the Marti scarf were trying to both silence and temporarily blind me.

"Enough past," I heard my mother say in my head. "Enough."

It was like a kick in the stomach, having to understand that I might never, thanks to Jacqueline's jealousy and possessiveness, get to speak with Picasso again. Might never tell him the truth of our relationship.

But maybe he knew. There had been moments during our conversation when he had looked at me strangely. He had, two or three times, touched me, my hand, my shoulder, not in a flirtatious way, but a tender, almost protective way. The way

Harry Olsen had put his hand on my shoulder when he helped me blow out the candles on my birthday cake; the way Harry had held my hand when he was trying to tell me something important, things a child doesn't always know to pay attention to: to wait for the pedestrian green light, not to talk to strangers.

There had been moments of tenderness between Pablo and myself. I might have to be content with that. Perhaps Anna's secret, now my secret, might also be his unvoiced secret.

Thinking of Pablo made me think of Jack at the inn. There had been tenderness in his hands as well, but a lover's tenderness, passion merging the tenderness and physical need. I missed him. Missed him in a way in which I didn't miss William.

What would it be like to love a complicated man, a man you couldn't predict? William's every thought and gesture could be guessed in advance. Perhaps that was what my mother had appreciated in him. His love was simple; his demands and moods would be as predictable as sunrise and sunset.

Jack, from our very first exchange, that hello over the reception desk, had kept me off balance. I never knew what he was going to say or why, aside from the requirements of innkeeping: *How many nights will you be dining with us?* That kind of thing. The unexpected things: that look in his face when he had brought me those flowers for Sara. When he had held my hand and followed me up the stairs to my room. Thinking of him made me shiver with desire.

After the mistral began to blow, I stayed away from Vallauris. I became a tourist, looking at the sights, shopping for souvenirs to bring home to friends. I took the local bus to Grasse and toured a perfume factory. I went to Vence and saw the huge column that had supported the ancient viaduct that had been blown up by the Germans. I saw the house where

D. H. Lawrence died of tuberculosis and the central square of Vintium, which had been the forum of the city the ancient Romans had built there. I saw them through my eyes and my mother's.

And all the while, the wind blew women's dresses into froths of cotton or linen, stole men's hats, chased handkerchiefs and scraps of papers down narrow cobbled streets. It seemed to be saying, "Go home. You are done here." Soon, I would. My cash was running low, and there was no reason to stay.

During my third week in Antibes, at breakfast, a large envelope arrived for me. The maid was just putting out the orange juice and bread basket when Madame brought it in, her face flushed. Her parrot sat on her shoulder, and between profanities in several languages, he pecked gently and affectionately at Madame Rosa's earring. She placed the envelope on the red-and-white-checked tablecloth and crossed her arms impatiently over her chest.

"Hand-delivered," she said. "I had to tip the boy." I knew the tip would be added to my final bill. I was fond of Madame and she of me, but there was no pretense that I was anything other than a paying guest.

"Well, aren't you going to open it?" she demanded, curiosity sharpening her voice.

The Parisian couple, like me, were early to breakfast, and they also looked at me expectantly, forks lifted and held in midair.

I held the envelope for a second, sensing that it represented one of the moments in life from which other moments flow, a decisive moment that changes things. The envelope was a decision that someone else had made, and I had no choice but to accept it. I released the flap.

It was a set of photographs, all of the pottery objects that Pablo had shown me, talked about with me, and a brief note from Jacqueline, giving me onetime permission to reproduce them for the article.

The message was clear. *You are finished here. No need to come back.* And I was to write about the pottery, not that summer in Antibes, the summer of Pablo and Anna and Sara.

Picasso had sent this, I was certain. As a kind gesture but also a final gesture.

Madame sighed. She knew what the delivery of the photos meant. I would not be returning to the Vallauris studio. Would not see Pablo Picasso again. I had come so close. I wished now that I had forced my way into his studio and declared, "I am your daughter!" that very first day.

But what would have come of that? There would have been no interview at all, no further meeting. Jacqueline would have seen to it. And he might have pushed me back out the door and slammed it. Even if he had welcomed me, embraced me, then what? Pablo Picasso already had plenty of acknowledged children: Paulo with his wife, Olga; Maya with an early mistress, Marie-Thérèse Walter; and Claude and Paloma with Françoise Gilot, who had just left him. Did I want to become a hanger-on, one of those frantic people who appear in very small articles in tabloid magazines, claiming to be Amelia Earhart's love child or the great-granddaughter of the dauphin of the French throne?

Enough.

My mother once had a lover, a famous artist. Later, she gave me a father who would help raise me, Harry, who held me during thunderstorms and looked at my mother in a way that made me hope that when I was grown, someone would look at me like that. My mother had taught me to love the art of my own time, not just dusty ancient masterpieces, and how to keep a secret. That had been my inheritance.

Madame Rosa took the envelope of photographs and thumbed through them. "But these are wonderful," she said.

"Yes. I have enough for my article. That's all I came for."

That day, I completed my other task in Antibes. I unpacked the small jar in which I had placed a handful of my mother's ashes and put it in my handbag. I walked downhill from Madame Rosa's guesthouse through town to the other side of Antibes, the ocean side, where the air grew salty and the everyday people of Madame's neighborhood, the housewives and butchers and shopkeepers, were replaced by tourists in skimpy bikinis and loud shirts.

Monsieur Sella's faded rose-colored hotel was still there, perched on a cliffside but now surrounded by larger, more luxurious establishments. The terrace where Sara and Gerald, Olga and Picasso, had had drinks and after-dinner coffees was empty except for a couple of hotel maids who were laying out plates and silverware on the tables. I walked to the spot where I estimated the photograph had been taken from, put my feet where Picasso must have placed his to get that specific angle.

With my eyes closed, I could see Sara and Olga clearly in the background, Sara smiling, Olga not quite, for the camera. The palm trees framing the terrace, the distant hills with cypress and pines behind them. I could see my mother, no longer a blur in the foreground but distinct, with her black hair and dark eyes, long, straight nose, the scar over her eye, still red and swollen because at that time the injury would have been only a few weeks old.

With my eyes still closed, I heard the mistral stir the palm fronds, and it sounded like a whispered voice in my ear, something from out of the past to greet me in this moment. My mother seemed very close, nearer to me than she had been since her death. It felt as if I already knew this place so well that I must have been there before.

Thank you, Sara, I thought. *You prepared me well for this.* In that instant, she was forgiven. She and my mother had been friends and then rivals. But now, that was in the past, and there was a future to be sorted.

The hotel maids ignored me and continued their work of setting tables for lunch. They carefully placed the heavy china plates over the napkins to keep them from blowing away and grumbled back and forth at each other. I stood in the shade of one of the palms, its fronds dancing far over my head as the wind toyed with it. It was too soon for lunch, and when I asked for a table, the maids were not pleased.

"Too early," one of them said, not even looking at me.

"Please."

She frowned but relented, and pointed to a table close to the edge of the terrace, where I could look over the balustrade and down to the ocean. The same view Sara and my mother had seen.

I sat and ordered tea; ever since that off-tasting cup of coffee, I had stuck with tea. I waited for my moment, listening to voices that had stopped echoing decades before, seeing people who were no longer there, feeling surrounded by them: my mother, Sara, Gerald, Pablo, Olga, Sara's boys, the dead mixing with the still living, all time becoming one.

"Anna?" Again, a voice called me by my mother's name, the way Picasso had. In the doorway stood a woman dressed in the white apron and tall hat of a cook. She stared at me in amazement. "Is it you? How . . . ?"

"I'm not Anna. I'm her daughter," I said, the same thing I had said to Picasso, except while I had a sense of who Picasso was, this woman was a total stranger. How did she know my mother? I started to rise from my chair, confused.

"Her daughter! Of course. Stupid of me. Anna would be . . . how old now? You don't remember me. Of course, you were too small. May I?" She sat across from me and made a gesture to one of the waitresses. "Tea with no biscuits? Bring some at once," she demanded, and the waitress scurried away, returning just moments later with a plate of *navettes*, the boat-shaped cookies of Provence.

"Made with real butter," she said proudly. "None of that artificial stuff in my kitchen. Not even during the war. Eat."

I wasn't hungry, but I broke a piece of a biscuit and put it in my mouth. I had so many questions. *One at a time*, I heard my mother say. I chewed thoughtfully and waited, letting this woman take the lead.

"How is your mother?" she asked after I had eaten two of the *navettes* under her watchful eye.

"She died six months ago."

"Oh. I'm so sorry." Her eyes reddened and she blinked until they cleared.

"How did you know her?" I asked. This cook was too young to have been working here thirty years ago. She looked to be in her forties, with just the beginning of lines in the corners of her eyes and no gray in her brown hair.

"My aunt Lorraine was the cook when your mother worked here as a maid. I remember Anna. More tea?" Again, that distinctive gesture, and the scurrying of a waitress who came out with a fresh cup.

A strong gust of wind struggled against her white cook's hat. She took it off and put it in her lap.

"It comes early this year, the mistral," she said. "Not a good sign. Maybe it means the Germans will be back." She made a quick sign of the cross on her forehead and chest for protection. "How did I know your mother? Sometimes she played with me. I was very small then. Hide-and-seek. I could hide behind that plant." She pointed to a large clay urn. "Every time, she pretended to be surprised to find me."

"You were here when my mother was here that summer?"

"Yes. My family lives in Issoire, but in the summers, I was sent here to live with my aunt. So, you are Anna's daughter. Grown up." She looked at me with careful assessment. "Yes. The black eyes. The same hair."

"How is Madame Lorraine?" Maybe, I hoped, I could speak with her, find out more about my mother as she had been that summer.

"She died. Many years ago. Your mother came for the funeral. You don't remember?"

When she said that, my old vague memory of sun and foreignness re-formed, expanded. The plane over the water. The long train ride. Warm sun, gritty sand, whispering ocean, and the prickling scent of wild thyme. I am so small my mother can lift me up under my arms and balance me on her knees. My mother's arms around me, the air warm like a bath, the blue sky. We were here, in Antibes.

It was Madame Lorraine my mother went to say goodbye to in the chapel. Madame Lorraine was the cold, still woman in the coffin for whom my mother had wept.

"What year was that?"

The cook frowned with concentration. "I think, yes, in 1929, the year that the Belgian, De Waele, won the Tour de France. My aunt had wanted to go to Nîmes to see the bicyclists go by, but she was already too ill by then."

I would have been five years old that year. Small enough to sit on my mother's lap, too young to form a clear memory, only impressions.

My mother had taken me with her. She had flown from New York and traveled here for a funeral. How had she ever afforded it? My father, Harry, had still been alive then. Probably, there had been enough money before he died. It was after she was widowed that dinner was sometimes only jam and bread, that the electricity was cut off sometimes—before the Marti line became successful.

"I think I do remember. It was the first time I saw my mother cry," I said.

"They were close, my aunt and your mother."

So, that was one thing Sara had gotten wrong, one fact she had misread. The cook may have shouted and stormed, but she and my mother had become friends, fond of each other.

"Please, what do you remember of my mother?"

"Not much. I was just a child then. Mademoiselle Anna was pretty, and sometimes she was frightened. She had been a student in Barcelona, I think, and got in some trouble. She talked sometimes about a boy named Antonio, and cried about him. She showed me her scars, where the police had beaten her."

Scars. Plural. More than just the scar over the eye. Scars she never let me see.

"What scars? Do you remember?"

"Over the eye. One on her back, a long gash. A small one on her knee. I remember that when she first came to Monsieur Sella's hotel looking for work, Aunt Lorraine put her to bed and made her sleep for two days. I wasn't allowed to play in front of her door, to disturb her. Before she came here, I think she had slept under bridges for a few nights and then on the train, sitting up."

I tried to imagine my mother, that fastidious, intensely private woman, curled up on cold, rough pavement, trying to rest as traffic passed overhead.

"I think she only stayed here for the summer," I said. "Do you know why she left Antibes?"

The wind had died down a little, and the sighing, sometimes the roaring, that we all had been living with for days grew silent so that we were able to speak more quietly.

"Things had happened that adults don't tell children," she said. "You know the kind of things. A man, I think. But more than that, your mother was not happy. She was never meant to be a maid. I remember she tried to teach me some Latin once, how to say, 'Gaul is divided into three parts,' and she told me Gaul was France. So, one day she was here and the next she was gone. That was the end of the summer, and Monsieur Sella was in a temper, trying to find a replacement. She left just as the true season was beginning."

She checked her watch. "Soon, the first people will arrive for lunch. I must go back to my work." She stood. "I'm happy to have seen you again. Your name is Alana, right? Yes, I remember. Little Alana. The first time we met, you didn't even come up to my waist. Stay as long as you like, Alana."

We hugged, and she walked back through the doorway. Moments later, I heard shouting, the clash of pans. She had inherited her aunt's style in the kitchen.

I sat, remembering and inventing at the same time, letting more light enter those dark places of my mother's history. After I finished my tea, the maids had also finished their work of preparing the tables for lunch and went off, I suppose, to have a cigarette before the busy dining time began. The mistral stayed quiet as if it knew that for a moment it must not blow except in the gentlest manner possible.

Alone on the terrace, I stood, took the jar from my purselet. I let my mother's ashes drift onto the hills below, onto the wild thyme and onto the distant lavender fields of Provence.

Anna. Marti. A woman of scars and secrets. My beloved mother, some of her now returned to where this part of her story began.

Go home, I heard her say. *This is finished.*

TWENTY-THREE

ALANA

I stayed in Antibes another week. Madame Rosa helped make this possible by giving me a slight reduction on my cost of room and board. "When you come next time, I will charge more," she promised.

I spent the time working on my interview notes and beginning to write the article on Picasso and the pottery in Vallauris. I was pleased with it. Perhaps Jacqueline had done me a favor with this redirection. For one thing, it meant I wouldn't have to worry about revealing any of Sara's secrets. Her affair with Pablo Picasso would stay private.

Spreading my mother's ashes hadn't in any way diminished my sense of her being close to me, and I was grateful for that. I felt that she was pleased about this new article as well. *Now and the future. Not yesterday*, I could hear her saying. I telegraphed David Reed, despite the expense, and told him I was writing about Picasso's pottery, asking if he would be interested in that, and he had replied with two words. *Yes. Proceed.* So I did.

I wished, though, I could get back inside the studio one more time, to look again at the pottery pieces, the urns painted with masklike faces, the platters with rims of olive branches. To speak with Picasso and tell him, *I know you had an affair with my mother. And you may be my father.*

I did go back to the studio once more. Jacqueline was standing in front of the door, smoking a cigarette. She crushed it underfoot when she saw me, and she would not let me enter. She slammed the door behind her, and I could hear her turning the key in the lock. I stood in front of it for a while, willing her to open it, knocking as hard as I could, calling through it. If he was there, inside, he was ignoring me, too. It wasn't just Jacqueline who had barricaded me out. Those words, *You are my father,* would never be spoken to him.

I felt like weeping for my mother as well as for myself. But she left him, I remembered. *Do the same thing. This is over.* Over before it began, really. I went back to Antibes knowing I had no reason to ever return to Vallauris.

The mistral blew, dislodging a roof tile and chasing away a pillowcase from the laundry line. My appetite disappeared completely, and one evening after dinner, after I had forced myself to eat Madame Rosa's rich cassoulet, I was ill. She found me outside on the path where she kept a woodpile for the old-fashioned stove, wiping my mouth and gasping.

She watched for a moment, then took my arm and led me to the porch steps to sit in the cool evening air.

"Do you mind if I smoke?" she asked for the first time. "Will it bother you?" The cat came out from its secret place in the shrubs and with feline dignity accepted the offering of garlic sausage from Madame Rosa. I had to look away as it ate.

The stomach upset continued for several days and grew even worse as I was repacking my suitcase and preparing for the flight back to New York, with a stopover in Paris. Madame Rosa had brought me breakfast in bed that morning since I was not feeling well. She had felt my forehead. No fever. Looked closely into my eyes. Not bloodshot. Just the nausea, the lack of appetite.

"Your appetite will return," she had pronounced. "Soon. And you will be eating for two."

"What?" I sat up in alarm. "No. That's not possible. Really. I . . ."

"Yes. Possible."

I thought. My period, usually regular as clockwork, was late. My breasts were tender. I sank back into the pillows, shocked into silence. Pregnant.

There would be no white wedding at Christmas for me. It would have to be quick and quiet at the town hall. William would not be happy about this. William.

"So?" Madame Rosa asked, sitting on the side of my bed. "Good news or not?"

I stared at her in wonder, speechless. She laughed. "You will get used to it," she said. "Mademoiselle, will there be a father for the baby?"

"Yes. I think. But . . ."

I counted months, remembering the last time William and I had made love. I had been out of town, and when I came back for my mother's funeral, William had been ill with the flu, and then he'd had a business trip, and then there had been quarrels . . . there had been a long chaste spell . . . and then Jack. It wasn't William's child. It was Jack's. *Oh God.* What would he think about this? Jack, who was married to Janet.

"Ah. A problem," Madame Rosa said, reading my expression. "Well, it's too late to worry about that. What will be will be."

With those words of wisdom, she left me, shell-shocked and terrified, in bed to rest, to think.

I half sat up, propped by pillows, and put my hands over my stomach. The future, uninvited, had found me. Had caught me and brought me down to earth like a child reeling in a kite.

Mama, I thought. *What do I do now? What do I tell David Reed, my would-be employer?* There goes that job. I'd be lucky if he still hired me as a freelancer. And what do I tell Jack and William?

All my work, all my plans, now derailed.

And yet . . . Jack's child. Ours. There would have to be new plans, work of a different nature. I felt frightened. But underneath the fear, promising to conquer it, was a different emotion: I also felt invincible, a creature of miracles. A maker of life.

My stomach was still completely flat, of course, but I imagined it growing, swelling, taking over me and my life as I had taken over my mother's. I thought of holding a child the way my mother had held me, singing to her.

I slept a couple more hours and woke up from a dreamless sleep, smiling. *Little one*, I thought. *I will do anything to keep you safe.*

Madame Rosa insisted I stay two more days in Antibes till she thought I looked sufficiently rested. Her timing, that delay of my trip to Paris, turned out to be fortuitous, because there was a second telegram from Helen.

"It will be good news. I will it to be good news," Madame said, handing me the folded paper. "The angels protect new mothers."

It was good news. Very good. Helen had telegrammed from New York.

Grippi released. Cleared of all charges. Not blacklisted. No names given. Over.

He had not lost his position at the university. Aside from already knowing that I had marched in a protest, McCarthy's men had no new information about me, no false charges.

Perhaps, I hoped, the "red scare" was beginning to die down. When, over the summer, McCarthy had begun to accuse and question members of the armed services, men of evident patriotism and service to the country, the public had paid attention and reacted. The tide of public opinion was beginning to turn against him. He had overreached. Whatever his goal had actually been, to create a dictatorship like Spain's, to "cleanse" America of anyone who did not look like him, think like him, he had failed.

It was a return to reason, a sign that we were finally healing all the war wounds. We had fought and defeated fascists and Nazis in Europe, and now we were defeating would-be fascists in our own country, and we could get on with the business of taking care of our families, doing our work as best as we could, dreaming of all that is possible to dream of in a free country.

Our families. My child.

"I was right? Good news?" Madame Rosa asked, standing in the doorway as I reread the telegram.

"Very good news." I refolded the telegram and slipped it into my pages of notes on Pablo Picasso. It would have been wonderful to be able to go to him, to say, *Look, your daughter is safe again.* But I was already teaching myself to steel my emotions against such thoughts. He had enough children. I had a father, Harry, and a mother, Marti. I did not need Pablo. My child would not need him.

Y ou will go home now," Madame Rosa said on my last eve-
ning at the guesthouse in Antibes. She had started knitting when we were sitting on the steps in the night, talking, because the smoke from her strong Gauloises made me feel ill.

The cat crept out from under the bushes and sat at my feet, licking his paws.

"Yes." Back to New York, my small apartment. And then . . . then what?

"First," Madame said, "you stop in Paris."

"Yes, I'm flying out of there. I'll be sure and see the Eiffel Tower."

"If you wish, of course. But I thought maybe you would like to visit with my friend Irène. She has agreed."

"You spoke with her?" I was eating a bowl of rice pudding, the only thing I was able to keep down that day. The cat sniffed at the rim of the bowl with carnivorous disdain.

"Yes, we spoke. And she would like it very much if you write about her. Enough, all these words about men artists."

"Yes," I agreed. "Enough about men."

We laughed and then fell into a companionable silence. There was no wind. The night was calm and velvety and very beauti-ful, so I could imagine my mother, and Sara, and Irène, in ear-lier years, enjoying this sky, this hint of salt in the air.

I would meet Irène after all. And begin the next article, the one I would write when I was finished with Picasso. That is how the future is constructed. One hope after the next.

"Make sure you bring plenty of pencils and paper," Ma-dame Rosa said. "She is a talker, my Irène."

I arrived in Paris on a Tuesday morning, disheveled and exhausted after taking the night train, my purse crammed full with a new notebook and a box of pencils. Madame Rosa had recommended a hotel on the Île de la Cité. "Small and not expensive," she had said. "They will look after you; they are friends." I lugged my suitcase onto the metro, yawned through several stops, and emerged again into the colder northern sunlight, close to Notre-Dame.

Religion does not come easily to me. My mother and I were not atheists, nor were we churchgoers. It was just something outside of our daily lives. But the ancient gray towers and huge rose window of the cathedral invited me in. I lit several candles. One for my mother. One for my child. One for me. Then, after stumbling down uneven cobbled streets that grew increasingly narrow, I found the hotel. Faded ocher paint, a cracked window on the first floor, a sagging window box of dead geraniums. The first sight of it was not encouraging.

It was owned and managed by an Algerian family and was as far from the beaten tourist track as a hotel could get. The reception area consisted of a small desk pushed up against the wall in the narrow entrance, and the only public area was a sitting room shared by family and hotel guests alike. The stairs up to my third-floor room were so narrow I could touch both walls at the same time. My bed was the size of an army cot, and the washroom was a floor below me.

But I had a view of Notre-Dame, and a chestnut tree, bare-branched now, tapped cheerfully at the window. There was a nursery school across from the hotel, so the street, twice a day, filled with children and their mothers coming and going. I could study them a bit, I decided, having realized I knew absolutely nothing about children. It was a good room for day-dreams, for making new plans.

At first, the spicy aroma of the meal being cooked in the downstairs kitchen made me queasy, but after my first day, I got used to it. In fact, I looked forward to it since the family asked me to join them at the table, to share their couscous and lamb stew flavored with coriander and cumin.

I had become quite emotional—Madame Rosa had warned me of this—as a result of the pregnancy and the hormones, and when Madame Nasri asked me why I had come to France, I burst into tears. It had become a year for crying, it seemed, first out of grief about my mother and now because of the child.

Madame Nasri began to cry in sympathy with me, wiping at her face with the corner of an apron spotted yellow with turmeric. "Life," she moaned. "It is so hard. I agree. But also, it is good, no? Very good."

"Very good. Yes," I agreed.

Unlike Madame Rosa, who had a spy's knack for teasing out secrets and intentions, Madame Nasri asked me no questions, sought no answers. If I cried, she cried with me for a moment and then went back to the kitchen. When I laughed, she laughed and then went back to her kitchen. Whereas Madame Rosa had filled our brief friendship with chatter, Madame Nasri preferred silence.

"Cook. All day," explained one of her sons, Samir. "It is her only pleasure, I think. She cooks both to forget and to remember. She is from the Maghreb, from a little village near the desert. Her family was not treated well by the French, in the Maghreb."

Samir, a tall good-looking man with wavy black hair and eyes as dark and intense as Picasso's, was in his thirties and not yet married, a condition his mother commented on frequently

during our mealtimes. But Samir had other plans. He explained
them to me when he came to my room to open a window that
was stuck shut. He worked as a busboy at Maxim's, had done
so since before the war and during the war as well, when he'd
had to clean up after the German officers who took over the
restaurant. He lived at home both because it was expected and
because he was saving as much money as he could to open his
own restaurant.

"Someday, if she lives long enough, Mama will cook for
me," he said. "For my restaurant."

His mother had come up the stairs to check on his progress
with the window. And, I suspected, to make sure our behavior
was aboveboard. Madame Nasri, unlike Madame Rosa, seemed
suspicious of the fact that I was traveling alone.

"Cook for a restaurant? Never," she said. "Let the Parisians
make fun of my food? Ha. It's enough that they stop me on the
street and ask, always ask, for my medical card to make sure I
am not tuberculosis carrier, that my papers are all legal. Cook
for them? No. You marry, Samir, make babies. I cook for
them."

Samir made a face behind her back and gave the stubborn
window frame a final thwack with the flat of his hand. The
window slid up, and a quick breeze whipped through the small
room. The mistral had not followed me up from Provence, but
Paris had her own autumn winds to contend with. This one,
because it was a city wind, carried the smells of bakery yeast
and car fumes. As soon as I smelled the car exhaust, I was
queasy again and sat on the bed staring up at the ceiling, another of Madame Rosa's recommendations for when the nausea
struck.

"Good, Samir," said his mother, eyeing me warily. "Now
you go back downstairs. Leave *Mademoiselle* Olsen to rest."

Her emphasis on the *mademoiselle* was prominent enough to make Samir duck his head in embarrassment. She looked at me suspiciously. She had guessed what that sudden queasiness was about. Guessed and disapproved. Mademoiselle. Unmarried.

Get used to it, I told myself. *Once your belly starts to show and you are not wearing a wedding ring, there will be plenty of judgmental looks.*

Irène Lagut had agreed to meet me at Café de Flore, not in her own home on the Avenue Montaigne. "She has a servant who is all ears and eyes," Madame Rosa had said after she arranged the day and time of our meeting from the tiny office in her guesthouse in Antibes. "Better to meet in a public place so you can talk freely. And Irène will bring a friend who knows English, so she can help. Your French"—she hesitated, not wanting to insult me, but in this instance the insult was deserved—"your French is like a child's. Worse."

Irène would be wearing a red carnation pinned to her coat so that I would know her. But the flower wasn't necessary. When she came into the crowded café at two thirty—half an hour late—I knew her instantly by her cloud of curly black hair and direct, confident gaze. She was sixty years old and still very beautiful, with a face like that of a classical Roman woman, one that could be seen in museum frescoes and on statues.

It was obvious why the young Picasso had fallen instantly in love with her. In addition to her stunning looks, there was great power in the way her long column of a neck supported that classical head with its heavy burden of hair, power in the intensity of her dark, bold gaze. I felt jealousy, not for myself, but for my mother, who had been his lover after, perhaps even during, that continuing affair with Irène.

His painting *The Lovers* was assumed to be a portrait of Irène, and the likeness was there, but he had changed her energy, taken that strength and boldness and turned it into something meeker, less confident. In the painting, he had covered that wild black hair with a scarf and turned her glance into a shy sideways look. He had tamed her, on the canvas at least.

The live Irène Lagut, older but still beautiful, paused in the doorway of the café, searching. She found me quickly, sitting at a table against the wall, surrounded by a courting couple on one side and on the other a noisy family of five who were celebrating the birthday of one of the children.

The friend Irène had brought with her was a second woman, taller, older, plainer, her gray hair knotted tightly on the back of her head. She followed behind Irène in a proprietorial manner, touching her occasionally on the shoulder to guide her through the maze of tables and chairs separating us.

"No," Irène said when she arrived at my table. "This will not do." She gave a withering glance at the loud family and signaled to a white-aproned waiter, who rushed over.

"There," she said, pointing to a corner table where a lunch party was just ending. It was a large table for six, not three, and I thought the waiter would refuse to seat us there. He did not. With a bow and a snap of his fingers, he had the table cleared in a matter of seconds and reset for three.

"They know me here," Irène said, taking the corner chair between myself and her companion. "They have respect for artists here. You are Alana Olsen? The one that Rosa has sent?"

She looked hard at me, squinting and leaning closer, then back, studying my face from different angles.

"You look familiar," she said after ordering coffee and cognac. "Why?"

I hadn't expected this. From Pablo, yes, because he had

known my mother intimately, knew of the hidden scars that even I, her daughter, hadn't known of. But Irène? They must have spent only a few minutes together when Irène came to the Midi and sat for Pablo in his studio there that summer.

"You may have met my mother," I said. "Thirty years ago. In Antibes at Sella's hotel."

"Ah! The maid? The one who caused all that trouble."

"Trouble?"

A quick exchange between Irène and her companion. "This is my friend, Tasha. She will help when there are difficulties. I just asked her the word for *discord*. She caused discord between Pablo and Olga. Your mother. Did you know?"

"Just recently, yes. I learned that she and Picasso were lovers that summer. She wasn't the only woman causing trouble."

"True. That man is a scoundrel," Irène said with great fondness in her voice. She looked hard at me again. "I adore him. But time with him is to be"—another quick conference with Tasha—"rationed, like sugar and soap during the war. He is overpowering. And not kind."

The waiter brought our coffees, bowing low before Irène Lagut as if she were a queen. She ignored him and continued staring at me as she stirred two lumps of sugar into her cup and then added a third, as if making up for the deprivations of the war.

"Does he know?" she asked, mischief lighting up her dark eyes. "That you are his daughter? Yes, I see that, too."

"Do you?" The directness and sureness of her statement startled me. "I look like my mother. But now it seems I look like him, too." It was still a strange sensation, realizing that all the time when I had looked into a mirror, seeing my mother, I had been seeing him as well.

I took a sip of my mint tea. "I don't know. I didn't have the chance to tell him. I saw him once in his studio, and we talked about the ceramics. After that, I was not allowed back in the studio. And then he left Antibes. He went to the bullfights in Nîmes."

"Bah. The bullfighting season is long over. He ran away. Or perhaps Jacqueline, the new one, took him away. I have heard she is formidable. Possessive, like a demon."

"I had that impression."

"And now what, for you?" Irène was already losing interest in our conversation. She checked her watch. Mumbled something to Tasha.

"Now I go back home. To New York. But first, I'd like to ask you some questions about your work."

"You know my work?" This topic interested her more than my parentage, and she sat up, her eyes wide with curiosity. "It is not usual, an American knowing of Irène Lagut. In America, it is only Picasso and Matisse they know."

"I found the catalog from the 1917 exhibit at the Bongard Gallery," I said. It seemed diplomatic not to tell her how hard it had been to find that catalog, finally unearthing it on a dusty shelf in the Morgan Library.

She interrupted eagerly. "Yes. A great night for me. My friend Apollinaire wrote the preface. Pablo was jealous, I think. He went to visit his family in Barcelona so that he wouldn't have to go to the opening. But Max was there, Max Jacob, and de Chirico. I showed some"—she hesitated, turning to her companion.

"Watercolors," Tasha said. "She showed watercolors that January. Mothers and children, mostly."

I had taken out my notebook and was scribbling like mad, jotting down not only what was said but the way Irène looked, her gestures, how she rested her arm on the back of her chair and leaned forward, watching, looking very like a photo I had found of her, taken in 1917, the year of that exhibit.

"We went away together, months before that show," she said. "Pablo. He was mad with love for me and took me to this terrible place full of spiders and cat piss. I pretended to fight him. It was a game. Oh, to be young again," she sighed. "Such fun we had, such wildness."

Irène and I talked for two hours, the waiter hovering occasionally to bring coffee, cognac, my tea, a plate of little sandwiches. Irène's friend shifted impatiently in her chair, obviously eager to be off, but Irène was equally eager to keep talking. She talked in great detail about the work she showed at Harvard in 1929, the group exhibit at the Museum of Modern Art in 1930. There had been shows in Paris at the Galerie Weill and at the Galerie Percier with a catalog preface written by Jean Cocteau.

"After 1930 it ends," she sighed. "The crash of your Wall Street. The Depression. No more buyers, at least not enough of them, though Pablo kept selling, of course. And I was married, you know. That takes up much time. I have a daughter. Smarter than me, very pretty. I worry, though."

She paused to drink her coffee and light another cigarette and then looked at me intently, her large dark eyes narrowing to slits of concentration. "You see, once you have a child, you worry endlessly. Will she get ill? Will she fall out the window? Will she eat paint or weeds in the park? You look forward to her growing up so that you can stop worrying. But you can't stop. My daughter, she works too hard. She is a doctor, too, like her father. And work, work, work. I worry. To avoid being like her mother, is she too much like her father? Daughters never want to be like their mothers. They think we do everything wrong. Maybe we do."

Her companion leaned over and whispered something to Irène, pointing to her watch. I thought of myself, young, vowing not to be like my overly cautious mother. What would my child see in me that she would spend her life avoiding? I couldn't wait to find out.

"She reminds me we must leave soon," Irène said, picking up her discarded gloves from the tabletop. She leaned closer so that only I could hear. "I have one great fear. That I will be remembered only as Pablo's model and lover. Not for my own work. You help with this?"

"I will help with this," I agreed.

"That painting. *The Lovers*. It is me, you know. He promised it to me, but never did he send it. Where is it? I don't even know. He will not tell."

I hesitated, not wanting to be the bearer of bad news, but Irène seemed to be a woman who could handle even a hard truth. "He sold it to an American, to Sara Murphy's sister. And then she sold it to the art collector Dale Chester." *Art Now* had done a small article on the sale, written by none other than David Reed himself.

Irène reeled back, astonished. "An American? It is not even here in France?" She puffed out an angry gust of air and hit the table with her palm, making the waiter look over at us in alarm. "That scoundrel," Irène said again, adding words I couldn't catch and Tasha didn't translate.

"I'm sorry," I said.

I felt a fleeting moment of affection, mixed with anger and irritation, for the man who had been my mother's lover. She had been right to leave him, whatever her reason. He was not the sort of man who would make a happy and secure home for her and her child. He would not have kept her safe, not in the long run, and that eighteen-year-old with her scars from a police beating, the family she could not return to, needed to feel safe. He was a scoundrel, as Irène said. And women adored him, though if they had any sense, they did not stay with him.

I had a feeling it would be different for him with that new woman, Jacqueline. He was older, and she was fiercer probably than any of his other lovers. She would stay, for better or for worse.

"My mother married a man, Harry Olsen," I told Irène, trying to change the subject. "Soon after her affair with Picasso."

She fell for the bait and calmed visibly. "Harry? I think I knew this man. He sold, what was it? Brushes?"

"Office supplies."

Irène forgot her anger over Picasso and smiled knowingly, reaching over to grasp my hand.

"Yes. He was here in Paris that year when your mother left Antibes. Why was he in Paris? I don't remember, maybe he didn't say, but many Americans were here—that woman Sara Murphy that you know and many others. He was having a good time in Paris before going back to New York. I was with a friend one evening at Au Lapin Agile, the nightclub, and my friend brought Harry over to our table. Harry. Big ears sticking out and very shy. He couldn't take his eyes off a girl who carried around a cigarette tray. At the Agile, they liked to hire foreign girls. They worked cheap." Irène flicked her ashes into the overflowing ashtray and closed her eyes, remembering.

"She was very young, this girl, and frightened. As she should have been. Agile was popular with artists, yes, but also pimps and thieves, and this girl looked like she would fall over if you looked too hard at her. A good girl, I thought, having a hard time. And then I saw she was the girl from the hotel, the maid who had caught Pablo's eye.

"I did not know that she had also been Pablo's lover. But then why pretend to be possessive of a man who cannot be possessed? I think it would not have bothered me that much if I had known. I brought her to the table and made her sit down, and my friend and I, we said they needed to know each other. Harry bought her a drink, but she wouldn't drink it."

Another story never told, at least not to me. It was difficult to reconcile this new image of my parents, my mother a frightened cigarette girl, my father enjoying R and R in Paris at a nightclub. But I had one more piece of the puzzle. How my mother came to America.

"But Sara said my mother went to Guernica after she left Antibes," I said. "To be with a friend."

"Did she? Maybe after that evening; maybe she was working to buy the train ticket. I don't know."

More secrets, then, this time with no one to supply answers. Marti had gone from Antibes to Paris, then to Guernica. And then to New York, where I suppose she and Harry had married. Had he, already smitten, followed her to Spain and brought her back with him to New York?

"More questions for me?" Irène asked. "You will come to my studio tomorrow. We will talk there. You will"—she jabbed at my notebook—"you will write about me."

"Yes," I said.

"Forget about Pablo," Irène said. "After that piece you write about his pots, forget him." She leaned so close I could smell the coffee and cognac on her breath, the gardenia of her perfume. "Forget him," she repeated, giving my hand a little pinch for emphasis.

I knew she wasn't talking about Picasso the artist, but Pablo, maybe my father.

I spent the next day with Irène at her studio taking notes, asking questions, listening to her wealth of information about art in Paris in the twenties, the personalities, the politics. None of it interested me as much as the stories of Anna had. But my mother had led me to art, and I would follow her bread-crumb trail. The lives those artists had lived! The affairs, the rivalries, the failures, and the successes. Irène's memory was encyclopedic. And as we talked—rather, she talked and I jotted page after page of notes—we paced through her studio, pulling out canvases.

"You like this one?" she asked, holding up a pastel of a dancer with a scarf. "And this?" A Harlequin in that bright geometric costume. "And this." A man and a woman seated on a bench, leaning closely into each other.

"They are about to kiss," Irène said. "I painted this in 1919. I call this *The Lovers*."

It was, without question, a painting of Irène and Pablo.

"Two years before he painted his," Irène said. "Mine first. And yet everyone knows his work, not mine. The world is not good to female artists."

I selected a dozen of what I thought were her best paintings, and we agreed that she would have them professionally photographed and sent on to me once I had the go-ahead from Reed.

"He doesn't know you are writing about me?" She slid the last canvas into place and frowned.

"Not yet," I admitted. "But I will write this."

A week later, I was back on a plane to New York, eager to be home and nervous to face the two men I now had to confront. Well, three if I counted Reed. All I had to do was sort out my future and find a way to earn a living if things did not go well with him. That was all. *Piece of cake*, I thought, burrowing my head into the skimpy plane pillow and trying to catch a few hours' sleep as we crossed the Atlantic.

I had retraced some of my mother's steps, learned much though not all of her story, which was also now my story. The past was done. The future was before me. I had no idea what it would be other than I would be sharing it with a child who would need everything I could give her, all the protection, guidance, and advice my mother had given me.

When I wake up, I told myself, *I will know what I must do.*

TWENTY-FOUR

·····················

ALANA

I met William at Agostino's to tell him. As usual, I was early and he was late, so I could watch him make his way through the crowded dining room, this good-looking ambitious man who would never be my husband. The same waiter who had served us the night of that disastrous conversation now pulled out the chair for William and waited, warily, for a repeat.

You don't know what's coming, I thought. *Hide the good crystal.*

"The trip did you good," William said, sitting opposite me. "You look great." He seemed disappointed, as if it were somehow disloyal of me to thrive when I should have been miserable and missing him. The engagement ring was on the table next to his water glass. The waiter saw it the same time William did and backed cautiously away.

"What's this?" William picked it up, frowning.

Okay. No preliminaries. Cut to the chase.

"I can't marry you," I told him.

William put the ring back on the table and leaned back in his chair, arms folded defensively over his chest.

"I thought you loved me," he said.

"So did I. But, William, I think we want different things. Different futures. And I've changed."

"Is it because of the *Art Now* account? If it means that much to you, I'll turn it down. Between us, I think that publication is a loser anyway." He gestured impatiently for the waiter, who had retreated to the other side of the room. "I want a martini," he said. "What about you?"

"Water for me."

We waited for his drink to arrive, not speaking, not even looking at each other.

"Okay," he said, when his martini was almost gone. "Why? And think carefully before you answer, because my patience does have a limit, Alana. You've changed. How?"

"I'm pregnant." I had decided in advance I'd have to tell him, that we had enough friends in common that he should hear it from me rather than them when I started to show.

William frowned and tapped the table, thinking. "Seems to me that should be an excellent reason to get married, not to cancel the wedding. It's a little sooner than I planned, but still . . ."

He was a clever man. I waited. The truth, when it hit, made him half stand and then fall back into his chair.

"Not mine," he said.

"No. Not yours."

He turned white and then red. His hand lifted as if he would strike me. He did not, but still, I was stunned by the threat of it. We didn't speak for several minutes. When he looked at me again, there was hatred in his eyes.

He grabbed up the ring with the too-large diamond before

he left, and he left without paying for his martini, leaving me with the bill. Part of me wished he had left the ring. I could have pawned it. I needed the money.

And part of me wished we could have been friends. But that hadn't been his plan, and William did not like to change plans, and everything had changed. I sat at the table, hearing that invisible door slam shut on the safety and security that William had promised.

Was it only three months ago that I had begun this journey? I had gone looking for Sara Murphy, whom I learned about only because of that newspaper clipping my mother had left in her book. I'd had a plan, a fiancé, goals. I'd had ambition and a sense that I could see beyond the horizon into an ordered future.

Now I felt like I couldn't see past the next hour.

But I had found the most important thing of all. Possibility. I thought of something Picasso had said to me that afternoon in his studio. I had been holding one of the ceramic urns painted with a woman's face. The piece had given him some difficulty. "To find is the thing," he'd said. *And that means you must keep looking*, I thought.

I waited two weeks to call Jack, testing myself every morning and evening with the need, the desire, to see him. This would be a point of no return for me, no changing my mind as there had been with William. I distracted myself with work and daydreams, and waited. I scrubbed the apartment, seeing for the first time all the sharp corners where a little head might be injured, the loose objects that might be pulled over, the rugs that my daughter might slip on. I found some copyediting work to tide me over while I wrote the Picasso article.

When I did call Jack, when the desire to hear his voice was as strong as my desire for food, for sleep, he sounded hurt.

"Why didn't you call before?" I heard the noises of his inn in the background, music from the bar, the clatter of dishes. "I want to see you," he said, not waiting for my answer.

"Good. Because I have something to tell you."

He drove into Manhattan that same night, ran up the stairs to my apartment, and pounded on the door.

"Alana," he shouted from the hall, waking me and the neighbors. "Alana, let me in!"

I opened the door, and we stood there for a long while, hugging, rocking in each other's arms, him kissing the top of my head, me inhaling the smoke and bay rum smell of his jacket.

"You think it will be a girl?" he asked when we were back in the apartment, sitting close to each other on the old chintz sofa.

"I think so. Every time I see something pink in a store window, I stop to look at it. My mother said she did that with me." I put his hand on my belly, just beginning to round.

He stayed for the weekend, and there were long days in bed making plans, daydreaming, but then he had to get back to Sneden's. We agreed that, for the time, we would travel back and forth, staying at my apartment when he could get away and at the inn when he could not. When I got Reed's notes from my article and was working on revisions, I could work anywhere. But first, we would take the train to Washington, to the National Gallery, so I could see face-to-face Picasso's *The Lovers*. What he had painted that summer of 1923.

The painting had originally been sold, directly by Picasso rather than his dealer, to Hoytie Wiborg, sister of Sara Murphy, just a few months after it had been finished. Hoytie had sold it to an art collector who had then given it to the National Gallery. I wondered if Picasso had sold the painting in a fit of temper, eager to be rid of what Sara had left behind after she had

ended their affair. He had told Irène that the painting was of
her, but looking at it, I thought that Picasso had used this tender image of lovers to express what he had felt for several
women, not just one.

"The woman looks like you," Jack whispered, putting his
arm around my shoulders.

"No," I said. "That's my mother. That's Anna Martina."

I grew big and clumsy and weepy and sometimes very frightened. I wished my mother were with me. The pregnancy was
not an easy one. The morning sickness grew worse rather than
better, all my joints ached, and I had so much trouble keeping
down food that, for a while, I lost rather than gained weight.
Jack fed me milkshakes made with the new blender he'd purchased for the inn's kitchen, rubbed my aching back and swollen feet.

We spent hours in silence just holding each other, overcome
with awe at the way the future had found us, claimed us, a future neither of us had anticipated, yet there we were, me as big
as house with a child given to me by a man I hadn't even known
a few months before. And Jack, so worried about the future,
about money, the wiring at the inn, the soft spot in a stairwell
that needed to be fixed, the slivers in the banisters. "What if she
falls? What if she chews on the old wallpaper? What if, what if,
what if?"

We took turns comforting each other, reassuring each other,
sometimes laughing, sometimes looking for an escape route
that we knew neither would use. Together. We were together,
and soon there would be the child.

Sara Murphy, busy with her new grandchild, sent me a layette blanket and a copy of Dr. Spock's book on baby and child care. She visited once, coming to the inn rather than inviting me to her house, and quizzed me about my meeting with Picasso, about the pottery studio, which she had never seen, and Jacqueline.

I was in Jack's and my room, and I hadn't gotten out of bed yet that day, so the covers were littered with crumbled pages and toast crumbs when Sara came in.

"You are huge!" she said. "Any day, right?"

I showed her the toy horse Picasso had given me, the keepsake he had kept all those years.

"He remembered," she said, pleased. "The party on the barge. When there were no flowers. I bought this at the market for a table decoration. And your mother, Anna. He remembered her?"

"Yes. When he first saw me, he called me Anna. But I didn't tell him that she had been pregnant when she left Antibes. He didn't give me the opportunity."

Sara folded her hands thoughtfully in her lap and watched me with her large blue eyes. "So, he doesn't know. About you."

"I think perhaps he does. There was something in his face when he first saw me. But I think it probably doesn't matter to him."

"Well. That's Pablo for you." She gave the little horse back to me and left soon after that, saying she didn't want to tire me. The conversation between us had come to a natural conclusion, and there was no more communication between us. We both had futures to think about, not the past. Whatever harm Sara had done to Anna was over now, healed by time and truth. There was peace between us.

In a fit of sentiment, I wrote to Picasso once just to see

what would happen. The letter was returned to me unopened, and I imagined Jacqueline standing in the studio door in Vallauris intercepting the mail, deciding what he would see and not see.

During those months of waiting, Jack was beside himself with joy and worry. We'd be married as soon as his divorce papers came through, he said. I didn't care, one way or the other. We were together, and there would soon be a child. That seemed enough, but he wanted it done correctly, ring and vows, the whole thing. "What your mother would have wished," he said.

I had been unwilling to follow this path with William. I hadn't loved him, not in the way I loved Jack. That needing to feel him next to me as soon as I woke up, falling asleep in his embrace, or not sleeping at all if he was not there. The sense that the world was made just for the two of us, the sun shone for us, and when it rained, the rain was for us, too.

I think, I hope, that Anna Martina never loved Picasso, either, not in a way that creates a future for two people, not just one. She knew he would not stay with her, that she would be one of many. And what woman chooses to live with that?

Did any of Pablo's women? I think they all believed, in their way, that they would be the last lover, the one that never is replaced. Maybe this would be true, finally, for Jacqueline.

The nurses reminded me frequently, and sometimes with a little too much satisfaction, I thought, that I was old to be having a first child. Thirty! Jack and I had celebrated my birthday at the inn, making very good use of the room that his father had kept private for his lady friend. The contractions began the day after my birthday, and the pain was like nothing I'd ever known, nothing that could have been expected. I descended into a maelstrom of tearing and clenching, the smell of blood, the hideous clanking of iron instruments, the smell of ether, the worried looks on the faces of the nurse, the doctor.

I wanted Jack to hold my hand, but he wasn't allowed into the operating room, just me and the nurse and the doctor, fighting to bring this new life into the world, the life-and-death struggle.

"Not breathing," I heard the doctor say when the child had finally been delivered and I roused from the last bout of semi-consciousness.

They held her aloft, that tiny bluish-white being who was as still as a wax statue, and slapped her again on the back, and still she did not breathe. Again, and she did not breathe, and the nurse looked close to tears, the doctor looked resigned. I thought of what Pablo had told me, about how as an infant he had not breathed, how his doctors had believed him to be stillborn.

"Again," I whispered, not knowing if I'd said the word out loud or just in my thoughts. "Again."

"Useless," the doctor said, laying the unbreathing newborn on the table next to his bloodied instruments.

"Again," I said, trying to sit up, and, knowing this time I didn't just think it, I said loudly, "It runs in the family." The nurse pushed me flat onto the bed, and it was clear from her frightened expression that she thought I was raving.

"Give her to me," I insisted.

"Just for a moment," the doctor agreed. He gently laid the infant, still not breathing, next to me.

I pinched her tiny leg as hard as I could. Again harder. The air in the room seemed to hold its breath just as the child was. Nothing moved. And then. And then. My child wailed in fury, flailed her fists against the air.

Welcome, I told her. *Oh, my precious. Welcome. This is the beginning of your story.*

Paris
1954

IRÈNE

So. Another child born of pain. The universe has a sense of humor, I think.

I remember when my own daughter was born, the pain that was like a curtain between life and death, then the years of her infancy, of childhood, when everything was a danger, a barking dog, an unknown weed plucked from a garden, a morsel of food swallowed wrong, a fever, a fall, a boy with wicked eyes. We bring our children through, knowing if we do not, we die ourselves, even if we go on living. Like Sara, when her two sons died. It ended everything for her, the sun and the sea, her love for France, even her friendship with Pablo, because Pablo does not accept the grief of others. If he can't paint it or sculpt it, it does not exist for him. But Sara has her grandchildren. She has survived.

I refold Alana's letter and look again at the photo of her baby. Huge black eyes. A black swirl of hair on top of the pleasantly round head. Unlike most infants, this baby has stared straight into the camera, giving it a look that is both imperious and full of curiosity. She makes me laugh, this baby, because that is how Pablo looked at me sometimes, in the old days, when he was planning another painting.

In the photo, she is being held by her father, a handsome man whose eyes are full of love and anxiety. The look of the new, first-time father. He will survive, I suppose. They usually do. Even Pablo did, though I remember Pablo on the floor, kneeling before his son, Paulo, gently rearranging the child's limbs into different patterns, different compositions, till the boy cried not in pain but newly revealed shyness. I remember the tenderness with which Pablo enfolded the child and kissed the top of his head.

I was jealous of that kiss, that tenderness. Pablo never gave himself completely, not to a woman. Perhaps it would have been different with Alana's mother, Anna. But Anna left, too.

Ultimately, all an artist has is her work. Everything else leaves. Even old friends. I may not see Pablo again. No more assignations in the studio, peering at each other over the bed-sheets. I think we have finished that story. And it will be a while before I know if I can forgive him, not for his infidelities, his lies, his selfishness, but for selling his portrait of me. *I will make you live forever*, he had said when he began it. And what woman would not want that?

Alana has promised that when she writes the article about my work, my career (Mr. Reed is a step closer to agreeing, she says in this letter), she will make sure it includes a reproduction of the painting *The Lovers*. Me and Pablo. No. Pablo and all his women. All the lovers of the world.

AUTHOR'S NOTE

Pablo Picasso is the artist we love to hate. Or hate to love. He did not treat his women well, and he earned a reputation for infidelity and emotional cruelty. Writing about Picasso does not mean the author condones his behavior. But as a novelist, I feel it is very important to accept people as flawed, as human, as something more complex than good or bad, since most people are a bit of both.

I've spent four concentrated years looking at his work, reading what other people have to say about him, and my opinion is that he earned his reputation as a visual genius and artist as well as that other reputation. The man could work miracles with a pencil and paper, with a single line. His different periods, from cubism to primitivism, represent revolutionary breaks from what went before. Picasso broke away from the past and created work that was the future. Even in the startlingly creative period of American art in the 1950s, artists were complaining that they couldn't visually go anywhere Picasso hadn't already been.

Would the world have been a better place if Picasso hadn't been born, hadn't become Picasso? I don't think so. Think of *Guernica*, the most visual depiction of the horrors of war in the world. Think of his very tender portraits of women and children, of his wife Olga, and that portrait I chose to emphasize, the young man and woman in *The Lovers*. There is affection there, and empathy. They were painted by an artist who was not saintly, but despite, or perhaps because of, his flaws of character, saw and then showed us a new and deeper way of seeing people and events.

Many characters in the novel do not live up to today's expectations. But I wanted to write about people in 1923 and 1953, two very different eras when standards and expectations were different. We should learn from history, and that is only possible when historical attitudes are accurately represented.

And, bottom line, after working with the characters, fictional and historical, I came to have a certain fondness for all of them, and an acceptance of their limitations as well as their quirky charms.

Readers of historical fiction often like to know what is real and what is invention in a novel. Sara and Gerald Murphy, Olga, Françoise Gilot, Irène Lagut, and of course Picasso himself are historical figures, and I kept my fictionalized versions of them close to the truth of their lives and their personalities. Alana and her mother and father are inventions, as are David Reed and his art magazine, and Madame Rosa.

ACKNOWLEDGMENTS

Writing this novel was, for me, an act of faith and determination, two qualities any writer needs to survive. I began it before the terror of the pandemic and the solitude of lockdown. I began it before I discovered that the person closest to me in the world would die soon. I put the manuscript away for months at a time, unable to come back to it, to come back to the me who was a writer, not just a grieving woman. Finishing it required all the strength and stubbornness I could muster.

I could not have done it without the support and encouragement of many people. So many, many thanks to Claire Zion for believing in this book, and my editor, Sarah Blumenstock, for her patience and understanding, and her ability to find where the story needed to be better sculpted and an image better phrased. My agent, Kevan Lyon, who always found the words needed to prompt me forward. The wonderful people at Berkley who made the manuscript into a book and then worked to place the book in readers' hands: art director and cover designer Rita Frangie Batour, interior designer George Towne, publicist Tara O'Connor, marketer Elisha Katz, production editor Lindsey Tulloch, and managing editor Christine Legon.

My friends in my writing group, Charlotte Greenspan, Hardy Griffin, and Nancy Holzner, who offered support and a glass of wine as well as critique. Thank you. You know how much it means, and I wish you joy and luck and success with your own projects. Thanks, too, to Tim, for his encouragement and insights and those wonderful conversations.

I am a shy person, not likely to step up and introduce myself to strangers, but if you are a gallerist, museum staffer, or librarian involved in the life and works of Pablo Picasso, there's a good chance that you have assisted me without even knowing it. So thank you, too.

PICASSO'S
LOVERS

JEANNE MACKIN

QUESTIONS FOR DISCUSSION

1. Which woman did you most identify with in this novel: Alana, her mother, Sara Murphy, or Irène?

2. Picasso could be cruel to his lovers. Have you known men like him? Were they ever happy in their relationships, and how did their partners respond to them?

3. Have you ever wanted or needed to meet a very famous person? Who, and were you able to?

4. What do you think of the relationship between Alana and her mother? Were there secrets in your family, and how did you finally discover them?

5. Of the various men in this novel, which did you find most and least appealing in terms of their ability to form a happy and loyal relationship?

6. McCarthyism, in this novel, is portrayed as an enemy of civil rights, including freedom of expression and the right to demonstrate peacefully. Have you ever participated in a demonstration for what you felt was a good cause? Did you feel any fear when doing so?

7. Do you think Sara Murphy and Alana have anything in common other than some form of relationship to Anna Martina? What?

8. Sara feels guilty for years because she felt she betrayed Anna and caused her dismissal from the hotel. Do you think she was justified?

9. What is your favorite painting? Why does it move you? What does it make you think of or dream about?

Jeanne Mackin is the author of several historical novels, including *The Last Collection*, which has been translated into five languages, and *The Beautiful American*, which won a CNY award for fiction. She has taught in the MFA Creative Writing program at Goddard College and won journalism awards. She lives in the Finger Lakes area of New York State.

Ready to find
your next great read?

Let us help.

Visit prh.com/nextread

Penguin
Random
House